E

"For anyone who has ever wondered how forgiveness is possible, even when the pain is overwhelming, wonder no more. *The Crying Tree* takes you on a journey you won't soon forget." —Sister Helen Prejean, author of *Dead Man Walking*

"In *The Crying Tree* Naseem Rakha uses grace and honesty to tell the gripping story of parents losing a son to murder and their desperate hope that an execution will provide closure, while allowing readers to consider the idea of forgiveness as a means of healing." —Randy Susan Meyers, author of *The Murderer's Daughters*

"Naseem Rakha writes with both clarity and sympathy about one of the most mysterious and evasive of human impulses: forgiveness. *The Crying Tree* is a memorable and deeply humane novel." —Jon Clinch, author of *Finn* and *Kings of the Earth*

"A powerful and stunning debut novel . . . replete with insights into the delicate family dynamics and suppressed emotions of those left behind. Written with wisdom and such sensitivity." —*Spokesman-Review*

"*The Crying Tree* is a fabulous family drama." —*Midwest Book Review*

"Ms. Rakha does a stunning job of nonlinear storytelling here, jumping back and forth between past and present to weave a strong tale that will make readers think while moving them more than once to tears. Not to be missed." —Lauren Lise Baratz-Logsted, author of *Crazy Beautiful* (review in *Red Room*)

Praise for

The CRYING TREE

"Each step of the book leads so beautifully to the next step that there are no natural stops when you have to go to bed or go to work or whatever task takes you away from this story. You really want to keep reading it—maybe for the rest of your life." —*Up and Away*

"*The Crying Tree* is hauntingly beautiful and sad as Rakha examines themes of hate, forgiveness, redemption, acceptance, and love. Here, Rakha brings hard questions for which there are no black-and-white answers to the fore. Readers are forced to question their own beliefs as Rakha's characters delve into their own." —*Deseret News*

"*The Crying Tree* is a powerful novel full of moral questions as well as surprises. Like real life, there are no easy roads for these characters, but they make their way, one step at a time." —*Las Vegas Review-Journal*

"Gifted storyteller Rakha has crafted a beautiful and passionate novel that never becomes maudlin or unbelievable. All of the characters are genuinely human, and the author even manages to save a few surprising plot details to the end." —*Library Journal*

"Rakha writes of one of her central subjects, 'and it wasn't anything she knew how to handle.' Not so for the author, who has crafted not only a compelling read, but one whose message lingers: At what point does that to which we cling for our survival become the very thing that robs us of our life?"—*The Oregonian*

"This is a gripping, well-paced tale, compassionate without being mawkish." —*The Guardian*

"This powerful book explores forgiving the unforgivable." —*Star*

The

CRYING

TREE

Naseem Rakha

BROADWAY BOOKS
New York

BROADWAY

This book is a work of fiction. Names, characters, businesses,
organizations, places, events, and incidents either are the
product of the author's imagination or are used fictitiously. Any
resemblance to actual persons, living or dead, events, or locales is
entirely coincidental.

Copyright © 2009 by Naseem Rakha

Originally published in hardcover in the United States by
Broadway Books, an imprint of the Crown Publishing Group,
a division of Random House, Inc., New York, in 2009.

Library of Congress Cataloging-in-Publication Data
Rakha, Naseem.
The crying tree / by Naseem Rakha.
p. cm.
1. Teenagers—Death—Fiction. 2. Grief—Fiction. 3. Loss
(Psychology)—Fiction. 4. Forgiveness—Fiction. 5. Prisoners—
Correspondence—Fiction. 6. Death row inmates—Fiction.
7. Oregon—Fiction. 8. Psychological fiction. I. Title.
PS3618.A435C79 2009
813'.6—dc22
2008040938

ISBN 978-0-7679-3174-8

PRINTED IN THE UNITED STATES OF AMERICA

Book design by Nicola Ferguson

5 7 9 10 8 6

First Paperback Edition

For my mother and father,
who taught me about the beauty of music,
the magic of words, and the gift of love.

Love is the prerogative of the brave.
—*Mohandas Gandhi*

PART I

PART I

CHAPTER 1

October 1, 2004

T HE DEATH WARRANT ARRIVED THAT morning, packaged in a large white envelope marked *confidential* and addressed to Tab Mason, Superintendent, Oregon State Penitentiary. Mason had been warned the order might be coming. A couple of weeks earlier, the Crook County DA had let the word slip that after nineteen years on death row, condemned murderer Daniel Joseph Robbin had stopped his appeals.

Mason dropped the envelope on his desk, along with a file about as thick as his fist, then ran his hand over the top of his cleanly shaved skull. He'd been in corrections for twenty years—Illinois, Louisiana, Florida—and on execution detail a half-dozen occasions, but he'd never been in charge of the actual procedure. Those other times he'd simply walked the guy into the room, strapped him down, opened the blinds on the witness booth, then stood back and waited. He'd worked with one guy in Florida who'd done the job fifty times. "It becomes routine," the officer told Mason, who was busy puking into a trash can after witnessing his first execution.

Now Mason slid into his chair, flicked on his desk lamp, and opened Robbin's file. There was the man's picture. A front and side shot. He had been nineteen years old when he was booked, had long scraggly hair and eyes squinted to a hostile slit. Mason turned the page and began to read. On the afternoon of May 6, 1985, Daniel Joseph Robbin beat, then shot fifteen-year-old Steven Joseph Stanley (aka "Shep") while in the process of robbing the boy's home at 111 Indian Ridge Lane. The victim was found still alive by his father, Deputy Sheriff Nathaniel Patrick Stanley, but died before medical assistance could arrive. The remaining family members—wife and mother, Irene Lucinda Stanley, and twelve-year-old Barbara Lee (aka Bliss)—were not present during the incident. The Stanleys, who were originally from Illinois, had been living in Oregon for a year and a half when the incident occurred.

The superintendent leafed through more pages—court documents, letters, photos—then leaned back in his chair and looked out his window. A squat rectangular building sat on its own toward the north end of the prison's twenty-five-acre grounds. The last time someone had been executed out there was seven-plus years ago. Mason had been working his way up through the ranks at the Florida State Prison out of Raiford, aspiring for a job like the one he had now—head of a large correctional institution, good salary, power. He blew out a long, disgusted breath. Why now? The Oregon penitentiary was way overcrowded, inmates doubled up in their cells, half of them out of their minds; fights were breaking out left and right, gangs getting tougher to handle; there were race issues, drugs—all while funding for counseling and rehab continued to get slashed. Why now, and why this?

Mason reread the warrant. The execution was scheduled for October 29, 12:01 A.M.

"Less than a goddamn month," he said, shaking his head. Then, as if to rouse himself, he clapped his mismatched hands, one as dark as the rest of his black skin, one strangely, almost grotesquely white. There was no complaining in this job, he told himself. No moaning about what needed to be done. No stammering or stuttering or doing anything that might show the slightest bit of reluctance or hesitancy. No. Everything in his career had been leading him to this kind of challenge: his demeanor, his words, his actions would all set a tone. And he knew exactly what that tone had to be.

CHAPTER 2

September 1983

S HE REMEMBERED THE DATE, SEPTEMBER 20, and the time, 6:00 P.M. The scent of the air was spiked with apples and over by the river geese were taking to the sky. Her son, Shep, thirteen and a half years old, stood in the field near the barn playing his trumpet. And her youngest, Bliss, was on the tire swing with her best friend Jeff. And she, Irene Stanley, thirty-two years old and trim as a pin, was making her family dinner.

Nate pulled up in their brand-new pickup, tugged off his wide-brimmed Smokey Bear–style hat, waved to his kids, banged through the back door, and smacked a U.S. map on the counter next to where she was cutting vegetables.

He was a handsome man, with fighter-hard muscles, copper-colored hair, and bright green eyes. She smiled as he shucked off his jacket, dropped it and his hat on the kitchen table, and announced that a buddy of his back in the service had called that morning.

"He's a sheriff out in Oregon. Says he wants me to come be his chief deputy."

Irene glanced up from her cutting. "Since when are you looking for a job?"

Nate had been a Union County deputy for going on nine years. Not *chief* deputy, but getting there. He was smart, gregarious, a war hero. He'd be elected sheriff one day, Irene was sure.

"Since I talked with Dobin. That's his name. Dobin Stubnik. We were pretty tight in Nam."

"Sheriff Stub*neck*?"

"Stub*nik*."

"Ooohh." Irene reached for a potato, sliced it in half. It'd be stew for dinner. Beef, with carrots, potatoes, and those little onions Nate hated but the kids loved.

"He's a good guy," her husband said. "Smart, quick, going somewhere." He pushed aside Irene's cutting board, then opened and flattened out his map—crisp and new, blue and red lines crossing the lower forty-eight. Nate traced his way from the middle of the heavyweight paper to its very left side, stopping on the word *Oregon*. "It's desert country out that way," he said. "Wide and open. Hell, parts of it are still considered frontier."

Irene looked at where Nate's finger stopped and imagined a scene from some John Wayne movie: cowboys, Indians, saloons with buxom barmaids. The farthest west she'd ever been from their home in Illinois was St. Louis, and that felt good enough.

"There's everything there, sweetie. Mountains, lakes, the ocean— you name it."

Irene set down her knife. She'd grown up in the house where she now stood. Her mom had cooked in this kitchen; so had her grandma. The place was built by her great-granddad, and it sat on a fine and fertile piece of ground with the Mississippi curving around it like a hand. And Nate? He grew up not three miles away. For fifty-five years his family had run Carlton's only butcher shop. Irene and Nate's two children, Shep and Bliss, went to the same school she and Nate had gone to. Had some of the same teachers, even. Southern Illinois was their home, their only home. And it damn well was going to stay that way. She turned to face her husband. *"Family,* Nate. We have no family out there."

Nate snatched up his map, then folded its creases tight and clean. "Yeah, well, we've always lived 'round family. Yours, mine—I mean, don't you ever just want to break out and see what we can do on our own?" He slapped the map against his hand. "It'd be good for us to get out of here."

Irene gave her husband a look, then pulled her cutting board back in place, wondering what in the world had gotten into him and, more important, how in the hell she'd get it out. Nate wasn't a tall man, but he carried himself with the sureness of one. A thick, sturdy neck holding up an even thicker head. Nothing got in his way once he made a decision.

"I don't know what you're talking about, Nathaniel Stanley. Moving wouldn't be good for anyone but you, if that."

Nate grabbed a carrot, bit into it, then walked to the sink. Irene sighed and cut into another carrot, her knife snapping the board loud and hard. "You don't just pull your life out of the ground like some kind of weed, Nate. I mean, I know people do it, but it doesn't make it right. This is home." *Snap.* "Everyone's here." *Snap.* "Your mom, your brother, aunts, uncles, cousins, nieces, nephews." *Snap, snap, snap, snap.* "Everyone who's anything to us, right here. It doesn't matter if we're tired of them, mad, bored, or what. They're family. *You don't leave family."* Irene scraped the cut rounds into her bowl and walked to the sink. "Anyway," she said, nudging her husband out of the way with her hip, "the kids are in school. Bliss just got voted class secretary, and Shep, well . . ."

She turned off the water, picked up a towel, and looked out the window. The sun, a burgeoning red ball in a scarlet sky, had turned everything—the ground, the barn, even the children—all shades of peach and pink. Bliss and Jeff were climbing the old maple, and Shep was still in the field with his trumpet. He was playing "Silent Night," and its long pleading notes made Irene clutch the towel to her chest. It was his closing piece to the day, and he'd either play it outside, when the weather was good, or inside on the piano. Nate often complained it drove him nuts to hear a Christmas song all year long.

"Shep." Nate spat the last piece of carrot into the sink, then slammed the window shut. "A place like Oregon? Hell, it'd be good for the boy, you know that?" He wiped his mouth with the back of his hand. "Fact is, Irene, I think it's just what the kid needs."

CHAPTER 3

October 1, 2004

SUPERINTENDENT TAB MASON'S RIGHT HAND had begun to lose its color while he was in his mid-thirties. It started in patches, making it look like the tall, muscular black man had been hit by bleach. Then the patches spread and merged until the entire appendage looked as though it could belong to any one of the white men on Oregon's death row. The only difference: his hand had never killed anyone.

Not that he hadn't come close. A memory triggered, a single flash of a smile, a scent of chalk, wood, and sweat. Tulane and that hideous garbled laugh of his . . . Mason tightened his grip on the phone receiver and shut down the images with a quick and nearly effortless efficiency.

"Mason, buddy." Dick Gefke's voice came over the receiver. "You going to the game?"

Mason rolled his eyes. He'd been on hold for four and a half minutes and didn't have time to talk sports.

"No, sir, 'fraid I can't make the game."

"Now, Tab, you have any idea what you're missing?"

Mason admitted he didn't, and his boss sighed. The way Gefke, a former college quarterback, figured, black men just had a natural affinity for sports. "An instinct," he'd said more than once. Taken as a whole, the superintendent considered the director of the Department of Corrections a kindhearted ass, just like a lot of people Mason had met since moving to Oregon five years earlier. Nice enough individuals, but so unused to being around blacks they constantly overcompensated, coming up with all kinds of comments that if said in another environment—Chicago, for example—would have gotten their asses kicked. That or just shot.

"I got other things going, sir."

"That's too bad, 'cause we're sure as hell gonna blow Arizona out of the water. Me and Suzie, we're heading to Eugene tonight. Avoid the traffic."

Mason imagined the big, bearlike man and his exuberant exclamation point of a wife cruising down Interstate 5 in their pine-green Expedition decked out with their alma mater's mascot. *The fighting fuckin' Ducks.* He shook his head. "Yeah, well, I'm sure it'll be a good game. Look." He ran his hand over his smooth head. "There's another reason I'm calling." Mason told Gefke about the death warrant.

"Well, goddamn. Stopped his appeals, huh?"

"Yes, sir."

"And we've got what, four weeks to get ready? Guess they couldn't have timed that any better. You know where the governor is right now?"

Mason picked a piece of lint from the sleeve of his suit coat, rolled it between his fingers. "No."

"Portland, talking with a victim's rights group. His staff just called a little while ago, wanted figures on the new prison. You know what he's doing?"

"Campaigning," Mason answered, dropping the lint into a small silver trash can.

"That's right, campaigning. It's a tough race, and with this thing coming when it is—Jesus. Well, let's just say you've got yourself one mighty big responsibility."

Mason nodded into the phone. He hadn't considered the upcoming election when he read the death warrant.

"When was the last time we had one of these things, anyway?" the director asked.

"Nineteen ninety-seven. Seven years, four months, two weeks, and two days ago, to be exact."

"What, you don't know how many hours?"

Knowing that it took an average of twelve minutes for a man to die by lethal injection, Mason glanced at the clock and did a quick calculation. "Eleven," he said. "And forty-eight minutes."

Gefke chuckled. "You're something, I'll give you that. You still have that container of pencils all sharpened up?"

Mason's gaze went back to his desk, where he did indeed have twelve pencils all honed to needlelike tips.

"That's what I like about you, Tab—no surprises. Look, you've probably thought of this already, but you should get hold of the superintendent in charge the last time we had one of these things. See how he handled it, 'cause I'm telling you, there can't be any slipups. Especially coming when it is. But you can handle that, right?"

Mason grabbed a pencil and began tapping it against his thigh. "I can handle it, sir."

"Good. So, from my end, what is it you need?"

Mason looked across the room at a picture of his daughter. She was seven in that one. Still tied her hair up with those colorful rubber bands. Still smiled. Now the pictures her mom sent showed a young woman with orange hair and an overload of makeup planted on a way too knowing face. Sixteen years old, and he swore she looked like a hooker. "You're supposed to inform the governor and the attorney general about the warrant. I'll have copies delivered."

"Right," said Gefke. "I'll handle the outside end, but I'm telling you now, I won't exclude you. I know you don't like it, but you're going to have to be front and center on this. Press conferences, interviews, all of it. And I'm warning you, those reporters—they'll be like flies on shit, no question about it."

Mason stopped drumming the pencil. He didn't like dealing with the press, but more than that, he didn't like the director's analogy. It felt too precise. Executing someone *was* a shitty job. Maybe not for others, but to him, right then, on that bright, clear October morning, that's just what the job felt like.

"So," Gefke said, "what are the odds?"

"Sir?"

"Hundred bucks says soon as you tell this guy Robbin his time's up, he'll hightail it to a phone and call his attorney. There's no way in hell he'll just sit back and let this thing happen. It's against human nature."

"I'm not sure," Mason replied. "He's not an easy one to figure out."

"Yeah, well, we'll see. Just be careful. Have a staff member or two nearby when you tell him, just in case he loses it or something."

Mason considered this. Robbin's record at the penitentiary was clean. Cleaner than clean, really—didn't bother anyone, read a lot, sketched. He'd even earned the privilege of taking a few classes. "I don't think there'll be trouble, but that brings up something else. Waters is supposed to be there with me when I tell Robbin—you know, as security manager. But he's off hunting with his kid. He won't be back for a week."

"That's your call. Have someone else there if you want."

"What about you?"

Gefke laughed. "I don't think so, buddy. Like I said, this is your baby. I handle the political end, you handle the procedure. Are we clear?"

"Yeah," Mason said. "Completely."

CHAPTER 4

October 1983

LAYERS OF SOFT, PULP-COLORED FLESH bulged and sagged around Pastor Samuel White's pale blue eyes. He was thinking— elbows on his desk, hands crossed, index fingers tapping. Irene sniffed and wiped her nose with a soggy handkerchief. How could she not be upset? They were moving. Nate had called from Oregon that morning. He had accepted the job and even signed papers for a house in some place called Blaine. "It's nice," he said. "Nice neighborhood, and the town, nice and small. Just like Carlton."

But Irene didn't want to live in Blaine. Didn't even want to hear its name. Moving made no sense, no sense whatsoever. But what was she going to do? She asked her pastor. "What? Tell me, what do I have to do to stop this thing?"

"Now, Irene." White folded his hands and leaned against his desk, a large old wooden platform covered with church bulletins, hymnals, and heaps of mail. "It's not going to do you any good to get all worked up over this."

She frowned. Her sister, Carol, had told her the same thing. "You go where the job is," Carol said. Completely ignoring the fact that Nate already had a job, and a home, and a church, and friends, and family. Irene could go on and on.

Pastor White looked over his glasses and counseled Irene to calm down and accept Nate's decision. It was her job to support her husband. "Your duty," he said, righting his posture.

"But my kids . . ."

"Bliss and Shep will be fine. You've got to remember, you-all wouldn't have been given this challenge if the Lord didn't think your family was up to it. I mean, who knows what waits for you out there? You just have to have trust, that's all." With that he lowered his head and began to pray for Irene and her family. And as she sat in that old wooden chapel, home to a thousand different memories, she could feel her will begin to bend and shape itself around her husband and his desires.

Just as it always had.

The next day Nate returned from Oregon with a fistful of postcards and a mortgage for a house at 111 Indian Ridge Lane. He described Blaine as rural and his job as "exciting, more responsibility, bigger region, that kind of thing." And from the postcards the place did look beautiful, with snowcapped mountains, trees as wide and tall as silos, and rivers as clear as cut crystal.

"It's really something," Nate told his family. "We'll learn to ski, go mountain climbing. The ocean's nearby, and there's rodeos all summer long. Heck, one of the biggest in the country's right out there in Oregon." He pronounced the name of the state just like he did the name of the old Wurlitzer at church, an *organ,* and corrected Irene when she said it otherwise. "Or-*ee*-gone, hell. You got to learn to say the name right. You never hear no one but tourists call this place Ill-i-*noise.*"

He had a point, but then, Irene hadn't ever met a tourist anywhere near Carlton. Southern Illinois was a quiet backwater filled
with lakes, swamps, hills, bluffs, and towns named after coal com-
panies and the thick carbon they hauled from the ground. Icy in
winter, thick with bugs and snakes in summer, the area simply
didn't draw people like the Ozarks did to Arkansas or Nashville to
Tennessee. Carlton didn't have lines of shops selling T-shirts and
fudge; there were no wooden Indians outside its storefronts, or cabins along its lakes. Its feel was small, its ambitions even smaller, and
Irene liked it for that. It made her think their life was safe. It made
her think it wasn't a good idea to leave.

But they did. On October 19, 1983, they boarded up their old
farmhouse, said goodbye to friends and family, and, under a cover
of autumn rain, left Carlton.

FOUR DAYS LATER THEY ARRIVED in Blaine, Oregon, population
5,000 and clearly declining. Nate drove a U-Haul with eleven-year-
old Bliss at his side, and Irene and Shep followed behind in their
Chevy pickup. They'd driven together the entire trip because Shep
had refused to ride with his father. And Irene couldn't blame him.
Not one hour before they left, Nate had dropped the bomb.

"Truck's full," he said, pulling down the U-Haul's door with a
big whacking clash. "Piano's staying. There's no room."

"No way!" Shep yelled through the rain.

"What do you mean, no room?" Irene grabbed the door, pushed
it back up. "There's *got* to be room."

But there was no space for their six-foot-long upright.

Irene offered to leave the couch, the dining room table, their
bed, anything. But Nate wouldn't budge.

"I'm not about to start hauling things out of this truck just to
make room for an old piano that will likely take up too much space
in our new house anyway."

A few minutes later, Irene found Shep huddled in the corner of his bedroom.

"I'm sorry," she said, pulling her cardigan around her as she slumped beside him. "You know it probably wouldn't have been good for the piano, anyway. Altitude change, and the cold, and with this rain . . ." She took a deep breath and looked around. The bedroom had been hers growing up. One window faced east, toward the road, and the other looked out on an apple tree she and her father had planted when she was little. The tree filled the window now, and the few apples that still clung to its branches looked like ornaments against the pewter clouds. It made her want to cry. "We'll get you another piano, son. I promise."

Shep's gold-colored hair fell forward as he tucked his head to his knees. "He doesn't like me playing."

"Now, Shep."

Her son had started playing the piano when he was two, pulling himself up on the wooden bench and fingering the keys, not pounding them, like most toddlers, but touching them lightly, then letting each note play itself out to nothing. This went on for weeks, one note after another, with Shep just sitting and staring at the yellowed ivories as if he could see the sound. Then, out of nowhere, he began putting notes together to make songs—"Mary Had a Little Lamb," "The Wheels on the Bus," simple one-handed stuff he'd poke out while singing softly to himself. Irene began singing more complicated tunes, then bought a few albums to see if he could copy those as well. Before she knew it, he was playing "Simple Gifts," "Für Elise," and "Ave Maria." At age four he began lessons with the church organist; then, when he turned seven, Irene brought down her father's horn from the attic, and with that she discovered she no longer needed evidence of God. She could hear him every single day declaring through that horn that there was more to this world than she would ever know.

Shep wiped his face with the sleeve of his flannel shirt. "He ever say why we're moving? I mean, the *real* reason? He ever tell you that?"

"The *real* reason? Shep, he's got a good job waiting. And it'll be good for us, seeing new parts of the country. It'll be exciting." She patted his arm. "You'll see."

He looked at her. "You know he hates me. You know that. Right?"

"Shep! You shouldn't ever talk like that. It's not right. Your pa, he was thinking of you, thinking of us all when he accepted this new job."

Years later, Irene would remember her son's look: disbelief, carved by a sadness that lay way beyond his years.

"I don't believe that, Ma," he'd answered. "I'm sorry, but I just don't."

IRENE FOLLOWED THE U-HAUL THROUGH Blaine, driving down a one-way street named Main South. Crippled-looking buildings lined both sides of the pavement, plywood nailed over many of the windows. She knew what it was like to live where people depended on what either lay deep in the ground or sprouted up out of it, and the quality of the smile in the market always depended on the price farmers got at the co-op or the chance discovery of another seam of bituminous. But Blaine looked different—harder and uglier in a way that almost seemed tragic. Even during the worst days of Illinois's farm crisis, with foreclosures everywhere and businesses shutting down one after another, Carlton's tree-lined streets and sturdy brick storefronts still held the promise of better times to come. Blaine, in contrast, looked incidental, an afterthought built by people who had no intention of staying.

Nate had told her before they arrived that cattle prices were down, and that Blaine's last remaining mill was knocking workers off the line as fast as it had once pushed through logs. And she knew

that in hard times the law—Nate and men just like him—would be
busy. Fights, abuse, suicide: all the dark stuff comes out when the
land can't provide. Irene had known all that before she came, but
still . . .

   She put on her blinker and followed Nate onto Tannenbaum,
driving past a grimy-looking gas station and a Dairy Queen. At the
end of the road they took a left into a neighborhood of flat, brick-
shaped homes lined up like abandoned railroad cars. Irene stopped
the truck and reached for Shep's hand as her husband backed into
the driveway of the third house on the left, a dirty-yellow ranch with
a chain-link fence and a FOR SALE sign pounded into the ground, the
word *Sold* smacked right across its face.

CHAPTER 5

October 1, 2004

THE OREGON STATE PENITENTIARY STOOD in the center of the city of Salem. One hundred and thirty-eight years old, it occupied its ground like a fortress, ringed by a twenty-five-foot-tall concrete wall and nine eight-sided gun turrets. Two thousand men lived in its stark confines, some for a little while, some for longer, and some, like Daniel Robbin, held for the rest of their lives in a separate building called the IMU—Intensive Management Unit— or, to people like Mason, death row.

A harsh metallic buzz signaled Mason's entrance into the IMU. A moment later there was a loud click as the electronic dead bolt slid back, then a snap indicating that the superintendent could open the door to the two-story, windowless building. Inside, an officer stood in a harshly lit alcove. He nodded, then handed the superintendent a clipboard with a chart, which Mason signed beside the date and time of day. The north end of the unit held solitary: one hundred and twenty cells with close to that many inmates, each too out of control to be kept with the general population. At the other end was death row. Mason took a deep breath of the caged air, handed back the clipboard, then proceeded down the south hall.

Three more doorways, three more officers. Mason gave each a cursory nod, then waited as the final door buzzed then snapped open. Mason entered a small oval room surrounded by thick bullet-proof glass looking out on two tiers of six-by-nine-foot cells. "The fishbowl," the inmates called the control room, though they had no way to see through its one-way glass. Instead, what they saw was a reflection of their own cells, reminding them, day after day, that that's all they'd ever see. *At least in this life,* Mason thought as the door clicked shut behind him.

Two men dressed in drab olive uniforms sat at a curved metal desk cluttered with clipboards, charts, and coffee-stained mugs. They turned and greeted their boss. The superintendent—"General," they liked to call him—made a habit of visiting the IMU at least once a month, always taking time to talk with staff, then getting a few inmates aside to talk with them as well. That way, Mason figured, his showing up was never a big deal, which was important when you had a couple thousand angry guys locked up on the same piece of ground.

Mason peered past the officers to the cells. Seven of the twenty-three inmates were out in the yard, Robbin among them. Of the others, most had TVs on, some were asleep, one was on the can, a few were yelling—some to one another, some to no one at all. Or at least no one anyone else could see. Most had demons, shadows lurking in some dark part of their minds. Confined as they were, twenty-three hours every single day, they were driven nuts. *Every one of these guys, different levels of crazy,* Mason thought. *Except one.*

The superintendent's eyes stopped at the bottom tier of cells, third one from the right. Daniel Robbin had a way with charcoal and pencil, and his concrete cell walls were covered with his work.

Mountains, forests, cliffs, and waterfalls were scratched onto whatever scrap of paper he could find. Some had a sparse Asian feel, trees reaching out over foggy crests. Some were flamboyant, almost chaotic—a tumble of stone, a waterfall crashing.

Since his move to Oregon, Mason had spent quite a bit of time traveling around the state, and a lot of what he'd seen was captured in Robbin's drawings. Slick, fern-lined paths; Goliath-sized trees with bark as thick and gnarled as elephant skin. He'd driven through a good part of Oregon's desert too, open country punctuated by blood-colored hills and vicious-looking outcrops of near-black stone. And just the weekend before he'd gone an hour west of Salem and watched the surf tear at what looked like the same rough volcanic rocks Robbin had sketched using nothing more than a paper bag and a pencil.

Mason took these little trips because doing so reminded him that he could. And it reminded him that there was something bigger and more permanent in life than any of the doors in any of the prisons he'd ever known.

Probably why Robbin draws, he thought. *Probably just exactly what keeps the guy sane.*

"That Robbin sure's got a lot of talent." Mason pointed at the man's cell.

Officer Pauly, fleshy lids swabbing bloodshot eyes, dug out a grunt. The other, a chiggery-looking guy named Stowenheim—cockeyed aviator glasses, oily hair—glanced where his boss pointed, shrugged, and went back to his charts.

Mason understood. The place—locks, walls, shit, piss, hate, loads of it heating up like a rank compost—got to most people. What the hell did they care about the talents inmates might or might not possess? By and large, the officers considered the men animals, heartless, cruel, and warped, and often enough they were proved right. Recently one of the staff had been struck in the leg by a shit-soaked dart. He was laid up in the Salem hospital for close to a month. Then last week an officer had been slashed while helping an inmate to his feet in the shower. The guy had hidden a razor up his ass. Whatever inkling of skill or capacity a prisoner might have was dwarfed by all that. Made insignificant. Robbin might have been an artist and might never have caused them any problems, but he was behind bars, and that's what counted.

Mason sighed. It used to be there was a kind of satisfaction in his job. The control, the punishment, even the brutality made sense in a world where people were doing all kinds of hideous things to one another. But lately the work just seemed fruitless. There were no good stories in this work. Just mistakes laid on top of more mistakes, with there being no way to make things any better.

"I got a death warrant from the Crook County Circuit Court today. It looks like Daniel Robbin's next."

The officers swiveled around in their chairs.

"Well, now, there's some news." Stowenheim yanked off his glasses. "They actually have a date?"

"October twenty-ninth, one minute after midnight."

The officer glanced at a calendar hanging by the door—picture of the ocean, big rocks, white waves, endless stretch of sand, all laid flat against a concrete wall. "That's just four weeks from now." Stowenheim turned toward Pauly. "Shit, I bet you it won't even happen. I'll bet you we get ourselves all ready for it, and some fuckin' judge will grant another stay, and there we'll be with our thumbs up our asses." The two men nodded at each other like park-tough kids, bored and pissed with being bored. Stowenheim glanced back at Mason. "How long's Robbin been in—fifteen, sixteen years?"

"Nineteen," the superintendent answered, articulating every sound in the two simple syllables. Mason hardly ever let his voice rise much above a whisper. "He came in when he was nineteen, and he's been in nearly nineteen."

Stowenheim rolled his eyes up toward the white bars of light.

"Half his life! Christ Almighty, see what I mean?" He knocked Pauly's arm. "I tell you, these things, they take for-fuckin'-ever."

The superintendent pulled his shoulder blades together, exposing a scar that ran down the left side of his neck from just below his ear to his throat. He snapped his head, right, left. Straightened. "These things take as long as they need, Stowenheim. We're talking about a man's life, and I won't be tolerating any talk that may lead someone to believe we are in any way eager to take on this job." Mason did not blink. "You got me?"

Stowenheim met his boss's stare. "I'm not saying I'm eager, I'm just saying—"

"I know what you're saying. I also know you've never been through this before, and I'm here to tell you, there's nothing easy about it. Understand? Nothing. And if it takes forever, then it goddamn takes forever."

Stowenheim sucked in his right cheek and nodded. "I gotcha, General. But I wasn't meaning nothing."

"Yeah, we'll see." Mason pointed to the monitor. "How much time they got left in the yard?"

Pauly glanced at the clock, its second hand moving with tight, steady jerks. "Five."

"All right. Have everyone brought in except Robbin. Play like it's routine—just a visit. Have someone stationed nearby. I'll give him the news out there." Mason pulled on the sleeves of his suit jacket and glanced again at the condemned man's cell. Among all the drawings Robbin had taped to his wall, Mason knew of only one human image: a portrait of a young boy with wide innocent eyes.

CHAPTER 6

May 6, 1985

THEY'D DONE A PRETTY GOOD job adjusting to their new life, Irene thought as she straightened a shelf of pickles at Glen's Market. It wasn't easy; that first night in Blaine the house was so filthy she wouldn't even let them sleep in it. And then all of them struggling to fit in—new school, new church, new jobs, new sights, sounds, smells. But now, a year and a half later, it looked like they were making it. Bliss was president of her seventh-grade class, Nate loved his job, and she had this one at Glen's. It helped with the mortgage, though it still bugged her to no end even to have to consider the word. But what the hell? They were all okay. Even Shep. He loved the desert, he told his mom. Liked seeing what he called "the roots of the earth," and he would take off on his bike for hours, exploring.

Irene was happy for him. Happy for them all as she wiped the shelves at Glen's and pulled forward the gherkins and relish to make the shelves look fuller than they were. *Facing*, it was called. When she heard her name paged on the intercom, she even paused to straighten a price tag before climbing down from her footstool. It was a Monday; a truckload of dry goods was due. Years later she would recall that "Ruby Tuesday" was playing on the radio, and that she hummed along as she walked to the back of the store.

Glen was waiting by the dairy cooler, looking agitated. He told her to come to his office. Her boss did as much work as anyone in the store. More, really. But he wasn't nice about it. "Harsh," she'd told her family over a dinner of Glen's best-cut Boston butt.

He pointed to the phone. "You have a call," he said, and then he left and closed the door behind him.

Irene shrugged, then leaned over Glen's desk, picked up the phone, and pressed the button.

"Get home," she heard Nate say. "Right now."

"Are you sick? You need me to bring something?"

But her husband only repeated himself, and something in his tone made her go cold.

When she stepped out of the office, Glen was waiting. "Let me know if there's something I can do," he said. Then his hand reached for her arm, and Irene looked at the place where his skin met hers, and without her being aware of it, the towel she'd been holding dropped to her feet.

AS IRENE DROVE, SHE DECIDED that Nate must have gotten bad news from home. His mom, maybe, or maybe something had happened to her sister, Carol, or one of the kids. She hit the Chevy's steering wheel, damning her husband for dragging them to this godforsaken stretch of desert, and separating them from everything and everyone back in Illinois. And as she stewed about this, she turned right off Main South, drove past the filling station with its faded green canopy and the Dairy Queen, strangely empty of kids, then turned left onto Indian Ridge.

Squad cars were everywhere—the street, the grass. An ambulance sat in their driveway, lights flicking off windows. And people— policemen, firemen, neighbors—stood huddled like small flocks of frightened birds. Irene slammed to a stop in the middle of the road, yanked on the parking brake and ran from the truck.

A deputy intercepted her. "Irene!" He grabbed her shoulder and walked her toward the driveway. "Nate's over in the squad car with the sheriff."

The passenger door was open; her husband sat inside, rocking his head back and forth. Irene dropped to her knees. "Oh my God, Nate. What happened?" Blood covered his shirt, his face, his hands. She knew this would happen one day—her husband, a cop, so tough. There must have been an accident, some bad seed somewhere doing something. "Tell me, where're you hurt?"

He didn't answer.

Frantically, she looked over at the sheriff. "Why isn't he in that ambulance?"

Dobin Stubnik's gaze went out to the street, where neighbors stood holding one another. A few were crying. She tugged on her husband's arm.

"Nate? What's going on?"

Her husband's bloodied hand went to his mouth, and she could see he was shaking. "I'm sorry," he whispered. "I'm so sorry."

"What? What are you talking about? Tell me."

Nate pulled himself from the car.

The blood wasn't his. She could see that now. There was no wound on him.

"It's Shep," he said, placing his hands on Irene's shoulders.

Irene's head began to shake.

"It's bad, honey."

Her breathing stopped.

"He's dead, Irene. Our son, he's . . . he's dead."

There was a moment of silence, like the quiet before a tornado. Then the impact, hitting her full in her chest, her gut, her stomach, legs giving way, chest heaving, releasing a sound that was nowhere near human.

Nate clutched her as she struggled. "It was a robbery," he said. "They tore the place apart looking for something. I don't know what. All I know is I found it that way, then I found Shep. He'd been shot. I tried to save him, but it was too late, Irene. Do you understand? It was too late."

Her husband, blood-soaked, eyes wild—she'd seen him that way before. Huddled in the corner of the bed pleading for someone, somewhere, to stop something. War dreams.

She pulled her arm loose and struck his chest, his arms, his face, yelling for him to stop lying. Sheriff Stubnik was suddenly there. "Where's my son?" she screamed. "You take me to my son!"

The man looked at Nate.

"Don't look at him! Look at me! Where the hell's my son?" Then the tiny woman who had never fought against anyone in her whole life pushed her husband aside and took off across the dry ground up to her front door.

Nate yelled her name. Shep yelled too; she could hear him calling. There was no way she would let her boy die. He was her life, her breath, her son. She would cover his mouth with hers and breathe life back. She could do these things. She *had* to do these things.

A mother does not let her child die.

CHAPTER 7

October 1, 2004

STEVEN JOSEPH STANLEY'S JAW HAD been cracked, his right shoulder dislocated. He was shot at close range, five or six feet. The angle and trajectory of the bullet indicated that the boy had been low to the ground, possibly kneeling, when struck. The bullet, a .22, had entered his left lung, penetrated his liver, then lodged in his spine. Daniel Robbin's rap sheet said his victim had died of asphyxiation.

"Drowned in his own damn blood," Mason muttered as he stepped into the rec yard.

Smoke raked the eastern sky, flooding it like something evil. "Damn shame to put so much crap in the air," Mason said as he approached the prisoner. He'd never get used to farmers burning off their fields.

"Used to be worse." Daniel Robbin stood. "Ten, twelve years

ago, they burned all summer." He licked his lips. "You could taste it. Even shut up inside, you could taste it."

"That's what I hear."

Robbin was a small man, medium height, thin, with sharp angular features and steel-gray eyes. He wore blue jeans and a denim shirt, the word *inmate* stenciled in orange across the front and back.

Mason reached inside his suit jacket, pulled out a red-and-white pack of cigarettes, glanced at the guard standing some fifteen feet away, then pointed the pack at Robbin.

The prisoner grinned and shook his head. "That's contraband, you know."

"You try keeping these things out of here." Mason tapped out a single cigarette, tucked it under his lip, flicked a lighter, inhaled.

"I didn't know you smoked."

Mason exhaled. "I don't."

A plane buzzed low. Geese honked. The rec yard was surrounded by two fences, each topped by coils of razor wire that caught and reflected the afternoon light like scraps of glass. Beyond the prison grounds, I-5 droned with its constant catalytic undertow, pulling at the imagination of every inmate in the place. In one direction the interstate led south to Mexico, in the other north to Canada. Either way meant freedom. Mason looked south, feeling the weight of the warrant in his jacket pocket, the stern, still pressure of what lay ahead, and the old, dull ache of just wanting to run.

Robbin broke into his thoughts. He'd changed his mind about having a smoke, and Mason, relieved to give the man something other than a death warrant, shook out another and flicked his lighter.

Robbin inhaled, then gagged. "You know," he said, hitting his chest, "you could get your job done a lot quicker if you just handed out a shitload of these." He looked at the cigarette, then took another drag. "So tell me"—his gaze back on the clouds—"they set a date?"

Mason rolled his cigarette between his thumb and index finger. "It's why you're here, isn't it?"

"End of the month," Mason replied.

"Halloween?"

"The twenty-ninth. First thing."

A breeze stirred Robbin's hair, and Mason noticed the gray that hid underneath, like a kind of down.

The inmate took another drag, then breathed out. "I see."

Mason didn't know what more to say, so he reached into his pocket and pulled out the letter. "You want me to read it to you? I'm supposed to read it to you."

"If you're supposed to, then I guess you should."

Mason looked at the envelope, turned it over, then handed it to Robbin. "You can call your lawyer when you get back inside. That, or first thing tomorrow."

Robbin dropped his cigarette, crushed it with the heel of his gym shoe, and took the letter. "Why would I want to go and do that?"

"I guess that'd be for you and your lawyer to decide."

Robbin shook his head. "There's nothing left to decide, Mr. Mason." He ran his hand over the envelope as if he were reading Braille. "I'm not fighting this thing."

Mason gave the inmate a sidewise glance, wondering if it would be easier to execute a man who wanted to die. And while he considered this question, Robbin pointed.

"Look at that, would you?"

Mason turned and looked, then whipped back his head. "Look at what?"

"Hummingbird. It just flew by—didn't you hear it?"

Mason locked his eyes on Robbin, taking him in whole. A man, even one behind bars, could have a weapon. A toothbrush filed down to a blade, a screw loosened from a piece of furniture. People had been known to mold instant coffee into knives. Mason had done it himself, once. A small shell-shaped blade that cut through flesh as easily as warm butter.

"A rufous," Robbin continued. "You know, mostly brown, bright red throat." The inmate looked past Mason. "What is it? October first, second? I don't remember ever seeing one this late in the season."

"A hummingbird?" Mason asked. "Here in the yard?"

"Yeah. A male, too. A male rufous."

"Right." Mason ground his cigarette under his shoe, pissed with himself for turning like that. Guard down. Vulnerable. Totally against instinct and training. "And why would a hummingbird be here? Look at this place—there's nothing for it to live off."

Robbin's gaze went back to the superintendent. Then he smiled. Not a full one, both sides of the mouth up, but one of those half-sized things, a lip lifting and something like a chuckle coming. "It's all right there, General. That bird'll find its way. We all do, eventually."

CHAPTER 8

May 11, 1985

THEY WENT TO BURY THEIR son on a cool, gray day, the clouds hanging like linen on the land. Sounds were an up-close, almost touchable thing, and Irene heard them all as they left Missionary Baptist. Footsteps . . . Coughs . . . Cars . . .

Nate helped his wife and daughter into their truck, then settled himself behind the wheel. Bliss sat between her parents, her twelve-year-old hands folded neatly on her lap. Irene looked down at her child's perfectly trimmed and painted nails. Her sister, Carol, had polished them. She'd also done her niece's hair and bought her a new dress at Runkle's. Carol had arrived within a day of Nate's call: a bus north to St. Louis, a flight to Portland, a rental car across the mountains, then into Sheriff Stubnik's guest room, where she'd found Irene and held her all night long.

Irene put her hand to her mouth and tore at a cuticle. Her own nails were unpolished, and her dress was something from Mrs. Stubnik's closet—a simple black sheath, polka dots like tiny stars covering a slice of night. Mrs. Stubnik had lent Irene a scarf as well, and it now hung down on either side of her face as Nate pulled behind the hearse and followed it out of the gravel lot and onto Main North.

They drove past the post office, Blaine Grain and Feed, Runkle's, other places either boarded up long ago or looking so empty and forlorn they ought to have been. They saw a tall, thin vagrant named Heath. He had a bristly beard and a weather-beaten hat that appeared molded to his head. He was a near fixture around town, but no one had known much about him, not even his name, until Shep had finally asked. She and her son were loading groceries into their truck when the aging vagabond walked by, hauling a garbage bag filled with cans. Shep introduced himself and his mother, then asked him his name. "Heath," he responded shyly, and from then on Shep always gathered whatever cans he ran across and left them near where he and the old man had met.

Heath stopped walking and looked up at the phalanx of vehicles led by the lone black hearse. Then he pulled off his hat, and held it to his chest.

"Look at that," Bliss said, pointing.

But Irene turned away. Her mission on this day was to stay upright. To bear this thing called a funeral with her mind as closed off to its sights and sounds as possible. Her lips trembled with the effort, and her pulse quickened as her daughter buried her face in Nate's arm.

They drove on, the sound of the truck whining as they climbed up out of town, past the mill and its empty lumber bays, and then left onto a steep gravel road surrounded by a still and lonely landscape of sagebrush, bunchgrass, and cindery blocks of iron-brown basalt—mile after mile, climbing and descending like wrinkles on a bedsheet. At a wide spot in the road, Nate pulled over. Nearby, a rocky path led up a ridge to a small cemetery bordered by a weathered iron fence.

"You can't tell with these clouds," Nate said, turning off the truck, "but from here you can see quite a bit of the Cascades."

Nate had picked their son's burial site, and Irene nodded her thanks. Shep loved the mountains, read everything he could about them, and was always out exploring. Just the autumn before, he had got the family to pile into the truck and head an hour and a half west, past cattle ranches and those huge red-barked pines. They all talked over each other as they drove higher and higher, curving around switchbacks and getting glimpses of Mount Jefferson, Three Fingered Jack, and other mountains with names Irene couldn't remember. Then suddenly the trees stopped and they were out on a wild and windy plateau covered in every direction with sharp black rocks tossed in a way that made her think it was where the state dumped its asphalt. Shep laughed when she said that, then explained that it was lava. "These mountains are still growing, Ma." He began climbing the jagged blocks, leaping and hollering into the wind. She'd never seen him so thrilled, going on and on about how exciting it was to live someplace where things actually change.

NATE GAVE HIS WIFE AND daughter a wan smile as he helped them from the truck, then hunched his back and walked to where the pallbearers were gathering, all of them in their Sunday boots and hats, western-style shirts, and Wrangler jeans held up by belts with buckles the size of saucers. Carol walked over from the sheriff's car and took Irene's arm in one hand, her niece's in the other, and when the time came they followed the men up the hill.

At the cemetery's entrance the gate opened with a screech that was echoed by the sound of a bird. A raven, possibly a crow, stared down at the group from the top of a lone juniper. Beside the tree lay a mound of sandy-colored soil. Irene held her breath as dizzying spikes of color flashed before her now closed eyes.

"No," she whispered. "I can't."

Carol tugged on her arm, but Irene's feet held fast to her spot of ground. "Come on now, sweetie." Carol's voice sounded muffled. "Come on, everyone's coming up behind us now. You can do this."

Irene conceded and stiff-legged it forward, one foot after another, the weave of Mrs. Stubnik's scarf obscuring everything but the sight of her own small feet.

At the grave she reached for her daughter, but the girl broke free and took off for the tree. It was a scraggly-looking thing, with a thick trunk and wizened branches holding fanlike tassels of green. A few minutes later, Bliss was back with a small handful of yellow, sap-filled pearls.

"They look like tears," she said, showing them to her aunt Carol and then her mother. "Like the tree's crying."

Irene ran her hand down her child's arm, then looked away. There are certain things you should never have to see in life. A crying tree standing beside your son's grave was one.

That was one.

THEY MADE AN ARC AROUND the casket, a small broken circle lined with grim faces. Then one by one people left the group and gravitated toward the Stanleys. "It's too sad," they said, picking up and holding Irene's hand as if it were a piece of old and tattered lace. "It's just too sad."

A short, pudgy boy about Shep's age, maybe younger, stood in front of the Stanleys, his hair pressed flat from the baseball cap he'd just taken off. He stuttered out an apology and Irene gasped. At his feet was Shep's horn. She'd recognize its case anywhere, beat up and bound with duct tape. The detectives had had Nate and Irene search their home for any missing items. Irene noticed the horn's absence right off. Then her mother's pearls, her father's watch, and the heart-shaped pendant Nate had given her the Christmas they moved to Blaine.

"Where'd you get that?" Nate's voice was ice.

The boy stepped back. "Sh-Shep. He lent it to me. I played it in church the Saturday before. He's been teaching me how."

Irene glanced from the boy to her husband. Shep had never lent out his horn, and he hadn't mentioned teaching anyone, either.

"You sure about that?" Nate asked.

The boy retreated another step. "Ye-ye-yes. My sister, she's over there." He pointed to a short, pink woman. "I played it at her wedding."

Nate stared at the boy a few seconds longer, then Irene picked up the case and pressed it against her chest.

"Thank you," she whispered. "I thought . . ." She swallowed at the image of her home, furniture overturned, lamps busted, blood. "I thought it'd been stolen."

"No, ma'am. Shep offered to let me use it for the wedding. I got my own, but it's nothing like his."

Irene smiled at the boy. The horn had been her father's. He'd played it in the Army Band, and perhaps because Nate once told Irene that being in the Army Band was nothing like being in the army—"He didn't do shit to save us from the Japs"—she'd taken particular joy in her son's playing.

"I-I meant to return it to him on Monday, but I got sick. I never did—" He turned his face toward the crying tree. "I never did get to th-thank him."

"I had no idea," Irene said.

Nate grimaced as if he'd swallowed something sour, then greeted someone else.

Irene looked back to the boy.

"Your son," he said, the tip of his gym shoe working its way into the dirt. "H-he could play like nothing I've ever heard. And, well . . ." He bit his lip. "I was wondering if maybe I could play his horn for him. You know, once the s-s-s-service is done?"

Irene stepped back as if he'd said something obscene.

"I-I'd play my own," he said, wringing his hat. "But like I said, it—it don't have nearly the sound of Shep's, and you know how he loved his horn. I thought maybe . . ."

Irene shook her head. "I'm sorry."

"What's going on here?" Nate was back on the boy.

"I-I was just asking if I might play something for Shep."

Irene watched her husband's face harden. "This ain't a talent show, son. Now you just go take your place over by your sister and never mind 'bout anything else."

The boy's ears turned a bright red. "Yes, sir. I-I'm sorry, I didn't mean to bother you. I mean, I'm sorry, real s-s-sorry about Shep."

"Thanks," Nate said, and turned away. Irene stared at her husband's rigid back, then at the boy walking away. She noticed that something about his leg wasn't right. Not a limp really, but an unevenness.

"What's your name?" she asked as she walked up behind him.

He turned. "E-Edgar. Edgar Siles, ma'am. Shep, he was my f-f-friend. He helped me." Edgar bit his lip once more, and a flutter of grief passed over his face. "He taught me a lot."

Irene held her breath for a moment, then released it, nodding.

"I didn't mean to offend. It's just that Shep, he was a real good musician, ma'am. The b-best I've ever heard."

"It's okay, Edgar. No one's offended." A gust of wind kicked up spurs of dust, forcing her to close her eyes. When it stopped, she looked at her son's trumpet case still clasped to her bosom.

"You know," she said, "I think you're right. Shep *would* want to hear his horn played one more time. I think you're absolutely right, and . . . I appreciate your asking. That took courage, and I'm appreciating it." She unfolded her arms and held the case out to the boy. "You play something for my son. He would like that. I think he would like that just fine."

THE ARC OF MOURNERS CLOSED around the grave like fingers around a stone. Irene stood on one side of Bliss, Nate on the other. Then the preacher, a sticklike being with long knobby hands, stepped into the center of the group, opened his Bible, and began to read from Psalms ("Blessed are the meek") and Proverbs ("Even in death the righteous have refuge"), then Isaiah ("Woe to the wicked"), before finally working his way into the story of Cain and Abel and God's call for punishment. But Irene couldn't keep up.

Shep was rolling a ball back and forth between his legs. He was crying because up beyond the trees the moon was all broken. He was tucked beside her as she read and laughing as she sang. He was riding his bike, and going to his first day of school, and playing the piano and the horn. Shep was smiling and laughing. Shep was her boy, he was just her little boy . . .

The preacher called for prayer, and all heads bent down. "He always had a smile," the man said, "a kind word, a hand. He was always in God's presence, and is there now as we pray in the name of Lord Jesus. Our Father, who art in Heaven . . ."

Irene's mouth moved with the others from prayer to song, like a child moves its mouth with its mother's, mimicking and miming but not understanding whats or whys. She only knew that she couldn't leave her son. Not in this place. Not alone. Not forever. And as she stood there, she swore she wouldn't. She'd be back. This ground, this place, they would share it. Together. Mother and child.

And as she made her promise, the plump boy with the crooked walk slowly emerged from beside that lone tree with its resinous tears and approached Shep's grave. Irene closed her eyes and steeled herself to hear the mournful call of "Taps," its four simple notes a kind of psalm, poetic and painful in its brevity. But "Taps" was not what young Edgar Siles played. Instead, it was "Silent Night." And suddenly Irene Stanley was back in Carlton, her son standing beside the field, a silhouette against the evening light. And in that moment, all that had been holding her from the ground fell off, like rain from a summer storm that finally broke itself free.

CHAPTER 9

May 15, 1985

NAPALM, GAS, GRENADES. SMELL OF *ammonia and diesel scorching eyes, nose, skin. Despite the wet. Sucking up to a swamp, thick with leeches and snakes, and floating in the rice grass, a child's hand.*

Just the hand. White and bloated as a fish.

And now gunfire, to the left, from the trees. Movement. People slithering like those damn snakes, copters clapping, ammo wet. Everything wet and slick and the gun grinding tendon and bone, pounding shots across the water, and the reeds, and the rest of the little kid's body, wherever the hell that might be.

Nate woke covered in sweat, sheets wrapped around his torso, pillows bundled and tossed. It was the first night back in their house on Indian Ridge and he hated it—the place, its size, its stinking little yard, and most of all . . .

Most of all . . .

Shep had died right across the hall, his eyes fixed on his father as he gasped for breath. Nate had done what he could, attempting to calm, to stanch the blood, to push life back into his boy. But it hadn't worked. He'd seen that kind of wound over and over in Nam, then once in Carlton, old man Droose cleaning out his gun. He hadn't been able to save any of them either.

Nate unwrapped himself from the sheets, sat upright, ran his hand through his hair. His memories of that day were nothing but a flash of horror and rage. Feeling sick and wounded and half insane. He had done everything he knew to save his boy. Every damn thing. But nothing worked.

Nothing had ever worked.

He glanced at the clock and swore. He'd spent the entire night thrashing and wishing Irene would come in. He slept better with her near—her scent, the small noises she made. She talked in her sleep, on and off, little words coming from her soft mouth. But she was too upset to be near anyone, Carol said. Too angry and depressed and lost for anyone to know what to do.

He flicked on the bedside lamp, looked around the small room, then put his head in his hands and wondered what he could have done differently to prevent all this. There must have been something. His father, he knew for sure, would have done *something* different.

Herb Stanley owned Carlton's only butcher shop and was as tough as they came. But more than that, he'd had a nose for trouble. Once a guy came to rob their shop, but Herb swore to the day he died he knew just what the guy was about before he ever stepped in. He told Loretta to handle the counter, and he went off to the side. The instant the guy pulled out the gun, Herb was on him. Cleaved three fingers clear off the guy. Threatened to do the same with Nate and his brother too, that time he caught them jerking off in the woods.

Nate stood, pulled at his boxers, walked to the window, and

yanked the sash on the shade. But the heavy vinyl just slipped lower and lower. So he pushed it aside. He had an idea that if the sun was coming up, he'd wake his wife and take her out back to watch the day begin. Just like they used to at the farm. But it was still dark, so he went to the john, took a piss, ran a toothbrush across his teeth, a razor over his face, then showered. Afterward, he dressed: khaki shirt and pants, white cotton socks, hiking shoes. Dobin had told him to stay home, but the hell if he'd listen to that. There was a suspect: a nineteen-year-old ex-con named Daniel Robbin. He'd worked as a mechanic right around the corner, until he disappeared on the afternoon of the murder. Their house had been full of his prints.

Nate lifted his gun from the bedside drawer, slipped it into its shoulder holster, then threw on his fishing vest and cap. It was the same outfit he'd worn the day before, and the day before that, pants torn and dirty from hiking, clambering over fences, searching caves and riverbanks. If he found the s.o.b., he promised himself, he'd kill him. Just put the gun to the fucker's head and pull the trigger.

In the hall he could hear Carol snoring. She was sleeping in Bliss's room; his daughter was at the Stubniks' for another two days, until Carol took her back to Carlton. He didn't want his little girl around all this, and he still hoped Irene would decide to go back home too. It'd be better that way. Easier all around.

Flat dawn light filtered through the living room's large rectangular window. Nate stared out past the houses to the singular peak of Mount Jefferson. He had hoped when he bought the house that its view and the vastness of the land that surrounded them would somehow make up for tearing his family from all they had had—that being without the coddling care of relatives would make them all stronger and clearer about who and what they were. But it hadn't worked out that way.

Irene lay curled in her recliner, her mom's afghan hanging at her feet. Nate picked it up, shook it, then placed it over her, tucking it around her shoulders the way she liked. She was the prettiest damn thing he'd ever seen. Always had been, even back when they were kids and all he could think to do was tease her about her tiny size and huge fawnlike eyes. There had never been a day when he hadn't had it for Irene Lucinda Crain. He leaned over and kissed her forehead, ran a finger down her cheek, hoping she'd wake so they could watch the sun light the mountains and he could take her hand and tell her all the ways he had tried to save their son, and then all the damn ways he'd failed.

CHAPTER 10

May 16, 1985

I RENE SAT IN A SLAT-BACK chair at her daughter's desk, watching Carol pack Bliss's suitcase. The American Tourister lay open on the bed among piles of summer clothes.

Carol tapped her fingers against her cheek. "She'll need her swimsuit."

Irene pointed. "Bottom drawer."

Carol bent over, a floral print dress covering her generous rear, and came back up dangling two tiny strips of pink cotton. "This little thing?" Carol smacked her lips, then tossed it into the case. "I'm glad you're letting me take Bliss for a while." She opened another drawer and pulled out a handful of underwear. "Poor thing's terrified. Margie Stubnik says Bliss just sits in their living room staring at the TV set. Hardly says a word."

Irene rubbed her temple, wishing her sister would shut up. For nine days all she'd done was talk, talk, talk. As if her words could somehow bury what had happened, like snow buries dirt.

"You'll see, though. She'll come 'round. Kids, they're resilient that way." Carol snapped a shirt in the air, pressed it against her pillowy chest, crossed its arms back, then folded it in half. "Plus it'll be good, her being back with friends and family." She set the shirt in the case and pushed it flat. "Don't you think?"

Irene's eyes settled on the suitcase, then closed altogether. She had no idea whether kids were resilient that way. Plus just thinking of their place back in Carlton—white clapboard, black trim, a good-sized kitchen looking out to the barn and the gnarled old maple with its tire swing and the dirt all trod flat beneath, the sounds of bobwhites and whip-poor-wills, and her garden and the land all around, 212 acres of river bottom as moist and fecund as a womb—it hit too many emotions at once. Like a pinball bouncing hard against her heart, her head, her throat, until it finally settled in her gut, heavy and cold.

They never should have left. She had known it when Nate first marched into their kitchen with that damn map of his. And she hadn't fought, not the way she should have.

"Irene?"

She opened her eyes.

"I was saying it's a good thing Bliss is going home. Don't you think?"

"Yeah, yeah, of course. No use being here."

Seven plastic horses stood in a line at the back of Bliss's desk. More stood on a shelf by her bed and along her dresser. Her daughter had been collecting them since kindergarten and would sit for hours playing with them. "You ought to pack a couple of these." Irene picked up a champagne-colored palomino named Jack. "And you might pack a sweater, just in case. She has a favorite in the hall closet."

Carol nodded. "Sweater's already packed. I also have some books she asked for. But she said she won't be needin' the horses."

Irene set Jack back with his line of mares, then looked away.

"I know." Carol snapped another shirt. "They grow so damn fast. She'll be wanting to go on dates before you know it. You should see Adam! He's taller than his pa now." Carol pressed her plump lips together, shook her head, continued folding. "It's something, really something."

Carol was taller than Irene and wider than her in every direction. Her cheeks were always lit with a bloom of blush, her lips always a candy-apple red. "Bliss did say she'd like a picture of Shep. Something recent. Is there any certain one you want her to have?"

Pictures, Irene thought. They were not a picture-taking family; no portraits or wedding photos were propped on the television set or lining the halls, as at Carol's. There were no baby pictures by her bed. She remembered Nate had taken a camera when they went to the mountains last fall, so maybe there'd be something from that. And he usually took at least a couple of pictures Christmas morning, though there was no saying if anything was ever developed.

Carol glanced at her sister. "You want me to look for one?"

"No," Irene said. "I'll find something before you two leave."

Despite her size, Carol moved around the room with ease, humming as she went from bed to closet to dresser and back. She reminded Irene of their dad—big, gregarious, happy almost all the time, and there, always right there, even if you didn't want him. In twenty-two hours, Carol and Bliss would be landing in St. Louis, where Carol's husband, Doctor Al, would pick them up and take them home. Irene drummed the desk with her fingers, wishing her sister and daughter were already gone, out of this bedroom, this house, this state, her sight. Irene just couldn't handle it, the snap of clothes, the humming, Bliss frightened and alone, with a mother too sunk in her own loss to even help pack her things. Irene sighed, then pushed herself from the chair and left the room. A couple of minutes later she was back, holding a red box the size of a cake. She set it beside the suitcase.

"What's that?" Carol asked.

"A kit with some books and Kotex and stuff. She hasn't started yet, but I expect she will before the summer's out. If she does, you can give her that kit. It'll explain everything she needs to know."

Carol straightened. "Irene Lucinda Stanley, you mean to tell me you haven't told her yet?"

Irene dropped down into Bliss's chair, painted lavender, just like her room. "They had that at the drugstore. I thought it'd do a better job explaining things than me."

Carol's forehead folded like a curtain. "You're just like Mom, you know it? Never telling us nothing about the birds and bees and then all the hell you and Nate caught when you went and figured it out on your own. I'll tell you what, I decided long ago that I didn't want that for *my* kids. Heck, Shelly and Ann have known what's what since they were eight."

Irene scratched her arm. "Bliss and me aren't like you and your girls."

Carol sucked on her front teeth and studied her sister, then opened the box. "I'll give her the books—the rest we can get at home. But I'm tellin' you, sis, you're the one who ought to be doing this."

Irene looked out the window where the rosebushes she and the kids had planted were wilting in the heat. There were a lot of things she ought to do, she thought, and she was not in the mood to talk about any one of them.

"You know how kids are, Irene," Carol continued. "You think they don't want you 'round when really they do. And that goes double for Bliss. She needs you. There's just no gettin' by it. The truth is, you really ought to be coming home with us."

Irene took a pen from a box made of Popsicle sticks and painted blue with a red heart that said *From your big broder.* Shep had made it in second grade. "I already told you, I can't."

Carol sighed, walked around the bed, and sat on its edge, knee to knee with her sister. The two Crain girls: one petite, one large; one quiet and passive, one loud and brash; one afraid to tell her daughter the facts of life, one so full of life that its facts just tumbled from her mouth years before her children had any idea what she was talking about. "What are you gonna do here? Tell me that. I've never seen a more lonesome place, and Nate . . . well, he's too busy to take care of you."

Irene looked down at her hands, nails bitten to the quick.

"Look at that. Lord, girl. You used to have the prettiest nails." Carol cupped Irene's hands. "You're not taking care of yourself, you know it? Not eating, hardly sleeping, and I know you've been drinking. And after all the trouble you had after Ma and Pa died. Remember that? How you tried to drown everything, and there was Bliss and Shep, so little. No, I tell you what—you should come on home for a while. Me and Al, we'll take care of you."

Irene pulled away from her sister. "I can't do that right now, Carol." She ran her hand back behind her neck, working her skin like she would work dough, or dirt, back when she lived in a place where dirt could grow something worthwhile. She hoped Carol would understand, thought that by being a mother, she would clearly see there was no way to leave this whole thing.

"But Bliss *needs* you, Irene. You know she does."

Irene's head snapped up. "Bliss doesn't need me."

"What are you talking about? Of course she does."

"Uh-uh. Bliss has hardly ever needed me. Been that way from the beginning. You remember how she fussed all the time, only'd calm down for Nate? I swear, it's like she and I, we're from different worlds."

"Oh, come on, Irene. All parents feel that way about their kids—"

"Not me and Shep. Nate always said that was my problem, that I paid too much attention to our boy. Babying him, he called it. Babying him and ignoring our daughter. And you know what? He was right. But I couldn't help it. It was just that Shep needed me more, and I'm telling you, Carol, I'm not leaving this place until my son stops needing me."

Carol leaned back, her lips silently counting to ten. It was a trick their mother had taught her daughters. Take time before responding, set a pace . . . think . . . breathe . . .

"Irene—honey, Shep needs you to be there for the rest of your family now. His sister, his father. He needs you to think about what *they* need." She put her hand on Irene's knee. "And more than anything else, your sweet boy needs you to start taking care of yourself. Don't you think? I mean, honestly, Irene." She paused. "Isn't that just what Shep would say?"

Irene stood. She didn't want to think about what Shep would say, and asking her to was wrong. "I gotta go look for that picture."

"Now hold on." Carol grunted as she pushed herself from the bed. "That can wait. I'm serious, sis, you can't go on like this. No food, no sleep. You come on back to Carlton. If you want, I'll have Ma and Pa's place fixed up in no time. Look, I know it's hard, but you need to start focusing on what you have."

Carol's face looked buttered with sympathy, and the sight of it made Irene want to scream. *Hard?* Carol had no idea about hard. Irene started counting, silently clicking through the numbers. Her son was dead and buried up on some godforsaken hill. Carol wanted to talk about what Irene had—well, there it was. A grave. That's what she had, and that was all she had. *Sweet Jesus, how can she not understand?* There was no way in hell Irene was leaving Shep. *Hard?* Carol's son was growing; he was taller than Al now. Shep wasn't. Shep would never get the chance to be taller than his father. He would never graduate from high school or go to college or get married. No, there was no goddamn way she was just going to leave Shep on that hillside alone. The sheriff would catch the creature that killed her son, and after it was all done—him hung or electrocuted, or whatever was done in this lousy state—she would go to that cemetery and join her little boy, because all she knew for certain was that once this was done, she was too. She'd made Nate buy the three plots next to Shep's, and she was damn certain she was going to use one of them soon.

"You're right," Irene said, forcing herself to measure her words. "But you've got to give me time. That's all. Just some time. *Alone*." Irene took a deep breath. "Look, maybe in a little while I'll be ready to come back to Carlton, be with you and the family. But not yet." She swallowed. "Now, if you don't mind, I think I'll take your advice and make myself a sandwich, then go lie down for a little while."

Carol cocked her head the way their mom would when she wasn't quite sure if her daughters were telling the truth.

"I understand what you're saying, Carol. I do. And you're right. We should never have moved out here to begin with. And maybe once this is all through I'll be able to get Nate to move on home."

Irene leveled her eyes on her sister, and after several beats Carol sighed and patted her arm.

"All right, then. At least we have a plan. A little more time here, then come on home. I can live with that." Carol smiled. "I don't pretend to understand what you're going through, sis, but I do know the sooner you start looking forward, the better off you'll be. Shep's not the one needing you now. I know it's not what you want to hear, and Lord knows I don't want to be saying it, but that's just the way it is."

THE NEXT MORNING BLISS SAT with Mrs. Stubnik and her three-year-old son, Calvin, on the Stubniks' front porch waiting for her aunt Carol. She had on her favorite summer dress and her brand-new gym shoes. And she had her purse filled with things for her trip: a *Seventeen* magazine from Annette, Doublemint gum from Tracy, and a twenty dollar bill Marjorie Stubnik had given her to get "something nice for herself" when she got back home.

"Do it again." Calvin Stubnik grabbed one of Bliss's braids. "Do it again."

Bliss pried the little boy's hand loose, then folded her own hands together. "This is the church, this is the steeple. Open it up—where are the people?"

The little boy giggled. "Show it the other way. The other way."

Bliss refolded her hands, making a steeple with her two index fingers, then opening her palms and wiggling the fingers inside.

"There they are!" Calvin shrieked. "Mama, see, there they are!"

Mrs. Stubnik looked up from her knitting. "Here comes your father, Bliss."

Her family's blue pickup pulled to the curb, followed by Aunt Carol in the little red car she'd rented in Portland. Bliss waved, then started down the porch stairs.

"Wait for me," Calvin yelled.

She turned and picked up the boy and headed toward the street while her father came around the front of the truck. *He looks pinched in*, Bliss thought. *Like one of those dried-up apple dolls.* She couldn't remember ever seeing him look that way before, but then again, everyone seemed to look different these days. Even her own face appeared strange to her, as if it had been buffed of expression and the eyes drained of color.

Bliss set Calvin down on the lawn and hugged her dad, pressing her face into his belly and suddenly feeling like she was going to bawl. Everything was all mixed up in her mind. She still didn't believe her brother was dead. Not completely. Her heart said yes, he was gone and everything was changed and ruined and life was never, ever going to be the same. But in her mind . . . in her mind it just didn't fit, and she kept waiting to wake up and find herself back in her room surrounded by her things and living her life the way she always had. No big problems. No real pain.

She heard the passenger door open, and she rubbed her face against her dad's belly and then looked over at her mom. Where her dad looked all squeezed in, her mom looked puffed out. Her eyes, her cheeks, even her hands, which were reaching for Bliss now, looked swollen. Bliss released her father and let her mother give her a hug.

"You go and be good for your aunt, you hear?" She talked into Bliss's hair, and Bliss nodded. "And be helpful. Clean up after yourself, offer to help with the cooking and cleaning."

"I will."

Her mother sniffed, then squeezed her again. "I know you will."

Bliss accepted this statement as true even though she had never been much help at home. She always had to be told to make her bed, clean her room, help with the dishes, or go out and weed. Not like Shep. He always seemed to anticipate what their mom wanted, and it always kind of bugged her. But now . . . now it just seemed like there was no other thing to do but be helpful. At least she'd be doing something, and something was better than the total nothing she was doing now. All day long just sitting around waiting to regain her sense of . . . what? Not sight, not hearing, not touch. Perhaps it was balance. Like when she would spin and spin and spin on the old tree swing at home and then wait for the world to refocus.

"I don't want to come back here, Mama. Not ever. You and Daddy, you need to come back to Carlton. You need to pack up our stuff and just come back home. I don't want to be there without you."

Her mother sighed, and at least in that Bliss felt the comfort of the familiar. Her mom's sighs had been the white noise riding behind every decision that had led them to leave Carlton in the first place. Bliss had gotten sick of hearing the helpless, meandering sound. Like water that had no choice where it would run.

"Don't worry, sweetheart." Her dad stepped up and patted her back. "You'll have plenty to do this summer. Jeff will be there, and all your cousins."

Bliss looked down and saw that Calvin was off chasing a grasshopper. "But I want you, Daddy. You and Mommy and, and . . ."

She wanted Shep. She wanted her mom and dad and Shep and home and everything to be back the way it was.

"We know, honey," her mother said. "But we'll be back together soon."

No, we won't, Bliss almost shouted. *We won't ever be back together, not the way we used to be.* But she didn't say that. She couldn't. She wanted to hurt someone for all the hurt she was feeling. But not her mom, and certainly not her dad. So she started toward her aunt's car. The trunk was open, and inside was her suitcase. She had used it once at a slumber party. She and three other girls had stayed up all night playing truth or dare and watching videos. She had made some pretty good friends in Blaine, and even kind of had a crush on Rupert Nolan. Plus she'd been made class president. But none of that meant anything now. It was like her eyes—the color, the excitement, the drama of her life had all been washed out, and she had no way of seeing how it would ever come back.

CHAPTER 11

May 23, 1985

DANIEL ROBBIN WALKED INTO THE Roadside Tavern in the middle of the day. The place was empty except for Bernie— barrel chest, tumbleweed beard—rubbing wax into a thirty-five-foot length of hand-planed walnut while humming along with Willie Nelson. Bernie owned the bar and tended it as if it were the only thing in his life, which it wasn't. He still had a daughter out in Tucson, a grandson too, thirteen years old now. And he had his customers: single guys always hoping, and married ones who knew better but kept hoping anyway; women, their long flannel shirts covering up what gravity had claimed; millworkers, cowhands, waitresses coming in off their shifts, tips jangling in their pockets. People, all of them, strung out on a line waiting for life to turn better, knowing full well how lucky they were that it wasn't any worse. The bar owner knew them all and considered them a kind of family.

Except for the guy walking in.

Sonofabitch, he thought. *It's him.* Bernie took a slow draw of the room's sour air as he watched the man approach: blue jeans, denim jacket, dirty light-blue T. He had long dark hair, a lean angular face, square jaw, silver coins for eyes.

It'd been all over the news these past couple weeks, his picture and what had happened out in Blaine, the break-in and the shooting of a deputy's son. Customers hung on the details, speculating about why it had happened, where the guy was hiding, and whether he'd get caught. Killings happened out their way; arguments could turn just as bad in the middle of nowhere as anywhere else. But the thing in Blaine felt different.

"Hot one out there, ain't it?" Bernie asked.

The guy closed his grimy hands around themselves, leaned against the bar, and looked around as if he hadn't a clue about the weather.

"So what can I get you?"

"Coors." He fished a crumpled dollar bill from his front pocket.

Bernie pulled a pint glass from a rack, filled it, plunked down a coaster, and set the beer on top. Then he pulled the crank on his register, a 1910 nickel-plated National. The newspapers said the suspect had worked as a mechanic. They also said he was armed and dangerous. Bernie eyed the drawer where he kept his gun, then closed the register with a quick shove, turned, and grabbed his rag.

He rubbed the bar with big, strong strokes, going around and around as he talked about the heat and the fire out by Sunriver. All those fancy homes just waiting for a spark. The bar got waxed once, sometimes twice a week. It wasn't that Bernie was a proud man; it was just that he cared about his place. The bar, and the twenty-foot-long brass inlaid cabinet behind it, had come from Europe in the late 1800s. Barged south across the Atlantic, around Cape Horn, north to the Columbia River, then on into Portland, where it was loaded onto a wagon train and hauled over the mountains. *You have to admire a thing like that,* he'd think to himself as he got out his rags. *Take good care it lasts.* Bernie glanced at his customer.

The TV news had shown a photo of the fifteen-year-old victim. They'd described him as shy. They'd also said he'd been a gifted musician. Bernie winced when he heard that. Winced, then picked up the phone and called his grandson, asked how he was doing in school and whether he needed money for a new set of guitar strings. His ma hardly ever bought him any, so the boy had to boil the old ones just to get some bounce back into them. He told his grandson he'd try to come out and visit sometime in the fall.

Bernie inched closer to his customer, his big bough of an arm buffing the wood to a rich chocolaty shine. Then, *whack.* He knocked over the kid's glass, sending it skidding across the gleaming wood, splashing everything along the way, then crashing and smashing on the pine floor.

"Shit! Oh, shit! Look what I've gone and done. Clumsy as all hell, I tell you." Bernie hurried around the bar, handed the kid a clean rag. "Sorry 'bout that. Look, the john's over there. You clean up, I'll get you a fresh beer. This next one's on me." He laughed at his own joke, hoping he didn't sound nervous.

Later that day Bernie would recount how he called the sheriff while the guy was in the bathroom. Five minutes later, Robbin back at his stool, fresh beer in hand, several deputies came in. "One, two, three, four of 'em. Loud as hell, I tell you. And the kid not even looking to see what the hell's up." Bernie squinted at the people who had gathered at the Roadside Tavern, every one of them eager to hear his story.

"And then, when they went and said 'Freeze,' you know what he went and did?" Bernie tilted a glass under the tap, thick caterpillar-like eyebrows crawling up his forehead. "He smiled. I swear to God. He just looked the hell up at me, and smiled."

CHAPTER 12

June 13, 1985

A FLY BEAT ITSELF AGAINST THE Stanleys' living room window. Up, then down, side to side. It dropped to the ledge, stopped for a second, then entered the dining area and buzzed around the table where Irene and Nate sat with two lawyers.

"Before we get started," District Attorney Arnold Brigham said, shucking off his jacket and draping it on the back of his chair, "my deputy, Miss Aaron, and I want you both to know how sorry we are about your loss. We know how hard it is, and we certainly wish it didn't happen. But it did, and we're here to make sure this Mr. Robbin is never able to do something like it again." Irene looked past the man and out the living room window to where the summer sun was battering the lawn and her pathetic row of roses: seven Abe Lincolns, planted to remind her of home. "But," the attorney continued, "for that to happen, Miss Aaron and I are going to have to ask you a bunch of questions. Things you'd probably rather not have to deal with right now."

Nate's foot started drumming the floor. "But I thought you already had all you need. Fingerprints, motive. That gun they found on him—it checked out, right?"

"It checked out, all right. And technically we don't even have to show a motive. But the guy hasn't confessed, so there's still work to do."

"Like what? What more do you need?" Nate asked.

"A witness would be nice. Someone who saw him flee the house, heard the gunshot, some screaming maybe. But so far no one seems to have noticed a thing until the ambulance showed up. But I can tell you one thing—this guy made a whole bunch of mistakes, starting by picking *your* house." The attorney pointed to the bright silver star pinned to Nate's khaki shirt. "Authority still means something out this way, and we're going to make certain everyone in that courtroom remembers that."

"In addition"—Miss Aaron glanced at her boss—"there's his history. In and out of foster homes, drugs, theft. He was locked up for assault and robbery when he was fourteen."

"Basically," Brigham cut back in, "we know what the guy's made of—how he ticks. Now we just need to make sure there's nothing the defense can dig up that would challenge a jury's . . ." He sucked in his bottom lip, making a loud smooching sound. "Sense of *duty.*"

Miss Aaron nodded in agreement. The young-looking attorney had called the day before to arrange "a visit," and Irene had stayed up most of the night thinking about what lay ahead. From everything she'd heard, it seemed they had the right guy. He had the gun, after all. And though he hadn't admitted anything, he hadn't denied it either. So Irene assumed it would all be over quickly. She needed it all to be over quickly.

"And what about him?" Nate asked. "Has this guy said anything? Anything at all?"

Brigham glanced at his watch. "Scuttlebutt is he hasn't uttered a word, not even to his lawyer. But you know how that goes—he could turn around tomorrow and deny everything. That or say he was insane, or that it was self-defense, possibly an accident—"

"An accident?" Irene straightened. "My son was beaten, Mr. Brigham. His jaw was broken, his arm pulled from its socket. Do you suppose he'd say that was an accident too? Or what about breaking in—you think he'd say he just accidentally broke into our house?"

The attorney glanced at his young deputy. "Actually, as far as the investigators can tell, your house wasn't exactly broken into. No forced entry, jimmied lock. Nothing."

"So? He was in there. A stranger in our house, taking our things."

"Look, Mr. Brigham." Nate leaned over the table. "We've already told Detective Macy that we just weren't in the habit of locking doors. Never even used a key in Carlton. But that doesn't mean our home wasn't entered illegally."

"True enough. I'm just saying we have to be prepared to prove he wasn't there for some other reason, that's all. You and I, we know Robbin's guilty. We just need to be able to convince the twelve people sitting on the jury of that as well."

The attorney smiled at Irene, and she held the man's gaze for a moment, then gave it up. She had no energy for any of this. No will or power.

"Anyway," Mr. Brigham continued, "I'm just rattling off here. The point is, we have to be ready for anything. You can never tell what Robbin's lawyer might try to pull, especially since we could be going for the big guns." The stocky attorney paused, then placed his hands on the table and leaned toward the two parents. "Capital punishment," he said. "Voters just reinstated it last year, and I have a sense this case could go in that direction."

"Death?" Nate's foot stopped hammering. "But his age—he just turned nineteen, right? Isn't that too young? I mean, you think a jury will really go for that?"

"We'll find one that will. This guy Robbin's a bad egg, and we'll make damn sure everyone in that courtroom smells it."

On cue, the fly cruised back into the dining area, buzzed the table, and landed on the DA's brown leather briefcase.

Irene closed her eyes. Shep had gone through an insect phase, checking out every book the library had on the creatures, then taking the books up to his room and reading them to her every night before bed. Flies had little hooks on their legs that enabled them to walk up glass. And cockroaches, they could live an entire week without their head. Something about their brain being all over their body. It made Irene squeamish, but Shep had been fascinated. He must have been, what? Seven—eight, maybe. She and he curled up in bed, reading about bugs . . .

"What about it, honey?" Nate squeezed Irene's knee. "Miss Aaron here was asking for a cup of coffee."

"Oh." Irene stood. "I'm sorry. Yes, yes, of course. It's Sanka," she added apologetically.

The attorney's eyes slanted in a smile. "That'll be fine," she said, rising and following Irene into the kitchen.

IRENE TURNED THE KNOB ON the range, then took a jar of Sanka from the cabinet. The lawyer's distorted reflection hung in the grease-speckled kettle. "You been an attorney long?"

"Nine years."

"You must like it."

The reflection grew bigger. "To be honest, I never expected to last this long. At least not out here—there aren't many Japanese Jewish Americans in central Oregon."

"That's some combination."

Miss Aaron leaned against the counter. "Dad's a Russian Jew, Mom was born and raised in Osaka. Anyway, I had always planned to join my father's firm over in Portland. But prosecuting just feels so much more important."

Irene grabbed a towel off the stove handle and unfolded and re-folded it. "I'm sorry," she said, patting the towel back in place, "but I'm not remembering your name."

The woman bit her lip and approached, taking one of Irene's hands in both of her own. "I'm Barbara," she said softly. "Barbara Aaron. But you're going to call me Barb."

Irene looked at their joined hands. "It's my daughter's name, Barbara. Barbara Lee. But we call her Bliss."

"I like that."

"Her father came up with it."

Miss Aaron released Irene's hand and let out a short laugh. "I can tell you my father certainly would never think to call me that. Torment, maybe. Is your husband the one who came up with Shep? I haven't heard anyone refer to him by his given name."

"That's right. Steven was my father's name, but Nate was never very fond of it. He started calling our son Shep once he was back from the service. I think maybe he knew someone by that name over there. I don't know for sure—he doesn't talk about those days."

"Your husband was in Vietnam, right?"

Irene nodded. "A marine. Spent the first two years of our marriage there."

"That must have been rough."

Nate had gone off to Parris Island marine training center three months after they got married. Six weeks later he came home, just in time to hold his newborn son. Then he was sent to Vietnam. "I had my family, and of course church."

The kettle started to hiss and sputter, and Irene unscrewed the top of the Sanka, spooned a mound into each cup, then opened a cupboard. Up on her toes, reaching back, third shelf up, she found a bag of Oreos held shut by a rubber band. She had hidden them from her children. Shep especially—he had loved Oreos and milk, and would have eaten them every day after school if she had let him. Irene placed a few cookies on a plate, then just stared at it all, stuck like a record with no more play. "You want to know what's rough?" she asked, her voice barely more than a whisper.

Barbara stepped closer.

"This kettle here," Irene said. "These cookies. That jar of coffee. They were all here, right in this house, when Shep was . . ." She paused for a long second. "I think of things like that all the time. Every damn minute."

The house shuddered as a couple motorcycles sped down the block.

"They shouldn't go so fast," Irene said.

"What's that?"

"Those motorcycles. There's kids that ride bikes on this street."

"Oh, yes. Of course. It's dangerous."

Irene nodded. "Dangerous."

The attorney tapped the Formica as if she were playing a chord on a piano. "Your neighbors, they had nothing but kind things to say about you and your family. Shep in particular."

Irene tried to smile.

"Look, Mrs. Stanley, I can't tell you how sorry I am about this whole thing—losing your son the way you have, the senselessness of it. There can't be anything worse. Frankly, I'm surprised you're even able to stand here and talk with me right now. I'm not sure I would be able to."

Irene gripped the counter. Barbara Aaron's words felt like warm water, and she had a sudden desire to dive in. There were cookies on the shelf, a kettle on the stove. She still hadn't changed the sheets on Shep's bed, couldn't bring herself to throw away his toothbrush, couldn't even sleep with her husband because she was so damn sure she wanted to blame him for this, forever and ever, until there was nothing left of either one of them.

The kettle built to a whistle, and the young attorney reached and poured its steaming water into the cups, stirring each to a dirt brown as Nate's voice came in from the dining room.

"He was flat out on the floor when I walked in."

IRENE OPENED THE DOOR TO Shep's room and flicked on the light. The shades were still pulled low from when Carol had cleaned the room. Her sister had had to get rid of a small braided carpet, a lamp, and a poster of Beethoven. "Damaged," she'd said vaguely.

"Is that his horn?" Miss Aaron pointed to the floor by the window.

Irene nodded. Each day since they moved back in, Irene had hauled herself from her living room chair and gone into this room, allowing herself to touch one thing: a book, a blanket, a rock, a piece of paper, the horn. Then, with that item in hand, she would close her eyes and conjure her boy, calling him, talking, praying, crying. A few days before, she'd sat on Shep's bed and read his copy of *Old Yeller*. It was a stupid thing to do. Each page of the book jamming her deeper into her pain—knowing what would happen to that old dog, and what had happened to her son, and having no way to stop either.

Barbara walked up to Shep's desk. Several arrowheads lay on a rusty saw blade; feathers poked out of one tin can, pens and pencils from another. Above the desk hung a series of photographs of Mount Saint Helens before and after its eruption. She turned and looked at Irene. "I want to apologize for my boss out there. He can be . . . brusque, I know. But it's only because he is so determined to get a conviction.

Irene looked down at her feet. She hadn't even bothered to put on shoes. Just her old slippers, cracked and torn and never replaced because she couldn't find anything like them around Blaine. "I didn't lock the door that day. I'm sure of it. I was in a hurry and I just left without even—"

"You need to forget about that. That man would have found a way into your house even if every door and window had been sealed tight."

"I don't know. Seems to me that's why he picked our house. I mean, why else? It's not like we had anything worth stealing. I just made it too easy for him."

"Mrs. Stanley, there could be any number of reasons he chose your house."

"Such as?"

"Such as proximity—he worked right around the corner. Maybe he heard you were new to town. Maybe he thought you might have something more than all these unemployed millworkers around here. Maybe he had something against your husband, or possibly the law in general. Or maybe he knew Shep. Robbin's boss seems to think he's seen Shep at the station a few times."

"At the gas station? Maybe to fill his bike tires, but he certainly didn't know that man. Not to have him come over, he didn't."

"That's probably right. But still, a random act like this, you know the question has to be asked."

Irene sat on the bed. "I suppose."

The attorney smiled sympathetically, then turned back to the desk. "He was quite the collector, wasn't he?"

"He'd take off on his bike all the time. Come home loaded with all kinds of things he'd find."

"Do you know where he'd go?"

"He liked to go fishing along Crooked River. I'm not sure where, exactly. And he mentioned some ridge he'd found out on the reservation. Said he could see forever from out there."

"And he'd do that alone?"

"As far as I know."

"No buddies he'd hang out with?"

"There was this boy he was teaching trumpet to."

"Edgar Siles."

"That's his name."

"Nice boy. We've talked with him. Seems Shep would work with him during band class. But he couldn't have gone off on Shep's little trips. He can't walk too far, let alone ride a bike."

Irene nodded, remembering the boy's awkward gait.

"Other than Edgar, did Shep have any friends?"

Irene shook her head. "Shep's always been a loner. Even back home, with cousins living so close and us knowing nearly everyone, he preferred just to be off on his own. Playing music, riding his bike. All of it alone."

The attorney walked over to the wall where a calendar hung from a corkboard. It was still set to May, and below the picture a couple dates were marked with tiny green checks. The last was May fourth, two days before Shep was killed.

The attorney reached for the calendar, then stopped. "Do you mind if I look at this?"

Irene bit her lip and shook her head, then watched Miss Aaron take it down from Shep's wall and turn it month by month, all the way back to the beginning of the year.

"These check marks." She pointed from page to page. "Do they mean anything to you?"

Irene shook her head again.

"A class? A job, maybe? Some project he was working on?"

"Nothing I knew about."

"What about this last one? Did Shep do anything special that Saturday?"

Irene ran her hand down the side of her face. "We got up . . . did chores . . . then Shep took off on his bike. I remember it was hot out, and that he got too much sun. Came home all red and complaining of a headache. He ended up going to bed early. Didn't even eat dinner. It was just me and Bliss. Nate had to work late."

"And he was okay the next day?"

Irene hesitated. Shep had opted out of church that morning, saying he felt "gross," so she, Nate, and Bliss had gone without him. Afterward, they ran a few errands. Shep was still in his room when they returned, but he joined them for supper and even offered to help with the dishes. But Irene had sent him off. "Get a good night's sleep," she remembered saying. "I want you all better for school."

"And the next day, that Monday—he must have been feeling well enough to go to school."

"I suppose so. I mean, he looked a lot better."

The woman slowly walked from one end of Shep's small room to the other, her finger tapping her lips. "Let me ask you this. What did Shep normally do after school? I mean, did he typically come right home, or do you think he did that because he still wasn't feeling too well?"

This question interested Irene. She hadn't thought about Shep's still maybe being sick and what that might have meant. "I don't know what Shep normally did after school. I work until five on weekdays. He was always home by the time I got here."

"So you don't really know if his coming home right after school was an anomaly? 'Cause if it was, that might explain why Mr. Robbin was in your house when he was. He might have cased your place, figured no one would be around till five or so. I mean, your daughter, Bliss, from what we hear, she stayed after school nearly every day."

"She's a busy girl."

"That's right, she is. But if you had some idea about Shep—"

The attorney's words struck Irene. She should have better answers to this woman's questions. Better ideas of what her son did with his time, where he went, and whether he was ever with anyone. A better sense of whether he still felt sick that day. "I failed him," she whispered. "You know how people say they had a feeling something was about to go wrong? Well, I didn't. Not at all. In fact, I thought everything was working out—the move, being away from home, all that. We were making paths for ourselves. I had no idea this was coming. Not a single goddamned clue."

Barbara Aaron crouched down on the floor and put a hand on one of Irene's knees. "But you couldn't possibly—"

"Couldn't I?" Irene stared at the woman: nice clean suit, pretty black hair, pearls at her neck. "You come in here asking about Shep's life. A lawyer, in my boy's room, asking about his things and his days and whether he had friends. And here I am, having not a single good answer for you. I thought he and I were so close, and yet I don't know what he did after school ... I never even knew about that Siles boy until Shep's funeral. I don't know a thing, Miss Aaron. Not a thing."

"It's okay, Mrs. Stanley."

"It's *not* okay. A mother should know these things. Needs to know these things."

Barbara's hand clamped harder on Irene's knee. "You can't blame yourself for this. Honestly. What could you possibly have known or done? Mrs. Stanley, the man responsible for this is sitting in a cell right now. He's the one to blame, and he's the one who is going to pay. People are outraged, Mrs. Stanley. *Outraged.* And they want justice. I know that doesn't sound like much right now, but it's something. Believe me, making sure Daniel Robbin is punished for doing what he did, that *is* something."

Irene gripped the ragged edges of a dream. The faltering ends, ripped and torn and giving way to something hard and sharp and real. "Justice?" Something like a sneer played at her lips as she began to rise from the bed. "My son is dead, and you want to tell me about justice?" She let out a laugh. "There's no justice for this kind of thing. A man steals, you can get your stuff back. A man beats someone, then maybe you can go on and find some way to make it all even out. But murder? Taking a young boy, a child? *Justice?* I don't know a damn thing about justice. Not a goddamn thing in the world. To me it's—it's just a word people like you say in order to feel better about things you can't ever make right."

"Mrs. Stanley—"

"It's true, right? Justice? My God. What I want has nothing to do with justice." Irene wiped her mouth with the back of her wrist. "You understand? What I want is *revenge.* God help me," she said. "But I want that man they've caught to suffer. I want him to plead and scream and beg and piss himself, just like he made my boy do. I want to wrap a rope around that sonofabitch's neck, Miss Aaron. And then—then I want to pull the lever and watch him hang. Do you understand? Can you possibly understand *that*? 'Cause if there is *anything* called justice, it's that. It's only that."

CHAPTER 13

October 2, 2004

SUPERINTENDENT TAB MASON LAY ON a vinyl-covered bench, a barbell held just above his chest. It was morning, early, some simpleminded reggae rhythm blasting too loud over substandard speakers. He closed his eyes, wishing the sound away. People had no idea what good music was anymore, and it pissed him off. Irrationally off. Hadn't-had-enough-sleep kind of off. All night Daniel Robbin had drifted in and out of his mind. The condemned man had taken the news about his own execution as Mason had expected: straight on. No hint of anything except—maybe—irony.

Mason's muscles tightened as he pushed the weight up, one hundred and eighty pounds, five more than the previous week. He held it steady. Then lowered it, slowly.

"Breathe."

He breathed.

"Deeper."

He looked over at his blond trainer, silver spandex clinging to every curve of her well-worked glutes. He paid her thirty bucks an hour to tell him how to breathe.

"Now up."

He huffed out a breath and his bare arms, one black, one white, extended.

The first time he'd met with his trainer, he'd worn a loose, long-sleeved T-shirt. He didn't like the stares his discolored arm brought, nor the unasked questions. He wished people would just speak up, say what was on their minds. But no one ever did, and the faked indifference or, worse, the casual avoidance of the half-white, half-black man bugged him. And it bugged him that it bugged him.

But Ms. Spandex had asked right off, grabbing his colorless hand and turning it like a washed-up starfish. "What's with this?" she asked.

She couldn't see the rest of it, how the discoloration stretched up to his shoulder, then down his back in large amoeba-shaped patches. She couldn't see how it had begun to affect his groin. So he'd explained, giving it its name, telling her how it was really quite common, an autoimmune problem, not painful or contagious.

She turned away while he talked, slapped weights onto a bar. Forty-five pounds each, no effort. Mason estimated she was five six and a half. Weight, 125, 127 tops. Maybe 5 percent body fat. She pointed to the bar, and as he grasped it, she asked him if it bothered him, "turning white like that."

"I'm not turning white," he huffed as he hoisted the bar.

"Whatever. Does it bother you? You wish it weren't happening? Or do you wish it would just take over your whole body?"

"I don't *wish* anything," he replied.

"You don't, huh?" She bent down to pick up a towel, and Mason noticed a tattoo of a snake working its way toward her ass. He hadn't been with a woman in three years.

"No," he said, forcing his eyes away. Mason refused to let his mind linger on anything he had no hope of ever having—or changing. So he was as spotted as a Holstein. So what? He was stuck with it, unless he got himself bleached like he'd heard that character Michael Jackson had done. And the hell if he'd do that. No. All his life Mason had felt separate and different, and all his life he'd continue to feel separate and different, and no amount of wishing was going to change that.

His trainer, however, was clearly unimpressed. "Okay," she said, walking around him slowly. "Then tell me this." Her hand went to his shoulder, over to his spine, then traipsed down each vertebra to his tailbone. "What's with this shirt?" She pulled his yellow T back so it clung to his chest. "I'm a sculptor, man. I got to see what I'm working with."

That had been almost a year ago.

Mason took another breath, pushed the weight back up.

"Slower," the woman demanded.

He went slower.

After the thing with the hummingbird, Robbin had sat down on the bench and read the letter. When finished, he folded it neatly and slipped it back in the envelope.

"Okay, now hold that," she said. "Good. Now down, slow. Slower!"

Mason dropped the barbell onto the stand.

"Fuck, you're ornery today. What's up—prisoner escape?"

Mason didn't answer. Mason never answered questions about his work, except to say what he did, or—rarely—why. Anyway, she'd find out what had made him ornery soon enough. The first press conference was in three days. After that, there wouldn't be anyone who didn't know the state was getting ready to kill someone. The media fed off that kind of thing. Newspapers, TV, radio talk shows—everyone would want a piece of the story. His silver-assed maven would know all about it even if she didn't read the paper—which Mason had a strong sense she did not.

"Come on," she said. "Let's finish this thing up."

He grabbed the bar.

News like this, there'd be no escaping it. They'd be talking about it in the sauna; it would be the subject of sermons. You wouldn't be able to get on a bus without hearing some mention of it. Executions—they caught everyone's imagination, then screwed with it.

Mason pressed out eight more, keeping his eye on a tiny loop of gold pierced through his trainer's navel.

"Okay, set it down. You're through." She slugged down some water from a hot-pink bottle, then wiped her mouth on her shoulder. "You ought to stop at the desk, see if you can get yourself a massage. You're one fucking hard knot. And I'm not talking the kind women like."

"It's work." He grabbed his towel, wiped his head.

"Yeah, whatever. Just leave it at the office, okay? You come here, you work here. That's what you pay me for. Tied up like this, you're not worth shit. Remember, you got to breathe, man—*breathe.*"

Mason watched his trainer's tight ass flex its way down the hall and around the corner.

Breathe, he thought. Robbin had told him the same damn thing, looking up from the letter with that smile. "Breathe, man," he had said. "You have got to relax about all this and just breathe."

CHAPTER 14

February 17, 1986

THE CROOK COUNTY COURTHOUSE SAT in the middle of a city block surrounded by an apron of brown grass. Three stories tall, boxlike and broad-shouldered, the gray stone building occupied its shelf like a sentinel.

Irene and Nate Stanley walked up a wide sidewalk, a silent and bent couple held together by the curve of the man's arm. She in a navy blue coat and white gloves. He in brown shoes and the same brown suit he had worn to his wedding sixteen years earlier.

Irene could see all this as if she were floating above herself and her husband, their setting and their woes. She could see it, but she couldn't feel it. Couldn't feel anything but the chill of the winter day and now stairs, eighteen of them, leading to a wide glass door and the icy grip of what lay beyond.

It had been nine months since her son had been killed. A nightmare of days and nights linked together by the same binding pain.

It was a physical thing. In her chest it felt like she'd swallowed something too large; in her abdomen an army was at battle; on her skin a rash had left her body splotched with weepy scabs. Her only comfort was that her daughter hadn't had to witness Irene's fall— the drinking, the depression, the inability to do much but wish she were dead. Bliss had stayed in Carlton, going back to her old school and routines while Irene and Nate remained in Blaine, waiting for the trial and everything to be settled. Yet, as Irene walked across the courthouse threshold, she felt about as unsettled as storm debris, uncertain about what was next—if anything. The attorneys had warned her and Nate that if Robbin was sentenced to death, the execution wouldn't happen right away. There'd be appeals and all other kinds of legal finagling. "It could take years," Mr. Brigham told them. "Maybe as much as a decade."

Nate squeezed Irene's arm and led her forward. Unlike him, Irene had not attended any of the preliminary hearings, nor had she gone when the lawyers had chosen the jury. The only thing that interested her was the trial. She wanted answers from Daniel Robbin, and she wanted to be there when he gave them. But most of all, she wanted him to see her. She had an idea that when they finally locked eyes, her son's killer would crumple and cry for mercy, knowing— absolutely knowing—the value of what he'd taken, and how in taking it he had altered the course of life. Not just his and Shep's, but something far more vast and irreconcilable. And then in this idea of Irene's—a dream, really; a kind of sinking, spinning vision that moved through her days—Daniel Robbin would experience all the agony he had caused and would continue to cause, from now until forever, all of it ravaging him as he had ravaged her son.

"Courtroom's upstairs." Nate stopped in front of a wide wooden staircase. "And the restroom's over there." He pointed to an oversized door, milky white glass marked *Ladies*. Not *Mothers*, nor *Mourners*.

It'd be good if they had that, Irene thought. *Someplace private to just go and wail. That, or bust things.* She walked up the stairs, imagining the restroom filled with china—plates, bowls, cups, saucers, fine old dishes the county would get at estate sales. Then, as they crossed the landing, she imagined herself destroying every last piece.

Two deputies stood in front of two large doors, arms crossed over their chests. They nodded at Nate, then pushed open the doors to the waiting chamber. The room was large, its ceiling high. From its center hung a globelike chandelier. Similar lamps were attached to the walls. Light from the room's long, narrow windows cut paths across the dark, pewlike benches. Irene searched the aisles, examining each tentative glance. She saw their pastor, a few of Shep's teachers, the man who owned the gas station where Robbin had worked. A group of people nudged each other, then turned in unison.

"Reporters," Nate said, leading Irene to the front row. Mr. Brigham and Miss Aaron sat at a table on the other side of a short wooden banister, files lined up like battlements. Nate helped Irene off with her coat, then she sat, pulled off her gloves, and folded and refolded them, checking her watch, brushing lint from her lap, watching the window light inch across the judge's bench. Five minutes, ten, fifteen . . .

"You know," Nate whispered, "if we were back home, this place would have been filled with family."

Irene stopped fidgeting. "What did you say?"

"I said, if this had happened at home—"

"Stop. Just stop." She glared at him. "If we were *home,* Nate, Shep would still be alive. He'd be *alive.* Okay? So just stop."

Her husband recoiled. Shrank, really—head down, arms on his knees.

Nate was built to save things. When his pa had had a stroke, it was he and his brother Earl who had run the butcher shop. When Irene's parents were killed, flattened by a car while they were out on their evening walk, Nate was beside her, making her get up, sober up, and take up their kids in her arms and be a mom again. And it was her husband, Nathaniel Patrick Stanley, Purple Heart in his topmost dresser drawer, who had run out in the middle of some soggy rice paddy, bullets flying, grenades tearing, sulfur, blood, screams, who knows what else? Irene had only her imagination and the few words he'd let slip from dreams. But she knew he had found his friend, carried him through the mud-water, saved him. And she knew he lived believing that that was who he was.

Until Shep.

Irene reached a hand to her husband's shoulder, and he took it and pulled it to his face. They had made choices. Their choices were wrong. And there it would always stand.

Just then a door opened. Twelve jurors—seven men, five women, young, old, fat, thin, mothers, fathers, sisters, brothers—entered the room in single file and sat. Irene studied them—their facial expressions, their dress, the color of their hair, their posture, anything that might indicate how they might feel about condemning a man to death. Especially a young man who, according to all reports, had been stitched onto a life so vacant of promise that pity might be considered a reasonable response.

A young girl nervously fingered the cross at her neck. Another woman, older and heavier, blew her nose into a Kleenex, then folded the tissue and tucked it back into her purse. A man sat and scanned the room as if he were searching for someone; another tapped his watch over and over; and a third, an older man with the leathery skin of a rancher, folded his hands in front of him, then bent his head forward. Irene focused on him, hoping he prayed to the same God she knew. Stern. Cold. Punishing.

She had been a good student at Creekside Baptist, accepting

her lessons about God with a wholehearted belief that if she did otherwise, lightning would strike her dead. The Almighty was all-knowing and uncompromising, hard and sometimes even cruel. But that was only because He knew the potential of the human heart and wanted nothing more than for His children to reach up and out and receive the gift of His grace. But that grace would be denied today. She was sure of it. Her son was God's child, he played in His orchestra, bringing joy and beauty into His world, and now this man Robbin would learn just how explicit and damning God's wrath could be.

A rumble of voices drew Irene's attention. Two deputies entered the rear of the room, then stood shoulder to shoulder in front of the double doors. A second later they stepped aside and in walked a thin, dark-haired man flanked by two more deputies, both of them taller than the man they bracketed. Boy, really—he looked so young. He wore blue jeans, a white shirt, and tennis shoes and had hair as black and glossy as crow feathers.

Irene's hand went to her mouth as she bit into the moment and everything it held—the steady march, Robbin's head down, jaw sharp and angular as the blade of a saw. She scooted to the edge of the bench, waiting for him to look at her, knowing he would, and certain that when he did there'd come that revelation. *God's finger. God's righteous, unyielding finger.*

She could feel it pointing toward this Robbin. Feel it sear the heat with greater heat. It scratched her skin, wrung the breath from her lungs, and she knew that Nate, the judge, jury, press, police, everyone in that courtroom could feel his vindicating presence as well. Poised midair, ready to grab hold of Daniel Robbin and buckle him flat under the weight of the horrific things he'd done.

But the young man did not buckle. Instead, with eyes immune to revelation or remorse, or anything approaching mercy, Daniel Robbin's glance swept past Irene Stanley and landed with a heavy and distinct weight on her husband. She gasped. The boy was the devil's progeny, grit of hell clinging to his glare—all hate, all enmity, all evil, all sin wrapped in a veneer of skin and bone. Unburdened by chain or cage, Robbin's look bored into her husband with a relentless and totally unjustifiable hate.

CHAPTER 15

November 5, 1989

YEARS GO BY. A TANGLE *of brush—osage and chinquapin— leaning and arching, one into the other. Sometimes lit with fire: crackling, sizzling, burning, bruising, baffling. Years. Sometimes frozen in silence. Her mother still stuck in that chair of hers, gnawing through the time like a dog biting away at its own lame leg. And her father a withered husk of pain. Unable to say his son's name, let alone admit her brother had ever walked, breathed, stood—lived. Years. Five of them, lined like tombstones: 1985, 1986, '87, '88, '89. Draining Bliss and her family, then drowning them in all time's waste: wasted days, wasted opportunities, wasted life.*

BLISS STANLEY SAT IN THE basement of Jeff Creal's home, a beer in one hand, his crotch in the other. It was her seventeenth birthday, and when Jeff called to say they had the house to themselves, Bliss knew where the night would go.

Just three weeks before Jeff had shown her what to do with what lay under the zipper of his Levi's. They'd been out at Turner's Pond, an old gravel pit by the river, sitting in the front seat of his dad's swamp-green LTD. Other than their ramshackle house, five boys, and a shopping bag filled with bills, it was the only thing the man had left his wife after twenty-one years of marriage.

Bliss and Jeff first started going to the pond as a lark, a "let's see who shows" kind of thing. They were friends, after all. Not boyfriend-girlfriend like all the others, but honest-to-god buddies. Jeff Creal was the freckle-faced kid Bliss had grown up with. They'd spent whole days hiking along the Mississippi, barefoot and covered in mud, digging holes, exploring caves, and hunting for berries, bears, and the fan-shaped brachiopods that lay fixed in the river's limestone cliffs. She still had the fossils in a box, along with a pill jar containing her baby teeth, a collection of plastic horses, several school certificates, and all the letters Jeff had written during that awful time in Oregon.

Bliss continued to feel haunted by the place: the ugly town, their miserable little house, that joke of a school. Then, hammered on top of it all, that terrible day in May, and all the days that followed.

Shep's death had twisted her family into an impenetrable knot, and on the outside sat Bliss, trying to unravel it so she could go on and live a normal life. That's it. Just normal. A teenager knocking around with her friends and butting heads with her parents. She wanted to worry about boys and clothes and parties and what she'd do once she graduated. Simple everyday things. Instead, she spent her time trying to exorcize a ghost.

Her mom was the worst. Shep's death had turned her upside-down and drained her dry, and the only things she ever found to fill her back up were her constant biting anger and a private stash of booze. Some days weren't so bad—dinner made, house picked up, her awake, aware, communicative. But then something would set her back—a photograph, a song, news reports of crimes or, worse, reports of someone getting off for some crime. The thing about the priests abusing kids put her off church for almost a year, even though they weren't even Catholic. And other things, little things. A book she hadn't opened in a while, some scent. Hell, the weather even. You never could tell what would drop her into a fall.

Just three days earlier, Bliss had come home with Jeff to find her mom sitting on the porch swing, swaying back and forth as if she were in a trance. She was still in her nightgown and slippers, her hair still uncombed. Bliss told her to get in the house before she froze to death. But Irene didn't answer. So Bliss reached out and jerked the swing to a stop.

"Hello, Mom, you in there? I'm home. You know me, your daughter, Bliss?"

Irene slowly turned her head, and Bliss could see it was one of the real bad days.

"You heard from the attorney, didn't you?"

Irene nodded, then let her gaze drift away.

Two or three times a year the Crook County DA would write to update the Stanleys on Daniel Robbin's case. Bliss had found a neat stack of the letters in her mom's rolltop, and after reading a few she could see why they would tear her mom apart. Their tone was abrupt and unsympathetic, their language—*pending the out-come . . . further appeal . . . judge's opinion*—vacant of any ache. None of them said sorry, and none made a space in her mom's heart for anything but more hatred and sorrow.

"That sucks," Bliss said. "Guess they didn't give us any hint of what's taking so long, did they?"

Irene didn't answer, and Bliss understood. Her mom wanted Shep's killer dead, and because he wasn't, it was killing her. One day at a time, breaking the woman down no matter what anyone said or did. And because of this Bliss didn't know whom she hated more, Daniel Robbin for doing what he had done, the attorneys for being so indifferent, or her mom for continuing to put Shep before everyone else.

And as for her dad—God love him, he had always been her rock, always the one she could run to no matter what. But lately he clung too hard and he clung too tight. She was his "sweet little girl," and there was a part of her that was tired of being all three. Having a cop for a father, especially *her* dad, had a way of shutting down opportunity. He had no tolerance, no trust for any of her friends except Jeff. Jeff he liked. Jeff he could count on.

As soon as Bliss had come back to Carlton with Aunt Carol, Jeff had shown up. He took her to Kessler's for sodas, or over to school to watch the baseball games. Just normal stuff, without all the sticky sympathy. Jeff would even talk about Shep, like that time everyone had been searching around the farm for him. They could hear his voice calling out, but no one could figure out where he was. Then they found him in the cistern, trying to save a goat that had fallen in. It made her laugh talking about things like that. And it made her almost happy at a time when she was not quite sure she'd ever be happy again.

And Jeff was like that for her parents, too. They'd moved back after the trial, looking old and all drifted apart. It scared and depressed her. But with Jeff around, everyone seemed to lighten up. Especially her dad, who would often take off with Jeff to go fishing, or have him help fix up some old car he had in the barn.

"Jeff's a salve," her mom once said, and because Bliss thought a salve was just what they needed, she never questioned the cadence of her relationship with her childhood buddy. And as it turned out, she didn't mind what she learned out by the quarry. Kissing was fun, then delicious, and like anything sweet, it made her want more. First the touching, light and tentative, then harder, more urgent. It amazed her how easily his cock could seize up, and how exciting it was to hear him beg her to touch it, hold it, anything. Anything at all. And it had felt good, real good, to know she was being both bad and loved at the same time.

So on her seventeenth birthday, with Neil Young on the stereo, she set down her beer and began kissing the downy plane of Jeff Creal's stomach, then up to his chest, his neck, his mouth. It was easy, so easy to be with Jeff. Playing or loving, it didn't matter.

"Oh—Jesus, Bliss, I love you." His hands slid under her shirt, cupped her breasts. They'd have beautiful strawberry-blond children. Freckles from Jeff, green eyes from her.

His mouth was on hers now. Kissing, licking, her leaning back into the couch, hand reaching for his belt, unhitching it, clumsily but still done. Then reaching under. He had taught her what to do with him. How to take him in her hand and move, and him, like a dog, pounding into her thigh or her stomach, then leaving that sticky puddle for her to wipe at and wonder about. He had even got her to take him into her mouth. It was salty and forbidden and made her want to do it all.

"Bliss, oh sweet Jesus, Bliss!"

She unzipped his pants, pulled his underwear down just enough. "Oh, please, Bliss, let's do it. We'll get married soon as school's done. Bliss, God, you got to know how much I want you."

He pulled at her pants now, fingers hurriedly snatching at the zipper, the panties, pink, lace-trimmed, and wet, his fingers reaching closer and closer. And her breath trying to latch on to anything, anything at all. They'd have children, and they'd live in Carlton, and things would be different for them than they were for everyone else. Better. It *had* to be better. Nothing, not a thing, could go wrong for her and Jeff.

He went to the floor, jerked on her pants, and began kissing along the inside of her leg, tongue flicking, diving, making her moan, then beg. "Please, yes, yes, of course." Of course she loved him, her Jeff, her friend, her dear, dear friend.

Then, there on the beer-stained couch, under the red glow of a Bud sign, Clydesdales marching on and on and Neil Young crooning about having a heart made of gold, he entered.

Afterward, his head resting on her chest, Bliss began to think of plenty of things that could go wrong. Chief among them, they hadn't used a rubber. Second, she realized with growing panic, she didn't want to marry Jeff Creal. It had never occurred to her before, because marrying Jeff was about as natural an expectation as completing school. More so, because her family needed Jeff more than they needed her diploma or anything it might bring. Jeff was their salve, and her dad's fishing buddy. Jeff was a smile and a laugh and a hand when anyone needed it. Jeff was the son her parents had lost, and everyone expected him to stay.

Jeff lifted his head, kissed her breast, and smiled, as Bliss reached for her forehead, thinking she just might get sick.

THE NEXT WEEK, BLISS AND Jeff were sitting at the kitchen table doing homework while her mom was making cookies. The baking, plus the way she moved around the room—light and with her head up—meant that Irene Stanley was in one of her good places.

"What's up, Mom?"

Irene wore an aqua-colored blouse she'd been given for her birthday the previous summer. Bliss hadn't ever seen it on her.

"I was just wondering," she replied, taking cookies off the baking sheet. "You two ever think of going to college?"

Jeff pulled his head up from his math book. "Are you kidding? And have to go and do more of this stuff?" He pointed with disgust at his assignment. "Or read . . . what do they have us reading now?" He glanced at Bliss.

"*Great Expectations.*"

"Yeah, that's right, Great Exasperations." He mocked a shudder. "God, it's boring."

Irene placed a few cookies on a plate. She'd made chocolate chip with oatmeal, butterscotch, and coconut. Jeff's favorite.

"What about you?" She looked at her daughter. "You ever think of going?"

Bliss worked her pencil around her fingers. "I guess so." Then, hearing Jeff turn, she added, "But not much. I mean, you know, not . . . *seriously.*"

Her mom set the plate on the table. "I see. And what kind of plans do you two have, if I may ask? I mean, you *are* graduating this spring."

Bliss glanced to her right. Jeff was smiling—glowing, if she had to say it—and she had a sudden urge to kick her friend. Smack him good right in the shin. But it was too late.

"Marriage, Mrs. Stanley." He grabbed a cookie, pointed it at her like a baton. "Soon as we're out of school and I get myself a job, I'm planning on marrying your daughter—I mean, with you and Mr. Stanley's blessings, of course." He grinned at Bliss. "Me and Bliss, we've already talked 'bout it, and—well, you got to know how much I love her, and I've always felt more a part of this family than my own. I can't even *imagine* a different life."

Irene's eyebrows arched like startled cats. "Well, now! Is that right, Bliss? You and Jeff, you're planning on *marrying*?"

Bliss shifted in her chair. "It's not like we've set a *date* or anything. It's just—you know . . . talk." Bliss could feel Jeff's eyes lying on her like a beggar's hands, so she reached for a cookie, split it in half, and quickly took a bite. "Real good," she said, avoiding both his and her mom's stare. For perhaps the first time in her life, Bliss actually felt like her mom knew what was going on—Turner's Pond, the sex, the whole thing. She swallowed and smiled meekly as Irene walked to the refrigerator, pulled out a gallon milk jug, and poured three cups.

"Well," she said, looking straight at her daughter, "here's to your future." Then she took a deep breath, winked, and downed the milk like a shot of whiskey.

CHAPTER 16

November 15, 1989

S IX DAYS LATER, BLISS WAS walking to class dogged by two friends. The girls had seen the Creals' LTD quite a bit at the pond lately, and "it wasn't simple talking rocking that ship."

The shorter of the two girls giggled, then knocked Bliss with her elbow. "Seriously, it's 'bout time you started taking advantage of that boy. Shit knows he only has it for you. Believe me, I've tried."

The girls exploded in laughter, and Bliss's permanently flushed cheeks drained of color. Then, as they passed the main office, the school counselor, Ms. Breedle, stepped in front of them, offered a greeting, and asked Bliss for a "moment of time." The girls glanced at each other as if they'd just been caught smoking, then the two unbeckoned ones bade their farewells and scattered like leaves.

Ms. Breedle is as thin as a needle,
and never will be loved.

The words had appeared on the side of the school shortly after the homely woman with the wickedly long nose showed up during the middle of Bliss's freshman year. The previous counselor had died of a heart attack while at the homecoming game. He had been at Lincoln High for decades, was well loved, and people knew what to expect, which, taken as a whole, was certainly not much. But the knock-kneed woman from Chicago, who lived with three cats and, it was whispered, *another woman,* was shaking things up.

Bliss followed Breedle's spindly figure into her office.

"Barbara." She pointed to a wooden chair.

Bliss dropped her backpack on the floor and sat, arms crossed, eyes roaming from one poster to another. There were four themes: Don't smoke; Don't do drugs; Don't have sex; and GO to college. Her eyes hooked on the third, the poster showing a sad-looking girl with a belly as big as a balloon. Bliss bit her lip and glanced down at her own stomach. It was flat. *And it had better damn well stay that way,* she silently demanded, imagining her uterus a hostile universe where nothing could survive.

Ms. Breedle sat with her hands clasped together. "I've taken a look at your schoolwork, Barbara. And I have to tell you, I'm impressed. Very impressed."

Bliss let out her breath. She had thought for sure she was about to get the sex lecture. Other girls had. It came with a warning, an evaluation of goals, and a quiet slip of a slim package of condoms. All very hush-hush.

"Yes, very impressed. And your test scores, ACT?" She pulled a piece of paper from a manila folder, placed it in front of Bliss, and tapped it with the tip of her index finger. "Very high."

"Yes, ma'am." Bliss twirled a curl of hair around her finger. "Mrs. Lingrin told me."

"Yes, well, Mrs. Lingrin and I have talked as well. She says your work just gets stronger and stronger."

"I wouldn't know about that." Behind the counselor hung three diplomas, gilded and framed.

"Your teachers and I, we've talked quite a bit about you and your work. And we think—that is, not just think, we're all fairly certain you'd be able to get yourself a scholarship to go to college. We're talking a *good* scholarship, to a *good* college," The counselor leaned back, picked up a pencil, rolled it between her hands like clay. "Do you ever think about that? Going to college?"

Ms. Breedle's nose ended with a buttonlike bump that just called out to be pressed. "No. Not really."

"Hmm . . . Can I ask why?"

Bliss bit at the pad of her index finger. Of course she'd thought of going to college. It was *the* gigantic dream. Like winning the lottery, or maybe beating Steffi Graf in the next U.S. Open, straight sets. The thought was as real as any of her fantasies, which meant it was about as windblown and distant as a cloud, and just about as hard to grasp.

"I don't know why, Ms. Breedle. I mean, I guess—well, you know, none of my friends are going."

The counselor tapped the pencil against her lips. "And that's your reason? Your friends?"

"Uh-huh. I mean, I guess so. Yeah, anyway, it's hard at home— you know. My parents, they need me around."

Ms. Breedle must have been told about what had happened to the Stanley family, because shortly after she arrived she called Bliss to her office and told her she was there for her if Bliss ever needed anyone to talk with.

That first encounter, Bliss didn't say anything. Not a word. She just nodded and, when the bell rang, got up and left. Sitting here in the office three years later, she was not that much more eager to talk.

"What if I told you your mother came in here the other day?"

Bliss looked up from her hand.

"Dropped in to talk about just this topic. Said it'd be a shame if you didn't at least *try* to get into college."

"My mom? In here?" Bliss's voice was pure doubt.

"Yes. In fact, she says it'd be a waste, you staying in Carlton."

"My mother came in this building and talked with *you*?"

"You shouldn't be so surprised. She cares about your future."

Bliss scrunched up her face. She couldn't imagine her mother coming and talking to Breedle. It would take a certain level of awareness to do such a thing. A certain degree of concern and energy. Her mom didn't have any of those things.

"You're a smart girl, Barbara. You could go places. Anyplace. Your mother sees that. Tell me, what interests you?"

"Interests me? I don't know. Lots of things, I guess."

"Name one."

Bliss's muscles tightened. "Tennis." It was a straight-arm slice, meant to take her opponent off-balance.

"Tennis? You play tennis?"

"No. But it interests me. That's what you asked, isn't it? Anyway, the courts out there"—she tossed her head in the direction of the door—"they're shit." She glanced up from her hand to see what effect lobbing a swear word had on the woman.

"But you like tennis."

"I guess so."

"What else?"

The seventeen-year-old took a deep breath, then spit it out in a way that indicated she was just about through wasting her time talking with some sick old lesbian. She had no idea if the rumors were true and felt pretty certain she didn't really care, but it served as a good enough reason not to trust the woman, so Bliss set her eyes that way—full of disgust and indifference.

"I like writing. I like history. I like Mr. Cantor's social studies class." She paused, then said it. "And *I* like *boys*."

Breedle smiled. "It's your *work* I'm interested in, Barbara." She pulled one of Bliss's midterms from a folder, an essay about the death penalty and all the common arguments for and against. Bliss had concluded the paper with her own feelings: "There are people who've been on death row for decades, appealing every move the state makes to end their lives. This must stop. The costs to the state are tremendous, and the costs to the victims endless."

"This is really quite thoughtful," Breedle said. "You present your thesis well, your grammar is excellent, research thorough. And, most important, there's passion in it. And not just this piece." She pulled out three other reports, each marked with a bright red A. "You have things to offer, Barbara, to give to the world. Your experiences, your intellect. Have you thought about what you might do with all that?"

Bliss pushed herself upright. "I don't know what you're talking about."

"Oh, I think you do. You have a way with words, Barbara, a way of making an argument. Your papers are good. Very good."

Bliss hated the way Breedle repeated herself: "Good, very good. Impressed, very impressed."

"My name is Bliss, and those were just silly midterms. They don't mean *nothing*." Bliss stressed the double negative. "And it sure don't mean I'd do well in college."

Breedle nodded. "You're right. College would be much more of a challenge."

Bliss's eyes dropped to the edge of the counselor's desk. "My dad, he hasn't come around asking about college, has he?"

"No, he hasn't."

She curled her lips into a satisfied grin. "Well, don't expect him to. He'd never want me going off like that. Have a fit knowing I was even in this office talking about it."

"But if he knew there were scholarships—"

"Wouldn't make a difference."

"He just doesn't believe women should go to college, is that it?"

Bliss glanced at the picture of the happy grads. "It's not like that," she said.

"Like what?"

"Like, you know, my dad being a chauvinist or something—he's not like that. It's just that . . ." Bliss's fist came down on the arm of her chair. "Look, I'm just not planning to go to college, okay? Once I graduate, I'm done with the whole school scene."

"And this is because you think your father wouldn't want you to go? Does that really sound right to you? Parents tend to want what's best for their children."

Bliss picked at the yellow stitching on her Doc Martens. She'd been saving her babysitting cash for months to get a pair. Then one day, her dad goes and asks her and Jeff to join him for a trip to Coldsprings. They went to an auto parts store and the Sears at the mall. They ate lunch at the Food Pavilion. Then, just when they were about to leave, her dad swung into a shoe store, pointed to the very ones she loved, and asked if he could buy her a pair. Afterward, they walked out to the parking lot, her with her Doc Martens squeaking and her dad up ahead, his arm wrapped around Jeff's shoulder.

"Bliss?" said Ms. Breedle.

"What?"

"I said parents generally want what's best for their children. Your parents, I'm sure, are no different."

Bliss closed her eyes to the woman and her words, floating like bubbles above her head. Trite messages pulled from some Junior League handbook. Comparing her parents to others was fucked. Just plain fucked. No one had parents like hers. How many times had she and Jeff come home to find her mom stuck in that chair of hers, not a thing done in the house? And the two of them, her and Jeff, taking care of the breakfast dishes or making dinner. Washing the goddamn laundry so her own mother would have some clean fucking underwear. And her dad? He was no better. "I really should be getting back to class."

Ms. Breedle relaxed in her chair and tapped her index fingers together.

"Look, you don't know my family," Bliss said. "If I weren't around, I don't know what would happen. I mean, I'm sure my mom probably *looked* normal to you, but she's not. Hell, she's been a damn basket case ever since my brother was killed. And my dad? Well, my dad just *needs* me, okay? Jeez."

It had been exactly five months since that time her dad had come into the barn to work on the truck. Bliss was up in the loft reading, hidden away in the hay.

Her dad turned on the radio, and the sound of the farm report and the sun and her sweet-smelling bed made her sleepy. When she woke, the sunlight had moved from where she lay and she shivered. Then she heard the sound. Like an animal caught in a trap, or like that time when the fox's den got plowed and the mama fox just stood over her dead kits, howling.

She crawled to the edge of the loft. It could be an owl, she thought. Maybe the radio? Down below, her father was sitting on a sawhorse pounding his fist into something over and over. It was small and brown, like a squirrel or a rat. But then she realized it wasn't the thing in his hands that was crying, but him. Sobs were raking her strong, fearless father, shaking him from head to foot.

"I'm sure it must tear at them both," Ms. Breedle went on. "It's only natural."

"It's not natural." Spittle flew from Bliss's mouth. "Nothing about my family is natural, or even normal."

After her father finally left the barn, Bliss climbed down from the loft and found what he had been hitting. It was a baseball mitt, stiff with disuse. And inside, written in her dad's hand, was Shep's name.

"You know we aren't even allowed to mention my brother? My dad gets up and leaves the room anytime Shep's name even comes up. Says we have to move on. Well, I'll tell you something—neither of my parents has moved on. Not one single step, okay?"

Ms. Breedle pushed a box of tissues across her desk, and Bliss sniffed and stared at it. "I have no idea what's in my mom's mind, coming in here like she did. Maybe she just figures it would be easier not having me around to remind her of the kid she really loved."

"Bliss."

She waved off the counselor.

"Bliss. Of course your parents are in pain. Losing a child—who knows if that kind of thing ever goes away? But I have to tell you, they *will* learn to survive without you at their side. They have to, and you have to trust them to do it. Besides, other than taking care of your parents, what would you do here in Carlton?"

Bliss sighed. "What everyone else does."

"And that would be? . . ."

"What else? Get married. Have kids."

Ms. Breedle tilted her head to the side. "You're not like everyone else, Bliss." She slid the midterm toward her. "Read this, then tell me you don't want to do anything but cook dinner and wipe kids' noses."

Bliss stared at the paper, knowing Breedle was right; she had no interest in marking her days with clothespins and wet wipes. She'd taken a good hard look at every single marriage she knew and had yet to find one—even one—that felt worth her sweat. She had no idea what kept her mom and dad together, except they'd grown into one another, like twisted old boughs on a tree. Or a burr worked up under the skin.

"Your friend Jeff—have you two talked about getting married?"

"It's been a topic."

"And it's what you want?"

She shrugged. "Could be. My parents like him, and he under-stands, you know, the way things are at home. He's a big help."

Breedle nodded. "You two ever talk about college?"

"Are you kidding me? I don't talk about college with anyone, Ms. Breedle. No one."

The counselor pushed herself back from her desk and stood. "Well, you've got someone to talk with now." She turned and took three books from a shelf. "Look through these." She set them in front of Bliss. "Then come back and see me. Maybe I'm wrong. Maybe you won't get offered any scholarships. Maybe you won't get admit-ted anywhere. There's always that possibility." She smiled. "But *if* you try, and *if* you get an offer, then you, your mother, and me—we'll work on your dad."

Bliss eyed the books, trying, really trying, to look about as un-interested as she knew how. "Shouldn't I be getting to class?" she asked.

Breedle put her two hands on the desk and leaned over. "You tell me."

CHAPTER 17

March 1990

THE FIRST RESPONSE CAME ON a snowy day in March. Thick and embossed with the University of Illinois's name and insignia, it sat on a diagonal inside the mailbox, too big to lie flat. Irene pulled it out and grasped it with both hands. "Yes!" she shouted to the large, feathery flakes falling and melting against her cheeks.

Irene figured the best thing she'd done in the past five years was to wake up from her depression long enough to push her daughter toward college. The girl was growing up, and Irene didn't need any more evidence than what had dropped onto her shoe last fall as she was outside hanging the laundry. She picked up the foil-covered package. *Gum*, she thought, glad it hadn't opened in the wash. Then she recognized it for what it was. "Shit!" Memories of her own early experience with Nate and how it ended up being a one-way ticket to the altar came back. Fast.

Irene threw the rest of the clothes over the line and ran into the house. There was no way she'd just let Bliss live out the rest of her life in Carlton without at least giving her a fighting chance at something different. The girl was smart, real smart. Doctor kind of smart, or lawyer, maybe a professor . . .

Getting the school involved, having her write an application essay, taking her on a trip over to Southern just to walk around the campus and get a feel for life as someone other than "the poor Stanley girl"—it was the most take-charge thing Irene had ever done. And one of the cagier. Both she and Bliss had agreed not to tell her father or Jeff about the applications until they'd heard back from the schools. Until then, it was just speculation. Simply dream talk.

So that night Irene waited until Jeff went home and Nate lay half asleep in front of the television before going upstairs and placing the envelope on the desk beside her daughter.

"Well?" she asked, after about a minute of Bliss's just sitting there ignoring both her mother and the package. "Aren't you going to open it?"

Irene couldn't see Bliss's face, eyes attempting to penetrate the envelope, mouth tense. She didn't notice Bliss digging a nail into her pencil before using it to slide the package toward her and slit it open. "They want me," she finally said, her voice as flat and colorless as the snowy fields they'd woken to that morning. "It says they've accepted my application and they're offering a scholarship."

Irene leaped to her daughter's side, took the envelope from her hand, and pulled out the letter. "On behalf of the staff and faculty of the University of Illinois . . ."

THE NEXT WEEK THEY GOT a letter from Kent State, then the University of Iowa, and finally Northwestern, up near Chicago. Each was stuffed with brochures and forms to fill out, and each was greeted by Bliss with a cool, featureless indifference.

By mid-May, Irene was frantic. "You've got to sit down and make a decision about school." It was a Saturday morning. Nate and Jeff were at the junkyard, and Irene and Bliss were at the kitchen table spooning through their cornflakes. "Because, you know, they're not just sitting around waiting for you to make up your mind. Besides, once you decide, we're going to have to tell Jeff and your pa. They'll need time to settle into this."

Bliss pushed away her bowl and put her head in her hands. She hadn't looked well these last few weeks—pale, listless, and she'd been more than a little forgetful.

"Bliss." Irene swallowed. "Honey, is there some *reason* you're not moving on this? I mean, you can't go wrong with any of those schools. And if it's Northwestern you have your heart set on, don't worry about them just offering a partial scholarship. I've been meaning to ask at the IGA about getting a job. We'll manage."

Bliss turned her head so that her hair fell on the table, just like Irene hated. "You? Come on, you haven't worked in years."

"I know, but with you going off to college, I figure I'd need something to do. Lord knows there won't be much for me to take care of here."

Bliss's big green irises swam around like koi in a pond. Then she stood and took her bowl to the sink.

"What is it, Bliss? I mean, aren't you at all excited by the possibility of going to college?"

Bliss set her dish in the basin, then dropped her spoon on top. "No-o-o." She started the water, hard, full, and loud.

Irene reached for the faucet and shut it off.

"What?" Bliss asked. "Don't you want me doing the dishes?"

"I want you to tell me why you're not doing anything about those offers."

The girl stepped away from her. "Who ever said I was interested, huh? This was all *your* idea, not mine."

"But I thought you wanted to go! You never once said—"

"Look, Mom, this whole college thing, it's a nice thought, and I appreciate your interest, but it's not happening. I'm not going to college, so quit pushing it."

"Of course it's happening. Just look at the responses. You've got your pick of some of the best schools around."

"Would you please drop it?" Bliss leaned back against the counter, arms crossed over her chest like a cage. "All this talk about college—I've had it, okay? I'm not going anywhere."

"Is it your pa? Is that what you're afraid of? If it is, you shouldn't be. I mean, I know it'll be a big surprise, but once he sees all the opportunities you have, he'll be first in line to help you get to wherever you decide to go. There's nothing in the world he wouldn't do for you—you know that."

"That's not what I'm talking about."

"Then what?" Irene watched her daughter work something in her head. "Bliss. It's not . . . I mean, you and Jeff. You're not *pregnant*, right?"

Bliss flinched.

"Well?"

"No, Mom, I'm not *pregnant*. Jeez. You say I'm smart, so treat me that way, would you?"

"You're sure? Because you look like hell."

"Yes, I'm sure."

"All right." Irene sighed. "But if you're not . . . expecting, then I have no idea what would keep you from jumping on the chance to go to one of those schools. I mean, I know you and Jeff are close, but that's no reason not to go to college. You can get married later if that's what you two are planning."

Bliss huffed out an impatient breath. "I'm not planning on marrying Jeff. In fact, I'm not planning on marrying anyone. Ever. Okay? *God*." She stuck out a leg and crossed it over the other. She wore pajamas, flannel polar bears on a baby-blue background, and an old T-shirt with a pink Mr. Bubble floating in front.

"O-kay." Irene took a slow breath. "It's not your dad and it's not Jeff. Then—"

"Leave it."

"No." Irene stepped up to her daughter and put her hands on her arms. "I'm not going to leave it. You want to stay here in Carlton, a girl like you, with more smarts than anyone in your school, then you're going to tell me why."

Bliss pushed off her mother's hands. "I said leave it." She turned and headed for the dining room.

"Bliss, don't you dare leave this room."

Bliss stopped and turned, her face crimson with anger. "Okay, you want to know why I'm not leaving? Why I can *never* leave, why I'm stuck here like some kind of prisoner? I'll tell you why. It's because of you. Okay? *You.*"

"Me? But I'm the one rooting for you."

"Oh, come on. All this talk about me going to college and you working. I know what it's all about, and it's got nothing to do with me or my future."

"What? Bliss, honey, why else—"

"Why else? To get me out of your hair, that's why. You don't think I see that?"

"Out of my hair?"

"Yeah, out and away so you can continue your slow slide without me standing around to watch. How many bottles are you up to, anyway, Mom? I swear, you're so damn wrapped up in yourself you never stop to see anything going on around you. You know that? You're gonna get yourself a job? Get real. You're like a zombie— the walking damn dead—and you have been ever since Shep was killed."

Irene's hand went to her chest. "Bliss."

"You want me gone so you can drink yourself to death. It's pathetic. You're pathetic. Stumbling around with a grief that never ends, no matter what you have in front of you. You're always look-

ing behind, *only behind*. And Dad? He's no better. I swear he's probably the loneliest person in the whole world. Never lets anyone into
what he's thinking or feeling. And you know why?"

Irene shook her head.

"Because of *you*. You're so stuck in your own world, you don't
have it in you to help a soul. Goddammit, Mom. Of course I don't
want to hang around here, but if I leave, who's gonna take care of
things? Huh? You? Dad? Give me a break. If it weren't for Jeff and
me, I don't know what would have happened to you two."

Irene, stunned and ashamed, looked away from her daughter.

"I've been waiting for it all to change. You know? Thought eventually you'd come around and start appreciating what you have, just
like you taught me and Shep, remember? All that talk about life and
God and the beauty in the world, seeing it, drinking it in like a cup
of cold water. You remember that? How you'd wake us in the mornings to hear the birds sing, or go out collecting leaves in the fall? All
because you wanted us to know how good life could be, to see it and
love it. But it's been five years, five damn years, and I don't see you
caring about a thing but getting me the hell away."

"Bliss, I'm—"

"Just leave it, okay? You wanted to know why I'm not acting on
those letters. Well, now you know. It's 'cause you're a drunk and
Dad's out of touch and neither one of you knows how to take care of
yourself, let alone each other."

Irene's hand went to her mouth, like a child caught stealing, and
Bliss rolled her eyes and left the room.

THAT NIGHT IRENE SOUGHT OUT her bottles of vodka, plus the one
thin flask she had tucked deep in her chair, and poured the contents
down the drain. She was determined to reform her life. Mold its
makings into some more accommodating shape. She could do
that. Take a pickax to her anger if she had to, but tame it, control

its force, line it up with the other emotions—the regret, the sadness, the guilt and sorrow—and let them all take a rest while she
went about the job of pretending, just simply pretending they didn't
exist. It was an idea, anyway. Keep busy, she told herself. Just keep
busy.

Two weeks later she started back at the IGA, working days like
she used to in Blaine, then coming home and making good solid
meals for her family. She engaged them in conversation, cleaned
the house, planted the garden, and started a sweater, a blue pull-
over for her husband, measuring him at night by the bed after he
had undressed. She started helping at church again, not just going
through the motions but actually trying to pay attention, then staying after to serve coffee with a few other ladies. She even went back
to Wednesday evening study with Carol. And she had her hair dyed,
and bought garden gloves so as not to damage her manicure, and
even got herself a new dress and a pair of slippers. And finally, when
she felt sure she could maintain this dance without utterly tripping
up, she went to Bliss with the envelopes and a promise she swore
she'd keep.

BLISS CHOSE THE UNIVERSITY OF Illinois. It had offered a full
scholarship, and it was closer to home than the others. She told her
father, who'd been prepped for the news by her mom, that she'd
come home weekends when she could, and of course holidays and
summer.

Then she went to tell Jeff. It was a Sunday after supper, and they
were sitting on the front porch stairs watching the occasional car
drive by.

He was talking about looking for work in Coldsprings. "Wal-Mart
is always hiring. We can look for a place to live near there."

Bliss dug her toes into her flip-flops. Ever since she had agreed to go to college, her whole body ached to get away from home, her parents, and—most of all—Jeff. He wore cut-off jeans, had soft blond hair, was gorgeous and kind, and had ambitions to work and live in Coldsprings, Illinois, goddammit. And at Wal-Mart, no less. She'd rather hang herself.

"Jeff, we've got to talk."

"Yeah, I know. The sooner we set a date and get married, the better. I can't wait to move out from home."

Bliss examined her nails. "I've been accepted to college."

"Huh?"

"I've been accepted to college, and I want to go. I don't want to be around here anymore. Not Carlton. Not Coldsprings, either."

"College? When did you apply for college?"

She clamped her hands together. "A few months ago."

"A few months ago? But you never mentioned . . . Wait a minute—you're joking, right?"

She shook her head. "I'm not joking. I applied to several places, and I got accepted to each one."

Jeff ran his hands up and down his arms. "Gosh, Bliss, I wish you had told me all this was going on. I mean, well—where are you thinking of going?"

"University of Illinois, in Champaign."

"But that's like two hundred miles away."

Bliss's hair fell toward her face as she nodded.

"Oh, okay. Then I guess we'll just move to Champaign. There's got to be a lot more jobs up that way anyhow." He smiled. "We can get married before you start."

A tractor drove by, pulling a chisel plow. Clods of red dirt fell off its tines and onto the road.

"I'm breaking things off, Jeff. I'm sorry, but I want to go to Champaign alone."

He turned to her and pushed the hair from her face and tucked it behind her ears. "What do you mean, alone? You don't want to get married right away? Is that it? We can wait, if that's what you want."

"Jeff."

"Right? I mean, okay, you want to go to college, that's fine. You're so smart you probably ought to go. But you know there's Southern not thirty miles away. That's a good school, isn't it? And, you know, that way you could go alone, and I could get up there whenever you want. What about that?"

"I didn't apply to that school."

"But you could, right? All those other ones want you."

"I've got a scholarship at U of I, Jeff. And I don't want to go to Southern. I want to get away. I'm sorry, I just don't want to be around all this anymore."

"This? You don't mean me, do you? You're not saying you don't want to be around me?"

She looked down.

"But why?"

She searched her mind, trying to find some way to explain. "I want to get away from my family, Jeff. And to me, you're family. You've always been family." She looked back up at him. "I know it's not fair, not right at all. You've done so much for us. But I can't be around here anymore. I just can't." Her voice broke, and she looked out and away from her friend and the road and the field beyond that, gluing her eyes to the horizon. She felt cruel, like someone who ties up and beats her dog. Loyal and faithful and true and filled with nothing but love and trust, and she's there slamming its head with a shovel. "I'm sorry, Jeff. Honestly. I am *so* sorry."

She heard him sob out her name. Then he was gone, taking off down the well-worn path that connected her home to his.

Four years later she would remember that day, and how after Jeff left she went out to the road and followed the mud clods all the way to where the plow was ripping at the ground. She remembered it pained her, watching that soil heave and tear and thinking of Jeff and knowing she'd done the same thing to him. But she noticed it was a very subdued and bearable pain, and then she understood the price of growing up as she had. She was heartless, she decided. Incapable of love or devotion.

Maybe, she would write in her senior college thesis, *a family is linked in ways we have no way to understand. Some unseen, cellular connection that binds us past and present. If so, perhaps when my brother died, those cells we shared died as well. And for us, that would have been the heart. Those fine, fragile walls that let us embrace life with fearlessness and faith. We suffer because our heart is dying, one small cell at a time.*

PART II

CHAPTER 18

October 5, 2004

FOUR DAYS AFTER MASON GAVE Robbin the death warrant, he sat in his office thinking. He had to figure out who would or would not participate in the "special project." Which staff members would take on the job with the proper attitude, who had the right discipline and temperament. He also had to figure out how to find professionals. A team to walk Robbin into the chamber that night, then strap him down and wait. A nurse willing to insert the IVs, someone else willing to sit in the execution booth and, at Mason's signal, start the drip. A doctor willing to lean over the man and pronounce him dead. A funeral home willing to pick up the body. Robbin didn't have family to take the remains, so that was another thing on Mason's list: find a place to store Robbin's ashes.

It seemed as if at least a thousand details called for Mason's attention, things that had to happen in a specific order and in a very specific way, and as long as he focused on them, one tight step after

another, he was okay. He could do it. He could pull everything together and get Daniel Robbin dead.

Mason tapped on his keyboard.

Just the day before, the warden at San Quentin had sent Mason
an e-mail offering to meet with him and a few key staff members.
"We've got things down to a system," the man wrote. "Ways for
dealing with the press, family, protesters, last-minute appeals, the
whole shebang. I'd be happy to share what we've come up with."
Mason typed out a thank-you. He'd gotten Gefke's approval for the
trip that morning. He and a couple of other people could be down
and back in a day, if they pushed it. And they'd have to push it.

In the seven years since the last execution, the chamber and its
holding cell had become the unit's dumping ground. Old desks, chairs,
boxes of files detailing who'd been in and out of the IMU, were piled
to the ceiling. All of it would have to be cleared out and the entire
place scrubbed, top to bottom. Then they'd need to set up.

Somewhere in that mess was the gurney, black vinyl and metal,
armrests that pulled out to the sides like wings. They'd need to make
sure it was in working order. Then there was all the medical stuff
to consider—the tubes, straps, and switches. When the time came,
the valves for the drugs would be opened from within an enclosed
booth so that no one could see who turned the switch. That meant
the IV lines had to travel at least five feet before getting to Robbin.
That all had to be set up and tested by someone from the infirmary.
Plus they'd have to get the video system up and running. The entire
procedure, beginning to end, had to be taped. But as far as Mason
knew, the recorders were all old-generation, so there was that to
deal with. And on top of all that, the phone company would need to
set up two direct lines, one to the attorney general's office, in case a
last-minute order for a stay came in from the Supreme Court, and
one to the governor's office, just in case he had a last-minute notion
to call a stop to the whole thing.

Like that's going to happen.

Mason had voted for the governor and would probably vote for him again, despite his ill-conceived idea of holding an execution before his election. He'd been around politicians enough to know how it was played. The governor's opponent was a tough-on-crime lawyer who'd helped get a bunch of strict sentencing laws passed. He'd done a good job of making the left-leaning poli-sci professor from Eugene look too weak to deal with today's level of criminal. An execution would dispel that notion. Or at least get people's minds off it for a while. Calling the thing off—it'd be political suicide.

Still, Mason hadn't been able to sleep the past few nights, hoping that somehow Robbin's order would be withdrawn. It wasn't that he was opposed to the process so much as overwhelmed by it. Maybe if it wasn't Robbin but one of those racist fucks who would just as soon stick him with a shiv as stand anywhere near him . . . *Maybe if it was Tulane* . . .

Mason shuddered at the reflexiveness of his thought. *All this damn time, and you're returning to that?* It disappointed him, the way his brother was still able to sneak up and hit him alongside the head even though he was locked up in a maximum security prison in Illinois.

Mason turned his focus back to his keyboard, wrote down some possible dates for going to San Quentin, then hit Send.

CHAPTER 19

March 19, 1995

IRENE DWELLS AT THE BOTTOM *of a river, hair moving with the current, flesh cool and soft, eyes lifeless windows. The soft scales of time drifting down and covering the remains of her days. The love, the inspiration, the hope, even the hate—all God's pliant gifts buried by the steady advance of time. Above her, sunlight breaks the river's dancing surface, travels down in snakelike patterns, lights her outstretched hand. She looks up . . .*

IRENE WOKE TO THE SOUND of Shep playing his horn. Clear, crisp, a clarion breaking the dawn with its call. High arcing notes dancing among clouds, trees, grass. Spirals of sound blending seamlessly with the wind and the birds . . .

Birds.

Irene Stanley opened her eyes to another day.

"Stupid," she muttered. It wasn't Shep. Of course it wasn't Shep. The birds didn't sound a thing like her son's playing. She put on her slippers, rose unsteadily, then dropped back to the bed.

"It's his birthday," she whispered.

A breeze moved through the open window, and sunshine played across the eyelets on the lace curtains, scattering seeds of light on the dresser and floor. She could hear the trill of a cardinal, the twitter of wrens. It was a fine day. It was always a fine day on Shep's birthday. The kind of day to plant peas, clean windows, have a picnic. For ten years she'd despised this irony—young, fresh light where she wanted only darkness. It ought to rain on such a day. Storm. The river should rise, wash out, flood everything in its path. There ought to be hell to pay. At least that's how she had felt back when she could feel anything at all.

Downstairs, Irene lit the stove and put on water for coffee. Yesterday's dishes sat in the sink; laundry lay heaped by the washer. She had not got around to cleaning the windows these last couple of years, because the idea of hauling out the ladder, climbing up, prying out the screens, getting the soap, the rags, the water—just the idea of it—made her tired.

Shep would have been twenty-five years old.

The words kept at her, following her around the house as she picked up Nate's slippers, straightened the cushions on the couch, put the magazines in order. They walked back with her into the kitchen, whispering while she spooned Sanka into a cup. They stood across from her, poking her in the chest as she sat on the porch swing watching her husband read the paper.

His belly pushed the newsprint out from him, and his khakis clung to his thighs. He was forty-three; so was she. Bliss was twenty-two, and Shep . . . *Shep would have been twenty-five years old.*

Birds sang; the swing creaked; clouds eased themselves across the mocking blue sky.

She no longer felt the manic terror she had when Shep was

killed. That sense of falling at every turn, always falling, unable to do anything but cling to whatever piece of her son she could find—a T-shirt, a book, the dirt embedded in his shoes. She no longer sneaked to the liquor store to get her "relief." And to her surprise, she didn't miss it. Instead, she just felt hollow. An empty and lifeless tree waiting for one good wind to knock her down.

Then, as she sat there thinking about what her son might have looked like if he had lived, she heard her husband's voice from behind his paper.

"It's Shep's birthday today, isn't it?"

The porch swing slowed, then stopped, and Irene hung above the old pine boards, uncertain how to respond. Shep, the subject as well as mere mention, was off-limits around Nate. Had been since shortly after they'd returned from Oregon. She remembered the day he had come back from a hunting trip and told her he was done with grieving. "Time to move on," he said. No one—not Bliss, not Irene, not his brother, not even Pastor White—could mention the boy around him. "There's only one way to heal from this kind of thing," he told them all. "And that's to look up and out." And that's just what her husband had gone and done.

Nate lowered his paper. "I said, it's Shep's birthday. Isn't that right?"

"Yes," she answered, unable to keep the surprise from her voice. "Yes, it is. His twenty-fifth birthday."

Nate smacked his lips. "Twenty-five, hmm. Hard to believe." He snapped his paper back into position, and Irene leaned back against the swing, figuring that was the end of it—a momentary flash of lightning skimming the morning air, nothing more. Nate had never mentioned any of Shep's other birthdays. And when she had brought them up in those first years, thinking that at least on *that* day he could pay some respect, some due, some *thing,* he'd silenced her not with a word or look but with just their opposites—that is, no word, no look, no response whatsoever. He'd silenced her with his own silence.

"You know," Nate continued from behind his paper, "it's been too damn long, that's what I think. All this waiting 'round—I don't get it. I mean, I know there's appeals and all, but hell. Ten years? Shep deserves better than that." He lowered his paper and peered at Irene over the top of his reading glasses. "What's going on over there in that damn state, anyway?"

Irene cocked her head to the side, like a bird listening for something. Part of her was exhilarated to hear Nate say Shep's name. Part of her felt afraid, knowing the moment would pass and she would be left alone, with only her tired memories for company. "I don't know, Nate. I mean, I've never really understood how all this works."

"You're the one who keeps tabs on it."

Irene's swing creaked back. "I had been, that's right."

"So?"

A small gray squirrel ran across the porch railing, then stopped and stared at the two people.

"So tell me," he went on. "What's going on with the case? Why is it takin' so long?"

The squirrel took off, and Irene looked at her husband. "I told you, I don't know. I don't follow it anymore. Haven't in a while."

Nate's eyebrows drew together. "You mind telling me why? I thought you were living for the day this all ended."

Irene ran her hand over the top of her head. He was right—there had been a time when all she wanted was to see Daniel Robbin executed and everything settled. Though what killing him would settle, she had no idea anymore. As the years had gone by, the anger that had kept her heart beating had faded to a dull throb, and the most she could muster now was an aching kind of lust. Robbin's death. Hers. It didn't really matter.

"I'm just tired, Nate. That's all. Just tired."

He laid his paper in his lap and frowned. "What's that supposed to mean?"

The swing shuddered to a stop, and Irene looked at her husband. It seemed impossible he wouldn't understand. It was so plain. Had been for so long. Life had dug itself out of her, and now she didn't even have the energy to wash the damn laundry, let alone continue to follow what was happening to that man over in Oregon. The dance she had started in order to get Bliss out of the house— the knitting and sewing, the cleaning and baking, the Bible classes, the hairdos—it had all ground to a halt. The last few months had been worse. Something about Bliss going off to law school in Texas, and Jeff getting himself married and now being their mailman. Something about Carol and Doctor Al having another grandchild, a beautiful little boy named Toby, who was born with the same golden hair Shep had had. Something about Nate and her falling further apart.

"It means I don't have it in me to call the DA's office every week, or read their letters over and over trying to make heads or tails out of them. It means I'm tired of keeping this whole thing in my sights like some kind of sniper, with you just . . . I don't know what. Absent, I guess. Just completely absent, like you just don't give a goddamn. That's what it means."

Nate's paper dropped to the floor. "Is that what you think?" He grabbed for the newsprint. "That I don't care?"

"I really wouldn't have any way to know what you think, would I? When was the last time we even talked about our son?"

"I brought him up just now, didn't I?" He thrust one page of the paper over another. "Remembered his birthday, didn't I? That sound like I don't care? It's just that . . . Hell." He attempted to refold the paper but gave up and shoved it at her. "You know how I am with these things, Irene. You got to move forward or it will just suck you back. You know that."

"That's what you say." Irene set her coffee on the floor and pressed and folded the paper back into a neat rectangle.

"That's what I say 'cause that's what's true. But if you had something you needed to talk about, I'd listen. He was my son, too. I just thought you'd know if maybe this Robbin guy's trying to . . . shit, I don't know, get out of this or something. You know, delay things by telling a new story. Something like that."

"That's why you brought all this up? To find out what's happening with Robbin?"

"Yeah. Sure. Why else?"

Irene sighed. "I'm sorry, Nate, but I can't help you. The lawyers' letters are all in the rolltop if you want to read them. Or you can call the DA's office. I've got the number."

Nate scratched his face, and Irene looked out at the yard. The lawn needed mowing, the fence mending. The daffodils she and the children had planted beside the house years ago needed thinning.

Nate leaned back in his chair and crossed his arms over his chest. "Are you doing all right?"

Irene didn't respond.

"It's just this past year or so, it's like the wind's gone outta you or something. Even Carol has noticed. Says she's worried 'bout you."

Irene's gaze slowly settled back on her husband. She had been not all right for so long now that it was just a matter of reality. Like a warp in a floorboard. And she started to tell him she was as well as could be expected, but stopped. "No," she said finally. "No, I don't expect I am all right." Her voice wavered. "I don't expect I'm all right at all." She grabbed the sash of her robe and began to wrap the terrycloth around her hand. She didn't know what she expected Nate to say, or even do. What tenderness or aid her husband could deliver. What was it Bliss had said? They didn't know how to take care of themselves, let alone each other? Yet suddenly Irene knew she needed something—a look, a word, a hand, an embrace, any-

thing to keep her from drifting off the edge of their world. He was
her husband, after all, and Shep his son, and it was their son's birthday. Twenty-five. *He would have been twenty-five years old.* Irene
pressed her hands together. Waiting. Wanting.

Nate took a breath, then reached for his hat. "Well, don't worry,
hon. I'm sure this'll all come to an end sooner or later. Bound to.
Then, you watch, everything will be okay."

He pecked her cheek, then took to the stairs, shouting over his
shoulder that she ought to call her sister. "Get outta the house. Go
shoppin'. It'll make you both feel better."

And then he was gone, and in the space he left behind, Irene
knew—it was over. There was no fixing her, and there was no one to
help her try. There was nothing to all this waiting. Nothing to make
things okay, and no one to understand. She slumped back into the
swing, letting her weight take her back and forth against its rusted
chain. There was just not much left to life. Hate had run its course
and depression had whittled her to nothing. After a while she looked
up at the rafters and noticed the dirty cylinder of an old bird feeder.
She and the kids used to mix up sugar, water, and food color, then
watch the hummers fight for a spot at its thin, flower-shaped straws.

She couldn't remember the last time she'd filled it. Probably
the summer before they moved to Oregon. It was impossible to say.
The years between Blaine and now were dead to her. She got up off
the swing and took the glass container from the bent nail that held
it in place.

Three steps led down to the walkway. She took them slow, slippers slapping against her heels, then rounded the path to the side of
the house, and dropped the feeder in the trash, wincing only slightly
as it shattered in the empty metal bin.

And what was it? The sound? Or possibly just the action? She
didn't know. All she knew was that she couldn't keep on with it
anymore. Empty feeders, empty days—she didn't need either. And
God knew she didn't want them.

Irene dropped the garbage can lid on the grass and turned. Cautious steps at first, then firmer, harder, faster, faltering once on her slipper but righting herself and walking past the daffodils and away from the sun and that damn bird still singing on and on and on . . .

Shep should be twenty-five, twenty-five goddamned years old, and she was done with it. Done with it all.

SHEP'S ROOM SMELLED LIKE A closet—dust, mites, old things just silently falling apart. His bed lay stripped of sheets and stacked with boxes. More boxes sat on his desk and in the corner of his room. All of it brought back from Blaine because not bringing it back somehow seemed wrong.

Irene stood in the doorway, swaying slightly. *A good mom would have unpacked those boxes a long time ago,* she thought. *Unpacked them, given away what others could use.* She sniffed and wiped her eyes. *A good mom wouldn't come to her son's room to die.*

Irene figured she'd taken at least twenty pills, maybe more. Her sister had been supplying her with Valium for years. A half-dozen pills one month, a few more the next. "They take the edge off," she told Irene with her most sisterly smile.

Irene aimed herself in the direction of one of the windows. It was glazed with grime, and outside the leaves and flowers of the apple tree she and her dad had planted pressed up against the screen. She reached for the window sash, put her weight into it, and pushed. It opened with a loud screech and her hands dragged along the glass, not quite feeling what she touched. Her mouth felt fuzzy, too. Like she'd been to the dentist. But the honey-sweet scent of the apple blossoms, that she could smell.

She must have been four or five when she and her dad planted the tree. He dug the hole and she tamped the dirt down with her feet. Then, year by year, she watched the tree's branches grow toward her room. She tried to reach it from her window once, but lost her balance and fell. Her ma ran out, folded Irene into her arms, and took her to Dr. Olson's, where he wrapped up her arm and commanded her to stop scaring her mother half to death. The bedroom was painted pink back then, and bookshelves held her dolls. She had a black metal fan she'd turn on summer nights when it was too hot to sleep. Other nights she'd just lie there and listen to the whip-poor-wills and the sound of barge horns signaling their way around the river bends. Irene grasped the windowsill and lowered herself to her knees. As a young girl she'd wake early each morning to the sound of her ma downstairs making breakfast and her pa calling for her and Carol to get going. Then, after she was married, she'd come to stay with her parents while Nate was off in Vietnam. Shep was just a baby then. A tiny breath of life, with flowerbud-shaped ears and skin as soft as feathers.

Irene laid her head against her arm, her eyes moving in and out of focus. First the apple blossoms, then the screen . . . blossoms . . . screen . . . She rested a hand on the dusty wire. *This is how it happens,* she thought. *This is how you die.*

Just then she heard a low buzzing. A hummingbird moved outside the window, busily working from one blushed blossom to another. Irene tried to follow its movement, but she couldn't. Then, as the last of her strength fell from her, like layers of skin, or hair, or worry—all of it insignificant in her growing haze—the bird was back, hovering before her hand.

"I broke the feeder," she said. "We used to fill it, but then Shep died and we just stopped doing things. And now—now I've gone and thrown it away, and it's broken, and, well, it's gone. It's all gone. Shep, Bliss, Jeff, Mom, Pop. Everyone. All gone." Irene's hand dropped and the bird darted away, and she looked at the place where it had been and saw her memories mix and blend, like watercolors on an abstract canvas. It had been so beautiful. Life had been so simple and so terribly beautiful.

"Get out of here!" a voice shouted.

Dizzy, disoriented, Irene swung around to the empty room. Her hand went to her temple. It could have been her mom, Shep, Bliss, God . . . A cold slice of terror cut to her stomach, and she doubled over, reaching for the floor, nausea rising like a sea.

Pathetic, Bliss had called her. *Pathetic.*

Irene crawled to the door, then reached for the jamb and pulled herself up. There are long paths to walk, she thought. The death of a child, the hate that comes, the despair, the infinite, immeasurable pain. There is family, and children, and hurts and injustices. There are hallways that last forever.

And then there is a tree, and a bird, and a memory of beauty.

CHAPTER 20

March 20, 1995

THE LETTER TO DANIEL ROBBIN came like instinct, flying from her hand and sweeping across the satin-white paper like a flurry of snow, hesitating only slightly when she wrote the date—March 20, 1995. The day after she nearly ended her life.

She had made it as far as the bathroom, before collapsing beside the sink. Hours later she woke up on the floor, vomit crusted on her face and clothes, shame folded into every cell of her body. She didn't have it in her to kill herself: not the courage, not the strength, not the clarity that comes from strong will. *I'm a fool,* she thought, grabbing the edge of the old claw-foot tub and dragging herself to her feet. Living to die, and then, when it's within arm's reach, running like a damned ass.

Only it wasn't that simple.

There in Shep's room, memories pulling and blending, she had discovered a reason to go on living that had nothing to do with revenge or hate, and that reason had shaken her from root to stem. Beat in her still as her pen moved across the paper.

"It was Shep's birthday yesterday," she wrote. "He would have been twenty-five years old. I thought about that a good deal throughout the day—what my son would have looked like, who he would have been, what he would have been doing if he were alive. He was a good boy, Mr. Robbin, and I'm sure he would have been just as good a man." She looked up at the kitchen ceiling, then leaned back toward the table. "There was a part of him that was an angel." She bit her lip, considering the word. She didn't want to sound maudlin, but she couldn't come up with anything else. So she continued. "I don't mean angel sweet, though he was that. What I'm talking about is something deeper. Like he had somehow got hold of a piece of something, some insight or vision into life that was beyond anything I could ever see or understand. That's what it felt like, anyway."

Irene nodded as she wrote, remembering her son's presence, the way he delighted in small things—the color of fallen leaves, the sound of the wind, the first crack of ice breaking off the river. His quiet way of being there for people. She remembered their first Thanksgiving in Blaine, and how angry she was, with no other family members around, and cooking in such a lame excuse for a kitchen. A tenth the counter space and an oven that didn't work right. She had burned herself basting the turkey, and as she stood there swearing, Shep appeared in the kitchen, grabbed some ice from the freezer, and had her sit and take care of her hand while he finished with the bird.

Her son was a self-contained, gentle soul, and it still tore to think of him.

"I think part of his specialness came from his music. He played the piano and the horn, and not just a little and fair. Shep had a way with those instruments that made people stop and sometimes even cry."

When Shep was about nine, his talent attracted a man who used to teach at the university, a well-known musician and conductor who'd traveled the world playing in different symphonies. He'd retired to a small ginseng farm up in the hills and would come down sometimes and give Shep lessons. He said Shep had a rare gift, and more than once Irene saw him wiping his eyes while he listened. And there were others, too. Her sister, people in church, herself. She hardly knew a soul who hadn't been touched by his music.

Irene set down her pen and read through her letter. There was no way to describe Shep, his music, or what they'd meant. She couldn't even come close, so she gave up and started in on her reason for writing.

"Hating you, Mr. Robbin, wanting to see you dead, and wanting to be there while it happened, has been all I've lived for these past years. It was the only thing that had any meaning, and the only way I could think to serve my son. It's a sad thing for a mother to have to admit, but it's an even sadder way to live. I see that now. I've sat through ten winters, ten birthdays, ten years of having no idea of anything but my hate for you. But that road is over for me now. It has not led me where I need to go. Though Lord knows where that might be."

She chewed her lip, suddenly sick with anxiety. Dread, even. There are things you don't do in life. Things you never do.

"Anyway, what I'm aiming to say is I'm done with it. I'm moving on. Leaving the room. And . . ." She took a deep breath. "I forgive you for what you did to my son. For whatever it may be worth, I understand people make mistakes in life, Mr. Robbin, and I forgive you yours."

IRENE DROVE FOURTEEN MILES EAST to Coldsprings. It had the closest Wal-Mart, a Denny's, the Pick and Pack, and the large-town anonymity needed for sending a letter off to a prisoner in Oregon.

She could never explain what she'd written—not to neighbors or people at church, not to her sister, and especially not to Nate. He'd never understand. And anyway, she'd been forced to deal with her despair alone, so it only made sense that her redemption would also be private. She nodded to herself as she drove past groves of strip malls and their acres of parking spots, a Dairy Queen, the Coldsprings library, and on into the heart of town, where brick buildings lined cobblestone streets wide enough for parades.

The post office was an old limestone structure sitting at the corner of Madison and Main, draped by catalpas with fresh green buds. It was a fine-looking building set up against a fine spring day. Irene pulled into one of a half-dozen empty parking spots, got out of the truck, looked around, then walked to a line of cobalt blue mailboxes.

Then she froze. She'd made a promise to see this thing through . . . A vow. A sacred vow.

"I'm sorry, son," she whispered. Then she reached for the slot and dropped the letter in the box.

CHAPTER 21

March 20, 1995

ON THE WAY HOME, IRENE stopped at the Coldsprings Kroger, pulled out a cart, and began walking the aisles, eyes alert to anything that could fill the empty sensation that rumbled in her stomach. For the first time in she didn't know how long, she felt hungry—deep down, ravenously hungry. Pregnant kind of hungry.

"Wouldn't that be a kick in the ass?" she muttered, yanking some chips from a display, then pausing midstride. It had to have been at least six or seven weeks since Nate rolled over in the middle of the night and planted her with a thick wet kiss and his heavy sleep-drawn breath. She did some quick calculations. No, she wasn't pregnant.

Irene tolerated Nate's occasional late-night disturbances, but she never enjoyed them. Once in a while, maybe. *Maybe.* She reached for a loaf of bread and squeezed. *Maybe a little bit more.*

She wound her way to the produce section, picked out a good

solid head of lettuce, a nice firm tomato, and a cucumber. She placed a single white onion in the cart. Used sparingly, it would last all week. Onions didn't sit right with Nate; peppers either. She grabbed a few apples, a bunch of bananas, then stopped at a display of tropical fruit: kumquat, coconut, ruby-colored pomegranates, and fuzzy brown kiwis. *Nate would never go for any of these,* she thought, picking up a speckled mango and holding it to her nose. It smelled ripe and succulent, and Irene had a sudden urge to peel it right there. Peel it and dig her teeth into its flesh, feel its juice fill her entirely. She lowered her hand and peered at the fruit suspiciously, then glanced around and tucked it between the bread and the bananas.

When she got home, she told herself, she'd make some iced tea, put on an album, and eat her mango. Afterward, she'd cook something special for dinner. A roast, maybe. Maybe something better. Nate deserved it—a good meal, a good deal more attention, a good bit more of everything all around.

She pushed the cart forward.

"Well, hello, pretty lady." Earl Stanley, short, squat, and round as a sausage, wiped his hands on his apron and walked up from behind the meat counter. Nate's older brother had started as Kroger's meat manager after deciding to close the family shop a couple of years earlier. People weren't raising their own animals as they once had, so there was no more need for the butcher truck. Plus nowadays women liked to get all their shopping done in one place—the IGA in town, or when they were in Coldsprings, the nice big Kroger. That, or the Wal-Mart. It wasn't the same, Earl said, working at a grocery store instead of the butcher shop, but he never complained.

"You never can tell what's good or bad," he told her and Nate the day he announced he was shutting down the sixty-eight-year-old business. And Irene remembered thinking Nate's brother was just plain stupid. "Of course you can tell what's good or bad," she just about screamed. "Of course you damn well can."

"Hello there, Earl. Beautiful day, isn't it?"

"Almost like summer."

"Almost. How are Rosie and the kids? I haven't seen them since . . . I guess since we were at your place for Christmas."

"Is that right? Now, that's a shame. She's been so busy with the grandkids these days, watchin' them while their mama's at work. It's wearin' her down, but you know her, she won't admit it. Still denies we're near fifty."

"Good for her."

"Yeah, I know. Still, she's plenty tired by the end of the day. 'Bout time for a vacation. We're thinking of renting a Winnebago and heading over to Branson. Take in a few shows."

"I swear, you two are always up to something."

He tucked his hands into his apron pockets. "It's easier, you know, now that I don't have the shop to keep up day in and day out. You and Nate ought to think of joining us—there'd be plenty of room, and anyway, it's about time my brother took you on a vacation. I've been telling him that for years."

"You have?"

"You bet. And wouldn't you know, he always has the same ol' excuse—'too much to do at home.' "

"It's true, you know. The place is always needing work, plus Nate's been talking about painting the barn."

"He's been talkin' about *that* for years."

Irene laughed.

"Seriously, Irene, gettin' away—it does wonders for a person's frame of mind, not to mention what it does for a marriage. I swear, me and Rosie, we'd be at each other's throats if it weren't for our little getaways. And just between you and me, I think Nate might consider doing something if he thought *you'd* be interested."

Nate's brother looked so sincere and trustworthy in his white hat and butcher's smock. Kind of like a doctor in that way, Irene supposed. You had to trust that both knew what they were talking about—best medicine, best cut of meat, best way to reset a marriage.

"When was the last time you two got up and out of here?" he asked.

She picked up a package of ground round, ran her finger over the cellophane. "That would have been Bliss's graduation."

"Sweetheart, I'm talking a *real* vacation. You and Nate were gone all of what, two, three days?"

"Two days, one night."

"See now, that ain't no vacation. Even Rosie and I made more of a time of it than you two. You know we went to Chicago afterward, right? Stayed at the Palmer House. I tell you, you've never seen such luxury." Earl waved at a customer, then leaned toward Irene. "Nice place like that, big bed, room service when you want it." He winked. "Does wonders for your attitude."

Irene blushed. "Earl, I swear . . ."

His eyes glinted like a naughty child's. "Oh, you know me— all talk. But I am sincere 'bout you and Nate. If you don't want to come with us, then hell, there's plenty else to do. We really liked that riverboat cruise out of St. Louis. Remember how Rosie won that bundle at blackjack? Or you could head north to Wisconsin, get yourselves a little cabin, go fishing."

"Wisconsin?"

"Why not?"

Irene imagined herself and Nate out at a cabin on some lake, fishing, reading, going on walks. It sounded so reasonable, something married couples do all the time—spend time together, enjoy one another's company, grow old knowing you've got each other to hold.

"You still don't have an air-cooler in that place of yours, do you?" Earl was on to the roasts, rearranging the butts of meat in a nice straight line.

"What?"

"An air-cooler." He shrugged. "Never mind. You ought to tell that brother of mine to step into the twentieth century. Get that house an air-cooler and take you on a vacation. I'm tellin' you, sweetie, it'll change your lives remarkably."

Irene placed her hands on her hips. Normally, Nate's brother's recipes for happiness irritated her. Earl was a simple man with very simple needs—a cool house, a vacation. "You know," she said, "I haven't yet been to Austin."

"There you go." He snapped his fingers and pointed at her. "Go see Bliss—that's a great idea."

Irene set down the ground round feeling as if something new and wonderful had come to her mind. Or better yet, that the recesses of her brain had been scrubbed clean. She took a deep breath. She couldn't tell Nate about her letter to Robbin, but she could tell him they ought to visit their daughter.

"I'll tell you what, Earl. You pick me out two nice steaks. T-bone, make them thick. I want to make my husband a real nice dinner."

CHAPTER 22

October 5, 2004

A STATE-ISSUED WHITE FORD EXPLORER SLID past the prison's physical plant, the laundry, the main rec yard, and into IMU parking space number two. Tab Mason turned off its ignition, palmed the keys, and eyed his passenger. The prison's security manager, Tom Waters, had returned early from his hunting trip with his oldest son. They'd been off in the Wallowas. Impossible to reach, except they went and stopped in some little town, and sure enough they had cell reception, and there was Mason's message telling him to come back to Salem.

Still, instead of moaning about having to return early, or even giving Mason some speech after he learned how he'd handled the warrant—giving it to Robbin while he was unrestrained, just one staff member for backup—the security manager simply listened as his boss explained how calmly Robbin had taken the news.

"Sounds about right." Waters pushed his arms forward and cracked his knuckles. "The guy never does let anything get to him."

"Yeah, but still. It was like I made his day."

Waters's head bobbed. His short hair was bleached nearly white by a summer of biking, kayaking, and climbing with his boys. He was divorced, like Mason, but luckier because he and his kids still had something. Mason's daughter didn't want to have a thing to do with him. She had been eighteen months old when he left Chicago. Kicked out by his wife because she was scared of him—his dark moods, his sudden anger. He'd hit his neighbor once; the guy had borrowed a broom without asking, and Mason knocked him clear across the hall. Broke his nose. And he'd hit his wife. Mason promised that he'd change, that he'd pull his life straight, get a good job, make a nice home. But Shauna would have none of it. Since leaving, he'd seen her and his daughter exactly eight times.

"You never know with these guys," Waters said. "But I see where you're coming from. Everything's so hard in this place. It feels weird when there's no fight."

"No fight at all. Not even a damn trace of fear, anger—something. It's not right. I mean, if he wants this so bad, it makes me wonder if we should be doing it."

"Come again?"

"This is supposed to be a punishment, right?"

"Yeah."

"So it's not much of a punishment if he wants it. You've got kids. When they do something wrong, do you go and give them what they want?"

Waters turned toward Mason. "No, but it's not the same thing. You can't even compare it. And anyway, I don't really buy it, you know? Wanting to die. I never buy it. Even when people go and kill themselves, I always think there's regret."

Mason's thumb ran down the jagged edge of the car key. He had seen his mom splayed out on the sidewalk like a dancer on the evening of his brother's conviction. She had come home from the courthouse, made Mason dinner, serving him on a TV tray so he could stay on the couch; then she had gone off down the hall. A little while later Mason heard the sirens but ignored them. There was always shit going on at the projects. Grim brick and steel, gangs, guns, prostitution, drugs—you name it, it was happening. But then the screaming started and he made his way to the window . . .

"Maybe you're right," he said to Waters. "I just know it's a stinking job."

"No question. But I'll tell you what, I think you're overanalyzing this whole thing. I mean, it's not gonna do you any good to start getting all philosophical. I know it's your nature, but I wouldn't recommend it. Not for this, I wouldn't."

Mason sniffed. "I know. We had rules about that back in Florida. The warden there, Luther Parsons, come time to set up Old Sparky, he'd always have us read the case, news clips, whatnot. Told us to keep the crime up front and center in our minds. Nothing else."

"I'd add Robbin's rap sheet to that list. He was trouble from the day the state got hold of him."

"He was seven," Mason replied.

"He was seven when he tried to set someone's house on fire."

"His mother was a junkie."

Waters held out his hands. "Ten, wasn't it? Ten foster homes in, what, nine years? Arson, assault, robbery—the guy was outta control."

"He saw his mother get shot in the face."

"Yeah, then twelve years later the poor misguided guy goes and shoots a kid."

Mason nodded his concession.

The first prison Tab had worked in was Pontiac, in Peoria. A sorry-ass place that held even sorrier-ass men who looked and acted a lot like Tulane had. Mean. Tough. Stupid. Mason didn't have an ounce of sympathy for them. Next he went to Louisiana—Angola.

Again he ran into the same pathetic lot. But some of the guys Mason started seeing differently. Confused, afraid, defenseless—it wasn't as if they'd somehow blown their chance, as much as that they had never had a chance from the get-go. Many of them couldn't read; a few couldn't even count; one cried for his mother every single night. Mason quit the job after two years and went to college. Six years later he came out with a master's in criminal justice and a job in Florida. Eyes open now, he listened more intently as the men told their stories. And he puked when it came time for him to tie one down to the chair.

Mason flipped up his sun visor. "You got to admit though, Robbin's a different person in here. That's all I'm saying. Just a hell of a lot different."

"I know. And all I'm saying is I think that dude—Parsons?—he got it right. Don't let this whole thing get to you." Waters slapped Mason's shoulder, then the two of them got out of the vehicle and stood staring across the prison yard at the snowcapped peak of Mount Hood some eighty miles away.

"How many times have you climbed that thing?" Mason asked.

"Six. Start out at timberline at two in the morning, get to the summit at dawn." Waters smacked his lips. "I tell you, there's nothing like watching the day begin from up there. Gives you perspective, you know what I mean?"

Mason squinted at the mountain, then shook his head. "I'm not sure I do," he said.

CHAPTER 23

June 10, 1995

BLISS STOOD OUTSIDE THE TRAVIS County Courthouse dressed in a black skirt and emerald suit jacket. In her hands was a briefcase. Nate and Irene stopped walking. They hadn't seen their daughter for close to six months and weren't altogether sure they had the right girl.

"She didn't!" Nate gasped. Bliss's long red locks had been replaced by a short, sassy bob.

Irene grabbed his arm. "Shhh, she looks . . . professional."

Nate had jumped on the idea of going to see Bliss and immediately started working on some car he had in the barn. When Bliss called in April saying she had a summer job in Austin, the deal was sealed. Nate and Irene took off for the eighteen-hour drive in a white 1968 Chevy Impala with an eight-track player and no tapes. She packed food for the road, and sunscreen so Nate's arm wouldn't get all burned hanging from the window as he drove, and somewhere around Texarkana they stopped and stayed in a motel with free HBO and a Magic Fingers vibrating bed.

Bliss set down her briefcase, hugged her parents, and asked about their drive and where they'd parked and were they tired and did they want to eat?

"Now hold on a minute," Nate interrupted. "What's with the hair? We hardly recognized you."

Bliss put her hand to her head. "Like it? I gave it all to Locks of Love. They make wigs for children."

"Wigs?" Irene asked.

"You know, like after cancer treatment? But mostly it's for children who can't grow their hair at all. The woman at the salon said red hair is particularly hard to get, so I'm going to do it again. Grow out my hair, then give it away."

"That's mighty generous of you." Nate ran his hand over the top of his own head. "Think you could spare some for your old man?"

Bliss laughed and hugged her father again, then pointed across the street. "Come on, let's get something to eat."

They entered a small restaurant where hanging plants covered the windows, photographs of fences covered the walls, and an immense woman in an orange muumuu occupied an entire corner. In her lap was some kind of instrument.

"That's Angie." Bliss waved. "She owns the place."

"Food must be good," Nate said.

Bliss elbowed her father as they followed a young guy with a beard and a braid to a table by the window.

"What's that she's playing?" Irene asked as she scooted into a booth. The thing looked like an oar and had a soft, whimsical sound that reminded her of rain.

"It's a dulcimer." The waiter smiled, then handed out menus. "Some people call it a zither. It's from Scotland originally, but used a lot in bluegrass. Angie's played on *Austin City Limits*."

Irene looked across the table at her daughter.

"It's a concert. They broadcast it on public television." Bliss looked up at the waiter. "Michael, these are my parents. They've come all the way from Illinois to visit."

"Hello," he said, setting down three Mason jars filled with water. "You've got one smart daughter here. She's always in here studying. I say she'll end up on the Supreme Court."

Irene cupped her chin and grinned. Bliss looked good, a little thin maybe, but healthy and certainly happy. "I like your hair," she said after the waiter left.

"Thanks. What do you think, Dad? You didn't say."

"I'm getting used to it."

Bliss nudged him again, and he tossed his arm around her and pulled her close.

"So." Irene leaned over the table. "Tell us about this job of yours. You were a little secretive on the phone."

Bliss bit her lip and smiled like she used to do when trying to pull something off. "I wanted to tell you earlier, but when you said you were coming to visit, I thought I'd just wait." She crossed her hands in front of her. "I'm working for the district attorney. Well, not for *him* specifically, but in his office. Not that I'm doing much of anything—just research, writing motions, that kind of thing. You know, basically grunt work. But I have to say, I've never been so excited to get up in the morning. The office just hums with energy. And the attorneys, they're the most dedicated group I've ever been around. Their work, it's like a mission with them."

"The district attorney's office. That means that they're—"

"Prosecutors, Mom. Criminal prosecutors."

"Your mom knows that." Nate let go of his daughter's shoulder and turned to face her. "So tell me, you think you might want to go into this line of work?"

"I'm certain of it. I mean, I know I've only been at this job for a month, but it's just exactly what I want to do. It's like . . ." She tapped the table with her hand. "Well, it just fits." She looked from one parent to another. "I don't know—it's hard to explain."

"But, honey"—Irene reached for her water—"it's only your first year in law school. You never know—you might find something else that really interests you."

"Sure," Bliss said. "Other things interest me. Constitutional law was pretty cool, but—"

Nate tapped his daughter's hand reassuringly. "You heard her, Irene, she's excited about this."

"I know. I'm just saying she doesn't have to decide right this second. There might be other things she wants to do with her degree, that's all."

"Of course, but let's not discourage her."

"I'm not trying to discourage her—"

Bliss held up her hand. "I know what you're thinking, Mom. That I'm doing this because of what we've been through, right?"

Irene glanced over at Angie and her zither.

"You're right." Bliss lowered her voice. "Shep's death has shaped a lot of my decisions, and this one's no different. But if I can make something good come out of it, what would be wrong with that?"

Nate picked up his fork and dug its tines into his napkin.

"I'm sorry, Dad. I know you don't like to hear about this, but honestly, I think I'd make a damn good prosecutor. Who better than someone who's been through what we have?"

"We're not through it yet," he whispered.

"I know. Believe me, I know. And that's all the more reason I want to do this. It's not fair how long everything's taken. It's not that way here in Texas. You know they had thirty-seven executions over in Huntsville last year?"

"Huntsville?" Nate asked.

"It's where the executions are conducted. Thirty-seven of them last year alone. You know how many Oregon's had in the last *ten* years?"

Nate shook his head.

"One. Just one. It's ridiculous the way they drag things out over there."

Irene's muscles slackened. Her daughter's words felt like a defeat. She wanted a fresh life for Bliss, not the same old wounds played out over and over. Besides, Irene had hoped to tell her daughter and husband how she had found her way through their loss. She would tell them about her letter and how the second she dropped it into that box the hair on her arms rose up toward the sun and sounds and smells sprang into different dimensions. It was like taking off ear muffs or rubbing menthol near your nose—everything became that much more vivid and alive. Her letter, she would say, was the reason they were in Austin, the reason she and Nate had held hands in the car, that he'd had mango in his salad and the house was clean and she was listening to music again, and even, up until a minute ago, considered getting herself something called a zither.

It was the reason she was still alive.

But there was no telling her family that story now. Forgiving Daniel Robbin was not part of the law-and-order world her husband belonged to and Bliss wanted to join. Irene's hand covered her daughter's. "You're choosing a hard road. You know that, honey."

Bliss bit her lip and nodded. "It chose me, Mom."

The two women sat staring at each other with Nate looking from one to the other. Then Michael came back and asked if they were ready to order.

"Yes," Nate said quickly, asking for a burger.

The women followed, Irene ordering gazpacho and Bliss a salad.

"Oh, and by the way, Mom, Dad, there's one more thing I need to tell you." Bliss laid her napkin in her lap, then looked up with an impish kind of grin. "I'm a vegetarian."

BLISS LIVED WITH TWO GIRLS in a bungalow near the center of town. Both were law students, and both were back home for the summer.

"Home?" Nate asked as Bliss unlocked the door. "Kids still go home for the summer?"

Irene gave him a look, then walked into the house. "It's sweet," she said. It had wooden blinds, an oak floor, a fireplace with a mantel and bookshelves running either side. In the middle of the room was a large Oriental rug. If she looked past its threadbare pattern, the piles of newspapers, the abandoned coffee cups, the dust and general disarray, it was a very sweet place.

Irene and Nate stayed in "Carrie's room," which was really a glassed-in porch surrounded by dusty bookshelves, wilted plants, and abstract art posters that had Nate scratching his head. They slept on a low-lying bed Bliss called a futon, and Irene found herself giggling at night as she watched Nate struggle to get up from the thing to go to the bathroom.

Bliss spent her days at work, suggesting once over dinner that she might bring her boyfriend home sometime. Both Irene and Nate looked up from their plates.

"Boyfriend?" Nate asked.

"Rudy, Rudy Kaplan. He's from Brooklyn."

"New York?" Irene asked.

"Yeah, and yeah, Dad, he's Jewish."

"I didn't say anything."

"You didn't have to." Bliss wiped her mouth with her napkin and rose from the table.

"Okay, mind reader, then why aren't you telling me more about him?"

"He's in his second year of law school, his parents are both cardiologists in Manhattan, he's handsome, and he's very smart. What else do you want to know?"

Irene set down her fork. "When did you two start dating, and what do you mean you *might* bring him over for dinner? We want to meet him."

"Oh, Mom, it's not that big a deal. He's nice, we get along, but it's not going anywhere. His mom has her heart set on him marrying some nice Jewish girl at Columbia, and I have my heart set on not getting married at all. Anyway, you two probably wouldn't understand a word he says."

"Why's that?" Nate asked, sounding defensive.

"It's his accent. It even took me a while."

"Not about that," he replied. "Marriage. You don't want to get married? When did you decide that?"

Irene watched Bliss turn into a child—a clever, sweet, knows-how-to-get-what-she-wants child—as she went up to her pa and wrapped an arm around his shoulder.

"You've spoiled me, Dad. What can I say?"

And Nate smiled and patted his daughter's arm. "There's that," he said, beaming. "There *is* that."

IRENE AND NATE LEFT AUSTIN six days later, after fixing up Bliss's home and making sure she had plenty of food. Bliss took Irene to the farmers' market, and Irene made her a few vegetable casseroles that she stored in her now immaculate freezer. And Nate went around the house checking all the door locks and outlets and putting new batteries in all the smoke alarms. They never did get to meet Rudy, and Irene never found an opportunity to tell Nate or Bliss about her letter to Robbin. But it didn't matter. Life was moving forward, and for the first time in a very long time, there was hope in it. Even joy. There was no reason to rattle that.

On the way home she and Nate stopped in Hot Springs, Arkansas. They roamed the streets, ate fudge, and bought T-shirts. Then, to Irene's surprise, Nate suggested they extend their vacation by a few days. "A second honeymoon," he said, forgetting that they had never really had a first.

So three hours out of Little Rock they found a nice little motel sitting beside a river where there was not much more to do than take walks, read, watch television, and sleep—which they did, not separately and apart but together, up close and comfortable.

CHAPTER 24

June 26, 1995

THE LETTER CAME WITH A few bills and an ad for the new Home Depot in Coldsprings. They were having an Independence Day sale, and Irene walked into the house thinking she might try to get out there, get some paint for the porch, maybe a bird feeder or two. She was in the kitchen when she got to the envelope from the Oregon State Penitentiary. It was addressed to her, and in the corner was Daniel Robbin's name and ID number.

"Dear God," she said, dropping the letter on the kitchen table, then backing away as if it had bitten her. "What in the world could *he* want?"

In the fervor of writing to Daniel Robbin, it had hardly crossed Irene's mind that the man might write back. "I'm so stupid," she said through clenched teeth. "So damn stupid."

She turned away from the table, staring outside to the yard and barn. "Of course he'd write back. A person like that. He would have to have the last word, right? Right? Shit!" She swung her fist into the counter, then grabbed her hand where it stung. "Shit, shit, shit, shit, shit."

In an instant she marched up to the table and grabbed the envelope. She wanted Robbin out of her life. *Needed* him out of her life. She had no interest in what he had to say. It was outrageous to write back. Wrong. An invasion. *Another invasion.* She imagined a wan, viperlike man scratching his venom into a few pieces of prison-issued paper. What did he care if she forgave him? He had never asked for forgiveness, never asked anything from anyone. She imagined all kinds of profane and ugly things in that envelope as she yanked at the paper and tore it in two. Then she froze.

What if he's explained? She stubbornly held the halves of the envelope apart from each other. *What if he's told why?* Her body tightened against a sliver of hope. "No," she said. "He's just trying to get something out of me. Some pity, maybe. Maybe something more." She imagined long wretched pages telling her how sorry, lonely, and ravaged by guilt he was. Telling her over and over that if he only had to live that day again, he'd never have broken into her house, never touched her son. She imagined him thinking hard about his words, calculating just how to turn her forgiveness to his advantage.

She looked at her hands, thinking. If it was hate he had written, then the letter was nothing. She would throw it away and go on with her life, just as she'd been doing three minutes earlier. And if it was meant to snare her in some web, he could forget it. But the chance that he had written that third thing—*a reason . . .*

Irene slowly lowered herself into a chair and pulled out the contents from each half of the torn envelope. Then she slowly eased the pieces together.

June 2, 1995

Mrs. Stanley, I'm writing you from Block B of the Intensive Management Unit here at the Oregon State Pen. It's a loud, rough place.
Cold because of the concrete, which makes it good in summer, I
guess.

Robbin's handwriting was tight and slanted so steeply to the
right the letters almost fell into one another. Irene remembered
reading somewhere that a slant like that meant the person was an
emotional type. Easily prone to acts of passion. Her own handwriting listed in the same direction, but not so steeply nor with the almost exacting tightness.

Two months ago I was given a copy of your letter. They don't give
us the originals just in case there's drugs stashed in the paper.
That's what people do here—eat their letters to get high. That or
kill themselves. That kind of stuff happens too. It's amazing how
creative people get in this place. Anyway, my guess is your original
letter is sitting on some shrink's desk.

Irene sneered, feeling armed and ready for what was coming.
You're a crazy damn bitch. She could hear the words before she even
read them, and she felt totally prepared.

I know your letter had me wondering about your state of mind.
I got to say up front, I didn't want to hear from you. Didn't want
to know what you had to say. And anyway, I was pretty certain I
could have guessed what you wrote. But I ended up being wrong,
and I got to tell you I don't think I've ever been so blown away.
    You can't imagine what it's like in here, how memories and
ideas can take hold and live like they're real. That's what that day
in Blaine is like. It lives in me like some kind of disease. It's something I hate, every bit of it—*HATE.*

He had capitalized and underlined the word three times, and
Irene coughed out a sarcastic laugh. "*He* hates it," she said, unimpressed.

> Then you come along telling me you forgive me for what I did that
> day, and for the life of me I don't know what you're talking about.
> How can the mother of a boy like Shep turn around and forgive
> someone for killing him? I know I wouldn't be able to, so your do-
> ing it—it just doesn't seem right.

She pulled back. "Who the hell do you think you are, mister,
pointing out right from wrong?" She twisted her mouth into a
lopsided frown, deciding that as soon as she got through reading,
she'd burn Robbin's letter. She looked back down, feeling some degree of satisfaction at the thought of Robbin's handwriting turning
to ash.

> The kind of thing you two shared, people think it's common, nat-
> ural even, but it's not. Not by a long shot, it's not. Kids, they get ig-
> nored and abused and forgotten in all kinds of ways. That's what's
> common, and that's what's sad. But what you and Shep had—my
> God. I don't know how you lived with losing that, let alone turn
> around and forgive the person who took it.

Irene worked the skin inside her cheek. Biting and pulling. She
hadn't lived with it, she thought. All those years in a stupor. *The
walking dead*—isn't that what Bliss had said? *The walking damn
dead?*

> For a long time I thought about apologizing to you for what hap-
> pened that day. But I didn't know how to say it. And anyway, sorry
> wouldn't bring back your son, or erase all the sadness that sits
> between the second that gun went off and now. Sorry is nothing,

worse than nothing, because after it's said people expect everything to be okay. But it never is. I know that. Even though you
say you've forgiven me, I know it's not okay and that there will
always be the ache of another birthday without Shep getting any
older.

Irene attempted to swallow, then looked away from the letter.
He knows where to hit, she thought, wiping her mouth and taking a
breath before piecing the last page together.

You're walking a lonely line, Mrs. Stanley. I've been in this prison
a long time, and I've never heard of others doing what you say
you've done. At least not for guys like me. And I can understand
that. That makes sense, it fits into the picture of the world that I
know. But thinking it over these last two months I guess what I've
come to decide is that maybe there comes a time in all that hating where a person realizes they have to give it up. Give it up, or
die. Maybe that's what made you write me and say what you did. I
don't know, but like I said, I was blown the hell away.

Irene closed her eyes, keenly aware of a sensation swelling in her
chest. Grief, yes. But something else. Something stronger and more
resilient.

Anyway, I wanted you to know I read your letter, and I hope you're
moving on means you've found life in this world. It can be a beautiful place out there, Mrs. Stanley, despite people like me wiping
out precious parts.

The letter ended with his signature—Daniel Joseph Robbin,
same middle name as Shep's. Irene stared at it, then beyond, to
somewhere so far away she had no idea where she was until the
mantel clock rang a single chime.

She'd been wrong. Daniel Robbin's letter was not vengeful or manipulative. It wasn't anything she'd expected, and it wasn't anything she knew how to handle. In all the years between Shep's death and this moment, no one had put into words how it had felt to lose her son. No one had even come close—until now.

CHAPTER 25

October 6, 2004

DANIEL PACED FORWARD THREE STEPS, turned, traced back the same route. Over and over, like a cartridge on a printer, his sneakers scuffing out a syncopated sound. Then he abruptly sat on his bed, picked up a piece of paper, wrote a few words, stopped, and stared at his scratches. Then he rose and paced some more.

The guards were watching, he knew it, and the idea filled him with an almost exquisite sense of irony. Give a guy notice they're gonna kill him, then suddenly take an interest in seeing he doesn't do the job himself. If he were cynical, he could feed off that, but he wasn't cynical. Just like he wasn't suicidal. He was just done with it, and the knowledge they'd finally set a date for his execution came like sweet air. Still, there was one problem. He glanced at the paper lying on his bed. Then he paced some more.

Over the years, he figured, he'd walked hundreds of miles within his cell, maybe thousands. Movement, his movement, forward and back, over and over, kept him sane. It was part of a routine—walk, breathe, think, not-think. Mornings were for meditation, then breakfast. After breakfast he would draw, that or read—papers, books, magazines, whatever he could get his hands on. In the afternoon it was exercise—stretching, isometrics, some yoga—then the pacing. It pushed blood harder and faster, and it even pushed out a kind of breeze that he could just about catch as he turned back into his own path. But most important, it pushed to the surface rock-hard shards of memory he could dig out, then discard.

Except one.

He stopped midstride, picked up what he'd written, read it, then tossed it back on the bed. He'd been trying to write to Mrs. Stanley for days, but it was all coming out wrong, mixed up with what he should say, which was simply goodbye, and what he wanted to say, which was the truth of what had happened in Blaine, Oregon, on May 6, 1985. It was the deep piece of shot he could not work to the surface. The one embedded memory he could never dislodge.

The stupid thing had been writing to Shep's mom to begin with. It was selfish. Greedy in every way. But that first letter of hers—it had felt like a kind of salvation, and it had brought him, quite literally, to his knees. Writing back didn't even feel like a choice. It wasn't until he'd given the pages to the guards that he'd begun to consider the consequences.

Among them, the possibility that she'd write back, letter after letter, keeping pace with his own. Nine years of correspondence, creating a cord that connected him to the world—the muddy smell of the Mississippi, the rustle of corn, the sound of whip-poor-wills going on and on all night long. He'd never actually heard the bird; there are no whip-poor-wills in Oregon. Yet he swore he knew the sound just by Irene Stanley's description; and sometimes, when he could no longer stand the sound of the screaming and yelling all around him, he'd lie in his cell whispering out the bird's call until he finally fell asleep. And there were other things he'd learned, like where Mrs. Stanley worked and what she did there, and what church she went to and why she wasn't going very often. He knew she had a bad knee and had started wearing glasses, and that her daughter was an attorney, and she worried about her not being married. And more important than anything else, he knew that Mrs. Stanley still had no idea what had really happened that day in Blaine.

"Truth," his mother had told him when he was seven, "is not necessarily what people want to hear." She'd said this after he'd just seen her lie to a man at the Kmart. She'd taught Danny that when they were walking around the store, he was to pick out certain things, certain *small* things, and slip them into her purse. She shouldn't see. In fact, *no one* should see. It was their "secret game." If he won, she'd give him a piece of gum and send him off to watch TV. Then one day a man with ears the shape of broccoli flowers grabbed his mother's arm and pointed at Danny, then at her purse.

"We're just playing," Danny said.

"Playing?" His mother grabbed her purse. "You call this playing?" She pulled out a silver watch and looped gold earrings, then struck him across his face and left him crying in an office all alone. When she finally came back she looked all puffed up, as if her clothes had been filled with air, and she explained the thing about truth.

"It's like a song people don't really want to hear, Danny. Afraid it just might stick in their head. You understand?"

Danny did. Truth could get you hurt. So three weeks later, when the police asked if it had been the man from the store who'd come to their home late that night, beat his mother with a beer bottle, and then shot her in the head, Danny didn't say. And twelve years later, sitting in a cell in Prineville, he'd refused to say a thing about the day he shot and killed Steven Joseph Stanley.

The problem was, he wanted to tell Mrs. Stanley. He wanted her to know why of all the homes in the world he'd gone to 111 Indian

Ridge Lane. That it wasn't the way she thought, or had been led to think. And most of all, he wanted her to know that he knew just how deep Shep's death cut. Knew it for a fact.

Robbin ran his fingers through his hair. Even still, it amazed him how little resistance he felt up there. In his mind he was still a young man, with thick hair cresting his shoulders, hard muscles, a lean body. Thirty-eight wasn't old, he knew that, and getting that death warrant made thirty-eight suddenly feel real young. Still, the thinning hair, the weak and lanky arms, his pitiful posture—they weren't a young man's.

Daniel dropped to his bed. The choice was simple. Take the truth to his grave, or make her choke on it. He shivered, then moaned. It was so hard to know what was right when it was all wrong. Every goddamned thing, wrong.

"She'd lose everything," he said. "Absolutely everything." He picked up his paper and crumpled it, threw it at the wall, watched it ricochet off the toilet. Then he clenched his abdomen and rocked back and forth.

They'd be watching him. Taking notes. They'd have him meet with counselors and the preacher and who knows who else. Afraid he was losing it—but he wasn't. He wasn't afraid of their gurney or their needles. If anything, he saw his death as a kind of peace. A quiet place where he could finally rest. And if he wrote Irene Stanley anything at all, he decided, he'd say just that.

CHAPTER 26

October 6, 2004

NATE'S YEARS WERE A HEAVY *and lonesome thing. A man at war with a dragline intent on scraping away what he'd buried. But Nate's secrets were stored deep. No shaft, no auger, no longwall dozer could possibly get to them. Still, he'd seen enough coal mines to know what happens when they try: farmland left so stripped and bare it was unrecognizable. Lunar. Dead. There are sins of commission, things that maybe shouldn't have been done, or possibly just done differently, and Nate believed he could justify those. But then there are the sins of omission. The things never done, not given nor said. "These are the things that will come and haunt you," Pastor White preached. "These are the things that will take you down."*

THE HOUSE WAS DARK WHEN Nate pulled up. No light coming from the porch or kitchen, nothing on upstairs. The truck was still there, though. He scanned the garden and barn. No one.

Maybe Irene'd gone with Carol to Bible class?

"No way," he said, slamming the car door shut and heading to the house. His wife hardly ever went to church anymore. It wasn't "giving her what she wanted," whatever the hell that meant. Irene was getting harder and harder to read these days. It wasn't like she was depressed anymore. Just the opposite. Humming away while she cooked or worked in the garden. He'd even found her reading poetry, and then once a book on meditation. But when he asked about it, joking about her joining some cult, she clammed up tight. If he didn't know better, he'd say she was hiding something. But Nate knew better. In their family, he was the one with the secrets.

"Irene, honey? You around?" Nothing was on the stove; no sound of a radio or television. He dropped his hat and keys on the table and stepped into the living room. "Irene?" The refrigerator purred, the mantel clock ticked. The uneasy sensation he'd been having lately, as if something bad were coming, worked its way back into his chest. "Honey?" He turned and took the stairs two at a time, rounded the corner, and thrust open their bedroom door. Irene was lying on the bed, her eyes closed and her mouth slightly open. Nate was beside her before she could lift her head from the pillow.

"What's going on?" he asked anxiously. "You not feeling well?" She blinked.

"Irene?"

"What time is it?"

"Nearly seven. Are you okay?"

She sat upright. "Seven o'clock? My goodness. I had a headache, so I lay down. I don't have a thing ready for supper."

"Jesus." Nate dropped beside her and undid his collar. "You had me going for a second. House all dark and all, I didn't know where you could be." He sighed, then patted her knee. "Don't worry about dinner. I can fry us up some eggs."

"No." She reached for her glasses. "There's still pot roast left from the other night, and I can pull together a salad."

"Whatever. Your head all better?"

Irene pushed her hair from her forehead and nodded.

She had stopped dyeing her hair, and it had come in a soft silver. *She's still beautiful*, Nate thought. Nothing like him, overweight and balding. He knew he looked like crap. "You sure 'bout that?" He put his hand to her temple, then tilted her chin toward him. "You look a little pale. I'll tell you what, let me take care of dinner. You just lie back and relax—I can reheat a roast as well as you." He got up from the bed and started toward the door, the dark feeling gone.

"Nate."

"Yeah." He turned with a smile.

"It's happening—Daniel Robbin's execution. We got notice from the DA today."

Nate's right eye twitched.

"I have it right here." She took an envelope from the nightstand. "It's at the end of the month."

He reached for the bedpost. "The end of *this* month?"

"That's what it says. October 29, 2004."

Nate watched his hand take the envelope, felt his other pull out his reading glasses, put them on. The words on the page floated in front of him, some clear, some not. Some jumping out and slapping him in the face. "So . . ." he said, lowering his hand. "It looks like they're actually going to move forward on this thing." He rubbed his bottom lip with his finger. "Nineteen years. Damn. Thought maybe they'd forgot about him, you know?"

Irene was looking at the ceiling. "I guess."

"Boy." He blew out an exaggerated breath, trying to act casual, calm, ready. "I guess we're gonna have to figure out what to do."

"Do?"

"Well, yeah. If this is as legit as it looks, then we'll have to get plane tickets right away, prices the way they are. And I guess I'll call Bliss with the news—that is, if you haven't already."

"I haven't."

He swallowed. "Okay, then I'll do that." He turned and took an unsteady step toward his dresser. The darkness he'd been harboring was no longer an imaginary predator but something very real and visible. "I gotta say, I thought you'd be more excited. That headache must have been pretty bad."

Irene picked a string loose from the bed quilt. Jeff had shown up with the DA's letter that afternoon, and as she signed for it, she knew what was inside. Over the years there'd been dozens of similar letters, all with the same official-looking insignia. But this one was different. She was certain of it. And as she stood there listening to Jeff tell her about his son not doing well in school, his wife, Juanita, losing some benefits, and him having to put in extra shifts just so they all could get by, she wondered what she'd do when she opened the letter and read what was coming.

"I don't want to go," she whispered.

Nate turned.

"The execution . . . I—I *won't* go."

Nate squinted over the top of his glasses. "You're not serious, right? I mean, you've always said you'd be there. That it was impor- tant, for Shep's sake."

"That was a long time ago." She looked away, wondering how to explain. In their world, people believed in taking responsibility for their actions, admitting when they were wrong and paying for it afterward. She'd heard it in church, at work, at the bank. "That man ought to be dead by now," people'd say over and over, until finally the topic lost its sheen and all that was left to say, if anything, was "What a shame, what a shame. What a goddamn shame."

Not one of them—not her pastor, her sister, or even her husband— had any idea she no longer agreed. Not that it wasn't a shame. It was all a shame. Every bit of it—the murder, the anger, the bitterness, the things people become or don't, or lose and never find. She and Nate, having no idea what each other thought or felt. All of it, a goddamn shame. It's just that she didn't think killing Daniel Robbin would solve any of it.

"I don't understand, honey. Nothing's changed."

Irene looked at Nate as if he'd struck her. "Oh, come on, look around. *Everything's* changed. Me, you, everyone around us. God, Nate, this whole world's gone crazy, and this thing they're planning to do in Oregon, it's all just part of it—more violence, more killing, and for what?"

"For what?" Suddenly there was no distance between memory and reality. No thick layer of overburden to cover and cushion. There was his son in that room, struggling to live. And there was Robbin. That sonofabitch, that damned sonofabitch. "For Shep, of course. That man shot our boy. Shot him and left him to die—in case you forgot." He was shaking now. Filled with rage, hate, sorrow, fear. Fear. It loomed in him like a rabid animal, digging its claws into his gut. "Irene, you used to talk about us standing there together, just like we did at the trial, remember?"

"Yes," she said. "I remember. Of course I remember. But Lord, Nate, there's a big difference between seeing someone sentenced to death and watching him die."

He knew that. Knew it like his name. Watching someone die, hearing it, knowing it never needed to happen. He knew it all. "Of course there's a difference." He sighed, trying to calm himself. "But it won't be a horror show or anything, if that's what you're worried about. I mean, the way they do it nowadays, with the drugs, it'll be like he's gone to sleep, that's all. There won't be any pain, any suffering. It will be easy, even." He nodded as if to reassure himself. "After that, it'll be over. All of it *finally* over and done with. No looking back."

Irene stood and grabbed her husband's arm. "Over? Do you honestly believe that?"

"Yes." He yanked his arm free. "Yes, I believe that. Of course I

believe that." Gut-shot, that's what he felt like. Gut-shot and bleed-
ing. *The things you don't do, don't say, the things you bury coming
back to bury you.* He dropped down to his side of the bed.

"I think about that afternoon every single day," he whispered.
"Every damn day. And every day I wonder what I could have done
different. Robbin took all our lives, Irene. Every one of us. All the
things we planned, all the ways we could have been. They all disappeared that day. And I hate him for that. I mean, look at us. Here
we are, nearly twenty years gone by, and I feel like we're strangers. I
don't know what you think anymore. What you feel. Hell, for all I
know, you could have been dead when I walked in this house. That
in all this waiting, you finally threw it in. I know you've thought of
it. I have too. Just say the fuck with it and go out to the barn with
my gun, just like so many of those old-timers. You remember, back
when all those farms were getting foreclosed left and right? I hated
coming on them. And their families, Jesus, it hurt them so bad. I
couldn't do that to you and Bliss. But you? I've never been at all convinced you wouldn't go and do it to us. And now, after all this time
waiting and worrying, you say you don't want to see this through. I
don't understand. I don't understand you at all."

Silence settled around them with the darkness resting in the
corner, waiting.

"Nate."

His eyes trailed up.

"Listen. There's things we have to talk about."

"No." He raised his hand to stop her words. "I don't want to
hear any more, Irene. I just want this over. I want this over so bad,
you have no idea. No goddamned idea."

CHAPTER 27

October 7, 2004

A BOX-SHAPED WOMAN WITH SPIKY BLOND hair stepped into Tab Mason's office stirring a cup of coffee. "A Mrs. Irene Stanley's on the line. Says she needs to talk to you about Daniel Robbin."

Mason's hand went to his face, then drew down. *Mrs. Stanley.*

"Should I tell her you're not available?"

His instinct was to say, *Yes, tell her I'm busy. Tell her I'll be busy for the next few weeks.* Robbin and Mrs. Stanley had been writing to each other since before Mason ever showed up in Oregon. The former superintendent had showed Mason a file filled with their correspondence. And then one evening Mason had taken that file home and read each and every letter. He was altogether too familiar with situations like hers—victims becoming so tied up, lost, and angry they begin to feel a kind of kinship with the person who hurt them. It never ended well. Still, he felt curious about the woman, and told his secretary he'd take the call.

She shrugged and shut the door behind her, and Mason took a breath and picked up the receiver.

"Superintendent Tab Mason."

The voice on the other end was brushed with the South. Not a strong accent, but curved around the edges, like his mother's had been. Mrs. Stanley thanked him for taking her call and apologized for any trouble.

"It's no trouble," he lied. "I understand the district attorney sent you notification about the execution."

"Yes. It arrived yesterday."

The woman hesitated, and Mason grabbed one of his pencils and scratched a circle onto a small square pad of paper.

"That letter," she went on. "Does that mean it's settled? That there's no chance for Daniel?"

"That's really a question for the district attorney. Have you called him?"

"No—no, I haven't. But I guess what I'm after is if you're actually moving forward with this, or if maybe—"

"We're moving forward, Mrs. Stanley. What the lawyers do, that's their business. My business is to plan as if things are happening."

"I see. So, can you tell me if it's pretty common for things to get this far and then . . . and then stop?"

Spikes came out from the circle. Spikes that turned to arrows. Arrow tips that turned to triangles. "Again, these are questions for an attorney."

Her voice grew hushed. "Yes. Yes, of course."

Mason shook his head while he methodically drew an X over each and every triangle. He had a press conference to prepare for, a meeting with the director and the governor. He had contingencies to consider, like a sudden stay of execution. What if one came in just as the drugs started to drip? What then? He'd need to meet with the state's lawyers and ask. He wrote down the AG's name and next to it the words *LAST-MINUTE STAY*.

She said something.

"Pardon?"

"I want to know what I have to do to see Daniel."

"You mean attend the execution? The forms should have been included with the notice."

"No. No, no, I want to *visit* him. Soon. As soon as possible. We've been writing for some time now. We, I mean, I—I want to see him, talk to him, face to face."

Mason sighed. Department rules clearly stated that victims were not allowed to visit their offenders, and he told her so.

"But there are exceptions, aren't there? I mean . . . *couldn't* there be?"

Mason glanced at his watch. "Yes, there have been exceptions, but not for capital cases and certainly not on short notice. There's a whole process to go through—applications to fill out, interviews, counseling for both parties. It's not simple."

"Nothing about any of this has been *simple*, Mr. Mason."

He rubbed his nose and leaned back in his chair until it creaked.

"Look, I know what I'm asking for is not . . . well, it's not normally done—"

"It's not *ever* done, Mrs. Stanley."

"All right. It's not ever *been* done. But I'm asking for an exception. I *need* an exception."

Mason tapped his pencil on his leg. The prison had quietly connected victims and prisoners for years. There was good research behind it knocking down recidivism big-time. But the reconciliation program was not something they did often, and never something they'd consider in a high-profile case like Robbin's. Justice, in the public's mind, didn't include forgiveness. It was not part of the public psyche, and any efforts in that direction would, Mason knew, be considered a waste of taxpayer dollars. "Like I said, it's just not done. And truth be told, I don't know if I'd approve of it if we could. You start getting yourself emotionally involved with your son's killer . . . Really, we're trying to protect you. It's in your interest." Mason's pencil tip drilled a dark hole through the paper.

"My interest? With all due respect, Mr. Mason, I don't see how you could possibly have any idea what's in my interest."

Again Mason thought of his mother. It was something in Mrs. Stanley's tone, a slogging kind of desperation too big and empty for any one person to hold on to.

"What about your husband, Mrs. Stanley? Is he interested in meeting with Mr. Robbin as well?"

Silence.

"Mrs. Stanley? Your husband, your family—do they support this idea of yours?"

"I wouldn't know, sir."

"Excuse me?"

"I wouldn't know."

Mason leaned forward, feeling something tug at the other end of the line. "But you've talked about it with them? They know what you want to do, they know you've been corresponding with your son's killer?"

No reply.

Mason could see her now. Dressed simply, sitting in her kitchen, faded curtains on the windows; gingham, perhaps a floral. He knew she lived on a farm in Illinois, and he saw an old house. Nothing fancy, but clean, well-kept. There'd be flowers blooming along the front in summer, a vegetable garden out back. In all respects, he was sure Mrs. Stanley's home and life appeared normal, pleasant, even pastoral. Something easy to look at, but apparently not so easy to live within.

"Mrs. Stanley, I'm not one to give advice—"

"Then don't. Just tell me what it will take for this to happen. It's all I'm asking, and all I'll be needing."

Mason drew a line across his paper.

"I'm sorry, but there's no use us even talking about your visiting Robbin if you don't have the support of your family. It won't happen. I won't let it happen. And even if you had their support, you don't have the time. It takes months, sometimes even years, to go through all the interviews, the counseling, all the forms that have to be filled out. It all takes time, and you don't have that."

He heard something drop. Maybe her hand on a table, maybe a book.

"You mean Daniel, don't you? Daniel doesn't have the time. Isn't that what you mean?"

Mason stiffened. "I mean if this ever *were* to have happened, you should have started the process a long time ago."

Mason listened to Mrs. Stanley breathe on the other end of the line. He hadn't planned on this. Hadn't considered that she might call, hadn't given her much thought at all, really. He only read her and Robbin's letters that one time, purposely filing them and all the sentiments they brought up someplace he wouldn't easily run into them.

"Does Daniel know?" she asked. "Did you tell him a date's been set?"

"Yes, ma'am."

"Well then, how'd he take it? How's he doing?"

"I can't talk with you about how Daniel Robbin's doing. I know you correspond and all, but technically the only ones I can say anything to are his family."

"But *technically* he doesn't have family, does he? Has anyone ever been in touch with him? His father, maybe? Did anyone ever find that man? What about any of his foster parents? He ever hear from a single one of them?"

"No, ma'am."

"Not even a letter, a Christmas card? Nothing?"

Mason rubbed his temple. "Nothing."

"So you're telling me I'm the only one who apparently gives a damn about the man, and you won't let me visit him, let alone tell me how he's doing?"

"Look, I appreciate—"

"Is he eating? Sleeping? Is he depressed? Suicidal? Dammit, I want to know."

Mason sighed. "Look, ma'am, I admire what you've done. It takes a lot, a whole hell of a lot, to come around to the place you have—"

"I didn't call to get a dose of your admiration, sir. There's a man in your prison who killed my son, and for good or bad I've come to terms with him. It's not something I expect people to understand, or even agree with, but I do expect that if there's a way for me to see that man before you go and *kill* him, you'll let me know how I can do that."

Mason shrank into his seat. It was only eight-thirty in the morning and he was already tired. "Can I ask why this is so important to you?"

Again there was silence, and Mason started to nod. The woman had no idea what she was doing.

She muttered something.

"What's that?" he asked.

"Forgiveness, Mr. Mason. Do you believe in it?"

Mason's hand went to his neck. "I've heard of it."

"But have you seen it, in your business? Do many people turn around and forgive?"

A siren took Mason's attention, and he looked out the window. A police car was racing down State Street. "Not often," he said.

"But it happens?"

"Mrs. Stanley, I don't know what you're fishing for, and I don't have any idea what you're looking to have happen by meeting Mr. Robbin. That man is in line to die, and there is nothing forgiveness can do to stop that. It seems to me you might do better to just move on from all this."

Her breath came out as a laugh. "And you have suggestions for doing that, huh?"

Mason glanced at the photograph on his bookcase. What would he do if Latiesha were killed? How would he get on with his life? Mason hadn't seen his little girl in five years, and the pictures he got now showed a different person from the one he remembered. He hated it, and hated her mother for letting their girl change so much. But there was no moving on from the pain of not being a family like they should.

"I'm sorry," he said, digging his nail into his pencil. "No, I don't have any idea what you should do."

"Well, I do."

"What's that?"

"I want to know if he'd like me to ask the governor to stop this thing. I'm willing to do it. Willing to tell him Daniel shouldn't be executed. That it won't bring justice to my son's death."

Mason nodded. It was his mother all over again. Pleading, begging, desperately trying to save what was left of Tulane's life. "You'd be wasting your time."

"What?"

Mason held his breath and dived. "Your trying to stop this thing. The governor's mind is made up on this and so's Robbin's."

"What do you mean?"

"Robbin's forgone his appeals, Mrs. Stanley. Doesn't want attorneys getting involved anymore. He says he's ready to die."

He heard something like a shudder, a cry maybe. Maybe not.

"Look, he's told me this himself, and your coming in trying to change that, it could make things harder for him in the end. Do you understand? If you care about him, you should think about that."

Mason could feel Mrs. Stanley nodding on the other end of the line. She just had to be. Had to see that nothing good could come from this quest of hers. Robbin would be executed in three weeks. Meeting him would only mean she would have to live through another loss. She had to see that.

"Send me the forms."

"What?"

"The forms to visit Daniel. I want them, but don't send them to my home. Daniel's letters all come to my box in Coldsprings. That's where I need the forms sent."

Mason's chest rose, flattened out his starched blue shirt, fell.

"Mrs. Stanley—"

"Don't take this away from me, Mr. Mason. I've been through hell and back, so don't you dare tell me I can't see the man who's taken me both ways."

Mason shook his head. This woman was in trouble. He could feel it, and he could feel himself feeling bad about it.

Shit, he thought. *Just goddamn shit.*

CHAPTER 28

October 7, 2004

THE LATE-MORNING LIGHT SLICED ACROSS the kitchen table like a hard road, slitting the salt and pepper shakers, a bowl of apples, a corner of a plastic place mat with a picture of a field of sunflowers. Irene placed a sweaty palm on the mat, pushed herself up from where she sat, and followed the sagging phone cord back to the wall. She could hardly believe what she'd done. To be so rude and demanding, to not care what the superintendent said so long as he promised to send the forms.

All night long she'd tried to figure out what to do about Daniel. It made no sense to kill him. None at all. All these years with the DA telling her the execution would provide "closure." That was their word. As if her son's life were a book that could finally be shut. And maybe that's what they meant. With Daniel dead, the attorneys, the jail keepers, all of them could close the book on her son and his killer. Isn't that what police called it? Isn't that how Nate considered it? Over and done with?

No, she had to see him, had to convince him to fight this thing. Then she'd get some lawyers, good ones who knew all about the death penalty, and together they'd march right up to the capitol and force the governor to stop this whole crazy thing. There'd be no way for people to ignore that, would there? A mother telling the state not to kill her son's murderer—people would listen. They had to listen. *Didn't they?*

"Dammit." Irene pushed her chair into the table, then in one swift move she reached for her coffee cup—a fine bone-china thing, old, probably her grandma's—and threw it across the room, where it shattered against the cabinet.

Coffee dripped. The screen door squeaked. Irene spun around to find Carol in the doorway, hands set on her hips, elbows poking out like burls on a log.

"Wh-what are you doing here?" Irene asked.

"What am I doing here? The question is, what the hell are *you* doing?" Her sister marched into the kitchen, reached into the sink, and turned around with the handle of the cup looped around her little finger. "You mind telling me what's going on?"

Irene looked down to her feet. "We got word," she said. "The execution's set."

Carol walked to the garbage can, stepped on its lever, and dropped in the cup's handle. "I know all about that. Nate called this morning." The lid slapped shut.

"Well," Irene said, "that's what's going on."

"And that's why you're breaking Mom's dishes?"

"How long have you been standing outside that door?"

"Long enough." Carol set her purse on the table and looked at her sister. "I swear, Irene, you look as if a snake bit ya."

Irene swallowed and pulled the collar of her sweater around her neck.

"Sit down. I'll clean up." Carol wiped the counter and grabbed the broom. "I guess you never really know how you're gonna react to news like this until it comes. You think you do. Think it'll be a big relief, but I guess there's more to it than that. Hmm, hmm, hmm." Carol shook her head in rhythm with her sweeping. "Course, I thought you'd have called to tell me."

Irene let the pause sit, then grow.

"Nate says you don't want to go to Robbin's execution. That right?"

Irene nodded, wary of her sister. Carol was good at pulling on threads, unraveling truths from whatever place they'd coiled.

"I can't say I'm totally surprised. If they'd have taken care of him back when they should've, it'd be different. But now? I don't guess you need to see all that. Hell, I'm not even sure I'd want to go if I were in your shoes. But your husband, he's worried 'bout you. 'Fraid you might have gone soft on the guy. I told him there's no way you'd do that."

Carol tossed a plastic dustpan onto the floor and used her foot to hold it still while she swept up the cup's fragments. "But now I got to say I'm wondering if I had that right." She dumped the dustpan's contents into the trash, then turned and pinned Irene with a look. "I'm asking you again, sis. What's going on?"

Irene drew her right hand up to her mouth and began to tear at a nail.

"Oh, stop that, Irene! You're not a little girl anymore. You tell me what's going on here. Who was that you were talking to on the phone? And why the hell are you asking them to send you stuff to a post office box off in Coldsprings?"

Irene placed her hand on the table and pressed down. "It's nothing."

Carol took a step forward. "Don't you tell me that. Don't you even begin to tell me that."

Irene suddenly felt foolish, like a child with some misguided idea about digging a hole to China. What the hell was she thinking, calling the superintendent? What in God's name did she really expect to do? Go to Oregon? Stop an execution? What was wrong with her? If she didn't have it in her to tell her sister the truth, she sure as hell wouldn't have it in her to confront a governor.

"Irene. I asked you what you're up to."

Irene's eyes burned into the table, pulled at the pattern in the wood, crawled into the grain, tightened on every particle. "You remember a while back when I was so sick, your husband had to come and help me out?"

Carol set the dustpan on the counter. "That must have been, what, six, seven years ago? Why?"

"Nine." Irene swallowed. "Nine and a half. You remember the date?"

"The date? Of course not."

"It was March nineteenth. Shep's twenty-fifth birthday." Irene began picking some grit off the table.

"You're not answering my question."

"I wasn't sick that day. Not with the flu, at any rate."

"So?"

Irene dug her fingernail deeper into the tabletop. "Do you know what it's like to live with hate, Carol? Every single day, nothing but hate?"

"Irene—"

"You don't know, do you? You have no idea."

"Oh, come on, sis. You don't think I hate Daniel Robbin? You don't think I hate what he did to Shep? It hurt everyone I love—you, Nate, Bliss, my family. You have any idea how scared my kids were when Shep was killed? He robbed them of something that day too, you know."

Irene looked up from her digging. "That's not the same. I'm talking about something that's as much a part of you as your spit. It's just there, always just right there, no matter what you're doing.

Waking, sleeping, it doesn't make any difference. Everything tastes of it, your eyes burn with it, your skin. Remember that rash I had? How it spread across me like a disease? And me clawing myself bloody? Remember that? That was hate covering me. Every inch of it, hate."

Carol's mouth closed up as if it had been buttoned.

"I'm telling you, I couldn't lift a finger without thinking about how I wanted to kill Daniel Robbin. I mean literally, not just see him dead or watch someone else do it, but me, kill him, on my own. I would dream of it, day in, day out, going over exactly what I'd say and how it'd feel to pull the trigger and watch him die. And after that I'd kill everyone else, too. Every single sonofabitch who had ever hurt a child. There was nothing in me that was sacred. If you had cheated someone, Carol, hurt anyone, I swear to God I would have thought of killing you, too." Irene wiped her mouth with the back of her hand. "I hated everything. Do you understand? Everything. My life, this house, anything that reminded me of Shep. Anything that reminded me life was so goddamned unfair."

Carol reached over and patted her sister. "Irene, hon, I know all that. Lord, it was as plain as day you were suffering. Who wouldn't be? You went through hell. You, Nate, Bliss, everyone. But you've been doing better. You're not so bitter, and it makes sense. No one can hold on to that much hate forever."

Irene grabbed a breath of air. Someone was burning leaves, and the scent of the smoke made her think of autumns growing up with her sister, raking up the leaves, then jumping in the piles. She looked out the window. "I took a bunch of the pills you gave me. Twenty, maybe thirty of them—I don't know. But I took them, all of them. I was done with it, Carol. Just done with it. But then I backed out, because you're right, I didn't have it in me to continue hating, and I didn't have it in me to kill myself either. I'm a coward. You've said it, Pa's said it, Nate—you've all said it, and if you haven't, you've thought it. I'm too weak. It was Shep's birthday and I took the damn pills, and then I threw them up. That evening Al came by, it wasn't the flu or food poisoning, like your husband thought. It was an overdose, Carol. An overdose."

Carol stood motionless for a good twenty seconds, then leaned forward. "You tried to kill yourself?"

Irene nodded.

"Lord Almighty." She slapped her thigh. "Why on earth didn't you come to me?"

Irene focused her eyes on her sister's. "What for?"

Carol stiffened. "You should have come to me. I've always said that, haven't I? Haven't I always been there for you and your family?" She stared at Irene, waiting for an answer. When it didn't come, she took a step forward. "You still haven't explained that call."

Irene took a deep breath, got up, dragged a chair over to the refrigerator, climbed up, and took a shoe box from a cabinet. "Here." She got down and set the box on the table.

"What's that?"

"I wrote him a letter the day after I took the pills. I figured if I didn't have the courage to kill myself, I didn't have the privilege of holding on to what made me so miserable. It was time for me to move on, Carol. Live or die. Forgive or hate. I had to make a choice, so I wrote him."

"Wrote who? What are you talking about?"

"Daniel Robbin. I wrote him and I told him that . . . that I forgave him."

Carol pointed. "And you're telling me that that shoe box there . . . has what? Your letter?"

"His. All his. I don't have mine."

"*His* letters?" Carol's eyes looked like they could drop from her face. "You two have been writing to each other?"

Irene nodded. "Nine years."

"Nine years? And Nate doesn't know?"

"No one knows."

Carol's hand went to her forehead. "Lord in heaven, tell me this isn't true. I'm serious, Irene. Tell me there are not letters in there from your son's killer. Tell me you have not been corresponding with that . . . that *monster*."

Irene opened the box and lifted out a handful of envelopes. "He writes two, sometimes three times a month. And I write back. You should read them. You should get to know the man."

Carol looked at Irene as if she were holding something she'd dredged up from the bottom of the river. "Have you lost your mind? You don't write to someone like that. Christ, I don't understand what's gotten into you!"

"Carol."

"I know, I have no idea what you've been through. I know, I know, I know. But to start a *relationship* with your son's killer? To forgive him for what he's done to you and your family?"

"He's not like what you think."

"Don't give me that. You think I'm fool enough to believe one word he's written? He's got you all tied up. For God's sake, people like him, they have no walls, no boundaries telling them right from wrong. Using you is just as easy as shooting Shep. Easier, 'cause he doesn't have to see your face." She turned and paced from one end of the kitchen to the other. "Goddammit, girl, you're being a fool."

"I told you, I had no choice. I couldn't go on like I was."

"So you go and decide the best person to turn to is the man who killed your son? That's crazy, Irene. You have the whole world supporting you. Me, Nate, Bliss, everyone at church—everyone's on your side. And who do you go and turn to? I can't even begin—"

"That's right! You can't even begin. Look at you—perfect marriage, perfect children, perfect, wonderful grandchildren. Jesus, Carol, you don't know anything about the miles that lie between losing a son and finally letting him go." Irene pulled a letter from one of the envelopes. "Look at one. Just one. He's just a man. A man who made a terrible mistake. He knows that and is sorry for it.

Something in him died when he shot Shep. Remember how he never tried to hide or nothing after Shep's murder? Walked right into that bar just asking to be caught? He'd just turned nineteen. Nineteen, Carol. He was just a nineteen-year-old kid."

"Stop it! Just stop .it." Carol halted two feet from Irene. "Who were you talking to on that phone?"

Irene's face tightened.

"I said, who. Were. You. Talking. To?"

"The superintendent there at the prison. I've asked him to let me see Daniel."

"No way."

"I'm willing to go to the governor, ask him to stop the execution. Tell him I've forgiven Daniel. Say what I know about him, how he's changed, made a mistake and changed."

"He's brainwashed you!"

"No. No, he hasn't. Me wanting to help, that's all my idea, he doesn't know a thing about it. Daniel's never asked me for help. Not once. In all these letters, he just writes about ordinary things—what he reads, things he sees. He's an artist, did you know that?"

Carol knocked her forehead with her palm. "An artist? Now why the hell didn't you tell me that earlier? God, listen to yourself. There are lines, sister—lines—and trying to save your boy's killer crosses each and every one of them. Tell me, when did you plan to drop this little bomb on Nate and Bliss?"

Carol's eyes lay hard on Irene, forcing holes right through her thoughts and dreams about saving her friend.

·   "I haven't thought that through yet."

"No kidding." Carol's arms dropped to her sides, dangling out of a wildly colored tropical top, large magenta flowers against purples and blues.

"You just said you've always been there for me. Well, be here *now.* I know there are lines, but lines get crossed, need to be crossed sometimes. I was dying. Do you understand how thin *that* line is?

Wrongs happened, I know. But at some point it was either forgive him or die. I didn't know he'd write back, had no idea in the world. But once I read what he wrote . . . well, I came to the other side of something I never thought I'd live through. These letters"—Irene slid the box toward her sister—"they've been my rafts. Giving me ways to see and appreciate the world again. That man, that *monster* in Oregon, the boy who killed my son? He's helped me, and I can't let him die without at least trying to help him."

Carol's face quivered. "Helped you? Um, um, um . . . now I just got to wonder what Nate would say to that. Or Bliss. Working herself to death trying to protect the world from people like this Robbin character, and you go and say *he* helped *you*. I bet it'd just thrill them to death to hear that. Uh-uh." Carol was close enough now for Irene to see her lipstick-stained teeth, and sweat—a thin line of it trailing down her forehead. "You listen to me, sis. You're gonna take that box of yours, and you're gonna burn every last thing inside. You understand? Robbin is getting his due, and there's nothing you can do to stop it. So you're gonna let go of that fantasy. 'Cause if you go ahead and try to do what you said"—she shook her head—"you'll lose everyone. Nate, Bliss—*everyone*."

A roll of thunder rumbled in the distance, and Carol nodded as if God were marking her words. "Destroy those things," she said. "Destroy them and forget about Robbin. Do it today, do it before Nate finds out the real reason you're not wanting to attend the execution. That man found his son dying and he couldn't do a thing to save him. You got to remember that. Remember how much that digs into him. No, there's no way he'd tolerate you turning on him like this, and that's what it is, Irene. That's *just* what it is."

Irene opened her mouth to speak, but Carol silenced her with a shake of her head. "You understand what I'm saying? I'm trying to save your ship, girl. But there's no doing it if you go ahead with your crazy ideas."

Irene held her sister's stare, then nodded, once, twice.

"Good." Carol brushed her chest as if she were cleaning off crumbs. "That's good. I'll check with you later today. Then tonight I'll call Nate and tell him to leave you be about all this execution stuff." Carol placed a hand on Irene's shoulder. "I know I haven't walked the path you have, Irene, but I also know no good can come out of all this." She nodded at the box. "Robbin is set to die. It's what everything's been leading toward. And as far as I can see, all you're doing is setting yourself up for another fall."

CHAPTER 29

October 7, 2004

IT MAKES SENSE, IRENE THOUGHT. *Get rid of the letters. It makes sense.*

It wouldn't take much, just rake up some leaves, strike a match . . .

She couldn't remember Carol ever sounding so disgusted. Befriending Shep's murderer—who wouldn't be shocked? And who was Irene to think she could possibly go and save the man? And for what, and at what cost? Carol was right, it was stupid. Stupid and wrong and deceptive and—and she didn't know what else.

Thunder rumbled to the west, and Irene glanced out beyond the crimson maple to see dark clouds building themselves into a wall somewhere over Missouri. She left the kitchen and went out the back door to get a closer look. She loved storms, admired how within a matter of moments the heat and dust of a day would relinquish themselves to the clouds. She sat on the back stairs and looked at the barn. It had once been painted white, but now, after years of neglect, it stood exposed and bare. If they didn't take care of it soon, it would start to collapse. Just like so many other old places along the river.

A bolt of lightning cut a silver gash to the west. Irene counted: one, two, three . . . Getting to twenty before the thunder.

She could burn the letters after the storm. Burn them, then get to the business of moving on. Talk to Nate about getting the barn fixed up, and the roof on the house—that was in bad shape, too. And while they were at it, they should attach a new rope to the tire swing. The one there now was old and frayed, and it made her worry every time one of Carol's grandkids headed toward the old tree.

Another bolt. Fifteen seconds to thunder.

Beyond the tree and barn lay a land Irene knew by sight, color, and smell. Placed there blindfolded, she'd easily find her way home. There was the fence line, warped osage boughs wrapped with wire, and the fields, all neatly plowed for the winter. Beyond that were the trees that abutted the river. They stood still as statues, bright reds and yellows against the darkening sky. Irene didn't need dramatic landscapes. Thunderstorms were her mountains, the rounded ridges that lined the Mississippi gorge enough for her. She loved the russet color of dried millet and sumac, liked seeing men in coveralls and seed caps, felt at home with the sound and smell of disks breaking soil. She loved it, actually. Absolutely loved it. And she didn't want to lose a bit of it. Not her sister, as overbearing as she was; not Nate, not her daughter, not her home or her life beside the Mississippi where storms often rolled in.

A streak of lightning. Four seconds to thunder.

A sultry-scented gust of wind pushed across the yard, bending the trees and littering the ground with leaves and dirt. Next came cold. The storm front collided full-force with the lingering heat, crashing in heaves of thunder, then breaking free with heavy, mineral-filled water. It pelted the dry ground, digging craters in the dust, thumping the leaves, the grass, the roof. Irene backed into the doorway, mesmerized by the rush and sound.

She bent her head toward the kitchen.

The phone was ringing, insistent as a wasp. She ignored it. A minute later it began again. She stepped into the house and picked up the receiver, but the line was dead. A crack of thunder sent a tremor through the rafters, and she hung up the phone and closed the kitchen window, then those in the dining room and living room. By the time she got upstairs her bedroom sills were soaked. She slammed the windows shut, grabbed a towel from the bathroom, and started wiping. Then stopped. Her face tingled, her head, her arms; everywhere on her body her hair stood at attention. She screamed and hit the floor as the room suddenly turned white and a shot of thunder rocked the house.

"Good Lord!" She looked up, then sniffed. "Something's burning."

She picked herself up from the floor and ran from room to room, finding nothing. Then she rushed outside. Wind whipped hard sidelong slices of rain against Irene as she dashed around the house, scanning the roof for damage. Then, as she came around to the back, she froze. A good half of the maple lay in the driveway, its red leaves splattered over the ground like blood. Irene wiped her drenched hair from her face and stared at what remained—fifteen feet of trunk holding the single low-hanging bough and its ragged swing.

"No!" She ran up to the smoldering stump. "No, no, no, no, no." Lightning flashed, and thunder came right on its back. "You sonofabitch!" she yelled to the sky—green now, thick as soup, clouds boiling over each other. "Look what you've gone and done. Look at it." A sob tumbled from her throat. "Can't you just let things be? Can't you? Do you have to go and destroy every goddamn thing?"

Her yelling was swept up and gone, trampled by the sound of the wind, loud as any machine—loud as a train, a jet, a monster roaring in her ear. Then something struck her neck, her legs, her arms. All around, dime-sized pieces of hail fell at her feet.

"You think you scare me?" she yelled. "Me?" Ice smacked her face and hands. "You've put me through hell, mister. You've put me through goddamned hell." The air swirled with leaves, dust, branches. A blast of wind knocked her sideways, and she fell into the fallen tree. "Is that all you've got?" She pushed herself up, thrust her fist toward the sky. "You sonofabitch. You sorry sonofabitch. I'm not running. You hear me? You don't want me around, then you come down right now and take me, 'cause I swear, I'm not running!"

PART III

CHAPTER 30

October 7, 2004

MASON LEFT HIS OFFICE AND went into the bathroom, took a piss, washed his hands. He couldn't get his conversation with Mrs. Stanley out of his mind. Her voice, so much like his mother's, determined and yet pleading, both at once. And her question: Do you believe in forgiveness? Of all the damn things.

Mason bent over the sink, splashed cold water on his face, then ran his wet hands over the top of his head. He closed his eyes, opened them, stared at himself, water dripping.

When he was ten he was thrown from a pier into Lake Michigan. It was January, the wind straight out of the Arctic and the water a frothing, slushy mass. Blue blocks of ice knocked into each other with each frigid wave as Mason, on his knees, begged the boys to leave him alone. He'd do something else, *anything* else. But they wouldn't listen, not when their leader was Tulane Mason, the sickest sonofabitch anyone could ever have for a brother.

It had started young. The punches, and kicking. The "jokes." Like the time he woke to find a dead rat in his bed. His mom lectured Tulane, punished him too. But it didn't make his brother stop. If anything, it only made things worse.

So on that cold January morning. Tulane's gang had dragged Tab to the end of the pier, punched him, kicked him till he fell facedown on the wooden boards, then with Tab screaming like a baby, they lifted him by his arms and flung him into the lake.

That was the first time his mother had begged Tab to forgive his brother, to "show him mercy—and not tell the police."

Mason wiped his face with a paper towel. "Forgiveness," he said to the mirror. "Like hell."

CHAPTER 31

October 7, 2004

S HE HEARD HER NAME AND opened her eyes to see Nate running toward her. Behind him, the patrol car sat sideways in the
driveway, lights spinning.

He pulled her to her feet and embraced her. "My God, Irene.
What the hell are you doing out here? Didn't you see that thing
coming?" His voice boomed against a suddenly silent world. "Look
at you—you look all beat up. Are you all right?"

She nodded and let go of the branches she'd been clutching like
reins on a wild horse. The whole experience had probably lasted
all of a minute, maybe two. There had been the solid force of the
hail, sharp and hard as nails, and that sound, as if she were caught
inside some horrific machine, blades spinning, ready to cut. No,
those were sticks—sticks and cornstalks and who knows what else?
She had fallen to her knees, grabbing at the fallen branches, the
ground, anything to keep herself from flying off into that chaotic

black mass. She thought for sure she was about to die. "I smelled smoke, thought maybe the house got hit by lightning." Irene felt the smallness of her voice.

"It was probably the tree." Nate wrapped an arm around her as they walked to the barn.

"Was it a tornado?"

"Hell yeah, it was a tornado. Passed right over our place. I tried calling. When the line went dead, I thought sure we got hit." He bent down and unscrewed the gas cap on his chain saw. "You *sure* you're all right?"

"I'm okay. But what about town? Don't tell me the storm went that way."

Nate poured some gas in the chain saw's small tank, screwed the cap back on. "Skirted by from what I can tell. But I'm heading to Drakes Crossing now. Got reports it's bad."

The crossing was nothing more than a handful of weather-beaten trailers used by migrant workers. It was just a couple miles away. If the tornado hit the crossing, the folks there would need help. Irene started toward the house.

"Where're you going?"

"To put on some dry clothes, grab supplies. You go and get down to Drakes—I'll be along in a minute."

"Hold on." He stood. "You're not going anywhere."

"The hell I'm not. I'll be along with some blankets. You go on."

Nate grunted. "Suit yourself. But hurry up. I'm not having you drive in this. The roads are a mess, and you never know, it might not be over. The weather service didn't see this coming at all."

Back in the house, Irene threw on sweatpants, a T-shirt, and one of Nate's seed caps. Then she grabbed a pile of old sheets and blankets and a gallon jug of water.

Nate was already seated when she got to the squad car. The radio was in his hand and the color gone from his face.

"What is it?" she asked.

"Coldsprings," he whispered. "It's been hit."

ROUTE 9 WAS SLICK WITH mud and covered with branches and debris. Trees and shrubs lay splintered and torn as if chewed by a mower. Power poles were cracked midway, their upper halves crowning a field of corn stubble. A half-mile off, a car was in a ditch. Nate pulled over and climbed down to it, but no one was inside. A mile or so beyond, a cow lay struggling in the middle of the road, its stomach gashed and its rear leg bent wrong. Again Nate got out of the squad car. Irene saw him pull out his gun, then closed her eyes as he put the pistol to the back of the animal's head. A moment or two later he got a chain from the trunk of the car and used the vehicle to pull the cow off the road.

"Fire trucks have got to get by," he said, then took off once more.

Drakes Crossing had been a shanty of six or seven beat-up-looking trailers surrounded by a small grove of trees. There was a volleyball net, a garden, and an old swing set with a slide. Irene gasped. Trailers lay tossed over and on top of one another, cracked in two, or just plain peeled open and discarded like someone's lunch. The trees, what were left of them, had been skinned of their leaves, some even of their bark. Others lay tossed about, their roots splayed upward like pleading hands. And everywhere else lay every-thing else—newspapers, plastic bags, mattresses, swings, cushions, chairs. Clothes hung from tree limbs as if they'd been placed there to dry, as did sheet metal and what looked like a child's bike.

Eight men and a woman, all of them Mexican, waded through the debris looking shell-shocked and disoriented. A woman and child sat on a muddy sofa, both of them crying.

"You stick in here," Nate said to Irene.

"But—"

"Uh-uh. I want to check it out first—you never know what's out there. Look, here comes Ethan. You just sit tight."

Nate and Sheriff Ethan Loveless perched on the embankment like hawks overlooking a freshly mowed field. The sheriff took off his hat and rubbed his bald head, and then he and Nate stepped into the wind-tossed debris, skirting a washing machine and an over-turned truck. A man with a bandanna wrapped around his neck came up to them and pointed to a ripped-open trailer. Then the three of them walked over to it, and that was the last Irene saw of them until she heard the sirens. Silas pulled up in an ambulance, followed by Fred with the pumper truck. Ethan waved them over, and they all disappeared behind the trailer.

Irene sat nervously listening to the scanner. Power lines down through the eastern half of town. Railroad tracks by Hudson blocked by a tree. A house fire on Kroph, and someone called saying she couldn't find her eighty-six-year-old mother. Irene pressed her hands down on her legs, worried that if she attempted a prayer she'd only make things worse.

Nate returned, his hat off and his face flushed. "We need to set up a shelter. Ethan's already checked with Pastor White, he says we can use the church basement. I'll drive you there so you can help get the place ready. Red Cross is coming, but they'll probably be pretty strapped. Silas got a call from his cousin in Coldsprings, says at least four or five blocks have been flattened."

"No."

"Yeah. So if we can take care of these folks, it'll be something, at any rate."

"How many people you think lived here?"

"Ethan is trying to figure it out—he speaks a little Spanish. I'm pretty sure most of the kids were in school. At least, that's what we're hoping."

Silas and Fred unlatched the back of the ambulance and pulled out a gurney.

"Was someone hurt?"

Nate wiped his forehead with his sleeve. "A woman. Her and her baby, but there's nothing we can do for them. Hopefully, we won't find anyone else."

Silas and Fred lifted the gurney over the debris. "I want to help here, Nate. Pastor White, he'll have plenty of volunteers. Let me stay here and help pull together these people's belongings."

Nate shook his head. "No way. It's dangerous. Glass, metal, who the hell knows what else. Anyway, it's not something you want to see." Thunder rumbled somewhere far away, and Nate looked up. "It's a hell of a life, you know? Come all this way, new country, hard work, family. You get all started, then you come home and find it's gone." Nate coughed, wiped his mouth with the back of his hand, then got in the squad car and pulled away.

THEY'D NEED SLEEPING BAGS, COTS, sheets, pillows, food. Lots of it. They'd need toilet paper, toothpaste, toothbrushes, toys. Irene's mind clicked through the list. Pastor White spoke Spanish, so there'd be that, but they'd need others, too. She chewed her lip, thinking.

They passed the cow, the car, the broken telephone poles. She reached for Nate's arm. "Let me stop at home and grab some stuff. It won't take more than a few minutes."

Nate pulled up to the fallen maple. "We were lucky," he said.

Irene looked at the tree and the mess all around. Trash and roof shingles lay scattered across the grass, along with leaves and branches, and then, near the apple tree, a lawn chair was set up as if for afternoon tea. It wasn't theirs.

Inside the house, Irene stuffed things into trash bags: sheets, towels, toilet paper, anything that looked useful. She found a sack of

clothes she'd saved for the annual firemen's bazaar and lugged that
along. Then she filled a small duffel bag with some stuff for herself.
No telling when she'd return. She dropped it all out the back door
and was almost out of the house when she spotted the shoe box.
It still sat on the kitchen table where she'd left it. Irene stopped,
stunned by how thoroughly the storm had blown thoughts of Daniel from her mind. She'd deal with the letters later, she told herself,
grabbing the box and shoving it on top of the refrigerator.

When she got outside, Nate stood brushing a film of debris off
the truck's windows. "You think you can manage these roads?" he
asked. " 'Cause I'm thinking you ought to follow me in the pickup.
That way you can come on back when you want. That, or head to
Carol's."

"Carol! I didn't even think—I mean, do we know they're okay?"

"Peggy just radioed. Your sister's fine. Says she has power, and
that she'll call Bliss and tell her what's happened. You probably
ought to just stay at her place. No telling when they'll get the elec-
tricity up and running out here."

"What about you?"

"State police have called for backup, so I wouldn't count on
my being around for a couple days, at least. Don't worry, though."
He dropped Irene's bags into the back of the truck. "I'll get word
to you."

"I was thinking someone ought to get ahold of Jeff's wife, Juanita. She could help with talking to those people. I know I won't be
able to understand much of what they say."

"Good idea," he said. Then, with no warning at all, he pulled
Irene to him.

"Nate?" She felt him shaking.

"You could have been hurt, Irene. That funnel, it was heading right to this place. I tried to race the damn thing here, but I
couldn't beat it. I was scared to death. You saw what happened back
at Drakes. That could have been here. That woman back there . . .

that could have been you." His words sounded choked, his voice like it had been filed rough. "I could have lost you."

Irene felt daunted by the intensity of his words. He could have lost her, and in that moment, right there, right then, the tree still smoldering and everything at their feet, she could feel the emptiness of that space, and she felt utterly ashamed. "Like you said," she whispered, "we were lucky."

CHAPTER 32

October 7, 2004

CREEKSIDE BAPTIST SAT ON THE corner of Second and Keen, surrounded by red oak and a platform of branches and leaves. Irene pulled into the church's parking lot and scanned the old wooden structure: the arched doorway she and Nate had walked through on a cold November afternoon under a rain of falling rice; the line of divided light windows that extended on either side of the sanctuary; the belfry her grandfather had helped build. Everything looked intact.

At the side door, Pastor White stood with a small group of men, gesticulating like a conductor. She turned off the truck's engine and sighed. White had come to their church as a young man with dark hair and a dark, brooding passion about God that filled her twelve-year-old mind with fantasies of the day he'd dip her body into Smidges Creek. It was a confusing, primal kind of desire, mixed up with puberty and a very real fear of God.

Forty-one years later, though, Irene just considered the pastor a sad and tired ringmaster. She wasn't quite sure what made her so cynical. Perhaps it was the cocky, almost offhand way he treated his parishioners, like a group of schoolchildren and he the long-suffering teacher. Or it could be his crown of white hair. The color had changed early, in his midforties, and the hair swam over and back behind his head in swooping waves. Women would pay good money to have hair like that. She had heard it plenty over at Racine's, back when she used to have her own hair done. But lately Irene had taken a dislike to men with well-coiffed hair. It was indulgent and typically indicated a level of confidence that never measured up to capacity. But her biggest reason for not wanting much to do with old man White was that the fierce and angry God he spoke to was not one she cared to be acquainted with anymore. She grabbed her duffel bag and slammed the door shut.

White broke into a wide grin as Irene walked up. Except for Christmas, Easter, and a couple of baptisms and funerals, she hadn't been to church in nearly two years, and her pastor made certain to point out that fact each and every time he saw her.

"Sister Stanley," he called out, "I trust everything is all right down at your place?"

"Yes, sir."

"That's good to hear. You know, no one saw this thing coming. Not a soul. We are blessed, really, God watching over us the way he does."

Irene tightened her grip around the handle of her bag. "I just came from Drakes," she said. "There's not much left out there."

The pastor straightened. "Yes, it's a tragedy, a real tragedy." His voice rolled like an empty barrel. "We must get our humble abode ready for those poor people. Do you know how many to expect?"

Chester Allister, the owner of the bowling alley, chimed in that there must be fifty of them living there, at least. "Maybe more. Probably more. You ever see how tight they can squeeze themselves in together? I've seen fifteen of 'em living in a chicken coop over by Eb's."

The pastor scratched his ear. "Hopefully we'll be able to find someplace else for them pretty quick. The church just has the two bathrooms, and only one with a shower."

"I can bring a honey bucket," said Soji Pike, the one and only Japanese man Irene had ever known.

"So can I," said Allister. "Possibly two."

"Sounds good," said the pastor. "As long as they get cleaned out regular. I don't want them creating a stink."

The men all frowned.

"We're going to need other things too," Irene said. "Don, what about you?" She pointed to Donald Alms, a neighboring farmer who often leased her and Nate's fields. "You have people work for you often enough. You have any cots, blankets, sheets, towels? Anything we can use?"

He turned his rubbery neck. "Yeah, I'm sure we do."

White looked excited now. "I tell you what. Why don't you men go out and start a collection? Go door to door, tell people the church needs help. In the meantime, as long as I have our Mrs. Stanley back with us for a while, she and I will start getting the basement ready. What do you say, boys?"

The men nodded: yes, sure, of course. They'd do whatever the pastor asked. And wasn't it nice to see Irene here? Yes, very nice. Very nice to see her back, indeed.

FOR THE NEXT SEVEN DAYS Irene scrubbed and washed and cooked and sorted through donations, working from dawn until well after midnight to help settle the twenty-three refugees, while simultaneously trying to keep away any thought of what was really going on in her life. The enormity of it all—the storm, the confrontation with her sister, the death warrant, and Daniel sitting in some cell counting out his days—was too much. So she kept herself busy helping the Drakes families, organizing volunteers, having kids from the high school come over after school and play with the children while their parents met with the pastor and Jeff's wife, Juanita. Juanita's brother had been able to line up work for some of the men up in Michigan harvesting Christmas trees. And Pastor White set up the rest with jobs picking oranges down in Florida. Donald Alms came through with a van for the families going south, and Nate offered up a Monte Carlo he had had sitting in the barn. He hadn't started working on it yet, but he figured it would at least get them to Manistee.

Then on the morning of the fourteenth, the families stood outside the church, smiling for the local paper as they waved goodbye to Pastor White and his church and the town that had brought them nothing but disappointment. When they were done with the photos, Irene handed each child a small bag filled with crayons, coloring books, and candy. *"Adios, amorcito,"* she said, using the words she had heard Juanita call her own children as they played in the church basement. *Amorcito*—little love. All of them, tiny, innocent loves wandering around in a world where clouds drop out of the sky and sweep everything away.

Back in the basement, Irene filled a bucket with hot water and grabbed a mop. Everything had been packed up, cots stripped and stacked, sheets sent off with Carol to get cleaned. All that was left was to wash the floor. Chester Allister had come by to tell her the power was back on at their place, and Irene wanted nothing more than to get home and take a nice long hot shower, followed by an even nicer and longer nap. After that, she'd sit down and figure out what to do about Daniel.

She began mopping in the corner of the room, working her way along the side and toward the middle. Getting down on her hands and knees to scrape paint from where the children had played.

"Sister Stanley." Pastor White traipsed across the wet floor, clasped a hand around her arm, and pulled her to her feet. "I would say we've done some mighty fine work in the service of our Lord, wouldn't you?"

Irene bent to pick up her pail and simultaneously break the pastor's grip. "I hope they'll be all right."

"We do what we can, my dear. We do what we can. I must say, it was good to see the community come together like it did. Volunteers offering up everything they had. And you here, working day and night. It did my heart good." He nodded to himself, then clapped his hands. "So let's say you and I have a little prayer for our friends' journey."

Irene squeezed out her mop and flopped it back on the floor. "I've already sent my prayers. And if you don't mind, I'd like to finish up here, then get on home. I haven't had a decent shower since the storm."

He laughed. "Yes, our old water heater barely kept up with the dishes. Well, you do as you see fit, but there's something I want to talk to you about before you go and leave our little home." He buffed his nails against his shirt, and Irene discreetly rolled her eyes. They had reached a kind of truce, she and White. She didn't mention the bourbon that sat on his breath every evening, and he didn't go on about her coming back to church. But clearly that was about to change.

"I hear Daniel Robbin's execution is finally scheduled."

Irene's mop stopped for a beat. Then resumed. "You heard right."

"That's mighty big news, wouldn't you say?" He walked over to a sagging armchair and dropped in with a sigh.

Irene swiped the mop by the pastor's feet, making him lift them up.

"It's been a long time since you and I talked about Shep," he said.

"I suppose."

"So I expect you and Nate will be headin' over to Or-ee-gone.

That could get hard, you know, being back there, seeing the man who did all this. You up to it?" His feet sank back down.

Irene peered at her pastor, trying to size up what he did or did not know. Carol had been helping around the church quite a bit, and though she never brought up the letters, that didn't mean she hadn't mentioned them to the preacher. Or maybe he'd heard about the execution from Nate. He'd been by more than once. "I don't plan on going," Irene said.

"Oh. I suppose that's one way to handle it."

Irene sloshed her mop in the grimy water, wrung it out, and slapped it back on the floor.

"There was a time you wanted to be there to see justice carried out."

"It's not justice," she muttered to the floor.

"How's that?"

"I said, it's not justice." She stopped mopping and looked up. "Killing Daniel Robbin. It's all about revenge, and that's it."

White hesitated a second. "So you're having some qualms about all this? Hmm. I guess I can see that. But I got to tell you, you're playing tricks with yourself. There's justice in Daniel Robbin's fate, you can rest assured of that. It's just too bad it's taken so long to finally get to this point. It hurts everyone—you, your family, even that man in jail, God save his soul."

"You really think God's up there with some kind of ledger, marking off who's paid what to whom?"

White's long eyebrows drew together like a drawbridge. "I think the Lord gave us laws and he's fully aware of who's broken them, if that's what you mean."

She twisted the mop handle. "The commandments say, 'Thou shalt not kill.'"

"Yes, that's right. Number six, 'Thou shalt not kill.'" He said it like Charlton Heston's Moses, finger pointed in the air. Then he crossed a leg over his knee and draped his arms around the back of his chair. "But let's not get confused. What they're planning to do to that man over in Or-ee-gone, that's not killing for killing's sake."

"It's pronounced *Oregon*, like your heart—an organ."

Irene watched him pick something from his teeth, look at it, then flick it to the floor. "My point is, what they're planning on doing out there, it's not murder. Not in God's eyes, it's not. In fact, it's kind of a mercy."

"Mercy?" She leaned her mop against the couch and stepped up to the man with the God-like hair. "What about turning the other cheek? What about Jesus telling people not to stone that woman for adultery? Seems to me that's mercy."

Pastor White tapped the chair next to him. "Come on, sit. You're getting yourself all worked up."

Irene obeyed, but only just. Her rear end balanced on the edge of the seat, her arms tense as electric wires.

"Jesus didn't say don't throw the stone. He told people to reconcile their own sins before dealing with others'. Straighten out your own house before you go cleaning up someone else's."

Irene glanced down at her reddened hands. The church basement smelled of stale coffee and sweat and she was sick and tired of cleaning it up.

"Nowhere in the Bible does it say capital punishment is wrong, Irene. If it were wrong, it would say so, but it doesn't." He uncrossed his legs and bent forward. "That man who killed your son—your *only* son—there's no other fit punishment. And if executing Mr. Robbin prevents other deaths, so much the better. Remember, we can't measure how many people are alive because of Daniel Robbin's sentence."

"I don't know what you're talking about," Irene said. A part of her wanted the brevity of the pastor's beliefs. An eye for an eye, a life for a life . . .

He put a hand over hers. "Robbin could be out of jail today if he weren't on death row. Criminals get paroled all the time, then they go and turn around and get in trouble all over again. Plus, this kind of punishment . . . well, it gives people pause, thinking they could end up just where Robbin is now. It makes an impression. Course, you can't prove it. It's not like you can count how many murders *don't* take place because of the death penalty, but it's common sense. Remember, you can't ever know how many boats a lighthouse might save, but you take it away and you'll sure find out how many sink without it."

Irene looked away. Pastor White had baptized her, and five years later married her and Nate. He had been there with his homilies when her parents were killed and there again when she and Nate had returned to Carlton without their son. He had always been there with his Bible and his prayers; this past week, even, he'd worked hard, cooked, cleaned, found those poor people work, even pocket money. There was not a thing Irene could point to that should make her want to slap him the way she did right now.

"Nate told you to tell me this, didn't he?"

"Your sister. She says you're confused."

"Confused, huh? And is that all? She didn't say that maybe I'm a traitor, or crazy even?"

The old man's mouth puckered. "No. But she did say she's worried about you. About you and Nate both."

Irene examined Pastor White's watery eyes for a hint of deceit. That, or collusion. It'd be just like Carol. Set God and the preacher out to do what she wanted done.

"I appreciate your taking the time, but you can tell my sister I'm *not* confused." She stood.

"Don't push me off like that, Irene."

"No. I'm sorry, but I'm done here." She grabbed the mop and bucket, then sloshed her way to the kitchen and dumped the dirty water into the sink.

White followed. "You came to me, remember? When you first got back?" He had his serious voice on, the God-will-come-and-get-you tone that turned his parishioners into a gelatinous mass. "You came, and I told you I'd pray you'd find your way through this. And I've done that. Every single day I pray for you and your family. You think I don't know? That I don't see how losing Shep has eaten into you and Nate? Two decades is a long time to carry this pain. But it's gonna be over soon, and then you two will be able to move forward."

Irene turned. "I don't need someone's death to move me forward, sir."

Pastor White smiled. "No? Then what do you need?"

"What's that supposed to mean?"

"Just that. You've been tortured by the loss of your son—anyone can see that. It's changed you, cast you off. Look at you, how angry you are right now. You never were like this growing up."

"I never was like this because I never spoke up for myself. But now I am, and I'm here to tell you I am not buying it, pastor. I don't think killing Daniel will make anyone in this world safer, and I don't think people will ever stop killing just because we go and hold executions. I know you don't agree, and God doesn't agree, and the whole damn world doesn't agree, but there it is. Move on? I *have* moved on. I've moved *way* on, and from where I sit, killing Daniel Robbin doesn't serve a soul."

White scratched his chest. "Sounds like you've almost forgiven him. Is that what I'm hearing? That you've gone and forgiven that man?"

"I figured Carol'd told you."

"Oh—I see." He paused, and she could see that he was genuinely surprised. "Well, Sister Stanley, forgiveness—now that's a different story. No wonder you're all worked up."

"Please."

"No, really." The pastor pulled on his wattles, stretching and working them like putty. "So you have no malice toward Mr. Robbin, none whatsoever?"

"That's right."

"And now, with a date set, how's that make you feel?"

"I told you. It's wrong. It doesn't make sense, it's hypocritical and ugly, and it doesn't do a damn thing to honor my son."

"Ah." He smiled as if he had just solved a riddle. "That's where you're thinking about this wrong. Daniel Robbin's execution has nothing to do with honoring Shep. Nothing in this world. Honoring your son—that's your job. Yours and Nate's. To honor your son's memory. But Mr. Robbin's punishment—that's between him and his Maker. No, what you need to do is pray, my dear. Pray for that man's soul. It's all you can give him and, at this point, all he needs."

"It's *not* all he needs. He's alone, pastor. He's got no one, not a single soul." Irene shut her mouth and turned back to the sink, picked up the bucket and mop, and took them to the closet.

"What are you saying?"

"Nothing."

"Irene Stanley, are you telling me you feel sorry for this fellow? I mean, forgiveness, that's one thing, but for you to spend an ounce of *pity* on the man, well, that's something else altogether."

Irene shut the closet door harder than she needed to. "What is it, sir? Altogether? What exactly is it when a mother decides to see the man who killed her child as a human being, not a villain? Can you tell me that? 'Cause I sure as hell'd love to know."

"You're not seeing straight, Irene."

"No?"

"No. That man needs your prayers, he needs all our prayers. Do I feel sorry he's had a hard life? Yes. I feel for everyone who's had a hard row. But do I pity him his fate? No. No, I do not. And I don't think you should waste a minute of your life doing so either."

Irene left the room, the pastor following.

"Irene Stanley, I won't have you walking away from me."

She picked up her duffel bag. "I sent Carol home with some sheets. She'll bring them back once they're clean. You should keep them on hand. And over there, the cots—three of them have been donated to the church, but the rest people will come and get later today or tomorrow." She stood and faced her pastor. She'd known him most of her life, and she didn't want to know him anymore. "It was a good thing you did here. Giving those people a place to stay, helping them figure out what's next. That was a real good thing."

White's voice softened. "It's my job. It's all our jobs, to be there for one another. Just like I'm here for you. Every day, I'm here. You don't have to go through this all alone. You come to me, we'll pray for Robbin and his salvation."

She looped the strap of her bag around her shoulder and walked to the stairs, took one more look at her pastor, and shook her head. "I appreciate the offer, sir, but from where I stand, what Daniel needs has nothing to do with our prayers."

Irene said goodbye to the slack-jawed man, then took to the stairs and flung open the door to a beautiful autumn afternoon— spangles of red and orange leaves, geese winging the air, their calls sounding like laughter.

CHAPTER 33

October 14, 2004

TAB MASON LEFT THE CONFERENCE room in a heat. He hated the press—their pens, their papers, their glib questions and cameras. Like they cared. Like they gave a flying fuck about anything but trying to make a name for themselves. Bloat up a story to something it should never be. They fed off attention, and he hated people like that; reporters and politicians, both of them the same kind of twisted animal.

He'd dealt with both plenty since getting this job. There had been that rash of suicides to deal with, then the AIDS problem, and the controversy over handing out condoms. That one really pissed off the right-wing nuts. Promoting homosexuality, they screamed. And the press and politicos feeding the frenzy.

And now, having to deal with reporters twice in ten days. First to make the announcement about the execution, then today to lay out more: procedures, protocols, and then take questions. They'd wanted to know if Robbin had changed his mind. "Has he asked to see an attorney? What about a chaplain? Is he depressed?" Then they wanted to know specifics about the night. "What goes first? His breathing? His heart? Are you sure," they asked, "there'll be no pain?"

Mason wanted to say, Of course there's pain, you assholes. There's always pain. The pain of knowing, the pain of waiting, the pain of anticipation. And then there's that other pain. The pain of planning out an execution. Even the word *execute* was a pain. Slicing so cleanly from throat to mouth, then landing in a grimace behind the front teeth. It was the perfect word for what it was, and what it was was a pain to say, a pain to think about, a pain to have to do. A job governors, kings, and heads of state have given to lesser men throughout time. Men never meant to sit with society—the pariahs, the recluses, the ones with the hoods, who either found a way to separate themselves from the results of their work or died from it, one execution at a time. That guy who'd done fifty executions in Florida had quit. Just up and quit one day. Told Mason that he couldn't get the eyes out of his head. Fifty sets of them, just staring.

There were tolls, Mason wanted to say. Tolls both sides of the road. But the press hadn't asked about that. And if they had, what would he have said?

That while Robbin appeared fine—eating, sleeping, everything pretty much normal—he himself hadn't had a good night's sleep since the day he had given Robbin the warrant? Or perhaps he could tell them that two people had already quit, said they couldn't work around there knowing they were setting out to kill someone. This wasn't California or Texas, where executions had become part of a machine no one really had to pay attention to. There are thresholds on the road to killing someone in Oregon. Doorways that hadn't been opened in quite a while. And everyone, from officer to cleanup crew, had to figure out whether or not he had it in him to cross over that line.

But instead of saying any of that, he'd kept to the script. "Four days prior to the event, Robbin will be transferred to a holding cell, where he will be under continuous surveillance. Forty-eight hours later the prison will go into lockdown, all inmates in their cells twenty-four hours a day until the morning after the procedure. Robbin's final meal will be served at eight P.M. Reporters will be told that evening what he ordered and how much he ate.

"No, he cannot get lobster," he replied to one wiseass. "Just regular prison food. He just gets to choose what."

A couple reporters nudged each other, then shook their heads.

Mason went on. "An hour before the procedure, the chaplain will join Robbin in his cell. Robbin will be shackled at this point, and electrodes attached to his chest so his breathing and heart rate can be monitored." Again reporters glanced at one another.

"You keep on calling it a 'procedure,'" an eager-looking guy with long hair said. "And I notice that you've also referred to it as . . . just a minute . . . Yeah, here it is, a 'special project.' Why don't you just call it what it is—an execution?"

Mason could have knocked a nail into the guy. "We call it a special project to lower anxiety around the *procedure*. These are not happy days around here, sir. No one's looking forward to this job. But we are the ones entrusted to carry out the law, and as long as I'm in charge of this place, I will use language that I believe causes the least disruption to my staff as well as the inmates."

Again, he went back to the script. "At eleven-thirty P.M. Robbin will walk the sixteen feet from the cell to the execution chamber, where he will be strapped down to the gurney and IVs will be inserted in both arms. Then, at eleven fifty-nine P.M. precisely, the blinds will be opened on the witness chamber. Robbin will have a chance for final words, and then, at my signal, the *procedure* will begin."

Mason slammed his office door and collapsed into his chair. They were a smart-ass group, those reporters. Know-it-alls who didn't know shit.

"Will we actually learn who turns the switch to start the drip?" the young guy with the pull-back bangs had asked. "I mean, who the *executioner* is? Or do you have another name for that too?"

Mason turned in his chair and kicked the windowsill with the heel of his shoe. "No," he had told the fucker. "You won't know the name of the person who turns that switch. And you never will."

CHAPTER 34

October 14, 2004

JEFF WAS SITTING ON THE back stoop flicking leaves with a stick when Irene pulled up. She waved from the truck, then reversed to the downed tree. "Taking a break?" she called as she got out of the truck.

"Yeah, I've been meaning to get a closer look at the tree. I swear I can remember spending whole days on that ol' swing."

Irene glanced at the maple's one remaining bough. Its leaves were brittle and curled in on themselves like old hands. "It could have been worse."

"There's always that." Jeff tossed Irene's duffel over his shoulder with his mailbag. "So the Drakes folks, they took off today, huh?"

"Yes, they did."

"Juanita said it was amazing how you pulled everything together for them. Said you were at it day and night."

"It was your wife and the pastor who made the difference. They found each and every one of those people a job and a place to live. I couldn't have done that." Irene kicked a shingle out of her way as they approached the house. "Still, you have to wonder if it was enough. Those people had nothing. And the kids—I felt so bad for them."

"It's the same in Coldsprings," said Jeff. "It's hard to see people hit so hard."

The screen door screeched open, and Jeff set down Irene's bag. "This fine?"

"Yeah, right there's good. I'll unpack later. First I've got to get myself a nice hot shower." She walked into her kitchen, opened the window above the sink. With the tree down she could see the back side of the barn, and beyond that, the pond. "So you've been out to Coldsprings?"

"Yeah, yeah, I have." Jeff knocked his knuckles on the kitchen table. "It's a real mess. Five blocks gone. Eight people dead. They're still looking for a little girl."

"I heard that." The two stood there not knowing what more to say about such a thing. Then Irene walked into the living room. She should get to Coldsprings herself. The forms the superintendent had promised could be there, and maybe something from Daniel. She sighed. "What about the post office—is that still standing?"

"Oh yeah. The roof got pretty beat up, and there was water damage, a lot of extra work 'cause of that. I've been there the past few nights helping out."

Irene's finger left a clean trail across the lid of the piano. "They call all the mailmen from Carlton over?"

Jeff coughed. "No. But you know, 'cause I've been working there anyways, I just went in."

She walked to the living room window, yanked it open, then sniffed the air, rolled its taste in her mouth. "I didn't know you've been working over at Coldsprings."

"Going on three years now."

"That right?" Irene's hand reached for the drapes, off-white lace, delicate and simple, just like her wedding gown had been. Her mother had made the dress. It was late fall, and she fit her for it in front of these windows, adding a little slack around the waist to account for the baby.

"I'm there weekends mostly, sometimes nights. It's the only way me and Juanita figure we'll ever be able to afford the kids' college."

Irene rubbed the lace between her fingers. She had saved her dress for Bliss. It was in a closet upstairs, packaged in plastic and waiting.

"So I've been out there helping. Like I said, there was some water damage, so a lot of the mail . . . well, you can't tell who it's for. Ink runs, labels come off—got to sort through that, and then there's always more stuff coming in."

Jeff had cried when Bliss told him she was going off to college. They were out on the front porch, Irene in the kitchen, and she heard him ask, "But why?" And then his sobbing as he ran across the backyard and off toward the river.

"Yeah," Jeff said, "if we're lucky we can reroute it, but a lot of it will probably never make it to where it was intended."

Irene released the curtain and turned. "Are you trying to tell me something? I mean, is there some *other* reason I found you sitting on my stairs just now?"

Jeff pressed his lips together, then pulled off his mailbag and sat down on the couch. "This has been sitting in your box the past few days." He held out a manila envelope. "I know you've been busy at the church, and with Coldsprings the way it is . . ."

The room suddenly felt smaller. "My box?"

Jeff looked left, then right. "Yeah. Like I said, I've been working over at Coldsprings for a while now. I know you have a box there. I mean, at first I didn't, but then one day you got some mail. I thought they had the wrong address."

"And now what do you think?"

Jeff didn't answer.

"Never mind, I know what you think."

"It's not my business where you pick up your mail, Mrs. S."

"What about who I get it from? You must have an opinion about that."

Jeff's Adam's apple slid up, then down.

"Go ahead, tell me, Jeffrey Creal. Just what *do* you think of my getting letters from Shep's killer? You must have noticed that. Says so on the front of every envelope—Daniel Joseph Robbin."

Jeff set the envelope on the table, and Irene could see it was from the superintendent.

"Mrs. Stanley—"

"Don't Mrs. Stanley me." She turned back to the window.

"You're tired. Everyone's tired."

"You know they're getting ready to kill him, don't you? Nineteen years, and they're finally going to do it. They have a date, time, guest list. It'll be a regular party." She whipped around. "Why, you delivered the notice yourself the day before the storm. Remember? And there you were, pretending you didn't know a thing about my little secret. Well it's October twenty-ninth. Midnight. You can take my place."

Jeff locked his hands together and nodded. "Juanita overheard Pastor White talking about it. She's the one who said I should bring you this letter. I wasn't going to, but with things like they are—she just thought you'd want whatever's inside."

Irene dropped into her chair, fingered its frayed upholstery, flowers and vines, faded and torn. After Bliss left, Jeff stopped coming around the house. She heard from Nate that he'd been caught driving under the influence a few times. And had even gotten into a fight with one of the other deputies. And Carol had told her that he tried to get into the army but didn't qualify because of an irregular heartbeat. A year or so later she heard he'd taken off to live with his dad in Kansas City, and Irene resigned herself to never seeing the boy again. Then one day he was back, a mailbag wrapped around his shoulder and a wedding band on his finger. Irene resented Jeff's wife at first, but then Juanita ended up being just what Jeff said: something special. A teacher, a mom, a good and kind soul raised up bunking it around the country, with her migrant family.

"You're right," Irene uttered almost soundlessly. "I am tired. Feel like I could sleep forever."

"You've been working hard. And with this news . . . well, it can't be easy."

"You don't know the half of it."

Jeff leaned forward, his arms laid flat along his legs.

"I'm trying to meet with him. That's what that envelope's about. It's from the prison superintendent. He's sent me forms so I can meet with Daniel."

The young man's eyes narrowed on her, and she tried to imagine what he might see. She had once been pretty, like Jessica Lange, Nate used to say. And she had held on to that thought for years, styling her hair in such a way as to maintain the impression. Now she expected she just looked old and drawn-out. Small in her oversized T-shirt and sweats.

"What do you want to say to him?"

"That's just it, I'm not sure. I mean, he already knows I've forgiven him. That's what started the letters. I wrote to him nine years ago, told him I couldn't live with hating him anymore. We've been writing to each other ever since."

Jeff leaned back into the couch. "Gosh, that's really something. You actually wrote and told him that, huh?"

Irene nodded.

"And you consider him what? A friend?"

She thought for a moment. "I suppose . . . I don't know. You know he never really had a family? Grew up in foster homes. He's got no friends. I think I'm the only one he's ever written to."

"He could just be telling you that."

Irene shook her head. "That's just it, he's never told me those things. Never complains about anything, really. It was the superintendent—he's the one who said I was the only one ever to contact Daniel. Can you imagine? Not having anyone in your life who cares whether you live or die?" Irene rested her head in her hand.

"So, if you don't mind me asking, what *does* this guy write about?"

"Oh, he's a pretty philosophical sort. I'm not even sure I understand all he has to say. He tells me about things he's read, what he's drawing, what he sees or thinks about. He thinks a lot." Her shoulders went up as she coughed out a laugh. "Course, what else would you do in that place?"

"He draws?"

"Yeah, I could show you. He's sent me a couple things. They're really something."

Jeff rubbed his leg. "Wow."

"Wow what?"

"I guess I never figured him to be so . . . I don't know. *Human,* maybe?"

Irene pushed on the arms of her chair and watched her feet rise up with the cushion.

"Still, meeting him, I don't see how that helps either one of you."

"It's crazy, I know. Lord knows how I'd even do it. Nate would never approve, that's for sure."

"Yeah, that's a whole other thing, I don't understand why you're so secretive about all this. It seems to me Mr. Stanley'd be happy to know what you've gone and done."

"I don't think so, Jeff."

"Why not?"

"That's just not the way my husband works—you know that.

It's law and order with him. Black and white. Forgiving Robbin—maybe I could get away with that, but writing to him, wanting to see him? No way. Nate would see it as a betrayal." She curled her legs under her. "You know, I used to think he really didn't like Shep. He wasn't the kind of son he wanted. Didn't hunt, wasn't interested in sports. 'Mama's boy,' Nate called him. And he was. I admit, I pampered him. Hell, you were more of a son to Nate than Shep ever was. But now, I almost think Shep's death cut him deeper than it ever did me. I would never have said that before, but Nate? He's not over it, and I really don't know if he ever will be."

The drapes waved in toward the room, and Irene stretched and yawned. "Used to be all I wanted was to punish Daniel Robbin, put him in as much pain as he did me. Then one day I woke up and realized what a lonely hole I'd dug."

Jeff pressed his hands together, brought them up to his mouth. "That sounds about right." The two locked their eyes on each other, then Jeff stood. "I want to show you something," he said.

"What?"

"Come on with me. You'll see."

"I'm too tired."

"No, really. I need you to see this."

Irene blew out a breath, then got up and followed Jeff outside, walking through the leaves to the maple. He dropped to his knees and began moving aside the grass and debris.

"Here, look." Jeff pointed.

Irene bent down. Cut into the tree about two feet from its base was a heart. In it, difficult to read but still there, were the words "Jeff and Bliss forever." Irene went to her knees and ran her hand over the scabbed bark.

"You have any idea when I cut those words in this tree?" Jeff asked.

She shook her head.

"Way back when you were in Oregon. I was heartsick when you all moved out thêre. Absolutely heartsick. But nothing like I was when Bliss went off to college."

Irene sat on the ground and plowed her hands through the leaves to the soil.

"I hated you, Mrs. Stanley. For years I cursed you for pushing her out that door. I mean really, honestly cursed you. I thought of doing things, things I'm too ashamed to even say. All my dreams had been built around your family, even back when I was a kid. I had tried to hang in there with it, you know? Got myself to Champaign as much as I could, even got her an engagement ring. But Bliss, she was in a different world, and all I knew was I hated you for putting her there. Then before long I found I hated everything else too."

Irene nodded. "You were right to hate me. Truth of the matter is, it wasn't just Bliss I was thinking of when I searched out that information on the colleges."

"That's what Bliss said."

Irene turned her head to look at the man sitting at her side.

"I didn't know what to think, 'cept that I didn't want her going away. But if you hadn't done it, she'd have found her own way out. I think I knew that even then."

Irene wrapped her arms around her legs and let her eyes follow the tree's charred trunk.

"And now? You, Juanita, the kids—it's all worked out?" Irene asked.

"That's just it. I wouldn't want it any other way. I found a life the other side of what I lost, and it's more than I could have ever dreamed. I wouldn't give it up for anything."

A shiver went through Irene, a knowing one, the kind that said she was in the presence of something good and true. Life, living, being happy with what you have. It sounded like such a rich, beautiful thing. She sighed. "Blue as a robin's egg."

"What's that?"

"The sky. Its color this time of year. It takes my breath," Irene said.

The two stared at the shell-blue dome reaching out, above, and over to the rest of the world, connecting good to bad, light to dark, sun to every drifting storm.

CHAPTER 35

October 14, 2004

THE SHAWNEE NATIONAL FOREST STRETCHES from the bluffs overhanging the Mississippi east to the Ohio River, then south to where Illinois tapers to an end. Inside this triangular region are farms, lakes, bogs, and prairies. There are chiggers hiding there, and snakes, and mosquitoes the size of nickels. And deep in the folds of its weathered hills, there are secrets.

Nate pulled his squad car off the state highway onto a narrow road. Trees arched overhead. A contrail of scarlet and burnt umber leaves followed behind. He drove downhill, sweeping around curves, then slowing where Stag Creek crossed the gritty pavement. He passed through the low water, turned left onto a gravel road, left again onto a smaller dirt road. A mile or so farther, he pulled over at a wide spot littered with beer cans, cigarette butts, and shotgun shells. Nate turned off the car, hit the steering wheel. Swore.

A pistol, handcuffs, club, radio—it all went with him down a

dirt path. Five minutes later he collapsed onto a flat rock sitting beside a motionless green lake. He took off his hat, wiped his forehead
with a handkerchief, lit a cigarette.

Fuck her, he thought. *Fuck her to hell.* Nate held the smoke like a
dragon holds its heat, then pushed it out through his nose. Once . . .
twice . . . He looked at the thing in his hand, then threw it on the
ground and smacked it with his heel.

Carol had told him to leave Irene alone about the execution.
"She doesn't have the stomach for it," she'd said the day after the
storm. And he had bought it.

Mostly.

Nate picked up a stick and began to peel its green bark.

Now he comes to find out nothing he knew about his wife was
true. "She tried to kill herself," Carol had blurted not a half-hour
ago. Pastor White suggested that Nate talk with his sister-in-law.
Said she might have something to share. But he didn't expect this—
a story of Irene trying to end her life, and then, when she failed,
turning to Robbin for comfort. *Robbin, by God.* She'd been writing
to him, and he writing back. Carol said she'd seen the letters, a box
stuffed full of them.

"Damn!" Nate broke the stick in two and stared at the water, the
sun, the trees, listened as some bird sang as if nothing were wrong.

*Tired. Isn't that what she'd said? Tired of all this? No mention.
Not one single word about suicide. And then this?*

White said, "Forget it, there's nothing to be done. Can't punish
someone for forgiving," he said. "Can't do that."

*But lying? Deceit? Keeping him in the dark about every damn
thing?*

Nate pulled on his collar as if he were choking. Pulled and twisted,
pulled again, coughed, then rocked forward and heaved out something like a sob.

Letters.

He had no way of knowing what his wife and Robbin had told

each other. No way of knowing what Irene knew or didn't. No idea what had been in her mind when she told Carol she needed to see the man. No notion of what to do next.

Nate imagined hitting his wife, smacking her across the face, pushing her onto the couch, watching her fall. He imagined screaming, raging. Then he covered his face and imagined something else.

He would sit her down; he would have his hands on her hands, maybe her arms. He'd need to be close so she didn't run. She'd want to do that—it was her nature. But not this time. He would hold her and she would listen. And after it was all said, they'd figure out what was left of their lives and how the hell they'd go on.

He'd wanted that for so long. To open his mouth and say what should be said.

Irene.

Nate chewed his lips. Life was mean and hard. Always had been, always would be. But Irene—she made it kinder. Still, it was that sweetness that drove him crazy. So damn naive, never seeing anything for what it was. She didn't have any idea about what the human heart could do. How it could turn from the world and become as slick and cold as a bloodied knife.

No fucking idea.

It was his fault. He shouldn't have let her hide in her own little world. But Irene was Irene. And Irene never would have believed anything that would break her pristine view of things. It was one of the reasons he loved her. It was one of the reasons he hated her. It was one of the reasons that every time he thought of leaving, he never thought long or hard.

Nate watched a heron fly low over the lake and then land, its long body perched like a dancer at the water's edge. He had wanted a good life. Quiet, undemanding, kind. Nothing like what he'd grown up with. He wanted his wife to love him, and he wanted his children to do the same. To be good, decent people that minded and obeyed because they loved their parents, not because they were scared shit-less by them.

The heron took a slow step into the water. Bass swam in the lake. Crappie, bluegill. He and Irene used to bring their boat out and cast and float without saying much. He liked that, the presence of company without the demands. Irene knew how to use a rod, and Nate enjoyed watching the sun come up and shine through her hair. His little daisy, he used to call her. He remembered the first time he kissed her, how he swore she tasted like honey.

The heron's head moved forward, one inch at a time. Then, quick as a snap, it propelled its sharp beak into the water and came up with a fish.

It'd been at least nine or ten years since he and Irene had gone fishing. Just about the time Carol said Irene had tried to kill herself. He rammed his fist into his palm. "Irene," he said. Then he yelled her name so loud it echoed across the lake, startling the heron to a freeze.

Nate bent down and picked up a leaf: red, purple, green, and orange. He didn't know what kind of tree it came from, never kept track of that kind of thing. It was something Irene knew. Irene and Shep. Something they worked on together—trees, plants, flowers . . .

Nate crushed the leaf in his hand, then tossed it in the water and watched it sink.

CHAPTER 36

October 14, 2004

"THERE'S NO WAY THEY'RE GONNA let me do this." Irene paged through the application for the prison's reconciliation program.

"Why not?" Jeff asked, twisting open an Oreo.

"It says here I have to go through counseling. There's no time for that. And here, right here"—Irene pushed a form across the kitchen table—"they want to know who in my family supports this."

"Doesn't anyone?"

Irene laughed. "Carol about had a fit when she found out about the letters. Told me to burn them."

"What about Bliss?"

"She spends her whole life putting people like Daniel behind bars."

"Yeah, I know. But that doesn't mean—"

"I don't want to drag her into this."

Jeff nodded. "Does she even know a date's been set?"

"Yeah, she reached me at the church. Said it was about time it was happening." Irene dropped her hands to the table and picked up the superintendent's letter. It had sat in front of all the other pages like a guard, warning her not to go further. She poked her finger at the note. "The superintendent says that my getting visiting privileges is a long shot."

"What did he say when you called?"

"Same thing. Wanted to know how much support I had, and when I told him none, he said I shouldn't even try. Said I'd be setting myself up for another loss. Carol said the same thing."

Jeff reached for the superintendent's note and read it. "This Mr. Mason . . . he give you anything to hang your hat on?"

"Nothing."

"But you want to try anyway."

Irene looked up at the kitchen light. "If he had someone else. Anyone, you know? A friend, a relative. But there isn't anyone. Just me. And because of that, I just feel . . . Hell, I don't know what I feel. Sad, I guess. For him, for me, for Shep—for everyone."

Jeff slid open another cookie, then scraped the frosting with his teeth.

"I can't believe you still do that."

"Habit. Remember those cookies you used to make? What did you call them? To heaven and back?"

"Back Home to Heaven."

"Loved those."

"My ma's recipe."

"Oatmeal, chocolate chip, and what else?"

"Butterscotch and coconut."

"Yeah, right. I remember your having them all ready when Bliss and I'd get home from school. It'd be cold out, and there you'd be with those cookies. You made a mean hot chocolate, too."

"It was just Hershey's."

"You put marshmallows in it. Those tiny ones, remember?"

Irene shook her head.

"I do. To me, coming here after school, it was just like you said—back home to heaven."

"You're thinking of someplace else, Jeff. Best I can recall, I spent most of those years stuck in that chair out there." She pointed toward the living room.

"There was that. But there was also knowing you were there. You and Mr. Stanley both. You always made me feel like I belonged."

"That was Bliss's doing."

"Some of it, sure. But not all of it. I can tell you this, I don't have a single memory of *my* mom ever having cookies waiting. Not even Oreos."

Irene listened to Jeff talk about days she couldn't quite remember.

"That's the thing with you, Mrs. Stanley—you were like my second mom. It's one of the things I missed most, you know, after Bliss left. I missed you so much, and I think that made me even angrier."

The house creaked as a slide of wind moved through the windows, and Irene shivered.

"This guy, Daniel Robbin, he's got no family at all?"

"None I know of. You have to remember the state got him when he was seven years old. And I guess none of his foster parents ever got in touch."

"So you're it for him?"

She didn't answer.

"October twenty-ninth?"

"Yeah."

"That's, like, in two weeks."

Irene swallowed.

"Let's say you see him. What are you going to do? I mean, what will you say?"

Irene looked over Jeff's shoulder, wondering if she should tell him her plan. "I'm not exactly sure, Jeff."

"Okay, so let's take it the other way. Say you don't go. You just stay here, and things move forward. What then?"

Irene tried to imagine what it'd be like the morning after Daniel's execution. It'd likely be cold out, the house quiet, and she'd rise knowing the man who had killed her son was dead. "It'd feel like I quit. Like I gave up after a long haul." She looked at Jeff. "I don't want to give up."

"Give up what?"

There was a chip on the rim of her coffee cup, and she ran the tip of her finger over it lightly, then harder. "There's something all wrong about this, Jeff. And I mean *all* wrong. I can't figure it out, but that man in jail? He doesn't match up with what I'd expect a murderer to be. It doesn't fit—not in my mind, it doesn't. Maybe it's the randomness of it, you know? I mean, why my house, my son?"

"What are you saying?"

"I don't know. I just have this feeling that there's something no one's ever said. Some explanation that would help sort everything out."

Jeff looked worried. "And you're sure he's not just trying to make himself out as something he's not? I mean, letters—you can't tell much in those."

Irene leaned back in her chair and dropped her hands between her legs. "Maybe." She sighed. "It's been a long time, and I'm tired. More than tired." She shivered, then got up and closed the kitchen window.

"I think you ought to go," Jeff said.

"What?"

"I think you should fill out these forms. Take them to Oregon and demand to see Robbin."

"You do?"

"Yeah, I do." He stood and handed her the envelope. "Forgiving doesn't mean accepting. If you got things to ask, do it. Do it while you can."

CHAPTER 37

October 14, 2004

DANIEL WAS SITTING LIKE SIDDHARTHA, legs folded, hands turned up toward the concrete ceiling. One hour, two . . . He wasn't sure. It used to be he'd know what time it was without ever looking at a clock. Could feel it, like some people can feel north from south. He had never owned a watch, never once set an alarm. Time for him was an internal thing, totally innate. But not anymore.

It could be the middle of the night, for all he knew. Lights always on, people always talking or yelling. Toilets flushing, doors rattling, then slamming shut with that hard definitive sound. Like a sledgehammer striking metal. Or a gunshot. Sleep always a half-ass thing, never done the way it ought, deep and full, his waking to bright morning light. He was so damn glad to know it would be over soon.

He got up and walked to the can. Unzipped his pants, held his

limp penis, aimed. When he was done, he was amused to observe
that he still reflexively thought about lowering the seat on the seat-
less stainless steel prison toilet, just like his mom had taught him.

He laughed and shook his head.

Sometimes he just fuckin' amazed himself. So much of his life
determined by a woman he had never really known. Not who her
parents were, or what she'd ever wanted out of life, or how in the
hell she had ended so short of anything that could be called a dream.
Some things he did know. Her smell, for one: chocolate mixed with
cigarette smoke. And her breasts—big, soft, and always pushed up
out of some shirt to show off her cleavage. When he was little he
tried to put his hand in that slit, thinking it was like a kangaroo's
pouch and that maybe his mom had a secret stash of candy hidden down there. He was, what—three, four? Still, she got mad and
slapped his hand, hard. Told him never to go reaching for people
like that. Ever.

Daniel dropped to the bed, wondering if it would've made a
difference, his following her advice. If his reaching out had been
the reason for all his troubles. The inchoate impulse to be a part
of something or someone, to connect, to bridge, and even—to
love. If he'd stayed free from all that, would he be in this cell now?
Wondering, always wondering, and having no idea how much time
had passed since the last time he had asked himself that question.

CHAPTER 38

October 14, 2004

T HE SOUND OF A CAR door slamming shut startled both Jeff and Irene out of their thoughts.

"It's Nate," Irene said, dropping the superintendent's letter into a drawer, and quickly brushing crumbs from the table.

"Well, if it isn't my wife and her mailman." Nate stood in the doorway scratching his unshaven face. His uniform was dirty and his eyes were bloodshot.

"Lord, you look like hell." Irene approached him. "When was the last time you saw a bed?"

"Two days."

"Two days? No wonder. Why don't you go on upstairs and take a shower? I'll make us up something for supper. I don't expect anything lasted in the refrigerator, but I'll figure out something." She reached to help him with his coat, but he pulled away, so she went to Jeff. "We've been talking about how bad things are out at Cold-springs. Jeff's been helping there at the post office."

Nate's eyebrows lifted. "That right?"

"Yes, sir."

"You know he's been working there for a while?" Irene smiled. "Pulling double shifts in order to save for the kids' college."

"No, I didn't know that. But it seems I don't know a lot of things that've been going on around here. Do I, Jeff?" Nate nailed Jeff with a look that Irene had never quite seen before.

"Jeff," she said, attempting casualness. "I imagine you're anxious to get back home to Juanita and the kids." She scouted the room. "Now where did you leave your mailbag?"

Nate hooked his thumbs in his belt and leaned against the refrigerator, the butt of his gun knocking the metal. "Yeah, Jeff, where'd you leave it? And more important, what's in it? Anything I should have a look at, or are you just delivering to my wife these days?"

Jeff cracked a smile. "I deliver to whoever it's addressed to, sir."

"So it's like that, huh?"

"Just exactly like that, Mr. Stanley."

Irene held her breath. In winter sometimes, they'd head out to the lake and try and go skating. Sometimes they could, sometimes not. It depended on how cold things had got that year. But even when it appeared the lake had set up pretty firm, it was still nerve-wracking. The ice could shift, cracks could open, anything could happen, and the next thing you know you could be falling into that frigid water.

"Come on now, Nate," she said. "Why don't you go upstairs, get yourself cleaned up? You'll feel like a different person."

Nate slowly locked his eyes on his wife. "When were you planning on telling me, Irene? Tonight? Tomorrow? Or maybe you thought you'd just give me a call from Oregon. Is that what you had in mind?"

The ice cracking, it made a sound like a whip. A snap and a buzz, then the tremor . . .

"I know all about the goddamned letters you and Jeff have been sneaking by me."

"Nate."

Nate's leg flew back and kicked the refrigerator, rattling it and everything inside. "What did you think you were doing, Irene? I mean, what the *hell*, writing Robbin? Writing to *him*? For what, almost ten years? And you—" He pointed at Jeff. "You were practically a son to us. Damned near lived under our roof, ate at my table, and you go and turn on me like this? Don't you think I had a right to know what was going on? Huh? I'm asking you, don't you think I had the damn right?"

Irene reached for her husband. "It's not like that, Nate. Jeff's not involved in this."

"Bullshit."

"He's not. He hasn't been delivering those letters. He didn't know anything about this. I specifically didn't have them come here so he wouldn't know."

"Bullshit, Irene."

"He's right, Mrs. Stanley. You don't have to protect me. I've known. I've known for years." Jeff crossed his arms over his chest.

"You hear that?" Nate asked.

"Jeff, you go on home. This has nothing—"

"Give me the letters," Nate demanded.

"What?"

"I want them. I want to know what that man's told you. How the hell he's messed with you."

Her fists clenched. "No."

"What did you say?"

"I won't. Not now I won't. Maybe later, after you've calmed down. You're not seeing this right. I know it looks bad—"

"Bad? You think it looks *bad*?" Nate jerked off his hat and threw it on the table. "Jesus Christ, Irene, it looks insane. Worse. Twisted, goddamned sick and twisted."

"Mr. Stanley—"

"Sit down and shut up, Jeff."

"Mr. Stanley, your wife's right. This isn't any way to talk about all this." He approached the table. "I know it's a shock and all, and that it looks like we've been hiding things from you, and I guess you're right. But now you know. Why, your wife here, she's gone and done a big thing. I mean, forgiving Robbin, that took courage, sir. You know how Shep's death almost killed her. Hell, everyone knows that. Her coming 'round like this, well, it's—it's a blessing, really."

"I said shut up, Jeff."

"But, Mr. Stanley—"

Nate took two quick steps and grabbed Jeff by the shirt. "I said shut the fuck up! You don't know what the hell you're talking about. Neither one of you do." He pushed Jeff off then turned away from both him and Irene, grasping the counter and shaking his head. "Getting yourself involved with Robbin. I swear to God, you have no idea what the hell you've gone and done."

Irene looked at Jeff and mouthed the word *leave.* But he didn't move.

"Show me, Irene," Nate said, his back still turned away. "Show me the damn letters."

Irene gritted her teeth. "Fine!" She retrieved the box from above the refrigerator and shoved it at him. "Go ahead, read them. That'd be good. You're right. Maybe then you'll understand. He's a sad man, Nate. Just a sad, lonely man who hates what he did and is sorry for it. Go ahead, read."

Nate held the box in front of him, staring at it with disbelief. "That's it? That's all he has to say, he's sorry?"

"What more do you want?"

"He doesn't explain anything? Give some reason—some *excuse,* I mean?"

"No. He just says he hates that day. Read them for yourself. You'll see."

Nate held the box for a minute longer, then dropped it on the table. "Tell me right now that you'll put a stop to all this. No more letters, no more trying to see that man. You tell me that."

Irene ran her hand across her mouth. "I can't do that."

Nate's face flushed.

"I'm sorry. I should have told you when it all started. It was wrong of me not to, and I'm sorry."

"I don't want to hear *sorry*. I want to hear that you'll put a stop to this thing. In fact, I want you to understand, you have no choice. I won't put up with your spending any more time on him. Not a second. You got me? You *understand* what I'm saying?"

"Mr. Stanley. Please. You can't ask her to do that. Your wife here, she has things she needs to resolve. You don't let her do that, well—"

"She tell you that?"

Jeff didn't respond.

"What else she tell you, Jeff? What else are you gonna tell me 'bout my wife?"

"I can tell you that her seeing Robbin is important. She has questions, things she wants to know, things she needs to have cleared up. That's all."

"And if she doesn't get her answers, what then? Huh? Well, I'll tell you what. She'll have to live with unresolved crap, that's what. Big fuckin' deal. That's what happens when shit happens. It sticks and it stinks, but no amount of damn answers will ever clean it up."

"You stop talking to Jeff like that. You just let him be. He's got nothing to do with any of this." Irene went up and put her hand on top of Nate's. "I didn't learn till just today he even knew I'd been writing to Daniel."

"Daniel, is it? And tell me, sweetheart, just what do you have to ask this Daniel? Maybe I can save you the trip."

"There's no way for you to help me, Nate. I'm sorry. I know,

I know, it's a mess, and you don't think I should ever have written him, but I did, and now . . ." She squeezed her husband's hand. "He's not like what you think. I mean, all those years we're imagining a monster. But we were wrong."

Nate wrenched his hand free. "Wrong? That S.O.B. goes and shoots our boy and *we're* the ones who are *wrong*?"

"I just want to see for myself. Hear for myself, that's all. You just asked if he explained anything. Well, he hasn't. And I need him to."

Nate grabbed the back of a chair, shoved it into the table. "Goddammit, Irene, he's not gonna have any more to say 'less he wants to play you, and it seems to me he's already done a hell of a job of that."

Her husband would know all this. Understand it about as well as anyone. Crime, criminals—it was his work. What did she know? Play her. She thought of Daniel's letters, dozens of them stuffed in a box. And slowly, one after another, she had come from accepting the murder and the murderer to wondering just what had gone wrong, and now feeling pretty damn certain that Daniel Robbin hadn't committed a crime that day. He had killed her son, yes, but it wasn't done as she'd thought. She felt it, but she couldn't say why. Playing her? Maybe he was. Playing her like a song.

She looked up at Jeff, begging him with her eyes to leave. But he shook his head, so she turned from both men.

Outside, the sun was sliding back behind the river trees.

"You ever think of your son, Nate?"

"What?"

"Shep, you ever think of him? What he'd be doing if he were still alive? What he'd be like?" She wiped her face. "I do. Not all the time like before, but often enough. I think he'd be composing music, and playing. Playing all around the world. I think he'd be famous. Loved for what he could make people feel."

Nate sighed and dropped into a chair.

"You ever hear of Wynton Marsalis?" she asked. "He's a trumpet player. Very famous. Plays jazz and classical, just like Shep did. I have a few of his tapes. They remind me of our boy . . . He wouldn't have turned out like you or me—married, kids, that whole thing." There were purples in the sky, greens too. Halos of light converging and covering the paling blue like a child's finger painting. "He'd have been a free soul, carving himself out a different path. Just as he was doing before he died. You know what I mean?" She turned. Nate's hands were cupped together as if he were praying. She was sorry for him. This coming as it had—it was nowhere near fair.

"He was gay," he said, so hushed Irene had to lean toward him. "Carving a different path, shit. Shep wouldn't have had a family 'cause he wouldn't have *made* a family." Nate wiped his mouth and looked up at his wife. "He was gay, Irene. A fag. Queer as a two-dollar bill." He paused. "You ever see that in your little dreams?"

Irene balled her hands into fists. "*What?* How dare you say that about our boy? What's wrong with you?"

"What's wrong with you, Irene? What the hell's wrong with you? I've been wondering that since the day I came back from Nam. Always treating the kid like a baby, never letting him outta your sight, never allowing him to take his own falls. You turned him into a goddamned fag, is what you did. And you never saw it coming. Never once."

Jeff stepped forward. "Don't do this."

"You really ought to get out of here, Jeff. These things here are between me and my wife."

"Come on, Mr. Stanley. This is no way—"

"I said get out!"

Irene stepped forward and brought her hand down on her husband's face. "Stop it!" she yelled, then raised her hand again, but Jeff was there, pulling her out of the kitchen, into the living room, telling her to go upstairs, calm down, he'd talk to Nate. "He's just upset."

"Upset!" she shrieked, wrenching herself from Jeff's arms and going back into the kitchen. "You should be ashamed of yourself, saying a thing like that about your son. And why? 'Cause he wasn't like you? So damn tough you can't feel a blessed thing? Well, thank God for that."

Nate looked disgusted, even bored, and it infuriated her. She would have expected yelling, swearing even, but this? Calling his own son a pervert? "I won't put up with this. You want to hurt me? Fine. I don't care, but it's not going to change my mind. I'm going to Oregon. And if I have to beg the governor to let me see Daniel, I will."

Nate laughed. "You're really something. You actually think I'm telling you this to hurt you?" He let out a breath as if he were just about done with everything. "If I wanted to do that, I could have told you years ago. No, you opened this box, Irene. Just remember, you opened it."

"I don't know what you're talking about."

"That man you want to see? Daniel Robbin? The boy who *killed* our son? He and Shep, they weren't strangers."

Nate's lips were moving, the sun was dimming, the house was cold.

"Your son and him—I warned them. I warned them both."

Irene raised her hands. "Don't do this, Nate. Don't—"

"I can't protect you anymore, Irene. I tried. You could have gone to your death with your sweet dreams of your son. A free sprit making new paths in the world, isn't that what you said? Well God-dammit, you've lost that privilege. Shep was queer. Had been for years. Why the hell you think I moved us out to Oregon to begin with? I had a good job here at home. We were settled in pretty well—friends, house, family. Remember? School had already started and you didn't think it was fair to the kids—the sudden move, the big change. Why the hell you think I did that?"

Irene was on a carnival ride, being sucked to the wall, glimpsing faces, colors, lights. His words were impossible, insane even.

Shep had been too young to be interested in girls. Too young to care about any of that.

"You remember the Culbertsons? The renters who lived down the road? How Shep was always over there?"

"He was teaching their son to play the piano."

"Yeah. He was teaching him to *play,* all right . . . I tried to break him of it, thought getting out and away, the West, the desert— thought he'd change." Nate sighed. "But then he found Robbin . . . They were lovers, Irene. *Lovers.* As sick as that sounds, that's just what they were."

"You bastard. Shep was your child, and you go and say this?" Her eyes held small wells. "I don't believe you. I don't believe a word you're saying. Don't you think I'd have known what was going on? Would have been able to tell? No, you're—you're just mad about the letters, that's what this is all about. Well, you can take it straight to hell. I'm going to Oregon, and I'll do whatever it takes to meet Daniel. And you know what else?" She stopped, her finger hanging in the air. "I'm gonna try to stop this execution." She nodded rapidly. "Yeah, that's right. I'm gonna do my level best to help that man live."

She had money stored in a drawer. Thirty dollars a month over ten years makes a lot. She would take it and she would get herself to Oregon, and to hell with Nate and her sister and all the others ready and willing to judge her. She picked up her duffel bag and headed out of the room.

"Robbin didn't kill him, Irene."

There was no kitchen—no wall—no floor. The doorway that had been there, right there in front of her, was gone. If there was air, she couldn't breathe it; if there was light, she didn't see it. The bag dropped from her hand, but it didn't make a sound.

"Didn't mean to, anyways. That bullet, it wasn't meant for Shep . . . Daniel Robbin was trying to kill *me.* He was aiming at *me,* Irene."

There are sounds inside silence—a buzzing, a whine, a sigh.

Suddenly Irene heard them all, and then, her heart. She could hear her heart. And her soul, it had a voice too, and she heard it crack open.

"They'd been together for months. Caught them the first time out on Crooked River. They were saddled up next to each other, shoulder to shoulder. Shep was leaning against him just like a little girl. Made me sick to my stomach."

"Stop."

"Then the Saturday before he was killed, I caught them again. Same goddamned place, but this time it was worse. Way worse, and I lost it. Beat the hell out of Robbin. Thought for sure it would be the last I saw of him, but then I dropped by the house that Monday, and there they were."

"I said stop."

She turned to see Nate. His hands were in a death grip now, clutched in front of his face, and his head was shaking from side to side, as if he didn't believe his own words. "It's not what I wanted. But when I found them there . . . Believe me, if there had been some other way—but to walk in and see them like *that*." Nate bit his knuckles. "I went nuts."

Bile, bitter and poisonous, filled Irene's mouth. She would kill him if he went further. She would kill him.

"I tried to stop them, scare them, you know? I was so mad. I grabbed Robbin, I remember that. I flattened him against the wall, got him good. And all the time Shep begging . . . that's what got me, his begging. I couldn't stand it. So I took off after him. I remember I hit him across the face, then I pulled him, pulled him hard. He fell to the floor."

"Stop it," Irene said. "The house was robbed that day. *Robbed.* Daniel did it, and he didn't know Shep from Adam. If you're trying to stop me from seeing him, it's not working, so stop it with your lying. *For Christ's sake, stop.*"

"That's what Shep was saying. I remember him screaming it.

'For Christ's sake, stop.' I thought he was trying to stop me from hitting him, and you know what I was thinking? *What right have you to ask God for anything?* That's how bad it was, seeing them there. What right did my own son have to call on anyone for help?" Nate was shaking now, visibly and desperately.

"That's when it happened." He looked up, tears cutting his face like acid on stone. And Irene backed away, one foot after the other, until she felt hands on her shoulders. Jeff pressed her against his chest, and together they watched Nate, hands digging into his face, voice choking out his son's name. "Shep. Oh dear God, Shep. He got in the way. Robbin's gun went off and Shep went and got in the way."

PART IV

CHAPTER 39

October 14, 2004

IT WAS UNUSUALLY QUIET IN the IMU, no banging or screaming. No catcalls as the officers made their rounds. News that Robbin's execution had been scheduled had filtered through the unit like a virus, laying all the men low. No one wanted to draw attention to himself. In the warped view of a prisoner's mind, anything that made him stand out—disciplinary action, illness, even the location of his cell—was part of a superstitious calculus that could very well determine who'd be next on the General's gurney.

Rick Stowenheim pulled his hand from a bag of sunflower seeds and pointed to the cell beside Robbin's. "Chavez's been off food for three days now. Says he's sure his number's next."

Miguel Chavez stood pressed to the steel-mesh grate that made up his cell door.

"Have you sent for the chaplain?" Mason asked the officer.

"Nooo."

"Why not?"

"He'll get over it."

Mason pulled out a chair and sat beside Stowenheim. It was a fancy ergodynamic thing that had cost the state twelve hundred dollars. The chair and about fifty others just like it were part of a union deal. Pay raises were on hold, but the staff could have more comfortable places to sit. It was stupid, Mason had thought at the time. Wasting money on chairs while drug programs and counseling were getting slashed to shit. But now, sitting there with the prison cells curved around them like a fist, the chair, with its lumbar support and specially contoured arms, felt comforting.

"Have you seen today's paper?" Stowenheim pushed the editorial section of the *Statesman Journal* toward Mason. "Five fuckin' letters against Bush. I swear to God, these people, they don't have any idea what it takes to win a war. Rather have that pansy-ass dick from Minnesota run the place. We get him as president, we might as well kiss our asses goodbye. He doesn't have the balls to handle those ragheads. It's like this place, you know? Can't give a damn inch, that's what I say. Not a damn inch."

"Massachusetts."

"Huh?"

"John Kerry," Mason said. "He's a senator from Massachusetts, not Minnesota."

"Yeah, well, wherever."

"And he probably knows quite a bit about war. He's a vet."

"I heard about that. Heard it was all a lie, too. They've got guys who served with him saying he was just out to make a name for himself. That's it."

Mason wiped his hand across his mouth and looked at the cells. Stowenheim had been the first one to sign up for a position on the execution team, and because of that Mason had been obliged to consider him for the job. "What's Robbin been up to?"

The officer reached back into his bag of sunflower seeds. "Same ol' shit. Reading, writing. Hasn't drawn in the past few days, but that always comes in spurts." He tossed a handful of seeds into his mouth.

"What's he reading?"

"*Old Yeller,* if you can believe that. Have a whole goddamn library and he goes and picks a kid's book."

Mason nodded. "What about eating, sleeping? Any changes?"

Stowenheim tapped his finger on a chart, then pushed it away. "Not a thing. I swear, you'd think he has no idea what's coming. I mean, not a clue. I even quizzed him a bit, just to see if he was as ready as he acts. You know what he said?"

Mason glanced at the officer.

"Nada. So I tell myself this guy is just playing us. Right? I mean, holding off on appeals and all that—I say it's an act." Stowenheim spat a mouthful of husks into the trash. "Just trying to get people to feel sorry for him. Least, that's how I see it. He's a smart one, that Robbin. Nuts, but smart. You know what I mean?"

Mason didn't reply. Could have, but didn't. Instead he pushed himself up from the twelve-hundred-dollar chair. Then, just as he stood, so did Robbin. And just as Mason put his hands together behind his back and stretched, Robbin reached his own arms back and out. Then Robbin walked to the can and Mason turned from the window.

"I'm moving you to the main house, Stowenheim. Admitting. You're gonna screen visitors for a while. Run background checks."

Stowenheim leaned toward the trash and spat once more, this time missing. "You're shitting me, right?"

Mason glanced at the scattered husks. "You begin tomorrow. Check in at C, they'll have your detail."

The guard didn't respond.

"You got that?"

"Yeah."

"Any questions?"

Mason could hear seeds split between the guard's yellowed teeth. He'd considered getting him out of the place altogether. Shift him off to Hermiston, maybe Pendleton. Anywhere Mason wouldn't have to run into his sorry ass. People thought working in a prison took toughness, and it did, but not meanness. Mason had run into plenty like the bug-eyed guy, dying to dig their teeth into something just for the fun of biting. Hell, he'd been like that himself. There was a thin line separating people like Stowenheim from the people they watched, and it didn't take much, Mason knew, to cross over.

CHAPTER 40

October 14, 2004

IRENE DROVE SOUTH ON HIGHWAY 3, speeding past river towns like Neunert and Grand Tower. Headlights made her squint, trains made her stop, and the words her husband had said made her shake with fury.

She struck the steering wheel, then struck it again. She had no idea what to do with Nate's confession. He might as well have told her they'd never been married, never had children, that he had no idea who in the hell she was—it had that kind of unreal feeling. Like driving up your road to find your home gone, your things, your life. Being stuck alone with nothing but memories and finding out they were nothing but lies. She raced down the road, yellow lines coming and going. Night all around.

"Damn brights!" She flashed her lights at an oncoming vehicle, then wiped the tears that squeezed from her eyes. Her life was disintegrating, bits and pieces of it flying off into the dark. She heard herself say, "If what Nate said is true . . ." Then stop, because anything beyond was just pure, volcanic rage.

Nate had been in the barn when she got back downstairs. She had packed her duffel in a frenzy: money, clothes, toothbrush and paste, and at the last second a box of Nate's razors. Jeff met her at the door, placed her bag in the truck.

"Is there something you want me to do?" he asked.

Irene wrapped her arms around herself and told him he'd already done enough. "More than I ever had a right to ask for."

"But what Mr. S. said—I mean . . ." He bit his lip and looked like he might cry. "If what he said is true, what are you gonna do?"

"I don't know, Jeff." She reached out and squeezed his arm, then looked toward the barn. "Is he in there?"

Jeff sniffed and nodded.

A few streaks of color remained tucked into the folds of the night. Irene drew in the cold air and willed herself forward.

Nate was sitting on a sawhorse, his shoulders hunched. He had something in his hands.

"I'm leaving now, Nate." Her jaw felt like it could crack steel. "I'm taking the truck and some things, and I'm leaving."

He didn't respond.

"I don't want you to try to stop me, or send someone out to get me. Do you understand? I will not be stopped."

He looked up at her. "Don't. Please don't leave, Irene. You know all there is, I swear. I know you think I was too hard on Shep, that I didn't love him. But you're wrong. I loved him, just the same as you."

She stiffened.

"I was doing what I knew to protect him. Doing the best I could. God knows you weren't—not in this, you weren't."

"You never gave me the chance." Her words felt like hot steam. "Not a word, not one damn word. My God, I was his mother. I could have helped him, talked to him, known where he was going, what he was doing, who he was with."

"You don't think I tried? Think about it. Think about all the times I tried to sit you down and talk about our son. But you always pushed me off like I was stupid. You were blind, always had been when it came to that boy."

"You should have made me see, forced me to, demanded it."

Nate's shoulders jerked as if she'd said something funny. "Like it would have made a difference? You never thought I had any right to have a say about that boy. Never once." He rose and walked past her into the dark of the yard.

"You're lying to yourself," she shouted. "Lying, just like you've been lying all these years. Holy Mother of Christ! You don't think I would have done something to help our son? I would have done anything for Shep. Anything!"

He turned. "Anything but listen to me."

"Oh, come on, Nate. I listen." She marched to where he stood. "I listen real well, and what I heard is, you killed our son. You. You and your secrets and lies."

"Don't say that."

"It's true, isn't it? Shep's jaw was broken, his arm dislocated." She grabbed the sleeve of her husband's jacket. "Threw him to the ground? You were beating him, Nate. *Beating him.* Seems to me if anyone was trying to protect Shep that day, it was Daniel, not you."

"I wasn't the one to shoot him. It was Robbin who did that, and it was Robbin who ran as soon as he saw what he'd done. He took off, leaving me holding Shep and having no way to save him. Uh-uh, you can't make me responsible for that."

"The hell I can't. You should have said what happened, what really happened."

"No. Now there's where you're wrong. You think Robbin would've been any better off if I told what he was doing with our son? Do you? See, that's where you just don't get it. Perverts like that, they don't last long. Believe me. My way, at least he had a chance."

"A chance?" The word caught in her throat. "They're gonna strap him down, pump him full of poison, and watch him die. That sound like much of a chance to you?"

"You don't think I've thought this out? Every damn day I've tried to figure how it could've been different, but there's nothing I can come up with. I warned them. Warned them both it wouldn't come to any good. I've seen it—Nam, policing—seen what happens to people like them. It's not good, Irene. It never is."

"People like *them*? You mean people like your *son*? Nate, people like *him,* they're bigger than us, don't you know that? Didn't you ever once see that? People like Shep end up showing other people things they never would have seen otherwise, feeling things bigger than they ever would. Didn't you ever once see that?"

Nate shook his head. "Listen to yourself. Just listen, then ask why I didn't tell you about Shep. You wouldn't have done anything to stop him. Not a damn thing." He wiped his nose on his shoulder, then looked down at his hands. "This is for you." He was holding a small box.

"What's in it?"

"Your jewelry. Your ma's ring, the pearls, that locket I gave you that one Christmas. And something else. Something you should see. I'm not lying about this, Irene. There'd be no use in it. Robbin and Shep, it's like I said. You go to Oregon, talk to Robbin, he'll tell you the same thing. There wasn't a burglary. I just made that up so people wouldn't suspect anything different."

He handed her the box. It felt heavy and made Irene want to cry. "Jesus, Nate."

"I know."

Up above, one remaining line of color wove through the trees like a ribbon. A breeze rattled some leaves. Irene turned from her husband and went to the truck, yanked open the door.

"Irene?" He stood next to the truck as she got in.

"What?"

"Try, would you?"

She sighed. "Try what, Nate?"

"To understand? Could you at least try? I didn't know Robbin had a gun, didn't even think it. And I was wrong to get so mad. More than wrong." Nate's voice caught and he coughed. "I can't do without you, Irene. I know I made mistakes, terrible mistakes." He sniffed, then folded his arms around himself, kicked the leaves. "But if you could try," he said. "Please. Just try."

IRENE CROSSED THE MISSISSIPPI AT Cape Girardeau, Missouri, stopped to fill the tank, then added a quart of oil and bought a U.S. map. Then, under the station's bright white lights, she charted a route to Oregon.

At three in the morning she crossed into Kansas at Fort Scott, and at sunrise she found herself near Wichita. She put in another quart of oil and took out her map. The sun was rising, but she couldn't rest. Her mind would not stop working over what Nate had said and what it meant. She kept seeing him come home with that job offer from Blaine. The move was "just what Shep needs." Isn't that what he'd said? *Just what he needs?*

And then there was the day of the move, Nate suddenly announcing there'd be no room for the piano, and Shep saying what? Something about his father hating him . . .

Irene's hand went to her lips, pulled on them as she thought and tried not to. Remembering and at the same time choking it back.

By the time she got to Salina, the undulating fields of wheat stubble had begun to lull her into a stupor. She pulled over at a rest stop, used her duffel as a pillow, her jacket as a blanket. Her last thought before falling under was to wonder what Nate was doing.

CHAPTER 41

October 14, 2004

J EFF FOLLOWED NATE INTO THE house, demanding that he call Bliss. "She needs to know what's going on, Mr. S. It's only fair."

Nate told him to mind his own business and get the hell home. But instead Jeff went into the kitchen. Nate could hear him rummaging around and then dialing. "There's been a problem at home," Nate heard him say. "No. No, they're okay. It's just your dad—he has something to tell you."

Nate glared at Jeff as the young man stretched the receiver into the dining room.

"What is it, Dad? What's the problem?" His daughter sounded panicked. "Dad? Jeff? Is someone there? Shit."

"I'm here." Nate collapsed into a chair.

"Dad? What the hell's going on? What's Jeff doing calling? What's wrong?"

He closed his eyes. "It's your mother . . . She's taken off for Oregon."

"Oregon? What do you mean she's taken off for Oregon? She told me she didn't want to go. And why aren't you with her?"

Nate glanced at Jeff, now sitting in Irene's chair, his head in his hands. Then he took a deep breath and told his daughter the rest: her mom forgiving Robbin, the letters, and then the news that had made Irene take off, gravel spitting behind her tires as she pulled from the drive.

Bliss didn't respond.

"Honey?" He pulled at his thinning hair.

"I have to hang up now," she said.

"Sweetheart? I'm sorry. I messed up. I totally messed up. I'm sorry. You can't know how sorry."

"Messed up? You did more than mess up, Dad. Shit. Just tell me this, who else knows?"

"You mean about your mom leaving?"

"No. About you and what happened to Shep. That sheriff back there in Blaine, was he in on this?"

"No. No one knew."

Again, she was silent.

"Bliss?"

"Obstructing justice, Dad. That's what this is called. You know that, right? You broke the law, Dad."

He knew this. Of course he knew this. But it was like knowing there was something dangerous in your house. And as long as you kept that one door closed . . .

"Are you going to try and stop her?"

"Mom? No. I promised her I wouldn't."

He heard Bliss sniff and thought she was probably crying. Or possibly trying not to. Either way, it was the last thing he wanted to hear.

"Look, I gotta go and make some calls," Bliss said. "You get hold of me as soon as you hear from Mom. I don't care what time it is. Do you understand?"

"Yes."

"And don't go telling anyone else this story. Not a soul."

"I won't," Nate replied.

"Okay. Now put Jeff back on."

Nate nodded into the phone, too choked up even to say good-bye. Then he handed the phone to Jeff and stumbled out the back door and into the barn.

CHAPTER 42

October 16, 2004

IRENE CONTINUED WEST ON I-70, closing in on Colorado some 270 miles farther. The idea of the growing distance between her and home felt daunting, and to prevent herself from thinking too hard, she turned on the radio. Stations came at her out of Fargo, Cedar Rapids, Denver. Some played music, others just talked about the weather, farming, the war, and politics. At some point she landed on a station playing music from some powwow that had taken place in New Mexico that year. *It's a whole other world,* she thought as she listened to drumming and the mournful wailing that accompanied it.

An hour or so later the station started to fade and in jumped "Praise the Lord, WGD, outta Tulsa."

Irene gave a sidelong glance at the radio. The station played "Be Still, My Soul" and a few other hymns she knew by heart. But after the drumming, the melodies sounded uninspired, so she turned the dial. But WGD was all there was. "Figures." She draped an arm over the steering wheel.

After the hymns, Reverend Tecumseh Evan Stow of Our Holy Redeemer welcomed his listeners with a voice as slick and practiced as a used-car dealer's. He asked them all to sit down and get comfortable, and Irene shifted in her seat, suddenly aware that she was anything but comfortable. Her right leg ached from pressing the accelerator, her back was stiff from sitting too long, and her eyes burned from lack of sleep.

Reverend Stow was sympathetic. "I know you're tired. That the road's been long, and there's so much more to go. But isn't it good to know you have a friend with you every mile of the way?"

Stow reminisced about his own journey. His papa working the coal out of Kentucky, his mama raising seven children, and he, the middle son, running off, losing his way: drugs, sex, stealing. "I was Satan's child," he said. "A burning flame in an empty field. But the Lord knocked me from my world of sin and into the glorious arms of redemption. How many of you are out there feeling alone, afraid, not knowing what to do or who to turn to?"

"How many ain't?" Irene said, imitating the preacher's thick southern drawl.

"Times are bad. Hard, hard, and harder. War, greed, drugs, terrorists coming in on our shores. Hating us for being Christian. Hating our freedom."

The reverend hitched up his tempo, drumming on the sin, the vice—prostitution, drugs, drink, abortion, taking us down the road to ruin. "And now this! Homosexuals! Gays and lesbians taking over our schools, libraries, churches, and TV."

Irene squeezed the steering wheel.

"Men with men, women with women. Having relations, sexual relations! That's right! Perverting God's creation! His word! His way! And now what are they trying to do?"

He paused and Irene waited, trying to think what *they* might be trying to do.

"Marry. That's right, they want to take the sacred covenant of marriage and pervert it. Men with men, women with women. It's happening now. Massachusetts, liberal judges are allowing homosexuals to marry. Oregon, it's the same thing. Vermont. California. All over this country these people are promoting their depraved ways—taking your jobs, sitting beside you and your children in your church, teaching them, even. That's right, homosexuals in your baby's class, teaching her it's okay if Bobby has two mommies. And it don't stop there. They own Hollywood, movies, television, the Internet, all of it designed to bring the gay agenda right into your home. Think! Mothers! Fathers! What are you going to tell your children? And I ask you, what are you going to do?"

"I'll tell you what I'll do!" Irene reached and turned the radio knob so hard it fell into her hand. Then she threw the plastic button to the other side of the truck and jammed the accelerator.

No wonder Shep hadn't told her he was gay. Every Sunday, every damn Sunday, there she was dragging him and Bliss off to church. And every damn time there was Pastor White telling them just what was right and what was wrong. Shep was wrong, beyond wrong—to the preacher, to God, and if to them, then of course to his ma.

Tears came to Irene's eyes. *Of course he didn't tell me.*

What he was, who he was, was a sin. Depraved. How could he tell her that? And if he had, what would she have done?

The pickup droned on. Denver, 170 miles. She hit the steering wheel, then hit it again. "Dammit anyway!" She yelled to herself and to God or whoever the hell was up there.

Irene knew what it was like to believe you were something wrong. Her pa had made her tell Pastor White about her situation—eighteen, pregnant, not married, going off with Nate to that old pond. No chaperone, just her and the handsomest boy in class . . . And her sitting in the preacher's office feeling the warmth of her own piss drip down her leg as the man of God leaned toward her with his slender arms and unsettling sliver of a smile and called her a whore.

And then she goes and raises her children in that very same church.

No wonder Shep kept quiet.

Irene drove, one empty mile pushing back another. Her son was gay. She tried to get her mind around the idea, but couldn't without feeling tight and uncomfortable.

Homosexuality was a big-city thing, brought about like all big-city problems—lost souls wandering around in too large a world. It sure didn't happen around Carlton, where everyone was either married, trying to get married, or busy getting themselves divorced so they could marry someone else.

What would she have done if Shep had told her? Nate thought nothing, and she hated him for it. But trying to imagine it, she couldn't think of what else she might have done. Have him talk with Pastor White, as her father had had her do? *Maybe.* Encourage him to go on dates, as Nate had always bugged him about hunting or playing ball? *Probably.*

Irene put on her blinker, got off the highway, pulled into a dimly lit motel parking lot, closed her eyes, and started to sob. She wouldn't have known what to do to help her son, and because of that, she probably wouldn't have done a thing.

Nate was right. Her hands went to her face, attempting to shield herself from the truth. *Nate was absolutely right.*

IRENE DECIDED SHE DID NOT want to see Daniel. It came to her in the middle of the night, under the too-thin blanket at the Moonlighter Motel. He deceived her. Nine years of letters and not a word about what really happened. She left the bed and stood in the shower, hot tears mixing with Ogallala water. A little card on the dresser asked guests to please conserve. "The Ogallala, the nation's largest underground aquifer, is running dry." And that, Irene decided as she dressed, was just what was happening to her. Her sympathy had run out. If she felt bad for anyone at all, it was Bliss, all the way out there in Texas, and she having no good way to explain to her daughter why she wanted nothing more than to close her eyes up on that hill outside Blaine and never open them again.

Irene packed up her duffel and got back on the road. At sunrise she could see the Rocky Mountains, pink-lit and menacing as a saw. But as she got closer to Denver the mountains vanished, hidden behind a whitewash of clouds that blended seamlessly with a skiff of fresh snow.

The only clear sky was to the north, so she pulled over and examined her map. Two hours later Irene crossed the Colorado border into Wyoming, where the flat hand of the land reached out to a completely unblemished horizon. She leaned back into her seat, letting the dry road and the monotonous miles slip by. Then, somewhere outside Rock Springs, things began to go wrong. Instead of the truck cruising up the hills as it had, the old thing seemed winded, making it necessary to downshift in order to help it over. Then, as if someone had flipped a switch, a wind kicked up, creating a situation Irene had never encountered before: a blizzard without the snow. Or at least no falling snow. Within an instant, the highway became almost invisible under a moving gauze of yesterday's snow. It was like driving on water, or within a low-hanging fog, but an undulating, quicksilver kind of fog that hid the slick parts of the road and was nearly hypnotizing.

Irene searched for an exit.

The Sinclair station stood alone on a corner, a lime-green dinosaur on its sign. Across the street was a restaurant named EAT, and beyond that a motel. Snow blew in great whiffs across the road, and there was not a person in sight. Irene stopped in front of the station and opened the truck door, only to have it wrenched from her hand by the wind. She got out, shoved the door closed, and took off for the station.

"You ought not to be running." A tall man in blue jeans, denim coat, and a large black cowboy hat held the door open for her.

Irene stepped inside and thanked him.

"Pretty icy out there. You don't want to slip and fall."

Irene rubbed her hands together, nodding. She wasn't dressed for the weather: a barn coat, tennis shoes, no hat or gloves. She glanced at her watch. It was nearly four o'clock and already starting to get dark. "I need somebody to look at my truck. It's not acting right, and I'm trying to get across the mountains."

The man shoved his hands in his pockets. "Um-hm. I hope you're not in any hurry. They just closed the road 'tween here and Green River."

"The interstate? For how long?"

"Till this thing blows through. I was just about to close up."

"Oh. Is there another place around here for me to get help?"

"Not that you'll be able to get to." The man took a breath, then walked to the other side of the counter. "So tell me what's going on with the Chevy."

"It's tired. Doesn't want to climb. It was fine up until a little while ago."

"How many miles she got?"

"Around two hundred and fifty."

The man ran his fingers down the sides of his mouth, drawing out his already long features so that he looked like a marionette.

"And you're heading west?"

"Oregon."

"Um-hm."

The room was filled with dead animals: a stuffed owl, a few mounted deer and an elk, some pelts. Raccoon she recognized, and maybe badger.

"Roadkill," the man said. "Every last one of 'em. Hate seeing things go to waste." He scratched the back of his head. "So it's Oregon, huh?"

"Yeah."

"I lived out there once. Roseburg. Friend was raising water buffalo. His girlfriend made cheese from their milk. They'd sell it for a bundle up in Portland and Seattle. Eugene, too. You ever been there?"

"No."

"It's like Missoula. College town. Anyway, I couldn't stick 'round. All those trees, they made me damn near claustrophobic."

Irene glanced outside, where there was nothing to see but a cinder-block motel and a restaurant someone didn't even have the ambition to name. "Where I'm ending up there aren't many trees."

"Pendleton? I've been there, too. The Round-Up—damn good rodeo."

The wind kicked open the door a few inches and let in a spray of snow.

"Blaine."

"Never heard of it." He pulled a pack of Camels from his pocket and pointed it at Irene. She shook her head, and he tapped one out and stuck it in his mouth. "Where're you coming from, anyway?"

"Illinois." Irene's fingers rattled the keys inside her pocket. Anxious, impatient.

He frowned. "Never been . . . So this rig of yours, if it's just started acting up, it could just be the timing's off. You start climbing, you need to adjust for altitude. When was the last time it had a tuneup?"

"My husband works on it quite a bit. At least he used to."

The man worked the cigarette from one side of his mouth to the other, never bothering to light it. "Like I said, I was about to head on home, but seeing as you may need some help . . ."

———

IRENE SAT. THEN STOOD. WALKED around the small gas-steeped office. There was a *Time* magazine with a picture of the World Trade
Center being hit by one of those jets. A bulletin board filled with
raunchy cartoons and business cards. A coffeepot black with hand-
prints. An ashtray brimming with crushed cigarettes, none of them
ever lit. And, of course, all the dead animals.

Irene buttoned her jacket and stepped out into the wind. Daniel
had been a mechanic. Worked right around the corner from where
they'd lived. Shep had probably stopped there to fill his tires. That,
or get a soda. Irene could see the machine in her mind, remembered
it had Dr Pepper, his favorite. He would have gone to the gas station,
and that's where Daniel would have decided to lure her son. Irene
clutched her arms around herself, carefully walking forward. Then
she stopped.

Shep had once mentioned wanting to be a mechanic. She closed
her eyes. They were bringing in groceries when he said something
about getting a job at a garage when he got out of high school. "I
think I'd be good at it," he said.

She remembered laughing and asking if he were kidding. But he
said no, he thought it would be interesting, "and anyway, don't you
think it would make Dad happy?"

Irene staggered back toward the garage, pushing away what she
had begun to pull. But there was no retracting the memory—Shep
standing beside her, a bag of groceries in his hands, and asking her
right out if she thought it was normal, him not being more like his
dad.

And her, loving him with all she was but still not giving him all
he needed—someone to sit down and look at him and listen and ask,
just ask, goddammit, What is this about wanting to be a mechanic
and not seeing yourself as normal? What is normal anyway, and
what difference did it make? *What the hell difference did it make?*

But there were groceries to put away and laundry to do. Dinner to start. And instead of talking with her son, she patted his back and told him something that had nothing to do with what he'd been aiming at. And then she asked him to bring in the rest of the groceries.

"I ADJUSTED THE TIMING, BUT I'll be honest with you, I wouldn't be trying to get over the mountains in that old girl. Least, not the way she is."

Irene turned from her staring match with the stuffed owl. "What do you mean?"

The mechanic wore coveralls with the name *Fletch* stitched above the pocket. He motioned for her to follow. "I'm not trying to sell you anything here, but take a look at these tires." He bent down, drew his finger along the rubber. "We're talking near bald. Dangerous even in good weather." He stood and pulled at a wiper. "These can't be doing you any good." Then he got to the engine. "And as far as this goes"—he sighed and leaned over the radiator—"it needs an overhaul. I mean, rings are near shot. You're probably going through a quart every time you fill up. Your gaskets are leaking, and your hoses . . ." He poked at a black tube. "Well, they're pretty old."

"I'm not looking to rebuild the thing."

"And I'm not looking to do it, neither." Fletch reached into the engine and pulled at a wire that seemed to have no place to go. "Look, you want t' get to Oregon, I can get you there. Try to, at least. But you'll need a new air filter, plugs, some hoses, a good solid tuneup, and 'cause winter's on, I'd flush out that radiator, get some antifreeze in it, change the oil, and at least get some retreads." He turned to face her. "Without at least that, you'd be pressing your luck."

A laugh jerked up through her. "Luck?"

"You got this far, you got something going for you. Course, I wouldn't go and try to drive her back to Illinois."

Irene folded her arms over her chest. Nate had been so good about keeping up their vehicles. But lately all he did when he got home was sit in front of the TV. "I'm not going back to Illinois."

"Just as well. You got family over in Oregon?"

Irene looked out at the darkened road. "My son. I'm going to go be with my son."

"There you go." Fletch pulled a cigarette from his pocket. "You get this rig fixed up a little bit, and it'll get you to your son."

CHAPTER 43

October 16, 2004

B Y THE TIME IRENE AND Fletch had determined just what would be done on the truck, the parking lot across the street was filled with cars and the roadside lined with semis belching smoke into the frigid night. The mechanic pointed.

"Doris has a room waiting over at the Hitching Post. I'll drop your rig by when I'm done. Could be late, though—don't wait up."

"What about the bill?"

"I'll leave it on the seat. You can stop by and pay in the morning."

Irene thanked Fletch, grabbed a few things from her duffel bag, and plowed through the wind to a single-story motel with a fiberglass horse kicking at a flashing NO VACANCY sign. Beneath it in big block letters it read, *God Bless America*.

Doris had hair the color of Pine-Sol, wore a bright red sweater, and big round glasses that reflected the light from the television set. *Dateline* was on. Irene recognized Stone Phillips's diesel-like voice

and wondered if Nate was watching. He liked *Dateline* more than
60 Minutes, and he liked Stone Phillips best of all. "It's all bullshit,"
he'd say each week. "But at least with this guy you know it going in."

Doris hit Mute and turned a lipstick-stained smile on Irene.
"You're the Illinois woman, aren't you? Off to see your son, right?
I'm Doris." She licked the tip of her index finger and pulled out a
sheet of paper. "Fletch called. Knew we'd be stacked up. Wind starts
up and you never know how long the roads will be closed."

"You mean it may not open by tomorrow?"

"Could open later tonight. But like I said, you never know.
Worst I've seen was four days."

"Four days?"

"Yeah, but I gotcha a nice enough room. Single with shower, TV
with cable. Phone. Forty-five for the night. You can have it for as
long as you like." She pulled a pen from behind her ear and leaned
over her form. Behind Doris an American flag was tacked to a
wood-paneled wall. Beneath it was a picture of a young boy.

"It's my Cody," Doris said without looking up. "He's on his second stint out there in Ee-rak."

"How old?"

"Twenty-three next month."

Cody wore a marine's dark blue coat, white belt, white hat, and
hard gaze. Irene knew it well. Nate had come home after his first
tour with that same look. Polished shoes, brass buttons, hair shaved
down to a thin felt. It had made her feel proud.

"It must be hard, having him out there."

"It goes with the territory. His pa was in Kosovo, my dad Korea.
But I got to say"—she clicked a bright red nail against the wood
counter—"it does feel different when it's your son."

"I hope he's doing okay. I mean, from what I hear—"

The woman slid the form over the counter and gave Irene her
pen. "I'll tell you what," she said. "You can hear a lot of bullcrap
about what's going on over there. People not interested in seeing

this thing through, not believing in our troops the way they ought, *or* our president. I stopped having anything to do with the so-called news a long time ago."

Irene glanced at Stone Phillips.

"Oh, that." Doris waved at the set. "I think that man's handsome, is all."

Irene chuckled as she wrote down her name and license plate number. "Do you hear from your son?"

"E-mails nearly every day. He tried for years to get me to sit down and learn how to use that computer." She pointed to a keyboard. "Now it's all I can do to stay away." She sighed. "Course I probably still have no idea what's really going on. You know boys, never really do tell their moms the truth, now do they?" She laughed as if it were some kind of joke, sons not telling their moms the truth of their lives, and moms not asking because they really don't want to know anyway. "Don't want us to worry, is my guess. And honestly, what can I do anyway but write and pray?" Doris took back the paper and a pen. "So how old's your son?"

Irene looked at the key in the woman's hand. It was strung on a chain with a rhinestone flag. "He's dead."

"Excuse me?" There were lines fanning from the corners of Doris's mouth.

"My son, Shep, he was killed out there in Oregon. He's buried there."

"Oh Lord, and here I am going on about my Cody. I am so sorry. It's just that I thought for sure Fletch said you were going to go live with your boy."

"I'm gonna go be near him. Near as I can, anyways."

The two women stood measuring each other, then Doris shook her head. "It never goes, does it? I mean, you hear about time healing. But it's not that easy, is it?"

Irene glanced at the picture of Cody, not knowing how to respond. The woman's son was off fighting a war. If she was lucky, he'd come back. But he wouldn't come back the same. "I admire your strength, having your son all the way out in Iraq. I don't think I'd have had it in me to let my child go. Fact is—" Irene stopped, ashamed of herself for wanting to challenge this woman.

"What?"

"Well . . ." Irene looked at her bitten-down nails. "I guess I don't think anyone's child should be there. Haven't since it all started. I'm sorry."

The woman's hand tightened around the key, and Irene figured she'd just blown her opportunity for sleep. She'd be seeing those mountains tonight. Once that road opened, it would be just her and it, climbing higher and higher until there was nothing left but thin air and stars.

"That's your privilege, of course. But the fact is, if it were your son out there, you'd have a whole different perspective."

"Maybe."

"There's no maybe about it. You'd support him and what he was doing, and you'd never let yourself think different."

Irene looked down.

"You say you've heard things." Doris turned toward the picture of her son. "Well, I've heard them too. How can you miss it? Radio, news, bumper stickers. War for oil. Oil! I'll tell you what— my son's not out there fighting 'cause some slicker wants to drive an SUV." She turned back to Irene. "You've lost your son, you can understand this. Us moms, we have no say. They grow up and they do what they're gonna do, and we can do nothing but keep loving and hoping and praying that somehow things work the way we've dreamed since the day we learned we were carrying 'em. There's no choice in it, 'cause we have no power in it. You understand what I'm saying?"

Irene did. No choice, no power. She understood completely.

"Anyway, I don't mean to go on. And here you are going off to see your son's grave and having a ways to go to get there. It's just that if you're right and Cody shouldn't be there, then I don't know how I'd live knowing that I didn't do something to stop him from going."

Irene nodded. She understood that, too.

Doris smiled sympathetically and handed Irene the key. "You look done in, and I bet you haven't eaten. You get in your room. My husband brought back an elk last week, and I've made a hell of a stew. I'll bring you a bowl. You eat it, get a shower, and get some sleep. Roads are bound to open up pretty soon."

A LIGHT SNOW CAME IN the middle of the night, covering the road and vehicles with a couple inches of powder. Irene's truck was parked in the lot with the others, and she noticed that most of the semis were gone. She turned on the television to check the weather, and as she washed up and dressed she half listened as people talked about safe Halloween treats and then something about the presidential race. After a commercial, a reporter began to interview some politician about a planned U.S. attack in a place called Fallujah. They were expecting a lot of casualties, and Irene wondered if Cody would be there and if it was true that Doris didn't listen to the news.

There was a knock on the door, and Irene shut off the TV.

"Coffee." Doris had on a beat-up cowboy hat and boots.

"You shouldn't do this," Irene said, letting her in.

"And why the heck not? All's I ever get through here are truckers and salesmen. It's nice having someone I can visit with." She handed Irene a mug. "I put creamer in—French vanilla. Hope you don't mind."

"No, that's fine. Thank you."

"So are you going to head out? 'Cause if you're thinking of it, I'd suggest hitting the road soon, before it gets too bad up on the pass. Otherwise I can heartily recommend the French toast over at Alma's. She dips it in cornflakes. You got tire chains?"

"No."

"Oh. Then you're not going anywhere. Got to have chains, that or studs, to get across. State police will be checking. You don't have 'em, they'll turn you back."

Irene dropped to the bed. Things were conspiring against her ever getting to Oregon. She could feel it. The truck, now the weather . . .

"You sleep all right?"

"So-so."

"More reason to just stay put."

Irene sighed. "I'll go get my bag. Didn't feel like hauling it across the street last night."

The two women, Doris in her well-worn boots, Irene in gym shoes, crunched their way through the scrim of snow. A deer stood by Irene's truck, nuzzling at something on the ground. Its antlers reached a good two feet to either side.

"Lord, he's big," Irene said, stopping.

"Nuisance, too. Eats everything I plant." Doris picked up a handful of snow, packed it as best she could, and threw. The animal looked at her, then sauntered off. "His ma was killed along the road a few years back. We took to leaving out hay. Now we don't have the heart to shoot him."

"We don't have them that big in Illinois."

"Like I said, a nuisance."

Irene got to the truck and looked down at the deer's tracks. They were nearly as wide as her hand, and beside one was something silver. Doris picked it up.

"Looks like a knob to something."

Irene pulled open the truck door. "Oh, that," she said. "It's for my radio. Must've fallen out when Fletch dropped off the truck." Irene pulled out her duffel. When she stepped away from the truck, Doris stepped forward.

"I'll snap this back on. When you go, tune it to 1150 AM. Weather and road conditions all the way to Ogden." She hauled herself up

into the passenger seat, making way for her feet among a heap of
paper sacks and Styrofoam cups. It was when she leaned forward,
snapping the knob in place, that her foot knocked something out
of the car. Irene heard it drop, and turned in time to see a strand of
pearls sink into the snow.

"Gosh darn, I'm sorry." Doris got out of the truck, bent over,
and snatched up the strand, a ring, a locket with a heart, and, scattered like a deck of cards, photographs. A boy, bare-chested, tanned,
sitting by a creek. Same boy, climbing a rock, jumping, beating his
chest like an ape. His smile was huge, gallant, strong. Beautiful.
And then the next: two boys sitting together on a stone, the younger
one's hand hooked around his friend's knee.

It was Shep and Daniel.

Irene reached for the door.

"You okay?" Doris quickly shoved everything back into the box
and grabbed Irene's arm. "Heavens. Come on." She took Irene's
duffel, threw the strap over her shoulder, tucked the box under one
arm, wrapped Irene with the other, and walked her into the office
and beyond, to her living room, where there were paintings of cowboys and horses on the walls.

Irene sat on the couch, the box in her lap. "It's Shep. In those
pictures. It's my son, Shep."

"I figured." Doris sat and pressed her hand against Irene's arm.

"I've never seen them before. My husband gave me that package
before I left, but I never looked inside."

"I'm sorry about kicking it out like that."

Irene tried to open the box.

"Here, now, let me help." Doris took the box and pulled out the
pictures. "Is this him?"

Irene nodded.

"It looks like he was a happy boy," Doris said, handing the stack
to Irene.

"You think so?" Shep's eyes were shaded by a thick curl of bangs.

He was tanned, and his jeans hung off his hips with room to spare. "I don't know anymore. Maybe he was. I don't know."

Doris leaned over. "Oh, sure he was—look at that smile. There's something rich in it. Reminds me of my own boy, out doing what he wants, knowing what he needs. How old was he in this, seventeen?"

Irene slid one photo past another. Shep climbing some rocks; Shep looking straight into the camera, eyes soft and full. "Fifteen," she said, rubbing the damp picture on her pants.

"And how old was he when . . . when you lost him?"

Irene looked at the next picture. Shep was curled on a blanket, sound asleep. "The same."

"Umm—no wonder you're upset. What was it, an accident?"

Irene turned to the next photo. It was an off-center shot of both boys, Daniel with one arm pointed toward the camera, the other around her son. Both of them shirtless, both of them smiling as if they had the world by the hand. Irene touched her son's face, his shoulder, his arm. Then she did the same with Daniel. Two boys. Two lives. Gone. "Yes," she whispered. "An accident. A shooting accident."

"Oh, sugar." Doris slapped her knee. "What a waste. Happens here all the time. Hunting, cleaning out guns, people just being careless. I won't allow the things in the house, least not where the grandkids can get to 'em."

Irene's eyes stuck on the two boys, and somewhere a bell rang.

Doris rose. "I'll be back in a minute."

Irene went through the pictures again, then once more. Nate had found the boys by this river, and later on in their home. There'd been a struggle. Daniel had a gun, and Shep got in the way.

An accident. Nothing more than an accident.

When Doris returned, Irene was standing. "I'm gonna need chains."

"What's that?"

"Chains or studded tires. Whatever it takes to get across those mountains."

"You're not serious."

"I am."

"But what's the sudden rush?"

Irene glanced at her watch. Daniel had only twelve days left. If she got to Ogden today, then she could be in Oregon by Tuesday, Wednesday at the latest. Then as soon as she got to Salem she would go to the superintendent's office and after that call the DA. They would have to do something to stop this when they heard what had happened. It had all been an accident. There was no one to blame, and no one to punish. "There's things I have to take care of. Things I should have taken care of a long time ago. And if I don't get there in the next few days, I'll lose any chance of ever doing it."

"But you don't understand these mountains. Could be a blizzard up there—likely is. And you know, it's steep, and just damn treacherous."

"I'll manage."

Doris's red nail clicked against a tooth.

"You're sure 'bout this?"

"Absolutely."

"Well, then, I guess we'll just work to make it happen."

FLETCH CLEARED A PATCH AROUND Irene's rear tire and showed her how to wrap the chain around the back, then hook and tighten it up front. "You don't need them now, but twenty miles from here, it's a whole other story. Pull over, get 'em on. Don't think twice about it. And don't push it. Nice and easy is the way. You don't want your son worrying." As a parting gift, he loaded the back of her truck with a few hundred pounds of Wyoming granite. "That should help plant you."

Irene thanked the mechanic, then climbed in her truck and got on I-80. Ten miles later she passed Rock Springs, and five miles after that she was in a full-blown snowstorm. Flakes as fat as catkins swept by, and the road was soon deep in the stuff. The truck pulled and swayed, but she kept her hands tight on the wheel and her eyes forward, looking for a place to pull over and put on her chains.

A few miles farther, flashing lights brought her to a standstill. One after another she watched people pull to a wide spot in the road, get out of their vehicles, chain up.

Irene put on the gloves and hat Doris had given her and joined the others.

Fletch had done a good job of showing Irene what to do, going over it all twice, then having her do it herself. But it didn't help. Wind blowing, ice scratching, and her dressed for a fall picnic, she fumbled with the heavy wire, trying to pull it up and over the back of the tire as she'd been shown.

When she couldn't handle the cold anymore, she got back into the truck, took off her shoes and socks, rubbed her feet, blew on her hands. By the time she was ready to try again, snow had covered the window. But she fought the death grip of the cold, pushed away the snow, then wrestled the damn chain around the tire, fastening it—not tight, but on. Then she went around to the other side of the vehicle to do the same. Twenty minutes later, hands aching with cold, Irene sat in her truck staring up at its roof, thanking whoever it was who helped women get chains on trucks and trucks over mountains—because she was certain she'd get over the mountains. Nothing was going to stop her. She had twelve days to try to save Daniel Robbin, and though she had no idea how she was going to do it, she *would* do it. She had to.

CHAPTER 44

October 19, 2004

BLISS STANLEY WORE A CRISP blue suit, a white blouse, low heels. Her posture was uncompromising, her briefcase black, and her hair pulled back into a stern bun. Still, unruly strands had slipped their leash, creating a burning halo around her heart-shaped face and bright green eyes, and Mason, taken aback by the sight, could see that no matter how seriously this woman wished to be taken, there would always be that first distracting thought: *Damn, she's beautiful.*

She reached out her hand and he took it, then quickly pulled back and pointed to a chair.

Ms. Stanley had called the previous afternoon to tell Mason she was flying to Oregon to talk to him. When he asked what about, she was abrupt.

"I think you know what this is about, superintendent. And I suggest you see me first thing tomorrow, before my mother arrives."

Now Mrs. Stanley's daughter slipped on a slim pair of glasses—
tortoiseshell, bookish—and clicked open her briefcase.

"I have a fax of some forms you sent my mother. Forms for her
to enter the prison's reconciliation program." She pulled out a file
and set her briefcase on the floor. "Why did you send her these, Mr.
Mason?"

"Because she asked for them," he said, sitting.

Ms. Stanley tapped the file folder. Her nails, he noticed, were
trimmed down to the flesh, each painted a soft, pale pink. Nothing
flashy or bold.

"When?"

"Two and a half weeks ago." Mason leaned back in his chair and
wrapped his own hands together. He watched the woman glance at
them, then look away. "She called after she received the death warrant. Said she wanted to visit Robbin. I told her it was against regu-
lations. Rules don't allow victims to meet with their offenders."

"But that's not altogether true, is it? I mean, you have this program." She tapped the folder.

"Yes, we have that program. She asked about it and I told her,
but it's not used much and takes a lot of time and work on everyone's part. It's a whole bunch of commitment."

"Yet you sent the application to my mother anyway."

"You have it in your hand."

She gave him a terse look. "Why send it if there's no chance of
her meeting him?"

"Like I said, she asked."

Ms. Stanley cocked her head. "You don't strike me as someone
who does whatever anyone asks."

"If they ask nice. Your mom asked nice."

Her eyes narrowed. "Look, Mr. Mason, I don't know what game
you're playing here. My mother is driving halfway across the country in order to see Daniel Robbin, and what I want to know is if you
intend on letting that happen."

"Do you think it should happen?"

The woman's lips tightened, and Mason watched her green eyes take in his office, coursing over the bookshelves, the neatly stacked files, the binders, his pencils, the incandescent lamp lighting his desk. She stopped on his daughter's picture. "I didn't know my mother had been corresponding with Mr. Robbin until last week. I'm still stunned." She looked back, and he saw that her eyes were flecked with gold and black. Like a stone. "My mother took my brother's death hard. About as hard as I've ever seen, and being a prosecutor, I've seen—"

"Hold on. You're a prosecutor?"

He saw a subtle flinch. "Yes."

"Capital cases?"

"Uh-huh."

"And you live where?"

"Texas," she said, as if daring him to take it further.

Mason whistled one long note and shook his head. "Hell of a career choice, isn't it? I mean, after what your family has been through?"

The woman took off her glasses, and Mason could see the gold in her eyes flash against the green.

"Doesn't everything we do come from what we've been through, Mr. Mason? I chose to put murderers behind bars, you chose to be their keeper. Executioner, even. There are reasons we do what we do, sir. I'm sure you must have your own story."

His fingertips reached out, barely touching one another. "Touché."

"I'm not here to spar with you. I just want to know, as a daughter, if my mother is going to be allowed to meet with Robbin."

"I don't think it's a good idea."

"That's not what I asked."

"Okay, then, I don't think the director will think it's a good idea, or the AG, not to mention the governor. Scheduled as it is, right before the election—you can guess what side of the fence he's on."

"I don't need a civics lesson, superintendent. And I'm not talking pardon, or even a delay. I'm simply asking if my mother has a chance of meeting with the man who killed my brother."

He noticed a thin gold chain circling Ms. Stanley's neck. "There's a lot of legwork in getting someone like your mother into this prison, and none of it's done. So, in answer to your question, you can stop worrying. She won't get to see him till the execution."

Bliss laid a hand on his desk and stared hard. "Actually, Mr. Mason, I'm here to ask that you *let* her see him."

He paused, wondering if she was joking, some sick kind of prosecutor humor. She didn't smile. "I see. I'm sorry. I thought she didn't have anyone who supported this idea of hers."

"She didn't. Now she does."

"Oh." Mason bit his lip. "Well, that's nice. I mean, I guess."

"It's not nice. None of this is *nice*."

"That's what your mother said."

The woman's nostrils flared, one quick breath's worth.

"You say she's driving here?"

"Left last week. My father found out about her and Robbin's letters, they had words, she left for here. She should be in Salem by tonight."

"Alone?"

"Yes."

"You try to stop her?"

The pretty woman in the Brooks Brothers suit gave him a look of exasperation, pain, and anger all wrapped together. "I told you, I just learned about the letters. My dad called after she drove off." Ms. Stanley's left hand went to her temple, and Mason noticed there was no ring.

"You have any idea why this is so important to her?"

"I can't tell you that."

This time he gave her a look, trying to determine whether she really didn't know or just wouldn't say.

"Look, I know of only one situation like this. Just one. And I have to tell you, Mr. Mason, I would never have guessed it. Not of my mom, not in a million years. She was so beaten down after Shep was killed—wanted nothing more than to see Robbin dead. She was damn near living for it. I had no idea she'd gone and forgiven the man."

"It's a noble thing, that's for sure."

Bliss nodded, mouthing out the word "Yeah" as if she weren't sure it was as much noble as desperate. She shook her head, then pulled some papers from her folder. It was the application for the reconciliation program, every page filled out. And where it asked for the signatures of supporting family members was the name *Barbara Lee Stanley,* followed by the word *daughter.* And after that, another—*Nathaniel Patrick Stanley, husband.*

"I thought you said your father and mother had words over this."

"They did." She paused. "She's never done anything like this. Just taken off. We had no idea where she was. Then yesterday morning she called me from Utah. That's when my dad faxed me these forms."

"What if Robbin doesn't want to see her? He may not, you know, especially if she's coming with ideas of getting clemency or some damn thing. She mentioned that to me on the phone, and that's a whole other reason I don't want her seeing him. I think there's more to this than you're letting on."

Bliss didn't respond.

"Robbin's not fighting this, you know. Fact is, he says he's relieved. I don't want you or your mom upsetting him."

"He's waived his appeals?"

"Yeah."

"And no one's trying to intervene?"

"ACLU's trying, but I doubt it'll come to much. Justice Department is looking into it as we speak. But unless there's a damn good reason—new evidence, mistrial, something—I don't see it stopping."

She nodded.

"You know what he did when I gave him his warrant?" Mason pulled out a pencil and pressed its sharp tip into his pale index finger. "Told *me* not to worry." He snorted. "Said he understood it was my job, and he was ready for it. *Ready!* I just about wanted to hit him, just to get him to react. I swear, he's the most composed s.o.b. I've run into 'round here, and I don't want your mother changing that."

"I understand."

Mason squinted at the woman with the amber-colored hair. "There's something else, Ms. Stanley."

"Bliss."

He swallowed. "There is one more thing, Bliss. Seeing him, saying what she needs—you sure that's good for your mother? I mean, have you thought about what it does . . ." He looked around, groping for what to say. "I've read their letters—procedure."

"Procedure." Bliss's voice was matter-of-fact.

"Victims writing . . . like I said, there's procedures."

"I realize that."

"And it's quite clear they've become close. So you got to wonder if seeing him won't make all this that much more difficult. I mean, in the end she's just losing someone all over again."

"You mean can my mother face another murder?"

Mason bit his lip. He hadn't meant that. He hadn't meant that at all. *Murder?* It was called capital punishment, emphasis on the *punishment.* Robbin's the one who had got himself into this mess. What the state had to do, what *he* had to do, was not murder. The death penalty was in the state constitution. Voters put it there. Who the hell was she to call it something it wasn't? A Texas prosecutor—she'd probably put more men to death than he had sitting in his entire unit.

Bliss looked down at her hands. "I'm sorry. That wasn't fair. You're right, it will be hard. But I guess my mom has learned to deal with hard."

They were silent, and they were both afraid. Mason could feel it. She in her world, he in his. They were facing things they didn't want to face, and they were doing it without anyone there to help. "I've never done this, you know."

She looked up.

"Run an execution. Worked it in other states, but I've never been in the driver's seat."

"And?"

"And I can tell you, I don't want to do it again."

Their gazes locked for a long moment, creating a kind of dark, uncertain haze. Then Bliss reached out and put her hand on his. Soft on hard. Woman on man. White on his own startling white hand. "I feel the same way, superintendent. I feel the same god-damned way."

CHAPTER 45

October 19, 2004

MASON WENT HOME AND DOWNED four antacids with a glass of Scotch. Nothing—not getting the execution chamber ready or taking the field trip to San Quentin, not meeting with doctors and hearing about injections and monitors and straps, not dealing with the press, not even giving Robbin the warrant—bothered him as much as Bliss Stanley's asking that her mother be allowed to meet with Daniel Robbin.

A prosecutor seeking mercy: it seemed such a compellingly courageous thing. And her mother, driving across the country like that, risking everything for the man who had killed her son. Mason felt obliged to help. More than that, it almost felt fated. Like it was part of the ongoing price he had to pay for the shit in his own life. He could just about see his mother looking down on him, telling him, "See, now I told you people can forgive." It was a stupid thought, and he had told himself that as he sat in his boss's office trying to convince him, the AG, and the governor's legal counsel to let Mrs. Stanley see Robbin. It wouldn't take much, he said. And he could probably get her to agree not to talk to the press. The daughter seemed reasonable. Smart . . . *stirring.*

But those bastards said no. There was no way in hell Irene Stanley would be allowed anywhere near the prison until the night of the execution.

Mason poured himself another Scotch and turned up the volume on his stereo. The Who was on. "Baba O'Riley." It started with Townshend's synthesizer looping an odd syncopated rhythm, which built in intensity as organs, drums, and finally Roger Daltrey's voice joined in.

Mason belted out the words, pounding the kitchen counter with the full force of Keith Moon's drumming, pushing away any thought of those two women.

> *I don't need to fight*
> *To prove I'm right.*

This wasn't his problem. None of it his. Not Daniel, not Mrs. Stanley, not her daughter. But they wouldn't let go. And neither would the feeling that came along with them. A creeping sensation that everything he had worked for—his job and prestige, his home and cat and furniture, even the fruit he had sitting neatly in a wide copper bowl—was all suddenly about to disappear.

The song ended and he braced himself against the counter, his chest rising and falling beneath his starched white shirt. A minute later he poured himself another drink, downed it while he went to his room, put on a pair of black sweatpants and shirt and a black stocking cap. He had to get outside. Move. Run. Get as far away from himself as he could.

Orange light from the streetlamps reflected in puddles all along the sidewalks and streets. Mason locked his front door and took off

at a good clip, crossing the street into Bush Park and running along
the bark-chip paths, soggy now and smelling like pulp. He crossed
Mission Street and walked through the university campus. It wasn't
that late, but the cold and wet were keeping people inside. He ran
on, past the capitol with its bowling-trophy-shaped dome, through
the commons, then west toward the river, along Front Street with
its warehouses. Mason ran on the empty road, zigzagging across the
freight tracks that meandered down its middle. At Market Street a
car rounded a corner, taking it fast, and Mason, suddenly faced with
the lights of the oncoming vehicle, jumped to the side of the road,
landing in a pile of pallets. The car pulled over and a middle-aged
guy got out, ran over, reached out a hand. But Mason didn't want
help.

"What the fuck is wrong with you, man?" he shouted.

"I'm sorry." The guy took a step back. He was dressed in a suit,
had neatly combed hair and a small belly jutting out above his belt.

Mason seethed. "Sorry? You fuckin' almost ran me over. Didn't
you see me?"

"No. No, I didn't. I mean, it's so dark, and with the way you're
dressed, all in black . . . I'm sorry. Really." The man's hands were
out, working the air with all kinds of apologetic gestures.

Mason took a step forward. "Dressed in black and *am* black.
I'll just bet you didn't see me." He grabbed the man by the sleeve of
his jacket, amazed and frightened by the surge of energy that ran
through him. He wanted to beat this simpering weak-kneed excuse
for a man. Lay him absolutely flat. It'd been so long since he'd tasted
the kind of exhilaration that came from hitting someone. It never
mattered who. Just as long as it was clear that *he* was the one to be
afraid of.

Mason shook him again, then noticed that it wasn't fear on the
man's face anymore, but confusion. Gripping the man's dark suit
jacket was Mason's stark white hand.

"What, you've never seen this before?" He let go of the man and held his hand up in front of the guy's frightened face. He could easily have curled up his fingers and squashed the man's entire head. Mason shoved the guy away, then dropped to the pallets in a sit.

"I'm sorry," the man said, then quickly ran to his car. His tires squealed on the wet pavement as he pulled away.

Mason buried his face in his hands, trying to stop himself from shaking. He had been that close, *that damn close,* to creaming the guy. A stranger. A weak, pathetic little businessman who suddenly found himself up against someone he had no idea how to handle. A madman, for all he knew. A predator.

Just like Tulane.

Over the years Mason had survived all kinds of attacks from his brother, but after the lake incident, things got worse—much, much worse—and Mason took to staying in homeroom, cleaning out beakers, sweeping, beating erasers out the window, whatever he could to avoid one more opportunity for Tulane to get him cornered while their mother was at work.

That's when he noticed the thing about the fish.

The tank, a hand-me-down from some restaurant, occupied a good section of the back wall of Mr. Acres's homeroom. Mason's eighth-grade teacher had filled it with things he'd gotten out of Jackson Harbor: twelve or so bluegills, a few perch, a crappie or two, and one big largemouth bass—*Micropterus salmoides.* It was colossal compared to the others, and when it swam past, Mason could see clear down into its chest. It seemed to him, at fifteen years old, and still unclear about the complex structure of even the simplest life forms, that the fish was hollow, moving without thought or motivation from one slimy end of the tank to the other. Empty of whatever it was that made life, life—until it came to killing. Then, and only then, the fish became an animated and sadistic monster. Once a week or so, it would get bored with the brine shrimp the kids put in the tank, and it would set its sights on a fish. Just one single small fish.

Mason never could figure out how the bass picked its victim, but once it did, the choice never altered. Slowly, patiently, it would stalk its quarry, nudging it slightly when it got in close, pushing it into the glass wall, grabbing a piece of its tail or a fin, tearing it down, bit by bit, until finally it cornered the doomed fish and swallowed it whole. The hunt over, the exhausted prey would simply lie in its predator's gigantic maw, its tail flapping against the bass's mouth like a white flag waving in a slender evening breeze.

Mason looked up to see a police car pulling to a stop. He stood. Brushed himself off. A guy got out, looking a little scared. But when Mason took off his hat, the man recognized him.

"We got a report of some trouble. A realtor in town said someone out here threatened him."

"That so?"

"You didn't see anything, did you, Mr. Mason?"

"Just some fast driving, that's all. Nothing anyone got hurt over."

"That's what I thought. You need a lift?"

Mason glanced at his watch. Eleven o'clock. "No," he said. "I'm fine."

The cop left and Mason started for home, his brother following right behind. He'd never get rid of him, Mason thought. His hand went to his neck and touched the scar that ran right over his jugular like the tracks cutting across the road. *Never in a million years.*

MASON WOKE THE NEXT MORNING with a headache. He pulled himself from bed, made a cup of coffee, and sat in his nook watching big fat drops of rain gather, then plunk off the leatherlike leaves of a magnolia tree. It had been spring when he had first seen the house on High Street, and that tree and about a dozen rhododendrons had all been in full bloom. Gigantic white, purple, and pink bundles of bell-shaped flowers stood upright from graceful branches. He decided to buy the place right then, not because he'd fallen in

love with it, but because he knew his mom would have. She had always promised that one day they would have a yard, someplace they
could sit and just be. And she said when they got one, she'd plant a
magnolia. Coming from the South, she talked about the trees as if
they were something magical, with flowers as big and creamy as a
bowl of fresh butter. She'd stretch out her hands, then close them
around her sons, laughing about trees she'd never live to see again.

Mason rubbed his eyes and wiped his nose on the sleeve of his
robe. Watched the rain.

At seven-thirty, Mason called Bliss. He asked if he had wakened
her, and she told him no, she'd already been for a run.

"My mom got in last night," she said.

"I imagine you two had a lot to talk about."

"Not really. We were both pretty tired."

"She still set on seeing Robbin?" He could hear movement, then
a door closing.

"She's counting on it, superintendent." Her voice seemed strained.

"Tab."

"Tab. Tab Mason." She paused. "I like the sound of that. Clear,
to the point."

"I like to think so."

"So tell me, Tab Mason, what have you and yours decided about
letting my mother in?"

He looked across the room to a small statue of three people
holding hands in a circle. It had been a Father's Day gift, back when
he, Shauna, and Latiesha were a circle, not a bunch of individual
arcs floating around with nothing to grab hold of. "I haven't yet
talked with Robbin, but I'm thinking if he says yes, we'll have to do
this quick. Tomorrow at the latest."

"Really?" She sounded skeptical. "Okay . . . So you'll call me?
Let me know what he says."

Mason's stomach cramped. "Yeah. I mean, no." He bit his lip. "I
want you and your mom at my office at one o'clock today. I'll have

talked to Robbin by then. If he says yes, then I've got questions, things I need to know *won't* happen. Do you understand what I'm saying?"

There was a pause, and she said she understood. "And if he doesn't want to see my mom?"

"Then I guess I'll explain his reasons." Mason eyed his surroundings. It was a nice, clean place. Solid furniture. A yard. He'd done okay for himself.

"That's kind of you, Tab. Going to all this trouble. Very kind."

His kindness, Mason thought, was going to get him fired. He hung up and clutched his gut. All night he'd tossed and turned. There was his brother sitting in a cell, his mother as shattered as glass. There was Robbin telling him to breathe, Stowenheim with his weasel-like grin, and the governor's counsel explaining to him how Mrs. Stanley's request just "wasn't part of the process." And now an unknown woman was working into him, making him feel there was more to getting on with life than just forgetting, and there was her daughter, Barbara Lee Stanley. Bliss.

Mason went to the bathroom, undressed, turned on the faucet, and stepped into the shower, forcing himself to take it while the water slowly warmed. Bliss Stanley. He could see her, but more than that there was the feel—the intensity, the determination, the rock-hard pieces of amber hidden in her eyes. The courage. His hand went down and rubbed slowly, then with more intensity. He felt shame, wanted relief. Yesterday, her hand on his—it had scared the hell out of him. It had made him want to cry; it had nailed him as he hadn't been nailed in what seemed like forever.

CHAPTER 46

October 20, 2004

IRENE AND BLISS LEFT THE Lamplighter Motel and walked east through a fine, cool mist. They were a few blocks from the prison, and the neighborhood looked it: law offices, pawnshops, army-navy surplus stores, all lined a busy four-lane street. Cars sloshed over the damp pavement.

At a stoplight Irene pointed to a billboard. "What the heck's that supposed to mean?" Bliss grimaced. The sign showed the glowing coils of a hot electric burner. Underneath it read, "Stoves Should Only Be Used for Cooking."

"Child abuse, Mom. It means don't put your kid's hands on a burner."

Irene pulled her coat tighter. "Lord in heaven, don't tell me that."

Bliss wore black jeans, boots, a black turtleneck, and a full-length trenchcoat. She tapped the sidewalk with the tip of her unopened umbrella as if demanding that the light change. When it did, she stepped into the street without looking.

Irene followed behind, feeling out of place in her barn coat, sweatpants, and Keds and feeling worried about her girl. The things she knew about, the people she dealt with—it had to take a toll. Thirty-two years old. No marriage. No serious relationship she ever talked about. In Bliss's world, a red-hot burner on a poster was a warning. Irene had thought it was just an ad for a stove.

"The state mental hospital's out that way a few blocks." Bliss pointed down a street. "You know, the one they used in *One Flew Over the Cuckoo's Nest,* with . . . what's his name?"

Irene could picture the movie and the actor. A famous guy, in lots of things, kind of crazy. The two women walked, each one biting the inside of her left cheek while they tried to remember.

"Jeez." Bliss kicked a stick. "I hate it when I can't remember things like that."

"Get used to it." Irene laughed.

"Anyway," Bliss said, "they filmed the movie right down there. Remember, with Nurse Ratched? God, she was a bitch. See, I can remember *her* name."

A few blocks farther Bliss pointed to where a wrought iron gate opened to a stately tree-lined drive. At the far end stood a large ocher building. "There it is."

"The prison? It looks like a university!"

"That's the administration building. The prison's behind it. The main one, anyway." Bliss glanced at her watch. "Look, we're early. I noticed a park when I went for my run. It's just a bit farther."

They continued along State Street, following a small creek that ran between the sidewalk and the prison wall. Locust trees arched overhead, their tiny chartreuse leaves dotting the ground like fine yellow feathers. It surprised Irene just how lush the landscape was west of the mountains. Trees were everywhere, and the grass was a bright, pungent green.

"You know we lost the maple out by the barn."

Bliss jumped a puddle. "Jeff told me."

"He ever tell you about carving your names in it?"

"Of course." She shook her head, smiling down at her boots as she walked. "I miss him sometimes, you know? Remember how he could always make us laugh, even when we felt like utter crap? He was a good person."

"Still is."

"You know he's back there taking care of Dad, don't you? Stayed with him the first few days after you left—him, Juanita, the kids, all of them right there in the house."

Irene kicked a leaf. She hadn't known, but it didn't surprise her. "You ever regret not sticking around and marrying him?"

Bliss stopped and turned. "Are you kidding me?"

Irene wasn't.

Bliss looped her arm with her mother's. "Don't you know the best thing you ever did was to get me to go to college? Me and Jeff, that wouldn't have worked. Not for the long term. I swear, it's like you gave me wings, Mom. Honestly."

Irene bit her lip and took a deep breath. "It's kind of pretty around here," she said. "Nothing like Blaine."

"Blaine," Bliss said, as if just hearing its name hurt.

As they walked on, the stretch of grass between the sidewalk and the creek widened, and on it were ducks—mallards, white domestics—and some Canada geese. Heaps of green droppings lay all over the sidewalk. Irene and Bliss slowed their pace. Thirty feet farther, they stood in a parking lot overlooking the creek, the birds, and the prison. The birds approached, quacking and honking.

"I don't think they want us here." Bliss backed up.

"They want food." Irene stepped toward them, arms outstretched. "Get out of here, go on. Get."

The birds made rowdy, feather-flapping complaints but then turned away from Irene and Bliss as two minivans pulled into the parking lot. Mothers popped out, unleashed children from their car seats, and handed them pieces of white bread, and off the kids ran across the excrement-strewn lot, throwing rolled-up scraps of dough at the birds, laughing, then shrieking when the birds got too close.

Irene was dumbfounded. "Is this the park you were talking about?"

"Um-hmm."

"Across from that?" Irene pointed to a gun tower perched on a tall concrete wall.

"You know how it is, Mom. People get used to what they have. Folks around here probably don't think twice about what's behind that wall. That is, unless they have someone inside."

Irene nodded, transfixed by the sight of children feeding birds just a stone's throw from a prison.

"I expect it'll be quite a bit different around here in a few days." Bliss poked a leaf with her umbrella.

"What do you mean?"

"Oh, security issues—there'll probably be a lot of cops around. The road might even be closed. Executions tend to draw a crowd."

"A crowd?"

"Protesters and whatnot."

"You mean people protest executions?"

"Sure. Abolitionists. They don't cause any problems. Usually just stand around with candles singing 'Kumbaya.' They don't believe in capital punishment."

"Abolitionists?"

"Yeah."

"Like the people who tried to free the slaves?"

"Yeah, like that. But now they want to free the murderers. Get them off death row, at least."

Irene nodded and mouthed the word to herself so as not to forget.

"But they're not the reason for the increased security. It's the ones who come half drunk and ready to celebrate. They think they're goddamn gladiators. It's sick."

"It's all sick," Irene said. She dug her hands deep into her pockets.

"Anyway, those mothers"—Bliss tucked her hair behind her ears—"they probably don't even see that wall. And the kids, they're too young to know the difference."

Irene turned from the group. "All I know is, I wouldn't be bringing a child here."

The mist thickened, so Bliss opened her umbrella and held it over them both as they walked back toward the prison entrance.

Irene watched the traffic. "What am I gonna do if Daniel won't let me see him?"

"I've been wondering what you're planning to do if he *does*. You know, they don't want you upsetting him. Mr. Mason says Daniel's ready to die. Is settled with it."

Irene stopped. "I don't believe that."

"I do. Think about it. What else does Robbin have? You're not going to get him out of prison. At best, he gets a retrial and is sentenced to life. You think that's what he wants—living with a bunch of half-crazy men all looking to do something ugly to one another? You're right. Those women back there, if they knew a *fraction* of what goes on behind those walls, they'd never come near this place. It's bad, real bad. And if you're thinking what I think you are, all you'd be doing is setting Robbin up for more pain. That's how I see it, anyway. Daniel Robbin is not going to get a reprieve, no matter what you do."

"But if people knew he didn't mean it, that it was all a mistake . . ."

"He had a gun. He was in our house. You get another trial, and all people will hear are two things: Robbin was in our house messing with Shep, and he tried to kill a deputy, a father, a father trying to protect his son."

"But Bliss—"

"Look, Mom, this is what I do for a living, okay? Right after Dad called, what do you think I did?"

Irene shook her head.

"I was on the phone with every defense attorney I know. And I can tell you they all agreed that even with what we know, Daniel Robbin will not ever leave this prison. You can try to fight it, drag Dad into it if you want, but it won't change a thing."

"It could save his life."

"There's a difference between saving his life and giving him a life."

A bus slowed to a stop and a woman and a little girl got out. The woman zipped the child's jacket and pulled up her hood, and then the two started toward the prison.

"So what do I say, Bliss? If he lets me see him, what do I say then?"

A gust of wind came up, and Bliss faced into it, hair whipping behind her. "You say goodbye, Mom. You say goodbye."

CHAPTER 47

October 20, 2004

MASON SLID A PIECE OF green paper across a dull gunmetal-gray table set in the middle of a small windowless room. Robbin sat across from him, hands cuffed, hair disheveled.

"I need to know what you want to do."

Robbin leaned forward, read, snorted out a laugh. "A will? You got to be kidding me. What the hell do I have that anyone would want?"

"There's the stuff in your cell, your drawings, plus whatever you came in with. Who knows, maybe you've got a fortune sitting in some vault you haven't told us about."

"Jesus." Robbin laughed.

"What's so funny?"

"You. This." He glanced back down at the paper. "Everything."

"I don't see anything funny."

Robbin sighed as if he were trying to teach a child something basic. "Kill me, but make sure what's left has a home? That don't strike you?"

Mason gnawed on the inside of his cheek.

"Okay, then you tell me." Robbin leaned back in his chair. "What *do* people do?"

"Typically, family takes everything. If they want it. Some don't."

"And if they don't?"

Mason put his hands between his knees. "If they don't, we store the remains, toss everything else."

"The *remains*?"

"Yeah, well, your ashes. I mean, if there's no family, that's typically what happens. Even inmates who die while incarcerated, if they have no family, they get cremated. Afterwards we store their ashes in the basement over in the main building."

Robbin looked shocked. "You mean some suckers *never* leave this place?"

This time Mason laughed. "Guess you could look at it that way."

"No way else to look at it." Robbin shoved the green sheet of paper back at the superintendent.

Mason looked at it, then at Robbin. He had the distinct sense he was on the edge of something—a ledge of a building, a cliff, toes sticking out, tie blowing in the breeze. "I have some news."

Robbin looked up.

"Irene Stanley's in town. Drove in yesterday. She wants to see you."

Robbin didn't move or blink.

"She's coming to my office at one. Her and her daughter both. If you want to see them, I can arrange that."

"They're here?" Robbin's words came out as if he were asleep.

"The daughter flew in from Texas yesterday morning. Mrs. Stanley drove from Illinois."

Robbin's forehead crumpled with worry. "She drove here? But why bother? I mean, they can't get in. It's against the rules."

"What?"

"The rules. I've read them. Mrs. Stanley can't come in here. Neither can her daughter. Not to see me, at least."

"There are exceptions, but it's your call."

"My call?"

The room was small and square as a box, with no window, no art, just the desk, two chairs, Mason and Robbin. "I was against the idea at first, still don't know whether it's a good one. I don't want her upsetting you."

"Upsetting?"

"I just don't want her making this whole thing more difficult."

"And you think she'd do that?"

"She may. And seeing you could make it harder for her too. That's a whole other thing to consider."

"So why the hell didn't you say no?"

Mason swallowed, and Robbin began to shake his head. "It's shower day today, you know. Hot water, shampoo. Can't miss that."

"You'll get your shower. But if we do this, it's got to happen right away. Five days from now, you'll be moved to the holding cell. No visits from anyone except the chaplain."

"Oh, that'll be a help."

"Don't write it off. He's a good man to have beside you when the time comes."

"Who's that, God or the chaplain?"

"Either one wouldn't hurt."

"Either one won't have a thing to do with people like me, General. Anyway, my cell's fine. I don't need to be moved anywhere. I won't cause a stir."

"Got to. Besides, it's a good place. Quiet, clean. You'll have your own shower, can use it as much as you want."

"Sounds like a resort."

"I'm just saying . . ."

"I know what you're saying. You just need to put me someplace you can make sure I won't kill myself, isn't that right? Holding cell, hell. I know what goes on in there. Every piss I take, your men will be keeping tabs on. Am I right?"

"That's the procedure."

"Procedure. So then answer my question, will you? Why did you tell Mrs. Stanley she could see me? You know as well as I that it's against your damn procedures."

Mason was caught. He'd spent the whole night asking himself the same question, and nothing came, except a solitary sense that he was in the presence of something larger than himself, and that he had no choice but to let that thing in. "I guess I admire what you and Mrs. Stanley have been able to do, and, well . . . she's come all this way." He paused, and because Robbin didn't respond he asked again. "So, what d'ya think? Can I tell her you'll see her?"

Robbin's temples held a network of veins trailing like hairs to his scalp. His arms were the same, pale blue lines underneath pale white skin. "What's the weather like?" he asked.

"Excuse me?"

"The weather, what's it doing? Cold, warm, rain, sun?"

"Cold and rainy, I guess. Not sure I noticed."

"You should."

"Should what?"

"Notice. I mean it. Don't take it for granted. You never know, you could be dead tomorrow. You just don't know."

Mason adjusted his long legs. From any other man he'd take Robbin's comment as a threat. "Yeah, okay. Look, what do you think? Do you want to see her? If so, it could happen by this afternoon."

Robbin's foot tapped the floor, faster and faster. Then it stopped. "Tell her no."

"No?"

"Nineteen years, cell the size of a john, the thought of seeing someone from the outside . . ." He shook his body as if someone had dunked him in water. "It don't come easy."

"I see."

Robbin began a slow rocking in his seat, back and forth. Lips working in and out.

"You okay?" Mason asked.

"Yeah. I mean . . ."

Mason waited.

"It's just that—shit. I wish she hadn't gone and done this, you know? I never said so, never asked, not once. Thought that her being all the way out there in Illinois, it'd never be an issue."

"Well, it is."

"Yeah." He shook his head.

"I tried to talk her out of it when she first called with the idea. Told her it would only make things harder for her, you know, in the end."

"And?"

"And the next thing I know her daughter's in my office telling me I got to let her mom see you."

"So tell her you can't. I mean, this shouldn't even be an issue. She can't see me. She just can't." Robbin kicked the leg of the table, and the heavy metal scraped across the floor a few inches.

"Calm down. No one's forcing you to see her. She knew it was a long shot."

"No. See, that's just it." He tapped the table with his cuffed hands. "She doesn't know anything. And I mean *nothing*. If she did, she wouldn't be here asking to see me. Couldn't be here. If she knew anything at all, she'd never have written me to begin with. You understand what I'm saying?"

"Not a clue, but if you don't want to see her, fine."

"It's not fine! Coming all this way—shit." He yanked his head to the side as if he were trying to work out some kink. "What about her husband? Where's he?"

"Illinois, I guess. They had words when he found out you two'd been writing to each other, then she took off for here. But he's come around. Signed the forms for her to be able to see you."

"He did *what*?"

"Signed some forms. Look, I don't know anything about what's going on in that family, I only know she's come an awful long way. But if you don't want to see her, I'll tell her."

Robbin took a staggered breath.

"Robbin, look, let's just drop it. I'll take care of Mrs. Stanley and her daughter. You just take care of yourself, okay?" Mason waited for Robbin to nod, smile, anything.

"You know that picture I drew?" he finally whispered. "The one of a kid? You once asked about it, remember?"

Mason nodded. "Yeah. What about it?"

"Well, it's him. Shep Stanley. Steven, really, but I always called him Shep. You know we had the same middle name? Joseph. I like that name—Joseph. Not Joe or Joey, but Joseph."

Mason swallowed. This was just what he'd been afraid of—Robbin getting unhinged. He'd seen men lose all sense of reality as their day came close. One guy was so out of it he had no idea he was being strapped in the goddamn chair.

"He's standing on Sumpter's Ridge," Robbin said to the ceiling. "It's on the res. Beautiful place, just a sea of trees all the way to Mount Jefferson. Not a single road or clear-cut in sight. Course, you can't see that in the drawing, but I can, in my mind."

"Robbin—"

"He liked to play his horn out there. Standing right on this flat stretch of basalt. It was something hearing him play in that place. Really something."

"Come on, quit it."

"It's hard not hearing music. If I had the money, I'd get me some tapes and a player. Some headphones, even. You ever hear of Aaron Copland? Shep liked Aaron Copland."

Mason slapped his hand on the table. "Fuck this, man. You didn't know Steven Stanley. Come on, get a grip."

Robbin wiped his eyes and slowly looked at Mason. "I knew him, General. I knew him real well. And that's only the beginning of the things I don't want Mrs. Stanley ever knowing."

OUTSIDE, MASON BLEW OUT THE shit smell of the prison. "The fucker," he said, gravel grinding under his shoe. "The goddamn motherfucker. Molesting the kid, that's what this is all about. He's nothing but a predator. Sonofabitch."

He jerked the Explorer's door open, then stood in the cold, staring at the building he had just left.

It was after school and Mason had been in Mr. Acres's room, wiping down the sides of the tank, when Tulane had come in. He was high; Mason could see it in the way his eyes couldn't stick on anything. *Like disco lights.* He bumped into a bookcase; a globe dropped and rolled across the floor; he kicked a chair. Then he caught sight of Mason and leered.

"There's my little bro."

Mason knew what Tulane wanted and decided right then it wasn't going to happen—not in this place, not now, not ever again if he could help it. He reached under the tank for his little science experiment: instant coffee mixed with water. He'd stirred it into a thick paste, poured it into a mold, let it harden. After it dried he'd spent afternoons honing it into a smooth, sharp sliver of blade. Black and hard as metal. He palmed it and kept wiping the tank.

Tulane stumbled around the room, picking up books, opening them, tossing them down. Some landed on desks; some missed and dropped to the beat-up wood floor.

"Mr. Acres is in the building," Mason stuttered. "He catch you in here, he won't like it."

Tulane lifted his head as if the news had caught his attention.

"No shit?" He turned heavily toward the door, and Mason let out a sigh. But then his brother shut the door and turned off the lights.

Streetlight drizzled though the room's ivy-covered windows. Mr. Acres always laughed about the vines, saying that those windows were the closest he'd ever get to teaching in an Ivy League school.

Tulane took a step toward his brother. There was a way to escape. Let him work his way across the rows, then push a desk into him and take off. But Mason didn't want to run. Not this time.

A line gets crossed, beating after beating, being torn up and down, every day huddled in fear like that damn little fish.

No more.

Mason fingered his blade. He would strike fast and he would strike deep, moving with deliberateness and sureness. He'd be the bass. This time, he'd be the fuckin' bass.

Tulane stepped closer; light cut across his hips and legs. His hand was on his crotch. "Come on, baby bro, I'll even help you out a little bit."

Mason winced, remembering his brother's hand coming around, and him not wanting it but doing it anyway, hot and horny and wanting nothing more than to crawl up inside himself and die.

Another step. A siren. A yell. Mason glanced out the window. Then, just as he looked back, his brother was there. A blow struck Mason's gut and he doubled over, struggling to breathe. Then Tulane was behind him, grabbing him at the waist. Mason turned, fast, furious, blade outstretched like a sword, swiping the air where Tulane should have been—but wasn't.

Tulane grabbed his arm. "What the fuck is that?" He wrenched and twisted Mason's hand, making the thing drop, then he let go of Mason and examined the shell-shaped object. "Where'd you get this?"

Mason didn't answer.

Tulane touched his finger to its point, pushed. "Whoa," he said, putting his finger in his mouth. "You shouldn't be playing with things like this, Tabby Cat. Someone could get hurt."

Mason knew he was in trouble. Big trouble. Bigger-than-he'd-ever-been-in kind of trouble. Frozen lakes, rats, being butt-fucked in the middle of the night, they were nothing. He took a step back and watched his brother like those fish watched that bass. Another step. Another. He felt the cool glass of the tank against his back.

"Don't be scared, little bro. Your big brother here, he just needs a little attention. This thing here"—he tossed the blade in the air and caught it—"it's just between you and me. You be a good boy and no one will ever know anything about it."

He pocketed the piece, then came up on Mason, shot him another blow to the gut, and kicked him in the balls. Mason dropped, and Tulane laughed. "You stupid motherfucker. You ass-lickin' stupid motherfucker." Mason felt himself being lifted by the back of his shirt. This was not going to happen. Not again. He turned, swung, missed, and fell once more.

More laughter, grotesque and gruesome, like the laughter of a madman in some lunatic film. Mason reached for something: a book, he threw it; a beaker, it splintered at Tulane's feet. A pencil, there on the desk. He was almost there, crawling, reaching. But Tulane pulled him back to his feet, yanking his arm behind him, his breath at his neck, hot and thick.

Then Mason heard his own voice, pleading, begging. He was weeping like a child, the weak, wretched child they both knew he was. Crying and blubbering, mucus pouring out of his nose, him sucking it in as his brother bent him over Mr. Acres's desk and did what he'd promised. And then, just as it ended, Mason felt the blade at his neck.

He tried to scream, but nothing came. He tried to breathe but only sucked blood. He grasped his neck and fell, his pants still draped around his knees.

MASON TOOK A DEEP BREATH of Salem's cold ocean-scented air. A storm was coming; he could smell it, and he had the sudden urge to take the prison's SUV out to the coast. The Pacific was an hour's drive west through densely forested mountains dripping with pine-scented rain. Four or five times a year Mason would rent an old cabin overlooking a rocky stretch of beach. The place was small, smelled of mildew, and was heated by a tiny wood stove. But for Mason it was a refuge. He knew to take razors to scrape the stove window so he could watch its fire; he knew the coffeepot didn't work, so he took his own; and he knew that the old Barcalounger on the left side of the lighthouse lamp offered the best view of the ocean and the storms he'd come to watch.

Summer was nice on the coast, a fine place to walk, but winter—it was something else altogether. He'd keep an eye on the weather, and when forecasters warned of high tides and gale-force winds, he'd get in his Jeep and go west.

The fierceness of the storms is what got to him, how the wind slashed at the trees and grass and any gull foolhardy enough to try to navigate it; how it kicked up pinnacles of water, stretched them out like taffy, then slammed them over and over onto the rough volcanic rock. He watched as logs the length of semis were picked up by waves and tossed into the air like toothpicks, and how the tide lifted the swelling ocean up and beyond former heights, breaking against trees, riprap, and pouring out into the roads. It was violent and dangerous and completely and totally gripping.

Mason grabbed the Explorer's steering wheel and squeezed. In front of him, the mist on the windshield had turned the IMU into a filmy Monet-like image. Mason closed his eyes. He wished he'd never heard of Daniel Robbin, or Irene Stanley, or her daughter. He wished he was sitting in that old cabin at the coast, having a cigar and a Scotch, and knew nothing about killing, or killers, or the forgiveness they demand. He wished he had a different kind of a life, built on something larger than what he had—a broken family, a broken-down kind of hate, or pain, or whatever it was he'd never been able to discard. He wished he could be more helpful and grateful and bigger and fuller than he was. He wished it would storm. Hard and heavy, the rain beating the earth itself into some new and more bearable form.

CHAPTER 48

October 20, 2004

IRENE STANLEY WAS A SMALL woman: small bones, small, finely carved face surrounded by a soft spill of nearly silver hair. She wore a canvas coat, sweatpants, and beat-up-looking gym shoes that gave a soggy squeak as she walked into the superintendent's office.

"Mrs. Stanley." Mason surrounded her hand with his. "Ms. Stanley. Both of you, please sit."

Bliss slipped off her coat, and her hair fell across her black sweater, unleashed and wild as fire.

"So, Mrs. Stanley, I hope your drive was uneventful."

"Little bit of delay in Wyoming, but that was it." She laid her coat on the back of her chair.

"I drove that route when I first came out here," he said, trying to find some way to ease into telling them about Robbin. "Florida to Chicago to Oregon. It took me a little over a week."

"Chicago's not exactly along the way."

"I was visiting family."

"Is that where you are from?" Irene asked.

"Yes."

"Bliss tells me it's a nice city. Remember how you used to go up there with your friends while you were in college?"

"Yes, Mom. It's a nice place. Big. Very big."

"Very big," Mason repeated.

Irene nodded, and they all fell silent until Mason took a breath and jumped in. "I met with Daniel Robbin this morning to talk about your request, Mrs. Stanley, and he told me to tell you how much your friendship has meant to him over the years. What a support it's been. But he says he'd rather not have you visit. I'm sorry, but he thinks it would be too hard."

The two women sat silently. Then Irene unfolded her hands and ran them down her thighs. "You're saying . . . a man facing his death would find it too hard to see *me*?" Her eye twitched. "I'm sorry, Mr. Superintendent, but that doesn't make sense."

Mason nodded. "In this kind of situation, it's hard to say what makes sense and what doesn't. What might seem like nothing to you could be almost impossible for someone inside."

Her face tightened. "I didn't say I was asking for nothing."

"I understand, but—"

"No, no buts, Mr. Mason. I didn't travel halfway across this country to hear buts. Daniel has got to see me. I don't care how hard it might be for him. There are things we need to talk about." She glanced at her daughter, then back at Mason. "That man didn't—"

Bliss grabbed her mother's arm. "What she's saying is, she wants to say goodbye. Isn't that right, Mother?"

Irene Stanley glared at her daughter.

"I'm sorry," Mason said. "But Robbin was quite clear. You've got to understand, he's under a lot of stress. Look, if you want to write a letter, I'm happy to make sure he gets it." He forced himself to smile. Wanting her to accept what he said without questioning it. He had always known this was a bad road—a victim opening herself up like this. She didn't need to know what Robbin was claiming. Whether it was true or not, she just didn't need it.

Irene leaned toward him. "Mr. Mason, do I look like a fool? I need to see Daniel, and I don't give a damn how *stressful* it might be for him."

Bliss uncrossed her legs. "Mom, Mr. Mason doesn't have time for this. He's been willing to let you in, probably bent the rules to do so, but Mr. Robbin doesn't want to see you. You can understand that, can't you? Facing what he is, he just wants to be left alone."

Irene pivoted like a knife flicked from its case. "Stop it, Bliss. For God's sake, you're just gonna accept this? You know as well as I do that that man shouldn't be on death row."

"Mom!"

"You're trying to protect your pa. Good for you, but you can't have it both ways—help me and help him too. We're on opposite ends of this whole thing, and I'm not going to keep my mouth shut if it means someone else dies."

Irene turned back to Mason. "You tell me what to do. Daniel didn't mean to kill Shep. I know it. He and Shep were friends. *Good* friends. It wasn't like they said in the trial. It wasn't like that at all."

Mason leaned his chair back and away from this woman.

"It was my husband who beat the living tar out of Shep that day. He caught Shep and Daniel together in our home. He says they were . . . lovers. He found them, a couple times I guess, and warned them each time. But that last time, Nate lost it. He just lost it. He wasn't like that normally. He's never done anything like that to the kids, me, nothing. But I guess the sight of his son . . . Well, he hit Shep. Then the next thing he knew Daniel had a gun."

Mason's chest felt heart-attack tight.

"Daniel Robbin was trying to protect my boy from my husband that day, Mr. Mason. Not kill him, *protect* him. But Shep got in the way. It was an accident, sir. Just an accident. Now you go and tell me if it's okay to execute someone like that, 'cause I sure as hell don't see it that way."

Mason looked from one woman to the other. Mrs. Stanley, her eyes on him. Bliss, her hand at her mouth. *Sonofabitch,* he thought. *Son of a bitch.* "When did you find this out?"

"Last week. Nate told me. He was upset when he learned Daniel and I had been writing. He told me then."

"And the DA, does he know anything about this?"

"No," Bliss said. "No, he doesn't. And we don't plan to tell him, do we, Mom?"

Mrs. Stanley didn't answer.

"Look, Mr. Mason," her daughter went on. "You know as well as I do that it wouldn't make any difference, a story like that, unless there's proof. But there isn't any. Nothing in the world will link my dad to that day."

"Are you saying your mother's making this up?"

She gritted her teeth. "I'm saying my dad would never tell you the same story."

Irene huffed out a breath and reached for her coat.

"Here's your proof." She slapped something on his desk.

"What are you talking about?" Bliss asked as her mother spread out a handful of pictures.

"Now tell me I don't have enough cause to talk to a lawyer. You need more? I've got the jewelry—my pearls, my ma's ring, all the things we thought Daniel had stolen. Your pa gave it all to me as I was leaving."

Bliss's head rocked back and forth. "Dad had these?"

"Yes."

"But he didn't mention . . ." Her voice trailed off.

"Look, Bliss, you've got to know it's not right to kill Daniel. Got to *feel* it, at least. The fact is, he shouldn't even be in jail."

Mason blew out a long impatient breath and looked out the window, where fat drops of rain splattered the stone sill. "Look, Mrs.

Stanley, if you don't think Robbin should be in this prison, you really should be talking to a lawyer." He turned back. "Not me."

Irene gathered the pictures, tapped them on the desk. "If Daniel wants me to go to a lawyer, I will. If he asks me to see the governor, I'll sit at his door until he lets me in. If Daniel Robbin wants to live another day, I'll find a way to make that happen. But first I need to see him."

She took a picture from the stack and slid it toward him. Daniel was sitting between her son's legs, leaning against his chest, his hand pointed toward the camera with what appeared to be a remote.

"You've got to understand, Mr. Mason, these two boys meant something to each other. I know it was wrong, and I know what they were was wrong, but it seems to me that the man in that cell of yours was the only one around who knew and cared for Shep for everything he was."

Mason pushed the picture back. "You know this could put your husband in jeopardy. You know that, right?"

She uncupped her hand as if letting go of a butterfly. "I know a man is in jail for defending someone he loved."

"No." Bliss was shaking her head. "Daniel Robbin's in jail for shooting Shep and leaving him to die. If he didn't mean to and instead wanted to kill Dad—a cop, a father trying to protect his son from a *molester*—that wouldn't have made things any easier for him." Her voice sounded frayed. "Robbin's had it, any way you put it, and I believe he knows that. Why else did he keep all this a secret? There was no reason for him to protect Dad, none at all. You can go and drag in an attorney, but anyone worth his salt will tell you what I've already said. The man doesn't stand a chance."

Irene Stanley put her hand on her daughter's knee. "I'm sorry, Bliss, but at this moment I'm not asking what an attorney would say."

Bliss's lips fluttered like a tiny bird's wings, then she pulled them in and looked away as Irene turned her gaze back to Mason.

CHAPTER 49

October 20, 2004

ROBBIN WANTED SILENCE. THE CLOSE feeling of nothing all around. No people, no sound, just a sense of space, like in the Ochocos. Thousands of square miles with nothing but juniper, pine, and abandoned mercury mines. You could stand on an outcrop and see as far as Mount Shasta to the south, Adams and Saint Helens to the north. Three states stretched out in front of you like wings on a plane.

He'd spent two weeks in those hills trying to figure out what the hell to do. Shep gone, and his own life now as empty as a shell. He followed cowpaths and creeks, stumbling around and broken. He remembered flowers—Indian paintbrush, lupine, things Shep would have noticed. Things that made Robbin bend to the ground and clutch his gut. And he remembered the nights, so still and silent. No cars, planes, birds, or even crickets. And so many stars—an infinite arc curving around the planet.

He had died the day that gun went off. Had felt it as clearly as if the bullet had gone into his own chest. Afterward, nothing mattered. So two and a half weeks later, he walked into that tavern knowing full well it was over.

Then came Mrs. Stanley . . .

"Robbin."

He heard his name, but he didn't move.

"Robbin, wake up."

The superintendent stood beside the bed, and next to him another black man. Equally as tall, but darker and heavier. Lewis, Duncan Lewis, his little finger wrapped with a Tweety Bird bandage.

"You're back," Robbin said, sitting up and rubbing his eyes.

Lewis jerked his thumb toward the door, and Robbin stood, reached out his hands. Once they were cuffed and his legs shackled, Mason and the guard walked him back to the interview room.

Robbin dropped into the metal chair, hands hanging between his legs.

"What happened that day?" Tab Mason asked as soon as Tweety was out of the room.

"What are you asking?"

Mason put one hand against the back of Robbin's chair, while the other, the white one, lay flat on the table. "That day the Stanley kid was killed, what happened?"

The chain of Robbin's shackle scraped along the floor as he stretched out his legs. "Oh, come on, can't a dying man get some peace around here?"

"I'm not fuckin' around, Robbin. Tell me."

"You've read the record."

"Bullshit on the record! I want to hear from you, right now. What the hell happened that day?"

"What difference does it make?"

"Fuck you, Robbin. Fuck you. You know, if you had told the

truth from the start, you wouldn't be here right now. You know that, don't you?"

Robbin tensed.

"Shit, man!" Mason shoved Robbin's chair. "Why the hell did you not tell anyone you were trying to protect that boy?"

"Where did you get that?"

"Where did I get that? From Irene Stanley, that's where. All your damn secrets. She knows everything. Okay? Every goddamn thing. You, Shep, her husband. She has pictures of you and the boy."

Pictures. He had taken pictures over to Shep's that day. Pictures of one of their afternoons on Crooked River. Such a great time. One of the best times of his life—until Nate Stanley showed up. Promised he'd kill Robbin if he ever saw him around his son again. And Shep scared out of his mind, begging his dad. *God, I hated that man.*

"Sonofabitch, Robbin. Is it true? You tried to save the kid? Is that right?"

Robbin felt hit in the head.

"I asked you a question!" The superintendent grabbed him by the collar and lifted him from the chair. "You stupid fuck. You think this is a game? We're set to kill you. Eight days, that's all you got, and you're sitting here trying to protect who?" He gave Daniel a good shake, then dropped him back into his chair.

Robbin wiped his mouth along his shoulder. He needed to think this out. Mrs. Stanley had never said anything about knowing. Not a thing. "How long has she known?" he asked.

"I don't know." Mason pulled the sleeves of his suit jacket. "A week, maybe? I really don't know."

"Damn."

"Yeah, damn." Mason went around the table and sat. "Why did you do this, Robbin?"

"What?"

"Lie. Why the hell have you been lying about all this? Not telling

the police, the lawyers, anyone? Why didn't you ever say anything
to defend yourself?"

Daniel stared at the fluorescent light. It gave off a buzzing sound
and flickered every once in a while. "It was a long time ago," he
said.

"So what?"

"Look, Mr. Mason, I didn't have a chance from the word go.
Think about it. What I was, what I *am*. You know I'm right, and you
know what? It doesn't matter. Didn't then and doesn't now. The second that gun went off, my life stopped. I should have killed myself
then, but I didn't have the balls."

"But you were trying to protect the boy!"

"No. Now see, that's where you're wrong. If I had wanted to protect him, I wouldn't have gone to his house. No, it wasn't Shep I was
thinking about that day, it was me. Just me."

"And when his dad walked in? What about that?"

"What about that, Mr. Mason? You don't think I hoped he'd
show up? Why you think I took that gun? I wanted to kill his damn
father and get the hell out of there—just me and Shep. Get away
from it all—Blaine, the state, who the hell knows what else. But don't
you ever think I was there to protect that boy. I knew better."

The two men looked at each other, then looked away.

"You were wrong, you know," Mason said.

"About what?"

"Mrs. Stanley. She doesn't hate you because of you and Shep. In
fact, she wants to help."

"Help?"

"Doesn't think you ought to die. Not now, not for this. In her
mind, you were protecting her son."

"She wasn't there."

Daniel had seen the fear in Shep's eyes when he'd showed up
at the house. But they were both so stupid. Him talking Shep into

just taking a look at the pictures, then watching a little TV, and then . . .

"She's something, I'll give you that. Doesn't look it, but strong. Real strong. She wants to get a lawyer, tell him what she knows. Says she'll go to the governor if it'll get you out of here."

Daniel clenched his cuffed hands. "When I got that letter from Mrs. Stanley, that first one, you know what I did?"

Mason shrugged.

"Cried. Cried like a baby. Couldn't look at it, couldn't even think about it without just breaking down. You ever done that? Forgiven someone even though they don't deserve it?"

The superintendent frowned, and Daniel wondered about the man and what he'd seen and done in life to make him who he was. There were his eyes, dark and deep; his posture, always so perfectly straight; and that scar poking out from his collar, a streak of cream against his coffee-colored skin.

"No," Mason said. "No, I've never done that."

"Well, I got to say, it fills you. Whether you want it to or not, that kind of thing, it just fills you. It's like pain and grace all tied up in one."

Mason nodded. "You know, you could fight this. You never know, something could change, and with Mrs. Stanley helping from the outside . . ."

"Maybe I could hang on? Go to more hearings, talk to more lawyers, live more days in my cage? No thanks, General. Don't get me wrong, I don't have anything against living, it's just that I got myself convinced I'd like what comes after a whole hell of a lot more."

"And what's that?"

"Rest. That's all, just rest. What Mrs. Stanley wants to do, it won't help, and it's not rest. I'm through, Mr. Mason. I'm sorry to do it to you, but you're gonna have to do your job next week, and you're gonna have to convince that woman it's what I want."

"Job?" Mason said. "You call this a job? It's an ordeal, Robbin. A goddamned nightmare of an ordeal, and you're not making it any easier." He shook his head. "No. You want to make Mrs. Stanley live with another death, you tell her. I'm not doing it." Mason rose, went to the door, banged it twice. "She'll be here tomorrow morning."

Duncan Lewis opened the door, Tweety Bird bright and yellow.

"And by the way, Robbin." Mason turned. "It's raining outside. Pouring. And the air? It smells like the ocean, like a big-ass storm right off the fuckin' ocean."

CHAPTER 50

October 21, 2004

T HE IMU IS OVER ON the north side of the grounds," the superintendent said, opening the passenger door for Irene. She looked at the SUV and stepped away.

"If you don't mind, I'd like to ride in back with Bliss."

He shut the door, and she climbed into the backseat, put on her seat belt, and grabbed hold of her daughter's hand, trying to decide whether she wanted to memorize all she saw—the parking lot, the gates, the razor wire coiled over the fence like claws—or shut her eyes. She wished she'd shut them during check-in.

The superintendent hadn't been able to meet them at Administration as he had said, and instead he had left word at the front desk to let Irene and Bliss through. But the guard on duty, a skinny man with fingerprint-smeared glasses, hadn't gotten the message, and questioned them both for at least ten minutes before letting them put their things in a locker and walk through the metal detector.

Then Bliss set off the thing, and he got her behind a curtain for more time than Irene thought necessary.

When Mason started driving, Irene leaned against her daughter and asked what she had on that had made the machine go off.

"Breasts," Bliss whispered. "Just breasts."

Irene shut her eyes.

When the vehicle stopped, Superintendent Mason turned around. "Ready?" he asked.

Irene's hands were shaking, and she noticed that nothing around her felt real. Not the upholstery, not Mason's worried look, not the white, two-story building, as hard and cold as a mortuary. Even her daughter's hand didn't quite feel like it was there in hers. She nodded and let herself out of the SUV, then she and Bliss followed the superintendent down a long steel-mesh tunnel. Above them, gigantic white clouds rode on a slow wind, lolling over the tops of each other like lambs playing. At the end of the tunnel, a buzzer sounded, then there was a loud *snap* and a large metal door clicked open.

Inside, a tall black guard greeted Mason as the three of them stepped into the building. Irene flinched when the door shut behind them. It felt so permanent. Like the punctuation at the end of a sentence. Mason pointed forward, indicating that she and Bliss should follow the other man, then the four of them went down a brightly lit, ammonia-scented hall. *Give me strength,* Irene thought, feeling the stagnant air close in on her. Halfway down the hall the guard stopped in front of a door. It buzzed, and he opened it and let in Irene, Bliss, and Mason. The guard left the three of them in an office with two chairs, a desk, and a glass window looking into a cell.

"Robbin will be moved in there in a few days," the superintendent said. "It's better than where he is now. Bigger. Quiet."

Irene nodded, imagining what it would be like sitting in that space. She shivered and turned. The superintendent walked to the other side of the small room and opened another door. Inside was a small rectangular room, lined left and right with windows. Dull white blinds hung down on the other side of both plates of glass, hiding whatever was on the other side. At the back of the room a metal chair sat facing one of the windows. In front of it was a ledge holding a black phone and a box of tissues.

"Robbin will be on the other side of this window." Mason tapped the glass. "You'll talk to him through the phone. Your daughter and I will be in the next room, but I got to tell you, nothing you say will be private. There'll be an officer with Robbin, and your conversation will be piped into that outer office where me and Bliss will be waiting." He looked at his watch. "Remember, you don't get more than ten minutes, but if you need it over quicker, you just say so."

"Okay," Irene said. "I'll remember." .

Bliss walked to her mother, hands out as if she were going to give her a hug. But instead she straightened Irene's collar, picked something from her coat. "If he wants to fight this," she said, "I'll help you. Dad and I both."

Irene bit her lip, unable to speak. Then Bliss and Mason left the room.

Irene stared at the door. Bliss had been on the phone with Nate for over an hour the previous night, pacing back and forth beneath the awning of the motel. She had come back looking like she'd been crying, but Irene didn't ask.

She turned from the door and walked around the small room. Gray walls, gray linoleum. A small vent up at the ceiling. The thick glass, the blinds, the metal ledge, the phone . . .

There was a sound on the other side of the glass, and the blinds shuddered and moved. Irene quickly went to the chair, took off her coat, and sat, her eyes fixed on her own reflection. Then, slowly, as the blinds rose, she came to see someone sitting on the other side of the glass.

She remembered his small build from the trial, and the eyes, bright and shining as beads. Everything else looked different, though. His hair was now thin and a little gray, and his face was not so much older as it was just worn down. She watched him reach his linked hands for the phone, tuck it between his shoulder and cheek. Then she picked up her own phone. But they didn't speak, not at first. Ten, twenty, thirty seconds went by, and all she could see were those eyes looking at her. Silence not a bother, but in itself a kind of word, and in it she knew. She knew.

"You don't want my help."

He looked down, and Irene thought he might be praying. "There's nothing I need, Mrs. Stanley."

"But . . ."

He mouthed the word *no*.

"There's a way out of here. You know that."

He smiled and shook his head as if she were a sad, sleepy child who didn't quite know where she was.

"But it was a mistake, Daniel. You never meant to kill Shep."

"You're right, Mrs. Stanley. It was a mistake. A terrible mistake. And I've regretted it ever since."

"And you shouldn't die for it."

"People die because of mistakes all the time. It doesn't matter."

"How can you say that? Of course it matters." Irene looked away from Daniel to the officer, standing with his arms crossed over his chest. She had told herself she would not cry in this place.

"Look, Mrs. Stanley—I want this to be over. I dream of it—going to sleep, not having to wake up in this place. Its sounds, its smell, never knowing if it's raining or the sun's shining. I can't do it anymore." He looked down. "Whatever you know about me and Shep, about that day, it doesn't change things. I killed your son. Nothing changes that."

"But you didn't mean to! That's got to count for something. If not to you, then to a judge or the governor. They've got to see, I'll make them see. And if that doesn't matter, then maybe just my telling them how I've forgiven you, how I don't think killing you will serve my son, not at all—they've got to listen to that."

"No."

"Why?"

He looked back up. "Because I'm ready."

Irene's heart pounded in her chest, harder and harder. "What's wrong with you? Don't you care that this isn't right? That you're gonna hurt more people? Me, all these people who work here. You think it's fair having to kill a man who should never have even seen a cell? Goddammit, Daniel, it wasn't you who did this, it was Nate."

"It's not that way."

"How can you say that? He beat you, beat you and then Shep. I know all about it. You were just trying to protect my little boy, that's all."

"It was all just mistakes. Just like you said, mistakes. I shouldn't have gone to your house that day. Shep told me not to, warned me over and over. But I couldn't help myself. It was me. I'm the one who hurt your son. None of it would have happened if it weren't for me. It was wrong, I was wrong, your husband, even Shep in his own way. All just people making mistakes. I've come to see that, Mrs. Stanley. You've helped me come to see that."

Irene swallowed, imagining Nate standing by the truck, a filament of fading light bending behind him.

"You wouldn't be in here if it weren't for my husband."

He smiled. "Neither would you."

He was infuriating. Coming all this way, going to all this trouble to see him, and he was trying to get her to see sense where there wasn't any? "It wasn't out of the goodness of his heart that Nate told me all this, you know. He found out about the letters, about you and me writing—that's what did it."

"So we all had secrets. That doesn't sound too unusual."

She pulled the phone from her ear, looked at it, then placed it back against the side of her head. "It's not the same. My letters and what happened that day, you can't compare it. Anyway, the only reason he said anything was to get me to hate you again. Thought if

I knew what you and Shep had been up to, I'd never again want to have anything to do with you. And it nearly worked. No, as far as I'm concerned, Nate killed his boy the day he gave up on him and decided not to tell me our son was a homosexual."

"But Shep didn't want you to know. He might have been afraid of his father, but hurting you, that scared him more."

Irene's head dropped to her hand, and she rubbed her temple. "Don't say that."

"I'm sorry, but you got to know that boy would have done just about anything for you. But he was afraid, you know? Thought if you knew anything about him and me, or what he was really like, you'd hate him."

She caught her breath. Held it. It was all too sad. Fear of loss causing more fear, more loss. "What am I supposed to do, Daniel? You tell me, what is it I'm supposed to do about all this?"

He opened his hands as wide as the handcuffs would allow, and she found herself staring at his palms. White as paste, the lines smooth and soft.

"Keep on doing what you've been doing, I guess."

"And what's that?"

"Just be there for people. That's all. Just like you've been there for me. Be there for others. And be there for yourself."

"Myself?"

"Most of all, yourself."

Irene's fingers went to her mouth as she searched her mind for some response, but the topography of the years that had brought her to that chair felt suddenly flat and totally without distinction. "That's it, then—that's all you've got for me?"

"It's all I can think of."

Daniel's eyes reminded her of stones shining under still water. "And there's nothing, absolutely nothing I can say or do to get you to fight for your freedom?"

"I *am* fighting for my freedom, Mrs. Stanley."

"You're fighting hard to die."

He nodded, then smiled, and she knew she'd lost.

"I have some things—some drawings, books and stuff. I'm wondering if you want them."

She thought of Shep's things. She'd finally got around to opening his boxes and cleaning up his room. It had been a hard day. A very hard day.

"I don't know, Daniel. I don't know about that."

"It's okay. They don't amount to much anyway."

She spotted the guard looking at his watch.

"That's the room, back there, in case you're wondering." Irene turned. "Witnesses come in where you are and blinds go up on the other window."

"That's where . . ." She turned back, unable to say the words.

"It's used for storage mostly, but it's probably cleaned out by now."

"And this room, where I'm sitting, this is where witnesses come?"

"That's the place."

Irene shivered. She had had no idea they were so near where Daniel would die. She thought it would be somewhere else. A long hall leading to a hidden chamber. Maybe a separate building. Certainly not a storage closet.

"That night, Daniel—what do I do? I mean, what is it you *want* me to do?"

He closed his eyes, and she could see his pulse working in the shallow dip of his neck. *He is just a man,* she thought. A man with skin and bones and a story that made her ache, and for the first time in what seemed a long time, she silently prayed. The tyrant she called God replaced by a thread of hope and mercy. Even love.

She heard a cough.

Daniel's hand was over the phone while he spoke with the guard. Then he was back, eyes bound to her own. "You saved me, Mrs. Stanley. I want you to know that. Your letters, they took me out of nothing and brought me back to life."

She pressed her arms close to her body. "Brought you back to life so you could let them kill you. That doesn't make sense to me. I'm sorry, but I just don't see it."

Daniel bit his lip. "Try to understand. There's nothing here for me. Even if I delay this or you're able to get me off the row, it wouldn't be a life I want. Believe me, I've thought it out. I know it's not fair, and I am sorry for that. Very, very sorry."

Irene looked away. Ten seconds . . . twenty . . . *She would not cry in this place. She would not cry.*

"Irene."

She looked up.

"G'bye."

The guard took the phone and set it on its cradle, then helped Daniel Robbin to his feet.

Irene stood and called out his name, needing him to turn and tell her, with a word or a nod, whether he wanted her there that night. But he didn't, and Irene wiped her eyes as she watched Robbin's shackled feet shuffle from the room.

CHAPTER 51

October 25, 2004

DICK GEFKE STOOD BESIDE HIS large arched office window, a stocky silhouette with a baseball in his hand. He tossed it up, caught it barehanded. Did it again. Then again.

"So," he said, without so much as glancing at Mason, "it looks like we've got ourselves a little situation." The ball thwacked the director's palm.

Mason had been called to his boss's office first thing that morning. No word on a reason. But he knew what it was about. And as Mason stood there, refusing to sit, he put on the face of a man who was patiently waiting to receive what was likely to be bad news.

"I mean, talking to those women, that was one thing. But taking them in to meet Robbin?" He turned. "What I want to know is what the hell you didn't understand about what I, the attorney general, and the governor's lawyer all said to you last week."

"I understood everything."

"Yet you decided the hell with it." He squeezed the ball, his veins and tendons bulging, then set it in a bowl filled with what looked to be cuff links.

Mason stared at the container and wondered what kind of man would collect cuff links.

"I don't like what you did, Tab. Not one bit. Goes against everything I thought you and I shared—an appreciation for rules, order, an understanding that in this business it's teamwork that makes the difference between getting things done right and fucking up altogether. I thought we agreed on that." The director eyed him. "Fortunately, this little incident's been . . . contained. If the press had gotten hold of it, there'd be a whole other level of crap we'd have to talk about. As is, this thing just stays right here, in the department. No need for anyone else to know."

Mason, waiting, slid his hands into his pockets.

"So here's what I'm gonna do. You'll continue on as superintendent of our dear old state penitentiary through December. After that, take a break. Go see family. Get yourself the fuck together. When you come back, you'll work in Pendleton. Jones just retired, so we can slip you right in. Same pay grade, same title. And better yet, no executions. I get the sense that'd be okay with you." He smiled. "Am I right?"

Mason sniffed loudly, like a dog sensing trouble. Pendleton lay four hours east of Portland, surrounded by wheat fields and filled with the state's worst sex offenders. "Why wait? I could start now," he said.

"That's right, you could. But you know what I figure? Why rush it? Let's get through the holidays, you take your break, then we'll get ourselves situated." He smiled. "What do you say?"

Mason studied his boss, the office, the bowl filled with cuff links. There was a time he had aspired to have the director's job. "I guess what I have to say is no."

Gefke crossed his arms over his chest.

"I say you're gonna have to find someone else for that job in Pendleton, sir. I don't want it."

"Your choice, of course."

Mason nodded. He was right. It *was* his choice. He thought of Robbin telling Mrs. Stanley how badly he wanted to die, and Mason sitting there too ashamed to look at Bliss. "And you can get someone else to handle Robbin's execution. I don't want anything to do with it."

His boss smiled again. "You sure? 'Cause I got to tell you, I've planned for that contingency. Just in case."

"What's that supposed to mean?"

"I sort of figured you might get your butt tied up in a bun 'bout this. Can't blame you. Handsome guy like you, single, what the hell would you want moving to some podunk town like Pendleton? There's nothing out there anyway but a bunch of rednecks and those army bunkers filled with mustard gas. You ever see those things? I swear, terrorists want to do some damage, they should crash a plane out that way." The director picked up and tossed his baseball once more, catching it with a hard forward slap. "But don't you worry. You can slip out quietly if you want. Leave today. It's fine by me. I already got myself another team all lined up."

Mason squinted. "Waters?"

"Yeah. Waters is ready to run the ship. I like him, even though he went to Oregon State. Plus I found a real good guy to head the tie-down team. A straight shooter. Name's Rick. Rick Stowenheim."

Mason smiled. "That's good, sir. Gotta give you credit. You go and pick the most sadistic sonofabitch in the place. That's *real* good."

"Glad you approve."

"And I suppose he's the one who told you about Mrs. Stanley's visit?"

"Very same. Poor guy, wasting his talents back there in Admitting."

Mason looked past Gefke and his ball and the window. "There was good reason to bring in Mrs. Stanley."

"There's always good reasons to do things."

"Not always."

Gefke shrugged. "Okay, not always."

"Stowenheim's sick—you know that."

"Could be."

Mason scratched the back of his neck. "So I stay. Do the job. What then?"

"Then it's your call. Keep the team you have if you want. I don't give a shit. Just make sure they're a team, not a bunch of fucking hotshots doing whatever the hell they please."

"Is that it, then? I stay, I do the job, I keep my team?"

"Well, there is one other thing." Gefke smiled in such a way that Mason knew he was screwed. "I don't want those two women around here anymore. No more visits, and no access the night of the execution. I don't want them near the press—not that night, not *ever* if I can help it."

"Come on. They have every right to attend the execution. And as for the press, you can't keep them away from reporters."

"You're right, I can't. But you know what I'm standing here thinking? I'm thinking that a man who'd break rules to get them in this prison might have a little bit of sway with those two ladies. Especially the younger one. I understand she's quite a piece."

Mason clenched his fist and took a step forward. Then stopped.

"That's right, buddy. You just keep your prick in place and this'll all go just fine. But you bring those women in again, I swear I'll cut you short. Stowenheim's more than eager to help you that night, and I'll make sure he's ready and waiting. You see, either way"— Gefke tossed his ball one last time—"I got my game plan all set."

CHAPTER 52

October 26, 2004

MASON THUMBED BACK THE LID on his bottle of Scotch and handed a glass to Bliss. He had put on Coltrane and she told him she liked it, then pointed to a painting. An abstract done by, of all things, an elephant. He had purchased it at a fund-raiser for the Portland Zoo.

"An elephant?"

"Yeah, Rama. He holds a paintbrush in his trunk. Then those splatters"—he pointed to an area that looked airbrushed—"those he did by blowing paint out his trunk."

She looked at him as if he were nuts. "Is that okay to do, I mean, having paint up its nose?"

"I guess. I mean, I hope so. Hadn't thought of it."

"And you like going to the zoo?"

"I liked the one in Chicago. Lincoln Park. No admission fee. It costs an arm and a leg to get into the one in Portland. The fund-raiser was to help kids pay for camp."

She slipped into a dining room chair. "Your friend Rama's got a lot more talent than I do."

Mason sat across from her. A copper bowl filled with tanger-ines, a few bananas, and one large ripe pomegranate occupied the space between them. Bliss had called about getting together. She needed to talk, she said. Her mom had been a wreck since seeing Robbin. "She thinks she ought to attend the execution. I don't know what to tell her."

Mason had half hoped he'd never hear from the two women again. But as soon as Bliss called, he suggested he pick her up and they come back to his place. "We can talk," he said. "Without inter-ruption."

Sitting across from her now, he listened as she told him about her life in Austin. She lived in an apartment by the university with a gray-and-black tabby named Toner. She'd never married and had little time for relationships. "Besides, all I know are lawyers, and who wants to hang out with lawyers?"

Mason was considering answering her question when his cat, Horatio, jumped onto the dining room hutch.

"Didn't take you for a cat owner," Bliss said.

Mason shrugged. "I'm not sure I am. He comes and goes when he wants. Sometimes I don't see him for days. Lately, though, he's here a lot. You should hear him talk. Goes on and on whenever I'm trying to get something done. I have no idea what he's saying."

"But you think it's something?"

"I guess so."

Comma-shaped dimples creased Bliss's cheeks. "Elephants and cats—I think there's a soft side to you, Mr. Tab Mason."

Tab blushed, though he was pretty sure she couldn't tell.

"I had pets growing up," she said. "A heeler named Karl. He got kicked in the head by a cow and went blind. Then there was a three-legged cat we named Trike. But what I really wanted was a horse."

"You ever get one?"

She laughed. "The closest I ever got was a herd of plastic mares and a stallion named Jack."

Mason liked the way Bliss licked her top teeth when she was thinking, and the way, when she leaned her head on her hand, her hair fell on the table like clothes tossed on the floor.

"They're probably back in my parents' home in some box."

"When was the last time you were there?"

Her smile disappeared. "Almost three years ago. Getting off work, it's impossible. Even now the office is calling all the time. I'm thinking of taking all my vacation, just to flip them out. I probably have at least a month coming."

He poured them both more Scotch. And she told him about growing up by the Mississippi, a pretty place that smelled of honeysuckle in the summer and mud in the fall. She had played along that river, barefoot and free to go where she pleased. Playing hide-and-go-seek in the corn, catching frogs in the boggy patches near the river. Snakes would migrate down from the hills every spring, so many of them that the highway department had to close an entire road. And as she talked, Mason tried to imagine things such as snake migrations and yards defined by the banks of a river.

"It was a pretty ideal life . . . For a while at least, pretty damn ideal." Her hand reached down and traced the table's dark grain. "Now I look back and I realize I had no idea what was going on in my house. All those years, and everything I believed about my family turns out to be wrong." She continued to trace the table's grain, over and around, her fingers pale and thin.

"I don't know what's gonna happen at home. My dad can't forgive himself. He was a tough guy, hardest shell you'd ever find. But now, when I talk to him, he sounds broken. Sad beyond belief. Says he's hurt everyone he's ever loved."

"Has he talked with your mom at all?"

Bliss sighed. "No. She won't talk to him. Forgave Robbin, but won't have a thing to do with my dad. I don't know what I'm gonna do."

"She'll come around, don't you think?"

Bliss's eyes filled like tide pools, kelp and anemones swaying. "I really don't know what to think. I've asked her when she's going home, even offered to drive her myself, but she says she's going to Blaine when it's all through."

"Blaine?"

"It's where Shep's buried. She says she needs to go see him. I can understand. I mean, we've never been back there. But she insists on going alone. And then she won't talk about what comes next."

"Oh," Mason said, trying to keep the worry from his face.

"She wants me to tell you that she's willing to take Daniel's things if he still wants her to have them. I guess he has some drawings or something."

"Yeah, he does."

"And I know she wants to attend the execution. Says at least that way she'd be doing something for Robbin. She was filling out the forms when you picked me up."

Mason gripped his hands in front of his face, aware that he felt no shame or awkwardness at this clear display of his disfigurement. "Your mother's something, that's for sure."

"Yeah, but Jeez—I don't think she can handle it. You know what it's like. I don't care how sanitized the process is these days, you're still watching someone die." She pulled herself short for a second. "Listen to me, will you? I swear, I sound like one of those anti–death penalty nuts."

"You sound like someone who loves her mother." He picked a tangerine from the bowl and examined its textured surface.

"Who's that?" Bliss's gaze had landed on a photograph of a young girl.

"It's my daughter, Latiesha."

"The same girl as in your office?"

"Yeah. She's sixteen now. Lives with her mother in Chicago."

Bliss leaned her head to the side, a question written on her face.

"Five. It's been five years since I visited." He dug his thumbnail into the tangerine's bright orange skin, and immediately the sharp scent of citrus filled the air. "I'm thinking of going to see her soon, though."

"Taking time off?"

"In a way." Mason took a deep breath and told Bliss about his visit to the director's office, the baseball, and the bowl of cuff links. "Anyway, it ends up we have a pretty significant difference of opinion regarding the management of the prison."

She looked stunned. "He fired you?"

Mason carefully expanded the tear in the tangerine's skin, lengthening it just enough to allow the fruit to emerge whole and unscathed, like a yolk from a perfectly cracked egg. He set the empty hide aside and began the task of gently working off the thin strands of pith. "In a way. Made it hard to stay, at any rate."

Bliss's eyes narrowed on the table as she considered Mason's words. Then she looked up. "Of course . . . They didn't want us visiting Robbin, did they?" She slapped her hands on the table. "Sonofabitch, Tab. They told you no, is that right? Jesus. Why didn't you tell us?" She stood up, walked to the hutch. She had on black jeans, boots, a green V-neck sweater that looked about as soft as new grass.

"The fucker," she said. "Tossing a baseball, you say? I can see it now. You weren't playing their game, so they're kicking you off the team. Shit." Horatio stood, stretched, and jumped off the hutch. "I hate their political pockmarked asses, you know that? And how the hell did they find out, anyway?" She ran her fingers over her lips. "Hold on, I know." She was pointing now. "It was that guy that checked us in, wasn't it? That slimy little prick! All his questions, and that damn smile when we said who we were visiting. A sneer, really. He called the director, I'll bet you any money. Probably got hold of him the second we were out of there. Goddammit, I should have known better."

She fell back into her chair, tapped her fingers against the table. Mason returned to his tangerine. There's an art to the perfectly peeled fruit. A tangerine stripped of every fiber of membrane is a succulent gold globe. It could take five minutes to get it right. And a pomegranate—hell, he could spend an hour pulling each individual seed from its brainlike cage. They were distractions, things he did so as not to think about other things, like losing his job or killing Robbin. Like Bliss and her brooding fury rolling over him in waves.

She leaned forward and grabbed his wrist. "Why'd you let us in? You didn't have to—you know that. Didn't have to do any of this. Hell, you never even had to take my mom's call to begin with."

He palmed the fruit and looked at her. "Didn't I?"

"What do you mean?"

"Stories, isn't that what you said? 'We all have stories.'"

She examined him with lawyerlike intensity. "So why not quit now? Tell your boss to fuck off. Let him do his own dirty work."

He shook his head.

"But how the hell will you live—" She stopped her question and let go of his wrist. Then the CD ended, and it was just the two of them and the clicking of the radiators and the loud purr of a cat sitting somewhere nearby.

Mason's body ached, he wanted this woman so badly. Not just physically, but something fuller, deeper than anything he'd ever known. Something about this woman right here, right now . . . He opened his mouth. "I've never been able to do what your mom has done."

She looked confused.

"Forgive." He looked at the fruit in his hands. "I probably should, but I never have."

"We can't all be saints, Tab."

He looked up. "No, but your mom's got me thinking that maybe we can be happier."

Bliss's pulse quivered along the vein in her neck. A causeway of blood and oxygen, feeding her heart and mind. So close to the surface. So vulnerable.

"You should know that if either you or your mother go to the execution, there'll be a change of plan."

"What's that?"

"Gefke, the director, has a different guy ready to head the tie-down crew, just in case one of you shows."

"And that would be?"

"That"—Mason pulled off one last piece of pith—"would be the man you just referred to as 'that slimy little prick.'"

Bliss leaned forward and put her head in her hands. "That bastard."

Mason looked away. The heart, he knew, was the most tender organ. Vulnerable, and never to be trusted. He learned that early from Tulane, then again from his mother, and his wife, then every time he got a picture of Latiesha. It was a trap, listening to its demands. Dangerous. But there he was, wanting nothing more than to reach for the woman sitting across from him. He leaned forward, took her hand, and placed the tangerine inside. An orange jewel, perfect and whole. "There is something else your mother could do for Robbin," he whispered. "I don't know if she'd be willing, but there is something."

CHAPTER 53

October 28, 2004

11:00 P.M.

Mason and the chaplain sat with Robbin in the observation cell, the three of them drinking Coke while Robbin told stories.

"You ever been whale-watching?" Robbin asked.

Mason and the chaplain shook their heads.

"You ought to go. Boats leave out of Depoe Bay. I went once when I was around eleven. It was a birthday present from this family I was living with. We went out on a fishing boat with a bunch of other people, then headed out past the jetties till all we could see was just birds and buoys. Then, toward the end of the hour, when we'd pretty much given up on seeing anything else, the captain shouted and revved up the motor—loud sucker. Spewed diesel all over us. Suddenly he cut the engine and we just sat there bobbing on the waves." Robbin paused, his hand held out in front of him as if he were still scanning the horizon.

"Anyway, this guy points to what looks like an oily spot on the water, said one just went down there. So we all pile up to the front of the boat to search. Then someone else yells about seeing a spout, but I can't see over everyone, so I run to the back of the boat hoping to get a better view, when all of a sudden this gigantic head comes up out of the water. I mean *huge*, like the size of a car or something, and she's only about as far away from me as you." Robbin pointed at the chaplain with his thumb. "And I just stop dead in my tracks. She had this huge mouth and it was open just enough for me to see inside. And her eyes—I've never seen anything like them. As dark as the ocean itself, and—this is gonna sound a little weird, but they looked wise. It was like that whale knew everything, and everything she knew made her sad."

11:30 P.M.

Irene and Bliss stood in the park by the prison, waiting for midnight. It was raining, misting really. A steady, soft drift of water that glowed under the institution's bright orange lights. *They're getting ready to kill a man,* thought Irene, cordoning off this comprehension and all the emotions it carried.

Two days after meeting with Robbin, she'd read in the paper that he'd been moved to the observation cell. The article said he appeared thoughtful and relaxed, spending most of his time sleeping, reading, or drawing. Over the years Robbin had sent her a few things he'd done. One was a portrait of a black man with a scar running down his neck. Exquisitely drawn in pencil, it came with a note describing the superintendent of the Oregon prison as "a decent man."

Irene looked up at one of the gun towers and wondered about that word and what exactly a decent man like Tab Mason would have to pay for doing what he was about to do. It had to stay with him. A person like that—it probably would stay with him a long time.

She reached for her daughter's hand. "I should be in there," she said.

11:40 P.M.

Mason, the chaplain, and Duncan Lewis walked Robbin into the execution chamber, then Lewis, as lead on the tie-down team, removed Robbin's restraints and asked him to get up on the gurney. Then the four members of Lewis's team strapped him to the table. Arms, legs, chest, held down by brown leather straps with buckles as large as a man's hand.

Mason had picked each member of his team. He had gone over their records and psych tests and asked each one all kinds of questions about his reasons for volunteering and what support he had at home or church. They all said they liked Robbin and thought it was their job to make sure things were done right. But no matter what support they had or how many times they had practiced their drills—walking each other into the execution chamber, strapping one another down, going through a countdown—nothing could prepare them for the emotional wallop they would feel when it was the real thing. Maybe it wouldn't come tonight, Mason thought. Maybe not even for a week, or a year. Maybe it wouldn't come until they were old men, waiting for their own time to pass. But it *would* come. And as Mason watched the men finish with Robbin's straps, he felt both grateful and awful at once. Especially after Robbin raised his head off the pillow and thanked them.

Mason had written his team a letter telling them how proud he was to have worked with them and asking them to extend the same service and dedication to his replacement. Then he wrote to Waters, telling him where certain files could be found and updating him on specific projects he hoped would continue. The prison was becoming a cage for the state's mentally ill. Certifiably crazy people who needed doctors and drugs were filling his cells. Mason had seen it with his brother back in Illinois. He should have gone to a state hospital, not prison. As it was, he only got in more and more trouble: getting in fights, attempting to kill an officer. It needed to change, the whole system needed to change, but the best Mason figured he could do was secure more funding for counseling. It was all in a memo Waters and the director would receive on Monday, well after Mason was gone.

Robbin laid his head back on the pillow and breathed deeply and steadily. Mason nodded to the crew and all but Lewis left the room. A minute later a nurse walked in, wearing green surgical scrubs, a green cap, and a mask. The woman had worked for the prison for ten years or so. Before that she'd been a pediatric nurse. Mason had always considered it a strange switch, and looking at her now, he also thought it strange that she was dressed as she was. She only had to hook up the monitors and start the IVs, after all. One line in each arm. The best the superintendent could figure was that the outfit gave her both the anonymity and the sense of authority she needed to take on the task at hand. Still, nerves got the better of her, and no matter how hard she worked, she couldn't get in a single IV. Mason tightened. If she didn't get it set soon, she'd have to cut directly into Robbin's vein, and Mason didn't want that. *Please God,* he found himself praying, *don't make her have to cut him. Not that.*

After another failed try, Robbin spoke up and told her to take a break for a second. "You ever been whale-watching?" he asked.

"I grew up in Newport," she said through her mask. "We'd see them all the time."

"That must have been something, seeing whales all the time."

"Yeah," she said. "I guess it was."

On the next try she got in one IV, then the other. She cleaned up his arms, threw away the balled-up cotton and alcohol swabs, snapped off her gloves. Then she stood beside Robbin and pulled down her mask. "You'll be in my prayers," she said, then left, her rubber-soled shoes squeaking against the shiny linoleum floor.

Mason went back to Robbin's side, glanced at the clock, snapped his head from side to side. His muscles were a solid mass and his stomach an acidic knot. He'd had a cup of coffee at 11:30 and could still taste its bitter sludge. He wanted to spit. That or cry. Maybe hit something. *All three'd be good*, he thought. He glanced at the phone, wishing it would ring.

At 11:59 precisely, the superintendent of the Oregon State Penitentiary nodded to Duncan Lewis, who turned and pulled a cord, and up went the blind. Three men and one woman stood in the witness chamber, their faces expressionless. Robbin raised his head and glanced at the reporters, then dropped back down.

"She's not there," he said.

"No."

"That's good. I worried she'd come."

Mason didn't reply.

"Do I have to say anything to those people?"

"Only if you want."

Robbin raised his head again, looked through the window, then lay back down on the pillow. "I'll think of something later," he said, then winked at the superintendent.

12:00 A.M.

Bliss looked at her watch. "One minute," she whispered, then through the swish of passing cars they both heard the singing. Chanting, really. A bawdy, drunken hooting and yelling done to some tune she'd heard at high school football games.

Na-na-na-na,
Na-na-na-na,
Hey, hey,
Goodbye

On the way to the park, she and her mother had driven by a crowd standing outside the prison's entrance. Some were huddled with candles, their faces grim. Others were festive, passing high fives and cans of beer.

Bliss closed her eyes and squeezed her mom's arm, imagining the superintendent, his posture as unequivocal as his character. His idea of duty, service, and justice was so much more generous than her own. She didn't know what made him who he was, but she knew she wanted to know more.

"Is it hard," her mother asked as the chanting continued, "being a prosecutor?"

Bliss opened her eyes and nodded. "I get tired. All that pain, lives twisted and broken every which way, and there not being any real good answer for it all." She hunched her shoulders against the wet wind. "It makes me tired, Mom, and it makes me sad."

12:00 A.M.

Mason looked down at his shoes. In thirty seconds he'd pull a pair of glasses from his pocket and put them on, signaling the moment the person in the booth would turn the switch and the valves on the vials would open and release their lethal mix. Measured by unseen hands and delivered by unfeeling, unassailable, un-understandable devices that push and whir and suck and snap, distinguishing nothing between life and death.

Mason had not reached out to Bliss that night in his home. Had not pulled her to him and slowly peeled away the layers that shielded them both from whatever it was they were running from. Instead, after he told her how her mother might be able to help Daniel Robbin, he drove Bliss back to her motel, and then he'd gone to his office. Once there, he pored over legal opinions, statutes, administrative rules, anything that would tell him just what would happen to Robbin during the last few days of his life—and then what would happen after. He made careful lists, divided and subdivided by hand-drawn lines.

Mason had once wanted to do big things. Free people, cure disease—it didn't matter what. As a child he'd admired Martin Luther King and Robert Kennedy, and he'd read about Gandhi. But then Tulane had slit his throat and his mother had committed suicide, and Tab Mason had decided he wasn't cut out for big things. If he could keep bad people locked up, he'd concluded, that would be enough.

He looked up from his shoes. "Are you ready, Daniel?"

The small man bit his lip and nodded, his steel-gray eyes watching as the superintendent reached for his glasses.

CHAPTER 54

October 30, 2004

THE CEMETERY SAT AS IRENE remembered, alone on a hill, hemmed in by an iron fence, with tumbleweed piled like fragile bones.

She dropped out of the old truck, pressed the door shut with a quiet click, and entered a silence so vast it almost felt like a presence. No wind to brush back the grass, no birds, not one insect or car. Just space spread out against an utterly formless sky. She buttoned her coat, pulled down Doris's hat, took a deep breath, and released it without a single sound.

Moments before the execution, Irene had wrapped her arm around her daughter as the drunken party outside the prison gate began its countdown. "Ten, nine, eight . . ." Each second closing off the last. Irene's body rigid as she thought about what was being done on the other side of those walls.

She had read a description of the procedure in the paper, how

they'd bring Daniel into the room and strap him down. A picture
of the gurney took up a quarter of the page: black vinyl and metal,
arm brackets pulled out to the sides. "It looks like a crucifix," she'd
said to Bliss. And that image stuck in her mind as they stood beside
the prison, and the seconds went by, and the counting stopped, and
a cheer rose from the crowd.

Irene wondered if Daniel could taste the drugs, and if he could,
what they tasted like. And she wondered if it hurt. The article said
most physicians agreed it did not. The first drug, the newspaper
said, would put Daniel to sleep, and the second would paralyze his
muscles, all of them but one—his heart. That would keep beating,
frantically reaching for oxygen until the third drug stopped it as
well. "If there's pain," a more ambivalent doctor was quoted as saying, "there would be no way to know, because of that second, para-
lytic drug."

Irene dropped her arm from Bliss and murmured something
about how she ought to have been with him. Then her legs faltered,
and Bliss, sad and strong and there for her after all, put an arm
around her mother and led her back to the truck.

THE CEMETERY'S GATE WAS OPEN, its bottom swamped by drifts
of dirt so it no longer swung or screeched the way it had nineteen years before. Irene stepped through, then stopped. The place
looked small and forgotten, hardly big enough for a barn. A few of
the gravestones were new; a couple held threadbare flags, another
a gaudy bouquet of bright plastic flowers. The crying tree, a wizened old lady in a scraggly cape of boughs, still stood beside Shep's
grave. Irene walked up and picked a pearl of sap from its frayed
bark, brought it to her nose and allowed its sharp scent to crack
open memories—the funeral, the clouds, the preacher's black Bible,
that young boy who played Shep's horn. She took in another breath
of the resiny scent, then looked down.

Dime-sized circles of lichen grew in and among the letters and numbers of her son's white stone, and instead of flowers, dry blades of cheatgrass stuck out from its base. Right at the edge of the mound sat several oddly shaped rocks lined up one after another. Irene counted nineteen, and she wondered who had placed them there year after year. Maybe that boy who had played Shep's horn? Maybe a teacher, or a neighbor?

Irene crouched down to the ground and brushed her hand over the stone. "I'm back," she whispered, breaking the silence with the only words she could say.

THEY DROVE THROUGH FORESTS RED with vine maple and up mountains bouldered with basalt. At the top of Santiam Pass it started to snow, and Mason slowed with the rest of the traffic. Then the road began its descent, the sun came out, and the trees opened up with the land. Ponderosa pine, bunchgrass, sage, juniper—the names came back to Bliss like the names of her friends in Blaine. In the little town of Sisters, they stopped, got coffee, and looked at the map. Blaine was fifty miles north and east, the cemetery a bit farther. It was almost three in the afternoon, the sun already drawing down to the west.

"Should take us about an hour more," Mason said.

"If I can remember how to get to the cemetery."

"Someone will know."

When Bliss woke that morning, her mom, her mom's things, and the truck were gone. It wasn't a surprise. Irene had told her that after the execution she was going to see Shep. And she'd insisted on going alone. Still, it alarmed Bliss, and she called Tab.

Bliss got back in the Jeep and glanced at the man at her side, his large discolored hand draped over the steering wheel in the same way her dad always drove. Tab Mason wore faded jeans, a dark blue sweatshirt, and canvas hiking boots. He listened to Lou Rawls,

Coltrane, and Bach. He had pencils sharpened to a fine point and a house with a cat and perfectly polished furniture. And he knew how to strip down a fruit in a way that made Bliss more than just hungry.

He began to tell her a bit about the night. Robbin had died very simply and cleanly. No fighting. "And the crew, they were something. I could see they didn't want to be there any more than I did, but they stayed professional. Even kind, if that's not too weird to say."

"It's not."

"I'll tell you, though, that Robbin, he had us all in the end. You'll never believe what he did."

Bliss silently ran through the things she'd heard people do: pray, plead, weep, scream, sing, piss in their pants.

"He sang 'Silent Night.' You know, the Christmas song? He had a fine voice, too. Began singing soon as the drugs started. He got as far as 'mother and child.' "

Bliss sucked in a breath, held it. Then, when she thought she could do so without crying, she exhaled.

IRENE HAD FORGOTTEN HOW QUICKLY the winter sun came and went in the Northwest. Rising, it seemed, as late as eight in the morning, setting before five. She glanced up, figuring at least an hour had passed since she'd arrived. Maybe two. She'd had her talk with her son. It started first with an apology for taking so long to return, then went into all that had happened between then and now—the move back home, her job, Nate still a deputy, Bliss a law-yer in Texas.

She slipped into the subject of depression, how hard it had been to live without him. Years had gone by with her so suffocated by pain she still couldn't remember much. She could recall his music, though. "It's like there's a radio in my mind. I can hear every note, without even thinking about it. It just goes on and on, keeping me company."

Then, with her hands held tight, she told him about her letters to Daniel Robbin—what had led to them and what they, eventually, led to.

She stopped and pulled some weeds. In many places the bare soil around his grave had crusted over with mounds of dull green moss. She bent down and examined its rough starlike structure.

"Daniel's dead, son. They say it didn't hurt. He just went to sleep." She wiped her nose with the back of her hand. "I know now why you thought you were different. And all I can say is I'm sorry."

She bit her bottom lip and shook her head. Her whole life, shaking her head from side to side. Things too sad to face, moving side to side.

"I'm sorry you couldn't tell me, and I'm sorry this world and me wouldn't have accepted it even if you had. That's not right, and it wasn't right your pa doing what he did. But he's sorry about that, too. You have to know that, Shep. His way of loving you may not have been what we would have designed. But you have to understand, it was all he knew to do."

A tear rolled down Irene's face and landed on a patch of moss, immediately turning that one spot a rich, soft green. She reached down and touched it, amazed by how little it took for something to come back to life.

"We all make mistakes, son. Every one of us. And we all pay. One way or another, we all pay."

She picked up a stone, rolled it in her hand, raised it to her mouth, then placed it beside the others. "I'm sorry you've been alone for so long, but it won't be like that anymore, Shep. You won't ever have to be alone again. Not ever."

Irene sat for a while longer, the shadows of the tombstones pointing east across the cemetery and onto the bareback ridge. Then she pulled off the hat Doris had given her, bunched it into a pillow, then lay beside Shep's stone, and closed her eyes.

THEY DROVE ON, THE TALL ponderosa country giving way to scrubbier trees and brush. Mason pointed to a ridge dotted with large log cabins. "Second homes," he said. "A lot of people in the valley buy out here. I thought of getting a place myself. Not one of those, but something small, maybe along the Metolius."

Bliss winced. The superintendent's life had been so set. His job, his home, his dreams. She had tried to apologize for her and her mom turning it all on its head, but he would have none of it. So she offered help. She knew people in Texas corrections who could get him a job. But he didn't want to hear about that either. He was glad to be moving on, he said. "It's time."

Then, as the land became more hard-bitten and brittle—barbed-wire fences and slack black cows, hipbones jutting like the keel on a boat—he told her about Robbin and some bird the man had seen the day Mason had given him the warrant.

"I turned my head, you know, to see. Still can't believe I did that. Should have known right then that it was time for me to leave that job."

"I don't get it."

"It was stupid. You don't turn your head. Not in my work, you don't. Not in yours either, I would think."

She shrugged. "So you trusted him—so what? That doesn't seem too unreasonable."

"It was for me." He stepped on the gas and passed a Winnebago with Florida plates, then after he settled back in his lane he glanced at Bliss. "You remember what you said that first day in my office?"

"I remember I wasn't polite."

He looked at her, and from across the distance of two feet, she felt suddenly sucked in and swallowed whole. It'd been less than two weeks since she had walked into his office, defiant and angry and so absolutely damn sure of herself. Now she wasn't sure of anything, except this singular sensation of falling into this man. Her lips parted in a smile, and he nodded.

"A pistol is what you were, and you had damn good aim." He dropped his hand to the shift and clenched it as if it were a ball. "You said we all have some reason we do what we do. We all have a story."

She nodded, then just looked out the window as he told her his. Somewhere in the middle, when it became clear that Mason hadn't had a chance with his brother, she laid her hand on his. It had dropped to his side as he had told of the beatings, the lake, and a handmade knife. "I'd have killed my brother. Without a doubt, I would have killed him and been sitting just where he is now. But as it turned out, he was quicker." He told Bliss how Tulane had grabbed the knife from him, and what he had done to Tab in the dark of the classroom. And then he told her about his mother.

"I blamed her. Blamed her and said I'd never forgive her . . . and that's the last thing I ever did get to say to her."

Bliss told him to pull over.

There are reasons we do what we do, she had said in his office. And she remembered thinking at the time she could probably guess Tab Mason's story. And maybe she could have. She'd heard worse. There was always worse.

But hardly ever did people come back and face their story to see it for all it was. Take from it all it could give. And suddenly she saw Daniel, her mother, Shep, Tab Mason, herself, and even her father as vines, destined to push, brace, and twine into one another. She saw the things Tab Mason had done for her mom and Robbin no longer as gifts but as improbable evolutionary steps—destined, ordained, and impossible to deny.

NATE SAT HUNCHED AGAINST THE window of a Greyhound bus traveling south on Oregon State Highway 96, over sand-colored hills and past pastures lined with irrigation pipe. Money had come to the region, he thought as they passed a billboard advertising a wine bar in Blaine, and then another for a casino out at the reservation.

"I hate those damn places," a man in front of him said to the woman at his side.

"I know."

"Gambling."

"Um-hmm."

The man huffed impatiently.

"You know," the woman said, "if you brought a book or something, it'd make the time go faster."

"Not going in for these treatments every damn few days would make the time go faster."

The woman sighed, and so did Nate. It was hardly a stretch imagining himself an old man, alone and so done with it all. He wiped his nose with his sleeve and looked down at his lap. Lying there, folded in half and feeling like it weighed about a thousand pounds, was the morning's paper. He'd bought it at the airport, then unfolded it and began reading while sitting around waiting for the bus. But he didn't get far before he stood up, stepped outside, and just leaned against the Portland terminal, shivering in the damp cold.

Nate stiffened his lips and opened the paper now. He studied the headline—"Robbin Dies by Lethal Injection"—then leaned his head back on the seat and shut his eyes.

He had been moments away from killing himself the night Irene left. Moments. But then Jeff walked into the barn and told him to put down the gun. "You have no right to run like that," he said. And he was right.

Nate lifted his head and looked out the window again. Blaine was eighty miles farther. It'd be dark by the time he got there, but that didn't matter. He could walk a dark road as well as anyone. He'd been doing it for years, after all. And once he got to that ridge, he'd figure out what came next. And if he couldn't, he felt certain his son could.

MASON COUNTED FIVE PEAKS, WHITE as sea foam floating over a dark brocade of trees and hills. He pulled over and parked beside Mrs. Stanley's truck, uncertain whether coming to the cemetery was a good idea. All he knew was that it was a small thing, and that maybe, in the end, it was only small things that mattered. A hand reaching out. A letter. A bird where no bird should be.

He and Bliss got out of the Jeep and walked up the trail, guiding each other around the cow patties and pumice stone. At the gate they could see Irene lying beside the tree, her canvas coat a deep russet in the fading light. Bliss let go of Mason and ran to where her mother lay.

When Mason had told Daniel what they'd agreed to do after his death, the man had just stared vacantly. "Are you okay?" Mason asked as Robbin dropped to the bed of his new, quiet, clean cell.

It was the morning before the execution, and things had finally been arranged with Mrs. Stanley, the funeral home, and Mason's neighbor—who hadn't been very pleased that he had given Horatio to her daughter.

"I asked if you're okay."

Daniel Robbin wiped his face and moved his head back and forth. "You've gone and done it now, General. You've *really* gone and done it now."

"What? What have I done?"

"Pain and grace, sir. Pain and grace."

IRENE PULLED A PIECE OF moss from her hair, brushed off her clothes, then stood and hugged her daughter. The sun was slipping fast—a ball, a crescent, a thin scrim of light.

They talked about their drives—the mountains, hills, and trees. "It's prettier here than I remember," Irene said. "Blaine even looked a little better. You notice the mill was operating?"

"I did," Bliss answered.

"And I drove by the house. It's blue now and has a trampoline in the yard. And you'll never believe this."

"What?"

"They still have the roses."

"The ones we planted? No way."

Irene shrugged. "Guess they were tougher than we thought."

"Guess so." Bliss knelt beside her brother's headstone and traced the letters of his name. "Did you line up these rocks here?"

"One, but not the others."

"Then who?"

"I'm not sure, but I'm thinking that young boy who played the horn at Shep's funeral."

Bliss rocked back on the bare ground, wrapped her arms around her legs, and gazed toward the mountains.

Mason remained by the front gate, one hand in his pocket, the other holding a box. Irene waved him over.

"Bliss tells me you've offered to be our chauffeur."

"Yes, ma'am. I figured since I'm going to Chicago . . ."

"And you think that's a good idea, us all driving together those long miles?"

"I wouldn't have volunteered if I didn't."

Irene nodded. "I expect that's right," she said. "And I understand you have a daughter in that city?"

"Yes."

"Well, I suppose we'll have a lot to talk about."

This time it was Mason's turn, nodding, telling her he expected that was true.

Then Bliss rose and tucked herself between her mother and the man, and the three of them stood, silent, shadowless creatures on a stark and open ridge, the sun burning a last fold of copper into the sky.

Bliss pointed. "Look at that." A star winked and shimmered like a spark of fire. They stared, then Mason opened the box he'd been holding.

There are roads to walk, Irene thought. *The death of a child. The pain that comes. The despair and immeasurable grief—*

"It's beautiful out here," Mason said. "Daniel would like that."

And then there is a night, and a star, and a moment of grace.

"I hope so," Irene said, accepting a round silver can from Mason's outstretched hands. One black, one white. One reaching for Bliss, one free to reach out for whatever was to come.

He's a good man, Irene thought. Nate would learn to like him. And she, Irene Stanley, setting the tin of Daniel's ashes beside her son's grave, would learn to call them all her family—Daniel, Mr. Mason, Nate, Bliss, herself, and all the people along the way who try and fail and then turn around and learn to accept both.

ACKNOWLEDGMENTS

I thank my friend Aba Gayle, whose story of struggle and survival was the seed for this book, my teacher Eric Witchey, who helped me understand how to tell this story, my friends Harriet Steinberg, Nancy Boutin, and Kate Davidson, who were never-flagging sources of support and ideas, my agent, Laney Katz Becker, whose passion for the book brought it to your hands, my editor, Christine Pride, who helped refine this story with graciousness and generosity, Perrin Damon with the Oregon Department of Corrections and criminal defense attorney Steve Krasik, who helped me better understand the state's penal system, and all the many people who willingly read and commented on early drafts. In addition, I want to thank the late Aaron Copland for creating music that inspired many scenes in this book. And most important, I want to thank my husband, Chuck, my son, Elijah, my father, Mohammed, my sister and brother, Shameem and Amir, and my dear in-laws, Sylvia and Lewis, for giving me the love, support, time, and space to write this story. I love you very much.

READERS' GUIDE

DEAR READERS,

In 1996 I was assigned to cover Oregon's first execution in over thirty years. At the time I had never given much thought to the death penalty and what it would take for the state to plan out, prepare, and then kill a man. After the assignment, I wanted to learn more so I began to interview death-row inmates, the people they had harmed, and the men and women we entrust to carry out our nation's most severe sentence. During that time I heard many stories, some of them abhorrent and some heartbreaking, but by far the most compelling were those told by the people who had come to terms with the murder of a loved one and no longer felt it necessary to seek retribution. This arc, from the most desperate kind of anguish to reconciliation and even love, stunned me and compelled me to write *The Crying Tree*.

I offer these questions because they are the very ones I asked myself as I wrote this book.

1. Why did Irene believe that she could not tell anyone about having forgiven Robbin? What did she think would happen? What was she afraid of? Have you ever forgiven someone but been afraid to admit it?

2. Do you think that, like Irene, you could forgive someone who harmed your family?

3. Irene tells her sister that forgiving Robbin was not a choice. What do you think she meant?

4. Do you think it is necessary to have a belief in a God or a higher power to have made the choices Irene made? Do you think the ability to forgive can be learned?

5. In the first chapter, Tab Mason describes his reaction to seeing his first execution. Have you ever given much thought to how executions affect those who must carry them out?

6. Secrets—Nate's, Shep's, Irene's—are the driving force behind the tragedy in this story. Do you think it is common for families to operate in such isolation from one another?

7. Nate says he moved his family west to help Shep. How did he think this would help?

8. How would you describe the novel's central message or theme? And how does the ending of the book impact your understanding of the novel's central message or theme?

9. Tab Mason has an unusual skin disorder. Why do you think I chose to mark him in such a way? What, if any, difference would it make if he were simply a black man? Or a white man?

10. Tab Mason is a man who offers "no surprises." He is painstakingly in control of his words, his thoughts, and his emotions. And this had paid off, giving him the job, power, and resources to live a very comfortable life. Why, then, do you think he was willing to risk it all to help Irene Stanley?

11. Bliss recounts a time she found her father having an emotional breakdown while in the barn. The event was heart-wrenching for her. Bliss loved and cared for her father more than anyone, yet she does nothing to try to help. Does it make sense to you that Bliss did not try to step in and help her father?

12. Irene and Bliss had a difficult relationship. How was this transformed by Irene's act of forgiveness?

13. Bliss feels compelled to forgo her dream of college so that she can stay in Carlton and help her parents. Have you had times in your life when you have given up your dreams to help others?

14. Why do you think Daniel Robbin refuses the offer to introduce new evidence that might overturn his murder conviction?

15. In the end Nate is in a bus going to Shep's grave. Why do you think he is doing this? Do you think Nate's character changed over the course of the book? If so, how? If not, why not?

16. Irene's relationship with her church and faith were challenged in this story. In the end do you think her belief in God was stronger or weaker?

17. Why, of all the people Irene had in her life, did she open up to Doris, the woman who owned the Hitching Post in Wyoming?

18. After Nate's confession, Irene leaves her husband. As she drives across the country, how do her feelings change about her son's death, about Nate, and about herself?

19. Irene had strong feelings about staying around her family ("You don't leave family," in chapter 2). Yet emotionally, Irene did leave her family. She was not there for her daughter through high school, she never turned to her sister for help, and she and Nate's relationship was estranged. In the end, what did this belief in family mean? What conclusions about Nate and Irene's future can you draw from this sentiment?

20. In the end, what do you think Irene's, Bliss's, and Tab Mason's actions meant to Daniel Robbin?